Wallace Family Affairs
Volume V
No Regrets

Carey Anderson

DEDICATION

I would like to dedicate this story to Joy.
From the moment you asked who Derrick was this volume
came to life. Your friendship and constant encouragement has
been a wonderful outlet for me. Your friendship is invaluable,
your loyalty and tenacity keep the Wallace's a live. Thank you
for being you. I love you and appreciate all that you do and
have done for me.

Cover design: Cover Couture

Join me on Facebook –
www.facebook.com/careythewriteranderson

Twitter - @CareyTheWriter

Blog - http://careyanderson.blogspot.com

Website – http://www.careythewriteranderson.com

Editorial – Treasures of Joy Editorial

ACKNOWLEDGMENTS

I would like to thank my baby-girl who is my life's ultimate expression of a dream realized. Thank you for sacrificing mommy time so that I could have the time to work some things out on paper.

I would like to thank my Soul Sistah #1 who has been my captivated audience since middle school. Without your love, support, encouragement, and FIRE I never would've completed Volume I or II, etc. Thank you for bringing me laughter when I couldn't get outside of my head.

I would like to thank my Sister-In-Law for taking time out of your busy family life to humor me with a read through of my latest thoughts and expressions. (SS1 & SIL THANK YOU for the trip to St. Helena where we spent the day lost in my imagination. I will never forget it, and it was exactly what I needed. THANK YOU!)

I would like to thank my dear cousin for reassuring me that my little hobby was relatable and entertaining. You are definitely a speed-reader, thank you for taking time out of your busy life to be entertained by my imagination.

I would like to thank last but not least Mrs. Laverne Dyes! Mrs. Dyes the day that you read my short story to my class changed my life. Thank you for giving me a positive outlet for all the angst going on in my life. You have forever changed my life, I am so thankful to have ever known you

Chapter 1

"The usual?" I asked him.

He gave me a funny look. "Usual?"

"Yes, it varies depending on your mood but normally you order the pineapple peach smoothie. Sometimes you'll order a strawberry banana smoothie, but that's normally when you're kind of sentimental. I haven't put my finger on what triggers your chocolate peanut butter mood yet."

He didn't smile; he stared at me for a minute like he was taking everything I said in. He looked at the menu, and then he rolled his eyes and looked at me. "I'll take the chocolate peanut butter smoothie." There was no smile or friendliness in his tone. He watched me for a minute then he paid for his smoothie.

Everybody else is scared of him; Shelly always breaks out in a sweat when she sees him coming. She says he's really scary. He's not so scary to me; actually, I think he's sexy as all get out. He's not like these goofy boys who run around here like kids. He always looks like he's thinking about something. "Someone will call your name when your order is ready." I said

He stood over to the side to let the next person order, but his eyes stayed stuck to me. I blushed cause I didn't know what to do. I wanted to get his attention, but now that I have it what am I supposed to do?

Shelly volunteered to take the rest of the orders so that I could make the smoothies. I knew she was trying to avoid making his smoothie cause she was that scared of him. So I decided to upgrade his smoothie to the largest size since I was making it. I turned around and I handed him his smoothie with a straw. "Here you go Derrick." I said with a smile.

"Thank you Chantel." He said then he walked away.

I was speechless; I didn't know he knew my name. I didn't have a nametag on and I never wore one here. How did he know my name? I looked at Shelly who was now wide eyed and scared. She said something had to be wrong with him. I didn't think so, but now I definitely wanted to know how he knew my name.

At the end of my shift, Shelly, Cadence, and I wiped all the machines down and closed up our station within the food court of the mall. Like clockwork, my brother Cyrus was there to pick me up. He worked in the shoe store on the other side of the mall. We both had two jobs here. I worked at the Smoothie Stand and Travel and Beyond, a luggage and travel store. Cyrus worked at the shoe store and the movie theater. Like a good big brother, he always watches over me and makes sure I'm taken care of. Most times, it's like we're all we have. Our mother works and works, when she isn't working she's resting. When she isn't resting she's working. Our father is there, but he's so selfish and self-centered we'd be better off without him. I don't know why our mother keeps him around; I guess she loves him even though loving him has gotten her nowhere. Cyrus and I do our best to ignore them and stay out of their way. We practically raise ourselves. Our mother doesn't have time and our father could careless.

Cadence gives all of us a ride home. Even though Cadence is older than Cyrus by a good four years, her obvious crush on him was ridiculous at times. I didn't say anything though, cause if I needed a favor her open relationship with my brother worked to my advantage. Cyrus liked Cadence enough, but he wasn't really feeling her. He just went a long with it because he's a horny teenager.

"How does he know your name?" Shelly asked

"I have no idea. Maybe he was checking me out." I said with a smile.

"Oh come on. A guy like that checking you out? Get real."

"What is that supposed to mean?" Cyrus asked upset for me.

"Don't get mad Cyrus. You gotta see this guy. Tall, dark, scary, and handsome. He's way out of all of our leagues." Shelly said matter of factly.

"Speak for yourself! My sister can have anyone she wants!" Cyrus barked. I thanked him with my eyes.

"Whatever! If you guys wanna live in a fantasy world, where guys like that want girls like us go ahead. But I live in the real world." Shelly said

"Shelly you could never be on my sister's level! Stop trying to tear her down to be as pathetic as you!" He was mad.

"Ok guys! Let's drop this." Cadence said trying to be the peacekeeper.

"Tell her to stop putting my sister down. Just because nobody would want her gives her no right to talk about my sister like that."

"Shelly you are out of line." She said

"Whatever Cadence you're only siding with Cyrus cause you're hoping to get lucky tonight. But you guys know I'm telling the truth." Shelly said

"No one said he was interested in me. He could've been checking me out because I knew his name. I was just saying I don't know how he knew my name is all."

"You don't have to apologize to her cause some guy was checking you out. Forget her!"

"Cyrus..." Cadence whined.

Cyrus rolled his eyes. "I'm just saying!"

"Well tell me how you really feel." Shelly said insulted. "Just because Cadence swings from your nuts doesn't mean you're all that Cyrus!"

"I do not!" Cadence gasped.

"You're just jealous! If I wanted to smash you right now, I could. You've been wanting me since you were in grade school." The car fell silent. Shelly had nothing to say to that not even a denial. Cyrus laughed but we all remained silent. Shelly got out of the car without uttering a word.

Cadence grabbed Cyrus' hand as she drove us home. When we got to our apartment, I got out of the car and I went inside. Cadence was in heat; so there was no telling when Cyrus was gonna come inside.

When I came in the door, my mother was in the kitchen heating up leftovers. "Where's your brother?"

"Outside talking to Cadence." I said as I sat on the couch to finish my homework.

"Your father said you didn't sweep the floor last night when you did the dishes." I didn't respond I kept my eyes on my homework. Cyrus and I did everything in there. All he did was knit-pick over everything we did. He was no help or example of how to do anything other than use somebody. "Make sure you sweep the floor." She said as she walked to her room.

Two hours later Cyrus came inside as I put my things away. He didn't look at me; he went straight to the kitchen. "If you don't like her why do you have sex with her?" I asked.

Cyrus shrugged, "just cause." Then he looked in the fridge. "What happened to the shrimp and pasta? There's only a little bit left."

"Ask your mother and father, I saw her in the kitchen when I came home." I said

"I had my mouth ready for that. I can't wait until we're out of here, no longer slaving for them." He said. I put my finger up to shush him. The last thing we needed was for them to hear us.

****

I was sitting behind the cash register working on my homework when I heard the bell chime that I had a customer. I put my book down and I stood up to greet my customer. My knees got weak when I saw him. "Hi" I said sounding completely surprised.

"Hi" he said not smiling or anything.

"How can I help you?" I asked not knowing what else to say. His eyes were scanning the store. "I need something for my father."

"Ok, does he travel a lot? Did you have luggage in mind or something more personal?"

"I was thinking something more personal."

"Is it for a special occasion?" I asked

"No, just because."

"What does he like?" I asked

"He's a lot like me; he likes nice stuff but nothing flashy." He said I loved the sound of his voice. It was deep, but not startling deep.

"How about a wallet, a flask, a money clip, or a brief case?"

"That sounds good, show me all of them." He said

"Is there a price range you want to stay within?" I asked as I led him to the left side of the store.

"No" he said.

Then Mona walked in the store. She was the owner's daughter and my supervision during my shifts. Normally she stayed on the phone or visited with her friends when they stopped by. Any customers that came in the store I was expected to assist them. She was walking towards the back, but slowed down when she saw Derrick. I was hoping she would keep moving, but I could tell she was curious about him. She walked to the counter and sat on my stool. She leaned on the counter watching us. Her top was loose so all you saw were breast when you looked at her. I showed Derrick our wallets; he picked a genuine leather one that was soft to the touch. He picked a flask and money clip that he wanted engraved with his father's initials. He said he would think about the briefcase some more. I got excited cause that meant he could possibly come back even after he picks up his personalized items. "I'll ring you up." I said motioning for him to follow me to the register.

When we got to the register, Mona sat up. "I'll ring him up. Go unpack those packages we got in today." She ordered.

I knew she wanted the opportunity to flirt with him, but also she wanted to take credit for my sale like she did with all my high-ticket purchases. "Can I ring him up, then do the unpacking?" I asked wanting to stand up for myself on this one.

Mona's face turned evil. "You heard what I said!" She said through clinched teeth.

I started to walk to the back, I was thinking of how good it was gonna feel keying her car and or busting out one of her taillights like I've done before. "Hold on." Derrick said in my direction. I stopped in my tracks and turned around. "Don't you get commission?" I shook my head yes.

"Kind of but not exactly. She hasn't been making her sales goals, so she's on her way to being fired anyways. It's not a big deal. I can give you a discount for the inconvenience."

She was so busy talking and removing tags that she didn't see his eyes turn evil. "How much of a discount?"

"I can take thirty percent off." She said still not paying attention.

"Naw! I'm good!" He started walking towards the exit.

"Wait! Why?" Then she looked at me. "Did she offer you a bigger discount?"

He walked back to the counter; she finally noticed his evil eyes.

"No, I was willing to pay full price. I liked the way she conducted business. You on the other hand are not trust worthy. I wouldn't spend anything in this store, and from now on, you can kiss your regular customers goodbye. Nobody's coming in here any more."

"What? Why? Just because I told her to go unpack some boxes?" She looked like she wanted to cry.

"I don't like the way you conduct business, you aren't to be trusted."

Then she sighed, "oh whatever little boy! You can't threaten me! A year from now my business will still be alive and thriving. You on the other hand will be outside begging for quarters." She said dismissing him.

"Chantel!" His voice boomed when he called my name.

Mona and I both jumped. "Yes?" I said nervously.

"Get your stuff; you don't work here no more. This place is going out of business. I got a job for you."

"Ooh! Scary! Too bad that job will only be in his lap. Go on if you're stupid." She said dismissing the whole thing.

I wasn't sure if what Derrick said was true or not, but I didn't have to take her treating me like this. I figured I'd find a job somewhere else in this big ole mall. I started grabbing my stuff. Mona huffed and said I was completely dumb for following him. I'm not gonna lie, I did feel a little stupid. But if I stayed after this, she would only treat me worse. When I had my things, I stopped behind Derrick waiting for him to lead the way. Then Derrick rattled off a phone number. "Robert K right? I'll call him and let him know why his business is failing." Then he started walking.

"How do you know my father's number?" She yelled.

"Only a fool underestimates a stranger!" He said then he walked out the store, with me on his heels. He slowed down so that I could walk next to him once we were in the mall. "Stuff like that happens all the time doesn't it?"

I shrugged, "yeah but it's no big deal. I would've gotten her back later."

"How so?" He pointed his eyes at me.

"I didn't have an exact plan yet. But I would've figured something out." I said

"Let's go tell your brother where you'll be working on Tuesdays, Thursdays, and Saturdays."

"You know my brother? How do you know my schedule?" I asked

"I know a lot of things. Come on..." He said leading the way to the theater. Cyrus was emptying the trash at the entrance when we walked up. "Hey D-Rick what's going on?" Cyrus said not realizing I was with him.

They shook hands, "nothing much. We just wanted to let you know that your sister just quit over there at the travel store, she's gonna work for my father at the Mitigated Staffing Services remote office here in the mall." He said matter of factly.

"O....k.... I guess I'll see you there in a little bit." Cyrus said to me. I had serious butterflies in my stomach as I waved bye to Cyrus and walked away with Derrick. "How do you know my brother?" I asked

"I know a lot of people for a lot of different reasons." He said. I guess that was supposed to be an answer. I decided to accept it for now. He held the glass door open for me when we got to the office space. An older Grandma looking lady was sitting at the receptionist desk. "Ms. Laverne this is Chantel. She's gonna assist you on Tuesdays, Thursdays, and Saturdays." Derrick said

"Hello baby, how you doing?" She said getting up to give me a hug.

She seemed like she was a sweet lady. "Hello" I said

"You can sit at this desk." Derrick pulled out the chair. I sat down. "You can put your stuff in the drawers; this will be your desk."

"Thank you." I said feeling somewhat funny about being here.

"Ms. Laverne can you give her a little orientation and show her what you need her to do. I gotta call Malcolm and tell him she's here."

Then a bigger and blacker man walked in the door, his face was even more serious than Derrick's as if that could be possible. His eyes were stuck on me. "Malcolm we just said your name." Ms. Laverne said

"Did you now?" He said, his voice was a lot deeper than Derrick's. "Malcolm this is Chantel." Derrick said plainly.

Malcolm finally looked at someone else. "So what's the story?"

"I went in, she's here." Derrick said

Malcolm looked at me, his face was serious. "So I guess this means you have a plan." Malcolm said walking to the back. Derrick walked with him.

I exhaled, Ms. Laverne laughed at me. "Oh honey you can relax. If you're here that means you're good people."

"It does? How would they know."? I asked

"Trust! They do their homework. Come on let me show you around." She said

Ms. Laverne showed me around the office. There was a bathroom, offices, a conference room, a small kitchen, and a room she called the mailroom. There was a ton of mail slots on the wall. She said some staff members drop by to pick up their mail. She told me to continue to dress like I was now. Slacks and a blouse. She said on Saturdays I could wear jeans. After talking to me for a while she smiled at me and said I was gonna fit in nicely around there. I smiled because I had no idea what she meant. I felt like I just joined a secret society without knowing I was signing up.

"How did you end up working for Derrick?" Cyrus asked as we made our way to the bus stop.

"It all happened so fast, I can't really tell you." I said scratching my head.

"Be careful, I don't know if I like you working there." Cyrus said thinking about it. "D-Rick is cool and all, but I hear things about him and his family. You remember Pearla?" I nodded, "that's his cousin."

"She's crazy!" I said wide-eyed.

"I know! But as crazy as she is, she doesn't jump bad with him, but then again remember Tim on my baseball team? That's his cousin too."

Boy, do I remember Tim. I had the biggest crush on him when my brother was playing. Tim was Asian and black and SO FINE! Tim was always respectable, well mannered, and focused on the game. He never knew I existed. His sister Tina was stuck on herself though. A little boy crazy, but you know how gorgeous girls are... It is truly a small world. I wondered how they all interacted. Was Derrick crazy like Pearla, or disciplined like Tim? And why did he notice me when he could've brought anyone in this office? As I was lost in my thoughts, I realized my mind had wandered off and Cyrus was now blank staring at me. I guess he said something when I stopped listening. I smiled a guilty smile at him. I was getting ready to say something when a beautiful old school car pulled up next to us. Both of us looked into the car. "Get in," Derrick said.

Cyrus looked at me like I did something wrong. I shrugged and then walked to the car, it was cold and dark. I knew he didn't want to be out here no more than I did. I got in the backseat. "Thanks man!" Cyrus said.

"No problem." Derrick said glancing at me. "Why don't you have a car?" That question was for Cyrus.

"Can't afford one right now. The bus works fine, sometimes we get rides."

Derrick nodded his head. "I hear you. You going to school after graduation?" Derrick was heading towards our apartment even though neither one of us were directing him.

"Naw! I gotta get a job. I gotta move out as soon as I can. Saving as much money as I can right now. I might loop back around and take some classes later though." Derrick nodded his head like he understood. "You going to school?"

Derrick exhaled, "yeah. I'm going." He said like it was no big deal.

"Must be nice." Cyrus said

Derrick glanced at Cyrus, "do you wanna go?"
"Yeah! I'd be a fool not to want to go. But school wasn't in my parent's plan for me. I gotta make my own way." Cyrus said sounding defeated like he normally did when it came to our parents.
"What about her? She always got her nose in a book, she going?" Derrick asked Cyrus like I couldn't speak for myself.
"We're hoping for a scholarship." Cyrus said
Derrick pulled in front of our building. "It's no problem to bring you guys home when you don't have a ride." Derrick said
"Alright man, thanks." Cyrus said
When Derrick drove away, we asked each other at the same time how he knew where we lived. Cyrus said he probably got it off my W-4 when I filled it out. I guess he's right.
Cyrus asked me if Derrick flirted with me, and I told him no. Derrick didn't even really look at me except that time when I told him about his smoothie order.

****

Our plan is to move out as soon as Cyrus graduates from high school, he says he's not leaving me to fin for myself while our dysfunctional parents forever ruin me. So I take my usual sixty dollars off the top, and then Cyrus and I put the rest of our money in our savings account to save for a deposit when we move out. We've been working on this plan since we were in middle school. We have over five thousand saved combined. Our parents only do what they have to for us, it's like they said lets have two kids, then afterwards they changed their minds. The basic necessities we have, a roof over our heads, and beds to sleep in. ANYTHING else we have to provide for ourselves. And since it is their house, anything we have that they may want they take. So if I cook the groceries I bought using their stove, electricity, or refrigerator it is their right to help their-selves to it. Even if they eat it up, it doesn't matter it's their house. Even my clothes the little bit that I have. Since my mom and I are about the same size, she helps herself to what I have and if she ruins it or decides to keep it for herself, I can't say nothing it's her house. They have to know we aren't staying here, and I really don't think they care all that much. As long as they don't get any bills behind us, they could careless.

I love working at Mitigated. I quit my job at the Smoothie Stand once Ms. Laverne said I was doing such a good job and she recommended that Derrick tell his father to give me a raise. I was expecting something like a twenty cent an hour raise or something like that. But they gave me four dollars more an hour, which made my take home more than what I was taking home from both jobs and still only working the days I worked. Cyrus suggested that I quit the Smoothie Stand and stick with the one job so I could have more time to study, work on my projects, and rest. I wanted to argue that we could stack that much more money faster if I kept both jobs. But the idea of going to bed like a normal person was appealing to me. Sometimes I would be up until all hours of the morning finishing school work, only getting a catnap and then rushing to school and then work. So I decided to take Cyrus' advice and my energy level at school has tremendously increased. Malcolm still hasn't warmed up to me yet although Ms. Laverne says he has. I can't tell, he says… "Chantel" when he walks in the door. He nods at me, and then he goes to his office. Sometimes I hear Ms. Laverne back there talking to him, going on and on about whatever, and laughing at her own jokes. The way she comes out of there you would swear he was back there laughing with her too.

I don't get it, but it's none of my business. It's not like he comes in everyday or anything. Sometimes a couple of weeks go by and then boom, there he is. He goes in his office; sometimes he conducts meetings in the conference room. One time I suggested to Ms. Laverne that we order snacks for his meeting and have them set up before the meeting started. When he went in the conference room he called Ms. Laverne in there, they closed the door. I thought he was mad about the snacks. I was sitting there panicking thinking I overstepped my boundaries, but Ms. Laverne came out and said that Malcolm loved the snacks and he was very thankful for them. I was SO confused I thought he was mad. That night when Derrick came out of the meeting he told me I did a good job too.

Cyrus keeps asking me if Derrick flirts with me or anything and I keep telling him no. Derrick talks to Ms. Laverne and I, but he doesn't flirt with me. Sometimes I catch him looking at me, but he doesn't do anything. Its more like he's thinking and happens to be looking in my direction, and then I look at him. I've seen his girlfriend, and of course she's beautiful! She seemed nice enough, who am I to judge? Derrick made sure he introduced her to me though. She kind of looked at him funny when he did it. It did seem like I was somewhat important, but I told myself to not put more on it than there actually was. Ms. Laverne smiles at me all the time whenever Derrick comes around. I ignore her hoping she's just assuming I like him and that she can't tell that I actually do like him. I try very hard to keep that to myself. I haven't even expressed that to Cyrus, although I think he knows too. As long as no one tries to confront me on it, it's all-good.

Chapter 2

My mouth fell open. It's like one-day they were here and the next day they were gone. I didn't even notice a going out of business sign or anything. Last I knew Mona was sitting at the counter looking sad and then the next thing I know the whole store is gone. I guess Derrick's words hit their mark. Ms. Laverne and I stood there staring at the empty store while I told her how I used to work there. She took a sip of her smoothie while she shook her head saying that was a shame. As we walked back to the Mitigated office we saw Malcolm and a white man walking into the office.
"Hey Tim!" Ms. Laverne called out
"Hey how you doing Ms. Laverne?" Tim said coming for his hug.
"Chantel this is Derrick's grandfather Tim." She said
I did a double take. When I looked at his face I could see Derrick in his face, but I had NO IDEA he had such a close white relative.
"Hello" I said
Tim and Ms. Laverne started cracking up. Malcolm went inside.

"It's ok honey people always respond that way when they see us. I don't know why, all my grandchildren get their good looks from me." He said with a smile
"I don't know about that Tim, your wife was gorgeous!" She said
"She was, wasn't she," he said pulling his wallet out his back pocket. He showed me a picture of a truly beautiful and breathtaking CHOCOLATE woman.
"Wow!" Is all I could say.
"Yep, they don't make them like this anymore," he stared at her picture, with nothing but love in his eyes.
"Tim, you gotta get back out there. You could find someone." Ms. Laverne said
"No one could ever replace Annette. I had a wonderful time with the love of my life. Now I'm just passing time. I'm not gonna pretend with someone else. Nope its pretty pointless." He said with a smile plastered on his face to hide his pain.
"I understand, well you gotta come over for dinner with Henry and I one of these days." She said as we walked towards the office.

"Naw, but thanks. Lately people only invite me over when they think they've got a friend they can match me up with. I'm just saying no these days."

Ms. Laverne laughed cause she knew he was talking about her too. "Well its an open invitation, you're welcome whenever." She said still laughing as she walked through the doors.

"How do you guys have smoothies and the mall isn't even open yet?" Malcolm said standing in the hallway

"Chantel's got the hook up, why you want one?" She said.

"Yes" he said to my surprise.

I moved backwards towards the door, "what kind do you want? Derrick always gets pineapple peach or strawberry banana or chocolate peanut butter?" I don't know why my heart was racing or I was talking so fast.

Malcolm looked at me without saying a word for the longest thirty seconds ever. "The first one, what about you Tim?"

"Same" he said with a smile.

"Ok, I'll be right back." I said hurrying away before he could get his wallet out.

I turned around and Derrick was at the door with a guy who looked like a little younger version of him. The guy smiled at me, "Where you hurrying off to?"

"I'm going to get smoothies, did you want one?" I said bouncing my eyes between them.

"We'll come with you." Derrick said calmly

My knees got weak a little. "Ok"

"So you're Chantel! Nice to finally meet you." He said

Derrick gave him evil eyes, which made him laugh. "Yep, and you are?" I said

"Darryl, his younger prettier brother." He said with a smile.

"In your dreams! You wish you were as fine as me!" Derrick said without a smile.

"Nice to meet you Darryl." I said, "oh Derrick. Did you see that the luggage store is gone?"

"I told that girl they were going out of business." He said unaffected.

When we got to the Smoothie Stand, Shelly's eyes got big. She hesitantly walked to the front. "Shelly I need more smoothies."

"Un huh" she said real nervous.

"What's wrong with her?" Darryl asked

"She always acts like that." Derrick said

"She scared of you D-Rick?" Derrick shrugged like he didn't care. "Aw! That's too bad." He tisked at her. "You can't judge a book by its cover. He ain't that bad." Darryl said

"Says who?" Derrick asked looking at his brother

"Momma!" Then they both started cracking up.

Shelly and I didn't get the joke, but they were both laughing really hard. I was tickled to see him laugh like that. I had never seen this side of him. "What can I get for you?" Shelly asked

"Chantel knows what I like." He said almost smiling at me.

"Aw! Ain't that sweet!" Darryl said looking at the menu. "Let me get an apple pineapple mango one." Then he looked at me.

"Chantel, what's my brother gonna have?"

Everybody looked at me. I looked at Derrick's face, he seemed happy with his brother. "Give him the pineapple peach, and I need two more." Derrick smiled quickly then his face went back to its normal seriousness. "Put them on my tab with Cadence." Shelly rolled her eyes.

"What's wrong with her? Its too early in the morning to be in a funky mood already." Darryl said

"Are you guys still hiring?" Shelly asked.

"No!" Derrick said looking her in her face.

"D is she that bad though?" Darryl asked.

"She's heck of negative!" Derrick said staring at her.

"You've been talking about me?" Shelly said to me looking hurt. "Nope, she hasn't said a word. I can tell. Instead of being happy for your friend, you over there pouting. I bet you always downing people and stuff. We don't need that in my office." he said

Shelly turned around and started making the smoothies. "Good thing she gotta make them right there and not in the back. I wouldn't be surprised if she spit in yours." Darryl said

Derrick stared at her, "she better hope she's never that dumb!" Shelly quietly made our smoothies, and then she handed them to us, then she went to the back. As scared as she was of Derrick I imagined her going to the back to cry.

****

"What you and your brother got going on tonight?" Derrick asked as Ms. Laverne and I shut down everything for the rest of the weekend.

Ms. Laverne had a goofy grin on her face. "Nothing, we were gonna go home, relax, veg out maybe. What about you?" My heart was pounding but I told myself to be cool.

"One of my cousins is having a kick back, I wanted you and your brother to come." He said

"A kick back?" I asked

"Yeah, another word for house party or just hanging out."

"What should I wear?"

"Whatever, its casual. Don't worry about dressing up. You could come as you are." He said

"I think Cyrus doesn't get off until later tonight though." I said

"You don't think he trust me with your safety?"

"My brother is very protective of me." I said

"As he should be, I can respect that. Do you want to go?" He asked me looking me in my eyes.

I felt embarrassed especially with Ms. Laverne over there listening acting like she wasn't. "Yes, but I feel like I should check with Cyrus."

"Ok, I'll walk you over. If he says no, I'll take you home."

We walked over to the movie theater, and Cyrus was working at the concession stand. The guy at the door let us in after Derrick shook his hand. I told Cyrus about the party. Cyrus said he didn't get off for another two hours. Derrick told him he'd send someone to pick him up and bring him to the party if it was ok with him. Cyrus asked me to give them a minute to talk so I walked away. Derrick's eyes were serious and so were Cyrus's, Cyrus was gesturing with his hands to get his point across. Derrick smiled and then they shook hands. Cyrus told me he'd see me at the party, but if at any time I felt uncomfortable all I had to do was raise my hand and say so. I gave him a hug and then I nervously walked away with Derrick. I tried to mask my nervousness, but I wasn't doing a good job of it. Derrick looked at me smiled and put his arm around my neck. I thought I was gonna die, he told me I needed to relax. When we walked past the Smoothie Stand Shelly's mouth fell open as she saw us walking with his arm around my neck. I smiled real big when that happened. I took in Derrick's smell and I impressed it on my brain. If this was as close as I ever got to having him touch my body I wanted to remember it always. When we got in the car, I turned to him. "Will your girlfriend be mad about you bringing me?" I asked hoping he'd say she wasn't his girlfriend anymore.

"Nope" he said focusing on the road.

"Is she gonna be there?"

"Nope"

"Will she know about this?"

"What's to know? I'm bringing my friend to a kick back with my family. It ain't none of her business." He said nonchalantly.

"Oh" I said feeling deflated.

"What about you?"

"Me what?"

"Where's your man at?"

"Nonexistent. Kind of really don't have time for one." I said

"Please! Who can't make room for romance? There has to be somebody."

"Nope, nobody." I said looking out the window

"You just don't be paying attention."

I frowned, "what do you mean?"

"Next time you go to the food court look over at the French fry hut. There's a guy over there who's got it bad for you."

"EEEWWWLLLL! You mean Wilbert?" I laughed

"Why Big Willie gotta be on yuck status?" He smiled

"I don't know, but he don't like me. He like Shelly."

"Are you sure about that?"

"Positive! He's asked her out a bunch of times. Every one hundredth time he's asked she's said yes."

"My bad, I thought he was looking at you." He said pulling up to a house that was full of people. It was a bunch of black people inside and a bunch outside. I looked at the house and swallowed. I was nervous. "You can leave your purse and jacket in the car."

"Excuse me, this is Oakland." I looked around.

"Look at that porch. All those Latour's up there ain't gonna let nothing happen to my car. You're with me, come on." He said getting out the car. A bunch of BIG guys looked at us getting out the car. They started calling out to Derrick, and he answered. It was interesting to watch, yet another side to him. "Everybody this is Chantel, Chantel this is everybody!"

Everyone started saying hi at once. I smiled and waved, and then
Derrick led me by the hand inside. Darryl was in the middle of the
living room dancing. Everyone else was sitting back and egging
him on. He danced really well. "What's up Chantel?" Darryl said in
the middle of his dance. I waved a shy wave, and then girl cousins
of Derrick came over saying hi. Some were older and some were
as young as me if not younger.
"Derrick she's pretty!' I turned my head to see who said that.
"Where's the stuck up chick you normally rock with?"
Derrick smiled, "she's not here is she?"
I wanted him to loop back around to the "she's pretty" part. He
didn't say anything to this woman to lead her to believe I was just a
friend. Then someone handed him a drink, the guy asked me what I
wanted to drink. I said water and he gave me a look like I had to be
kidding. Derrick told him to bring me water. When the guy
brought me water back he said, he'd be back in a minute to find out
what I really wanted. Derrick asked me if I've ever had a drink
before and I told him I hadn't. Darryl came over, snatched my
hand, and pulled me on the dance floor area with him. They were
playing hit after hit on the house stereo that pumped out bass like
you wouldn't believe. One girl kept eyeing me like she was trying
to figure me out. She stopped dancing and sat over to the side
watching Darryl and I dance. I couldn't tell if she was nice or not.
Darryl noticed her watching and he made her dance with us. "Lanie
be nice, this is our friend Chantel." He said to her just over the
music. "Chantel this is our goofy cousin Lanie, she's always leery
of new people excuse her." I smiled and gave her a hug telling her
it was nice to meet her. She looked like she was digesting my
niceness then she focused on her dancing, but I knew she was
watching me. Two hours flew by and before I knew it Cyrus
walked in the door with a tall caramel brown guy that everyone
was calling Drew. Cyrus said hi to everyone as he came over to
me. He shook Darryl's hand and then he asked me how I was
doing. I told him I was fine. Then I told him that someone offered
me a drink, but I asked for water. Cyrus smiled at me and patted
my back. Then he walked away as Darryl and I continued dancing.
Cyrus came back with a red cup and said "screwdriver." I tasted it

and it tasted like weird orange juice. Derrick was watching me with a smile on his face. Cyrus asked me if I liked it, I told him it would do. I downed my drink and then I put my cup on the mantle. Darryl asked me if I've ever drunken before. When I said no, he smiled and said this was going to be fun. Cyrus was dancing with an older woman; he was an older lady magnet for some reason. My drink had me feeling GOOD! I let go and did all the moves just like I wanted to without reservation. I heard Lanie tell Darryl so far

I was cool, I don't know why that picked my spirits up, but it did.

After a little bit Derrick cut in on Darryl and I's dance, my heart started beating again. He moved like butter, he kept smiling at me telling me I was gone. I tried to lie and say I wasn't, but I knew he was right. Then the cousin that said I was pretty stood in the middle of the floor. "Alright! This is the last song, and then all ya'll gotta get out!" She said

"Aw man! Come on Renee!" Someone said

"Whatever! You heard me!"

The music cranked out a lighter tune than we had been listening to. "Could you be the most beautiful girl in the world? Plain to see, you're the reason that God made a girl." Derrick swept me into his arms and danced close to me while the song played. I melted in his arms, it was like a dream come true moment for me. I expected Cyrus to object, but he kept a watchful eye on us, but he didn't say anything. When the song went off, I screamed internally. I didn't want the moment to end. Derrick introduced me to his other brother Drew. Drew looked more like Malcolm than Derrick did, but all three of them favored. Drew was the only light brown-skinned one. But they all had curly hair, and fresh haircuts. Drew told me it was nice to finally meet me.

I looked at Derrick and asked him why people keep saying "oh you're Chantel? Or she's Chantel?"

Drew smiled at Derrick, Derrick smiled back. "Cause they know we got a new receptionist."

"Oh," I said not masking my disappointment.

"And..." Drew said rolling his hands like he was telling Derrick to say more.

Derrick frowned at Drew, "And, I've been telling them about the good job you've been doing."

Drew smiled, "and...." he chuckled

Derrick sucked his teeth, "SHUT UP NIGGA! AIN'T NOBODY ASKED YOU NOTHING!" He said halfway laughing. I could definitely get used to his smile.

****

Derrick convinced me that Cyrus and I needed a phone. So I got a basic phone line. The only time it rang was if Derrick or Cadence were calling. I had the phone company come out while our mother was at work and fortunately our father wasn't home. I only plug the phone line in when I'm home, and I keep the ringer off. I got one of those phones that lights up when it rings, so that I'd know if someone was calling. If my parents knew about the line they'd take it over. Sometimes Derrick calls me and we talk for hours. My heart pounds out of my chest when I see the phone glow. I'm disappointed every time it's only Cadence, but I enjoy chatting with her as well. Derrick and I talk about all kinds of things. I feel a sense of accomplishment if I make him laugh. Since he's always so serious you wouldn't expect him to laugh or be silly. But now I guess he's comfortable enough around me where he shows that side too. I think about him all the time. In my dreams he loves me too. We're married and just the whole happy scene.

Cyrus got a job at the airport, so now he only works one job too. But that also means that I ride home with Derrick all alone. JOY! Sometimes we sit in his car in front of the building talking for hours. The first time Cyrus came home and saw Derrick's car sitting with the windows all foggy he almost lost it. Derrick almost smiled at Cyrus when he saw we were just talking and that nothing was happening. If Cyrus only knew how much I wished something happened, but alas Derrick only sees me as a friend. I know this because sometimes we talk about his girlfriend, if he liked me I don't think we'd talk about her. Ms. Laverne gives me that goofy smile whenever Derrick comes in the office and when he's there to pick me up.

****

"Welcome to Mitigated Staffing Solutions, how may I help you today?" I said as a guy walked in the door.

The guy was slightly tall, cocoa brown with long dreads. "I'm here to pick up mail for Lamont Jenkins." He said with kind but serious eyes.

Ms. Laverne smiled, "how you doing baby?"

"I'm good Ms. Laverne, how are you?" He said. I walked back to his mail slot. It was full of envelopes. As I walked towards the front I stopped. It looked like the mail had gotten mixed up. As if he could read my thoughts. "It's all mine Jeremy, Lamont, and Yussef."

I looked at Ms. Laverne and she nodded to confirm his statement. "Malcolm's in the back baby, go ahead and go in." She said

"Thank you," then he looked at me. "When did you get here?"

"A few months ago." I said

He looked like he made a mental note of it, and then he went to the back.

Then another guy walked in the door. "Welcome to Mitigated Staffing Solutions, how may I help you?" I said

The guy looked at me for a few minutes like he was taking me in. Then he smiled at me, "my name is Kevin. I need a job." He said

I grabbed applications, a clipboard, and a pen for him. "Please fill out these applications and have a seat. I'll take them when you're done."

While he was filling out his application I caught him looking at me a few times. I blushed and so did he. Ms. Laverne laughed out loud at us. When he was done he walked back up to the counter. I gave the clipboard to Ms. Laverne, she determined appointments, etc.

"So what's your name?" He asked

"Chantel" I said

"I don't believe in beating around the bush. You got a boyfriend Chantel?"

"No," I said

"Uh hem!" Ms. Laverne said, "you might wanna find out how old that girl is before you get too deep."

His smile kind of dropped. "How old are you?"

Suddenly I felt self-conscious. "16" I said

Kevin looked up at the ceiling exhaled and then back at me. "I'm 23"

"Un huh, go ahead and have a seat sweetheart. I'll be with you in a minute." Ms. Laverne said shooing him to sit. She went over his application. "Who referred you?" She asked him.

He was still staring at me from his seat. "Curtis" he said not taking his eyes off of me.

Ms. Laverne got up and gave him a card. "I'll call you after the background check."

"Thank you" he said, "it was nice meeting you Chantel."

"Bye, nice meeting you." I said

"I hope to see you around." He said

****

"I'm going to LA with my family for a quick weekend trip."
Derrick said

"Ooh! Sounds like fun. Can you bring me something back?" I
asked

His face was serious, but that didn't bother me so much any more.
"What do you want?"

I rolled my eyes around like I was thinking. "Surprise me."

"What?"

"I wanna see what you think I would like." I said

He rolled his eyes, "my point is that I won't be able to pick you up
Saturday. I've arranged for a car service to pick you up."

"You don't have to do that. I can take the bus." I said

"I know I don't have to, but your brother has entrusted your safety
to me. So I've made arrangements for you. When you leave, go to
the parking lot where I normally park. You'll see a black car with a
driver."

"When are you coming back?"

"Most likely Sunday." He said

"You're missing school to go with your family?" I said in fake
shock

His face softened, "my parents… I think they may FINALLY get it
right. Malcolm bought a condo that my momma is too excited for

us to see." He looked down and smiled, "it's finally happening like
it should've been all along."

I LOVED his smile, I LOVED how sentimental he was about the
idea of his parents being together. I LOVED that he was sharing
this information with ME! I put my hands on his, "I'm happy for
you guys. Sounds like you've been waiting for this to happen for a
long time." I said

"They've gotten close before, but it was always something. Now
there shouldn't be anything standing in their way." He smiled
harder.

"Look at you smiling and showing a softer side, I like it." I said

He quickly dropped his smile, and the coldness returned to his
face, "what?"

"Oh come on Derrick, if you can't be vulnerable with your friends…" I smiled while rubbing his hands.

He looked at my hands, "why don't you talk about your parents?" I made a "oh crap" face. He smiled, "Aw! The tables turn…"

"What do you want to know? I think I've told you everything." I said

"You haven't told me anything really." He said

"Which shows that there isn't much to tell." I shrugged sitting up straight in my chair.

"You know you're gonna have to do better than that." He said preparing himself for what I was gonna say.

"My mother is an only child, she married my dad right out of high school. Before long they had Cyrus and right after that they had me. My mother is in love with my father, so much that it doesn't bother her that he doesn't even provide for her. I think she wants him to stay no matter what. When it came down to choosing between him or us, she chose him. We've never been the same since." I said

Derrick leaned in, "how did she have to choose?"

It felt like I instantly burst into flames. "Derrick! I can't!" I started fanning myself. I felt like my air was leaving me. Derrick eyed me closely. "I can't!"

He touched my hand; his touch was strong, deliberate, and protective. "It's ok, I think I get it. I've seen that same reaction from my momma once. Tell me when you're ready." He said with soft eyes. I wanted to leap off my chair and into his lap. The only person I've ever been willing to talk to on this level has been my brother, and well we both live this hell of a life. We don't talk about it. I tried to pull myself together; I didn't want him to think I was weak. "So you gonna miss me?"

"Of course! Don't you know how expensive chauffeurs are in this town?" I said with a smile

He smiled.

****

"Thank you for calling Mitigated Staffing Solutions how may I direct your call?" I said

The caller was breathing hard, "Chantel!"

Derrick was angry, my heart dropped for him. "Yes?" Derrick didn't say anything but I could hear him. "Derrick?" Ms. Laverne looked at me with a question mark on her face. "Are you ok?"

"Yes…. no…. I don't know." He was all over the place.

"I can come over tomorrow when you get back in town. What's your address?" I said picking up my pen.
"I'm already back."
"But you left yesterday morning." I said
"And we were back by last night." He paused. "She's really upset and I don't know what to do."
"Just be there for her." I said

"She…." he was quiet. "I gotta call you back." Then he hung up.

Ms. Laverne was on the edge of her seat, "What's going on?"
"Derrick's back already. His mother is upset about something, and he sounds really upset." I said
"Oh Lord! What did Malcolm do?" She said
"You think he did something?" I asked
"I can't imagine what. He's been real excited lately haven't you noticed?"
I blank stared at her. "How in the world can you read moods on him? He always looks the same to me."
She smiled, "how do you read Derrick then?"

I blushed, "he's different. It's little subtle things, but now he smiles and laughs around me."
"You two are a mess." She chuckled
"What do you mean?"
"Your little love thing, you got going on." She said
I scrunched up my face. "Love thing? We're just friends." I unsuccessfully tried to say nonchalantly.
She gave me a knowing look, "UN huh!"
"Ok! Ok! Ms. Laverne you twisted my arm, I'll tell you that I might have a tiny itty bitty, barely even noticeable crush on him. But he has a girlfriend, and she's gorgeous. He's not checking for me."
She looked at me like I insulted her. "You say that like you're not."
"I'm not on her level. I understand it, and I accept it."
Ms. Laverne got up and locked the door. Then she made me get out of my chair and she took me in the bathroom. "LOOK IN THIS MIRROR!" She looked and sounded mad. "Look at your face!"

My eyes dropped to the floor. "DO I HAVE TO GO GET A
BELT? LOOK AT YOUR FACE!" I looked by force. Her face and
voice turned tender. "Look at your eyes, they're so exotic and
wonderfully big. If you look closely they look like they reflect
specks of gold. Those high cheekbones, this beautiful chocolate
skin, and those beautiful full lips, you look like you come straight
from a beautiful island. You are gorgeous! But! Even more
important than that, you're smart, a hard worker, and a good
person. All of that is why Derrick likes you."
My eyes got big, "He does not."
"When have I lied to you?" She said with her hands on her hips.
"How do you think he knew your name before you told him? He
made it a point to know who you are before you knew him. "
I stood there staring at my face; I wish I could see what Ms.
Laverne saw. All I could see is what everyone has always poked
fun at; I don't really look like anyone from around here.
At the end of my shift, I followed Derrick's instructions. But
instead of a car service he was there. He was standing next to the
car, I gave him a big hug, and his body was trembling. He held on
to me real tight not letting go for a LONG time. He wasn't crying
but it seemed like he wanted to. "Is your mother ok?" I said
looking in his eyes.
His eyes glazed over; "no" then he slumped into his car. "Malcolm
and Andrew are the stupidest people when it comes to love.
Malcolm can't get it right to save his life. Drew had a good woman,
for the most part, and he messed that up for some hood rat.

Malcolm keeps breaking my momma's heart! I CAN'T TAKE IT
NO MORE!" He was angry and his eyes were evil. "I could've
killed him tonight! If it wasn't for my momma we were going to."
Even though I wanted to shrug it off like he was just kidding the
look on his face said he wasn't joking at all. "I'm glad you didn't."
He squinted his eyes, "why?"
I swallowed, "from the way Ms. Laverne paints the picture of your
mother and father, he is so in love with your mother."
"You don't even know what he did to the last man who hurt my
mother. Why does he get a pass? Just because he's Malcolm?"
"Did he intentionally hurt your mother?" I don't know why I felt
sorry for Malcolm in that moment. It seemed like Derrick was in
full protection mode. I imagined all three of them guarding his

mother like angry dogs ready to attack. There were three of them and only one Malcolm.

"That's not the point!" Derrick said still angry

"Thank you for coming to pick me up. You're such a good friend." Derrick looked at me his eyes were piercing. Then his face softened. "I see what you're doing."

"What am I doing?"

"You're trying to poke holes in my anger. You keep distracting me with positivity." His eyes stayed on me.

"Is it working?" I smiled

He hugged me in a bear hug, "I'm glad we're friends." Then he kissed my cheek. "Thank you."

Chapter 3

"Hello hello hello!" Caprice said walking in the door with a big smile. "Is Malcolm in?"

"No, not yet. You want your mail?" I said standing up.

"No it's okay, I can get it." She said walking to the back. She slowly walked back. "Where's Ms. Laverne?"

"She called in sick today." I said returning to my computer. Caprice sat at Ms. Laverne's desk opening her mail and reading. "You're in high school right?"

"Yep" I said

"When do you graduate?"

"Next year, I'm a junior." I said

"What are your...."

Cyrus walked in the door and she stopped mid sentence. "Chantel, what time do you go to lunch?" His face was really excited.

"Whenever, this is Caprice. Caprice that's my brother Cyrus." Caprice got up and walked to the counter. She stuck her hand out, "nice to meet you."

Cyrus looked stuck like he couldn't take his eyes off of her. "Likewise, you work for Mitigated?"

"I sure do." She smiled still holding his hand.

"I thought only men worked here." He said

"Temping is not just for men." She said, "Where do you work?"

"The airport. I'm still in school."

"High school? How old are you?"

"18, I graduate this summer." Then he gave her a knowing smile. "Is that a problem?"

I was sitting there taking notes. Caprice smiled at Cyrus, she found excuses to touch him. If the counter wasn't there I imagined her finding an excuse to put her body on his. She definitely had Cyrus' attention. I imagined Derrick looking at me like I was crazy if I tried that with him.

Cyrus told Caprice he was taking me to lunch. He invited her to come along. He told us he'd be back at twelve thirty. When he left, she started drilling me with questions. In the middle of her interrogation Malcolm walked in the office. He's slimmed down a lot, and now he seems easily excitable. Where before he was a little mellower. His eyes pointed at Caprice, "why aren't you on assignment?" His tone was serious.

Caprice straightened up. "My assignment ended yesterday."

Malcolm squinted his eyes, "that's premature! What did you do?"

Caprice swallowed, "Nothing. I've been waiting to discuss it with you."

Malcolm stood there like she was working his nerves. "Get in the office! You waiting for a special invite?" He had no patience.

I felt nervous for her. "Chantel!"

Hearing him suddenly say my name made me jump. "Yes Malcolm?"

His voice softened. "Ms. Laverne has a cold. Can you call Lamont with a grocery list to take to her? Tell him to get stuff to help her feel better."

"Of course. I'll make a list." I said

"Thank you," he said then he closed his door.

I wrote out my list, and then I called the number on file. A girl answered the phone. Lamont got on the phone, his voice was sad. He listened like he was writing as I slowly went down the list of things. When I mentioned the bouquet of flowers he asked what that was for. I told him we heal by sight as well. I could hear his smile through the phone, he said he liked that and he was gonna have to use that as well. He asked me how Malcolm was today. I told him he was very short with Caprice. Lamont laughed and said she does goofy stuff sometimes, but she's good at what she does. I told him that Malcolm looks like he's wasting away. He was concerned; he asked if Drew or any of his boys were coming by the office. When I said no, he asked about Tim. I told him Tim still comes.

I didn't mention when Tim came by the first time after they all came back. He was mad, and Malcolm looked like he was in trouble with his father. They went in the conference room, every once in awhile I heard Tim. They were in there a long time. When they came out Malcolm was sad and Tim looked sad. They hugged then Tim left. I told Derrick about it when he came to pick me up. He was real quiet for a while, and then he told me was going over to his grandfather's after he dropped me off.

Lamont asked me if I wanted something for lunch, I told him I was having lunch with my brother and Caprice.

Cyrus was waiting in the chair when Malcolm and Caprice came out his office. Cyrus said hello to Malcolm, they were chatting when Lamont walked in with lunch. Malcolm frowned at his bags. "What's that?" He barked

"You need to eat." Lamont said with sadness in his eyes.

"I don't need you to take care of me!" He barked again.

"Fight me if you want, but I got you food." He said walking past Malcolm to his office.

"Not in there, I don't want my office smelling like cheap takeout." Malcolm barked.

"You guys go to lunch, I'll man the phones while you're gone." Lamont said

When we walked out the mall, there was a black sedan. Cyrus was extremely excited. "This is my car!"

"What? How?" I said excited for him.

Caprice wasn't impressed, but she smiled. "I got a raise and right after graduation I'll start my new position." Cyrus said excited.

I gave him a huge hug. "So how much did the car set us back?" I asked

"Nothing, it's a perk." He said

Caprice smiled a knowing smile. "This has Malcolm written all over it."

I started to say something, Cyrus was so excited. "Thank you Malcolm! We can find a place now!" He said excited.

I got real excited and started jumping around. "Really?"

"Yes, we'll talk about it tonight when I pick you up." He said

My celebration stopped. "Derrick's gonna pick me up."

"Now that I've got a car he doesn't have to. Think about it, he can have his nights back." Cyrus said not picking up on my sadness.

I looked forward to getting off work just so I could spend time with Derrick. I didn't want to steal Cyrus' thunder, but I had to find a way to tell him I didn't want him to pick me up. I was quiet the rest of lunch thinking on my quandary.

When we got back to the office I convinced Cyrus to let Derrick pick me up tonight, and then Cyrus could pick me up after that. When Derrick met me in the parking lot that evening, I told him about Cyrus' promotion. He was happy for him until he heard about the car. I told him that Cyrus wants to pick me up from now on. His eyes got evil, "his schedule was changed?"

"I guess so, cause Cyrus is convinced he'll be able to pick me up on a regular basis." I said. We were in the right turning lane, Derrick threw the car into a sudden hard left turn. "WHAT'S WRONG WITH YOU?" I yelled.

Derrick had his hand out to steady me so that I didn't sway with the car but he didn't say anything. He drove top speed back to the mall. As if Malcolm was waiting for him, he was leaning against the hood of his car in the parking lot. Derrick got out the car angry. Malcolm watched him but he didn't move. Derrick didn't yell he walked up on Malcolm though, both of their eyes were angry. I WISHED I could hear what they were saying. All I could hear were low rumbles from their voices. Derrick leaned against the hood of his car matching Malcolm's stance. They went back and forth for a while. Then Malcolm stood up. He held both hands out like he was saying he came in peace or something. Derrick stood up and braced himself, and then he took a step to the left. Malcolm put his hands down. He started gesturing with his hands. Abruptly Derrick walked away, Malcolm got in his car. Derrick got in the car his eyes were red but he wasn't crying. He told me that Malcolm set up Cyrus' job at the airport, and he set up his whole raise. I asked him why that made him angry. He said it was all fine until he switched his schedule that was a jab at him. I looked confused, and then he said Malcolm knew that if he interfered with our friendship he'd have some thing to say about it and he did. "I value our friendship."

"Me too. Once I had time to slow down I realized Shelly is my only friend, and I think that was only because we worked together. You and Ms. Laverne are my only friends these days."

Derrick nodded his head. "So where you think you guys gonna move to?" He said changing the subject before it got too deep.

"I guess we're gonna talk about it tonight. But I would prefer somewhere close to school for now. So it won't be difficult to get to and from school." I said

"You want a car? That way you can keep your options open." He said nonchalantly.

"Eventually, but for now walking will do. I don't know how to drive." I said

We pulled up to the light, Derrick squinted his eyes at me. "Why don't you know how to drive?"

"Hello? Who was gonna teach me? Cyrus just got a car today." I said

"How did Cyrus get his license then?"

"Cadence" I smiled.

Derrick shook his head, "she let your brother walk all over her! What is she gonna think about Caprice?" He asked

I frowned, "we only had lunch."

Derrick looked at me like "yeah right." He pursed his lips. I wanted to bite them. "Five dollars says Caprice will be your first over night guest."

"Cyrus and Cadence go way back though." I said

"Don't matter Caprice is new booty." He said

"Is that what you would do?" I asked hoping he said no.

"Depends."

"On?" I said

"Who the old booty is. If I'm just passing time with them, who cares. I got needs; she got needs, who cares, but no one would come before my woman."

"What category is Abby in?" I was hoping he said he was passing time with her.

"Its hard to say?" He said flatly.

"Why?"

"It just is."

"Derrick that's not an answer." I said trying to mask my frustration.

He exhaled, "I like her enough to call her my girl and friend, but never enough to call her my woman."

"What is the difference between a girl and a woman?"

He smiled then he dropped the smile and looked at me. "You really wanna have this conversation?"

"I'm asking, so I'd say yes."

He shrugged, "you asked for it. I'll be nice to a girl; I'll take her out. Spend a little bit, and I do mean a little bit of money on her. NOTHING DEEP!" Then he licked his lips, "but my woman!" He readjusted in his seat, "that whole experience is on a whole other level!" He shook his head like he was remembering someone.

There was a lump in my throat, "what's her name?" I tried to ask like it wasn't gonna hurt to know there was someone in that space.

"*Raquel*!" His whole face lit up, and I started sweating. "Her family moved away some years ago. You can't do long distance on that level as little kids."

"Do you guys still talk?" I was hoping he said no.

"Every once in a blue moon, but nothing like before. She lives in a dorm so it's only so much talking we can do. " He said

"She's in college?" I don't know why I expected her to be his age or younger. I thought Cyrus was the only old lady magnet.

"Why you sound surprised?" He smiled

"I don't know, I guess I didn't expect her to be grown." I said feeling like an infant. "What made her special?"

"She's smart, sweet to me, got along good with my family. She was everything Drew's girl wasn't. There's more, but that's in the past."

"Are you guys going to get married?" I asked

"I doubt it, we've both grown in different directions since we last laid eyes on each other."

"But you should see the way everything about you changed when she came up. You still got feelings for her." I said hoping he'd argue with me.

"For who she was, and I know some of that may still be there. But we've both changed, I don't know who she is anymore. Especially once she decided to go by Brooklyn, she changed her name and a lot seemed to change with it."

"Seems like if she was here right now, you'd be with her."

"I don't have time for a relationship right now. Especially when I start college in the fall. I'm gonna be on the other side of the Bay with my head stuck in books. I may find a couple minutes for a girl, but I know better than to think I'll have time for a woman." He said looking at me.

"Oh," I said.

****

"So how does it feel to be in your own place?" Ms. Laverne asked. Last night was our first night in our one bedroom apartment. Cyrus and I were so excited. So what if we had no furniture, only our clothes, and the few things we bought at our parent's place. We were away from the selfish people! Yes! We didn't even say bye. We grabbed our stuff and left. The cold-blooded part is that it will probably take them a few days to realize we were gone. Cyrus insisted that I take the bedroom although I wanted him to have it since he paid the rent. But he said I should have the room. So our plan is to set up the dining area next to the kitchen like a small bedroom for him. Our place was nothing fancy at all. But it was ours, I cried a little when Cyrus gave me his speech about us finally being free from our parents. This morning Cyrus said it was the first night he slept peacefully. He said he didn't know sleeping could be so peaceful. He dropped me to school and then I caught the bus to the mall afterwards. "Ms. Laverne it feels WONDERFUL!"

Ms. Laverne smiled, and then she went to Malcolm's office. She came back with a manila envelope. "Everybody chipped in to give you guys something, but you know Malcolm he kicked it up a notch." She said with a big smile.

Inside the envelope was a bunch of regular sized envelopes. Each one was marked with a store name, a furniture store, a couple different department stores, and a grocery store. Each envelope had gift certificates, and the furniture store had the most in it. Tears poured out my eyes. "You guys didn't have to do this!"

Malcolm walked in as my tears poured over the envelopes. He saw my face and turned around. "Oh no you don't! Come here!" Ms. Laverne said.

Malcolm exhaled, "why did you wait so long to do this?" He sounded irritated.

"Cause I knew you were trying to avoid this." She said

When he got close I gave him a hug. Malcolm stood there letting me hug him. "Thank you Malcolm! Thank you from the bottom of my heart!" He felt like a rock. "Not just for this, but for everything!" I said

"Ok! Ok!" Malcolm said trying to get free. "Let me go!"

Then Derrick walked in the door. He had a question mark on his face. "Do you know what your father did for Cyrus and I?" I let go of Malcolm and handed Derrick the envelope as he came behind the counter.

Malcolm hissed and walked in his office. Derrick smiled at the envelopes. "Derrick knows he was in on it too." Ms. Laverne said giving Derrick a goofy grin. "I know I said it before, but you were gone too long. Don't ever let anything keep you away from here that long again. You hear me?"

"Yes ma'am." Derrick said almost smiling

"How's Amber?" She asked

"She's just as bad off as he is." He said nodding towards the office. "I told her I want him to come to my graduation."

Malcolm shut his door. "How did she respond?" She asked

He frowned, "she got all dramatic, that's not exactly her style."

"Matters of the heart will make you act that way."
Then the phone rang and I answered it. It was Cyrus and he wanted to know if Derrick could bring me home. I asked Derrick if he would take me home. He agreed. When we approached his car he handed me keys. "You better not hit anything!" He said giving me evil eyes.
My heart sank, "NO DERRICK!" I screamed running from him. He stood there looking annoyed. "You gotta learn some time." "But I'm scared!" I said

"You can't let fear rule you! Now stop playing and let's go!" He said tossing his keys to me. My hands were shaking I was nervous, and the fact that Derrick was watching me only made me more nervous. He gently put his hand on mine. "You can do this, relax!" Then he sat back.
I started the car, he told me to check my mirrors and make sure I could see. He calmly guided me through each step. We circled around the parking lot a few times until I got a better handle on stopping. Then he told me to drive us home. Sweat was pouring down my back. I managed to get us to my place without incident. I parked very crooked behind Cyrus. "This day has been amazing!" I said then I leaned over and kissed Derrick on the cheek. His face was serious, but I didn't know what that meant so I kept talking. "Thank you for everything! I truly appreciate it." Derrick was still staring at me. "You wanna come up?"
"Ok," He said.
As I opened the door I heard a female voice. Then I saw Caprice sitting on the floor with Cyrus. Derrick looked at me with an "I told you so look on his face." Cyrus was shirtless and Caprice's hair was all over her head. They were sitting on the floor eating Chinese food. "Did you eat?" Cyrus asked
"Yes," then I turned to Derrick. "This is our living room. Cyrus is going to have a make shift bedroom right here." I said walking over to the area. "That's our kitchen of course." Then I walked back across the living room with Derrick on my heels. "The bathroom, and that will be my bedroom." I said pointing at the door.
"Can I see it?" He said
"I don't have any furniture, there's nothing to see." I said opening the door.

He looked around and smiled. "Nice" Then he looked at me. "I got you a specific house warming present. But it's in the car. I'll be right back." He hurried out the door.

"He coming back?" Cyrus asked

"Yes, he went to get something out the car." I gasped as Derrick walked back in with a big box. "What did you do?"

"Whoa Derrick! That is nice!" Cyrus said

Derrick bought us a stereo system; it was a REALLY nice one too. Top of the line system. It was perfect size not too big, and not small. "Oh my God! Somebody has a crush on Chantel!" Caprice said

"No he doesn't, we're just friends." I said defending him.

"Where do you want it?" Derrick asked ignoring Caprice's comment.

"Out here…"

"In your room." Cyrus had the same goofy look Ms. Laverne gets.

"But…. it's for the house." I said

"This place ain't that big. It should go in your room." Cyrus said

Derrick brought the box in my room. "Thank you Derrick! You are the sweetest! Thank you for everything." I said

"This is in no way connected." He took a deep breath. "My family is going to throw me a graduation party. My parents are still gonna be beefing I can already tell. Do you wanna come to my party?"

"OF COURSE! Why would I miss it?" I said

He looked relieved, "but I won't introduce you to my mother yet. With them funking like they are, who knows how dramatic she'll be. "I don't want you to have the wrong first impression."

"That's fine," I said

****

I walked into the auditorium with a lady who had a large family with her. She handed a stack of tickets to the person manning the door, instead of counting them and the amount of people she had with her they just let us through. They went to the right and I went to the left. When I found a seat, I spotted Darryl talking to one of their cousins across the auditorium. The lady and her large family all came over to Darryl and hugged him and this really light-skinned woman. That had to be Derrick's mother. I liked how he called her momma. I couldn't wait until he was GROWN still

41

calling his mother momma. I promised myself to tease him about it later. Slowly but surely their section started filling in. I saw his grandfather walk in with Malcolm. When the graduates entered the auditorium Derrick was focused on the section where his family was sitting. Then my heart stopped when he stood up to give his valedictorian speech. When he stepped up to the podium his face was serious, my heart was racing cause I thought he would be nervous, I was. By the way he spoke you would have sworn he did it for a living. I was melting in my seat, his voice, his eloquent way of speaking, his gestures and voice infliction. I had a little pep talk with myself telling myself to get it together. Everyone was on their feet at the end of his speech. I knew I couldn't have been the only female affected by him like this. That thought made me calm down a lot. After the ceremony I gave him a hug in the auditorium before he went out to his family. He looked me in my eyes with his normal serious expression and asked if I was coming to his grandfather's house for the party. I told him I had to go run an errand with Cyrus but he would drop me off before he went to work. He said ok and then I walked away, a couple of girls nervously approached him saying bye. I saw no hint of a smile in his expression as he looked at them. That made me feel good. When I got to Derrick's grandfather's house I saw Kevin standing out front. "Hey you remember me?" He asked

"Of course I do how are you?"

"I'm good. I got a job." He smiled

"You're not here for the party?"

"Yes, in so many words."

"Ok so then I'll see you inside." I said walking towards the gate. When I walked inside the gate everybody was having a good time. Derrick's mother's family was all over. But Malcolm's people were here too. Malcolm was talking with Tim and two other relatives of Tim's; they all favored. Malcolm nodded at me when he saw me, but he continued on with his conversation. Derrick's cousin Tina came over. "Don't I know you from somewhere?" She was still gorgeous.

"Yeah, our brother's used to play baseball for the city together. I'm Chantel." I said

"Right I remember. Are you here alone?"

"Yes."

"Come sit with us." she motioned for me to follow her. They were all gorgeous. "This is Chantel, Chantel this is Sasha, Zoey, Tanisha, Erica, Pearla, Lanie, Liz, and Paulette." I said a general hello, but I felt under dressed. Although we were all wearing jeans and tops, theirs seem to go further. Everyone was nice, but Lanie and Pearla stared.

"Don't I know you?" Pearla asked while searching her mental Rolodex.

"We went to the same middle school." I said

"And remember when Tim was playing baseball with all those big kids? Her brother was one of the few nice ones on the team." Tina volunteered

"Somebody was mean?" Sasha asked

"Yes, they didn't like little Tim playing with them, and we were new to the area." Tina said

"Oakland doesn't like new comers." Paulette said

"What city does?" Liz said, and then she looked at me. "How you know Derrick?"

I felt like I was being interrogated. "I met him at the mall. We're just friends."

They all smiled. "Derrick makes friends you guys." Tanisha said with a smile. Then she pulled out a chair, "have a seat."

"Yeah... but..." she snapped her fingers like a light bulb went off.

"You're that girl from that night at my house."

"What girl?" Paulette asked

Pearla made her eyes big, "THE GIRL! The one Derrick was dancing with..." Pearla said bouncing her head.

"Oh!" Paulette smiled at me. "That girl!"

Pearla described the night very colorfully to everyone else. The way she explained it was like I didn't come as just a friend. I knew better, so I didn't say anything. I wished everything she was insinuating were true. Lanie didn't say much she kept watching me like she was trying to figure me out. Fortunately the interrogation kind of stopped, but Pearla and Tina kept looking at me. They weren't looking at me in a mean way, but like they were picking apart my face. Liz was telling the group something when Tina rudely interrupted by blurting out, "you're really pretty!"

Everyone stopped talking and looked at me again. If I could've ran I would've. "Thank you!" I said blushing, and hoping she wasn't trying to be funny.

"I can see why Derrick likes you." She said

They all smiled at me again. "Thank you, but we're just friends. He has a girlfriend."

"What girlfriend? Wouldn't a girlfriend come to her man's graduation party? The only girl friend I see here is you." Liz said

I swallowed, "Stop doing her like that." Tanisha barked, "if they aren't claiming each other it's for a reason."

Then Derrick walked over, serious face like usual. "When did you get here?"

"Just a little while ago. Tina invited me to come over and sit."

He put his hand out, "come on." I got up and took his hand. I could hear them whispering, but I was too embarrassed to look back. He took me over to his grandfather who greeted me with a hug. Then he introduced me to his Great-Uncles. Although they all had serious faces, his grandfather and Uncle Jeff seemed the nicest. Derrick didn't smile just like Malcolm and his Great Uncle Frank. Even though they were white you seemed to forget it when you talked to them. They talked just like Derrick and Malcolm. Derrick introduced me to a lot of cousins and Aunties and Uncles. Even his cousin Tim was there, who until seeing Derrick I thought he was the cutest guy ever. But now seeing him next to Derrick he isn't even a close eighth place. The song changed and Derrick pulled me to the dance area. We were dancing for a long time. At one point I saw his mother and a woman, most likely a relative, looking at me and whispering. I wondered if Derrick would introduce me. But when I realized that she looked upset, I didn't see the point in asking. Derrick kept me at his side the rest of the party. When I went to the bathroom inside the house it seemed like every person I walked past was smiling at me like they knew something I didn't. As I came out I saw his immediate family taking pictures. There was tension in their demeanor. But hey at least he had family to have tension with. Not that I think they care, but my parents haven't even attempted to reach out to Cyrus and I. At some point they have to notice that we're not sleeping in those bunk beds and that we don't live there anymore. Maybe they're relieved that we're gone. As we were leaving the party at the end of the night, Kevin was still outside. "D-Rick is this you?" He said to him in regards to me.

Derrick's face remained serious, he told him we're finishing up inside; but he didn't answer the question. Derrick had me drive us to my house. When we walked inside my place I had him have a seat on the couch while I went in my room. I was at a loss as to what to get him for his graduation. I hope he likes my gift. I put the hand held box in his lap and then I sat next to him on the couch. He looked at the box like it was suspicious, and then he asked me what was in it. I told him he would have to open it to see. He slowly opened the box like he didn't want one part of the wrapping to tear. He smiled real big when he revealed a wallet a lot like the one he picked out for Malcolm. He gave me a hug and thanked me. I was relieved that he liked my gift.

****

"Hey Chantel, fancy meeting you here." Pearla said as she walked into the office.

"Hey Pearla." I said watching her eyes bounce around the office. I wondered why she was here, and if at any minute her craziness would flash. "What can I do for you?"

"What time do you get off work?"

"In a couple of hours. What's up?"

"Liz, Paulette, and I are going to the movies. You wanna go?"

"My brother was gonna pick me up, can somebody give me a ride home?"

"Of course! I'll come back when it's time for you to get off work. Is Malcolm here today?" She asked

"No, but you never know when he'll show up." I said

Ms. Laverne came around the corner from the back. "Hey Pearla, how you been sweetheart?"

Ms. Laverne walked over and gave her a hug. "I'm better. How have you been? How's Henry?"

"He's good, tell your momma I said hi. Malcolm's not here right now."

"I know, I came to invite Chantel to the movies after work."

Ms. Laverne's smile dropped a little. "Chantel is a good girl. You better be on best behavior, I don't want none of your ways rubbing off on her." She said sternly like a mother.

"Ms. Laverne am I really that bad?" Pearla asked like she was getting a kick out of Ms. Laverne reprimanding her. Ms. Laverne blew air. "I'm good. I told you I've been doing better. Besides I think Derrick would kill me." She said with a smile

"He's not the one you should be worried about. He'll have to take a number. That girl is highly favored over here." My heart melted listening to Ms. Laverne talk about me like I wasn't there.

Pearla put her hand up, "Scout's honor!"

Ms. Laverne started laughing. "You were never a scout you nut!" She said giving her another hug.

"I hear you though. I'm glad to hear that you guys like her." Then she looked at me with a serious face. "It would suck to be her if that ever changed."

Ms. Laverne sat down at her desk. "See you in a little bit." She said waving her off.

When Pearla came back she was excited and energized. Cyrus didn't sound too happy about me hanging with Pearla, but it's not like he could tell me I couldn't go. The movie was fine, and then we went to get something to eat after the movies. Whenever I said something they were paying attention, like they were trying to figure me out. But they were all nice to me. Pearla said if I'm gonna be a part of the family we were going to have to hang out more often. I didn't realize I was petitioning to be a part of the family, but I loved the idea of it. I only had Cyrus; it would be nice to have more family.

****

Today is a R&B day. I turned on my stereo this morning and I couldn't stop singing. I sang while eating my breakfast. I sang in the shower. Cyrus smiled at me but he didn't object. He's always said that he loves my singing voice. But my parents would always tell me to shut up and that I sounded like a horse dying. So I never sang in front of people other than Cyrus. It was Sunday and Derrick and I were going to go look at apartments near his school, and get a feel for the area. I had my permit and I was going to take my driving test in days. The top to my lotion rolled under my bed. I bent down to get it; this old school jam had me going. I was belting out my tune for a minute while I was on the floor on my hands and knees. When I stood up Derrick was standing there with BIG eyes. I was completely embarrassed! I light weight screamed when I saw him. I didn't mean to torture him with my singing. "How come I'm just now finding out you can sing like that?" He said still looking awestruck.

"Sorry, I didn't mean to hurt your ears." I said hurrying over to the stereo to turn the music off.

"Hurt my ears?"

I didn't want to talk about it. "I'm ready, are you ready?"

"Sing something else." He said staring at me.

"No Derrick, let's just go." My face started stinging.

"You have a beautiful voice I wanna hear more."

I put my eyes on the floor and shook my head. "I'm too embarrassed. I never meant for you to hear that. I'm sorry."

"What are you apologizing for? I just told you that your voice is beautiful. I wanna hear more." I kept my eyes on the floor and I stood there feeling stuck. Derrick walked up to me and lifted my chin. "I have no reason to lie to you. If I tell you it's beautiful, then it is. I'll leave it alone for now, but you will sing for me again." Then he almost smiled at me.

I exhaled and grabbed my sweater. Cyrus was sitting on the couch smiling while he watched TV. I could tell he was listening to our conversation. Derrick asked him if he wanted to come with us, and he said no. Cadence was coming over any minute and they planned to stay inside all day. Then he confirmed that I would be out until late tonight. The rest of the day was normal; we drove around the Stanford area looking at apartment listings. As we drove past some nice and fancy looking apartments I jokingly asked Derrick why he didn't apply there. He said his uncle owned them and he didn't want to live that high profile. I laughed like I thought he was kidding but he never said anything to change it up. Then he said that his cousins, the "Twin Terrors" lived there, he wanted his own space. He reminded me that I met them at his graduation, but I couldn't place them, he's the one with the photographic memory not me. Every chance he got he had me practicing parallel parking and maneuvering his big ole boat car into tight spaces. I amazed myself with how well I was doing. Derrick kept saying there was nothing to driving, I guess he was right. When we drove up to our last listing the building was huge, there were two swimming pools on site, and lots of stairs. The manager said that they mainly rented to students since they were so close to the school. She showed us a model unit for the studio, one bedroom, and the two bedroom. Then she showed us where some of the available units were. The building and units were simple enough. Derrick told her he wanted to apply for the one bedroom. He gave her a check to hold the unit on the second floor. Since he was only seventeen the manager gave him instructions on how to apply for the apartment. Derrick assured the manager he would bring his mother back tomorrow to finalize everything. We both agreed that this place was going to be nice. He made me promise to visit him at least once a month. I gladly agreed, but I feared that once school started he wasn't going to have time for a little high schoolgirl. He watched my face for a minute, like he was reading my mind. Then we went over his

cousin Eric's in the apartment building I pointed out earlier. Eric was nice and friendly, he kind of reminded me of Darryl. There is only one Darryl, but I guess most of the guys in this family got the funny bone except Derrick.

Chapter 4

"Why are you going all the way to El Cerrito to take your test?" Cyrus asked sounding irritated.

"Oakland DMV is overbooked, so they redirected me to the El Cerrito office. Its not a big deal Cyrus stop tripping."

"This is starting to not feel right. All of a sudden you're little miss popular. If you're not with Derrick you're with his family. They're starting to have their hands in everything we do. You don't see that?" Cyrus was frustrated.

"Yeah, but I don't see anything wrong with it. Derrick and his family are fun, besides they give me something to do while you're in here getting your freak on."

"My company bothers you?" He asked with a guilty face.

"No, but that's because I'm normally gone. It's not why I'm gone most of the time. We can talk about this later. I'm sure Derrick's outside." I gave him a kiss on his cheek.

Like clockwork Derrick was outside in the passenger seat, I smiled at him and said hi.

He said hi but he stared at me. "What are you wearing?"

I went shopping with Pearla and Liz; they talked me into buying this orange sundress that they said looked amazing on my skin. I thought it looked good, but now with Derrick's question I was second-guessing myself. "Do I look horrible? Should I go change?"

Derrick adjusted in his seat, "no, no it's nice. I just…. you don't normally dress like this." He cleared his throat

"Ok" I said feeling relieved. Derrick directed me to the DMV in El Cerrito. When I went inside they told me I would be testing with a lady named Judy.

When she came out to inspect Derrick's car, she kept looking me up and down. I didn't know why she was doing that so I watched her. I could see Derrick looking out the window. When she got in the car she kept taking deep breaths to calm herself. She told me which way to drive. Then she had me parallel park on a hill. Before she told me to move she asked me how I knew Yussef. I looked at her with no idea of who she was talking about. She stared in each individual eye for a minute, I guess checking to see if I was lying then, she asked me if I knew Lamont. I told her I knew a Lamont, but I wasn't sure if we were talking about the same guy. She asked me if I was dating my Lamont or if I ever had. I told her no, and then I looked annoyed. Did this lady really think she could hold my license hostage? I felt myself get angry, I guess Pearla was rubbing off on me. "I'm not dating nor have I ever dated Lamont. Can we please get back to my test or do I need to call him?" I said with as much attitude as I could muster.

She stared at me for a long time. Like she was trying to figure me out. She turned red, and then she huffed. She directed me back to the DMV and then she told me that I passed with one hundred percent. I started screaming I was so excited. I hugged her, and she rolled her eyes. I came back inside the building bouncing as I hugged Derrick. I threw my arms around him and I kissed his neck I was so excited. He stiffened a little then he told me congratulations. I smiled nicely for my license picture, and then I bounced back over to Derrick. I was too excited. Derrick said we needed to celebrate. When we got in his car he asked me where I wanted to go. I was so excited I didn't care where. He thought for a minute. Then he told me to drive. He took me across the city, and then we hopped on the 580 freeway towards San Rafael. We got off the freeway by a refinery. We made a left and went under the freeway, and suddenly it looked like we were in an old town. He had me park on a small hill, and there was an old school hotel. When we went to the hostess station Derrick asked to speak to the manager. When the manager came down he looked at Derrick like he was crazy for requesting him. "How may I help you?"

"My name is Derrick Mason, I believe you know my father Malcolm Latour and my grandfather Tim Wallace." The guy's demeanor changed. "I'd like to have lunch in your private room, the one with the piano."

The guy swallowed, he looked at the hostess schedule. "For how many people and when?"

"Two people and right now." Derrick said staring at the guy.

The manager looked at the list, "um it looks like we have a small party in the room already. Are you sure I can't...."

"No, I want that room and I want it now. Make it happen." Derrick said staring at the manager.

"One moment." The manager said walking towards the bar with the schedule. I looked at Derrick and his eyes were focused on the manager. The manager gestured one moment to Derrick and then he walked to the back. Then you heard people in the hallway. I peeked my head in the hallway and I saw people holding their drinks and talking. No one looked angry or upset about the move. They were placed in the other room, and the manager explained that they needed to clean up. and it would be ready for us in ten minutes. Derrick pulled out his phone. He called Malcolm and told him we were at the Mac Hotel in Point Richmond.

They set a table for two in the middle of the room and there was a piano in the corner. We sat at the table and had a lovely a lunch; my entire meal was delicious. Derrick ordered a cocktail; he asked me if I wanted one. I was too chicken to order one, so I stuck to lemonade. Derrick kept watching my face like he was studying it. He seemed kind of emotional slash sentimental, but I didn't know why he was looking at me like that.

Derrick sat at the piano and told me to sit next to him. I swallowed cause I knew what was coming next. "What do you want me to play?" His face was serious as usual, but I didn't have a choice in the matter.

"You know how to play the piano?"

"Yes," He said watching my eyes.

"Wow! I had no idea." I said, "Where did you learn how to do that?"

"We used to take classes at The Center, there isn't an instrument I can't play. What song?"

I put my head on Derrick's shoulder, my heart wouldn't stop beating. "Derrick!"

"Its now or never? You gonna let this moment pass us?

"What does that mean?"

"It means I'll be moving into my apartment in a couple weeks. We both start school not too long after that. We won't have too many more moments like this. I'm asking you to do this for me." Then he looked me in my eyes. "Won't you do it for me?" He tried to make his face real sad and pathetic.

I laughed at him and I nudged him. I sat up trying to think of a song, but my brain was mush. I couldn't think of a song to save my life. Then one popped into my head, so I told him how the song went. He knew immediately what song I was talking about. I screamed slightly then I tried to stop smiling. I was embarrassed, I reminded him that he couldn't hold me accountable for his ears bleeding when it was all said and done. He stared at me; I guess he was ignoring the comment. He tapped his foot, and then he started playing. I got caught up watching his fingers glide over the keys. I missed my cue to start singing. Even the piano obeyed his command; I was awestruck about that for a minute. He gave me a slightly amused look and said we were going to try it again. This time I was ready. "Time after time when I'm feeling low,

something inside of me lets me know, it's alright love is on my

side…." Derrick smiled as he kept playing. After the first chorus he seemed like he was into it, so I kept going. When the song was over he asked me if that was so painful. If he only knew how much my heart was beating. "I bet you regret asking for that don't you." I said not looking at him.
He raised my chin, and then he kissed my lips, "it was beautiful!" He watched my face for a reaction.
I looked confused like did that just happen? Then an employee walked in the room. She looked startled realizing she interrupted a moment. "Can I bring you anything else, something to drink? Dessert? Or do you need a few more minutes?" She said with an apologetic expression.
"More lemonade." I said
"For both of you?" She asked backing away.
"Yes" Derrick said, and then he returned his eyes to me. "Can we talk?"
I felt like my heart was going to jump out of my chest. "Of course! You can talk to me about anything."
"I value our friendship." He said watching my face.
"I do too."
"I like you."

"But?" I could hear the "but" coming.

"I'm gonna be on the other side of the Bay. I feel conflicted. I keep weighing the logical and the emotional. I think you like me too, but it wouldn't be fair to you."
"Why do you say that?" I wanted to scream!
"I was prepared to continue admiring you from a distance, once I walked in that store I couldn't walk away from you. However, I

couldn't deny that I was leaving. I was hoping you ended up getting on my nerves or something. But I don't want you waiting on me. I'm not telling you any of this for me."
"Then why tell me, its been almost a year?"

"Every time you look at me, you're searching for confirmation. It's not fair to you to keep you guessing." He said, "I've been dying to kiss those lips." He looked at my lips like he was tipsy.
"So what am I supposed to do with this new information?" I didn't know how I was supposed to feel. I had been dreaming of this information since forever, but now that it is happening I still feel robbed. "You're telling me you like me, but we can't be together. Why tell me at all?"
"I didn't want to leave without giving you confirmation."
"You're accepting me and rejecting me at the same time." I stood up, "do you have any idea of how that makes me feel?"
"Yes" he said deflating. Then he looked at the table; "this isn't going the way I saw it playing out in my mind." A reckless tear fell from my eye, and I tried to wipe it away before he noticed. I walked over to the table and put the menu in front of my face. I sat there for a minute, but it wasn't working, I was about to explode into tears. I told him I was going to the bathroom, and then I walked out. I went in the stall and I put my hand over my mouth. I cried a disappointed cry. I heard the bathroom door open and close. Then there was a knock on the stall door. I opened it expecting to see our waitress looking like she was ordered to check on me, but it was Derrick and he looked sad. I started to ask him why he would come in the women's bathroom, but he rushed me and kissed me. I felt unequipped to handle this. Derrick was my first real kiss. "I'm sorry! You're right this is selfish. I'm sorry. Let me take you home." I didn't say anything the whole car ride, but neither did he. When he pulled up to my apartment, I got out the car before it stopped moving completely.
When I came in the door Cyrus was cooking, he called out asking me if I passed my test. I told him I did and I needed to go lay down. Then I went in my room and shut the door. I laid on my bed facing the wall leaving my shoes on. Cyrus came to my door and asked if everything was ok. I told him I was fine, and I wanted to take a nap. A few minutes later my door opened and it wasn't closed, I could tell by the touch it was Derrick. He laid down

behind me spooning me. I was happy he came after me, but I was still disappointed all the same.

We ended up talking that night and no matter how he tried to explain it to me it felt like he was showing me my dream, but telling me I couldn't have it. I felt myself shutting down. I did my best to convince Derrick I was ok. He stayed for the rest of the day. I even made dinner that night, and he said it was really good. However, my disappointment was undeniable.

Ms. Laverne said it was for the best. She said the last thing I needed was to be waiting for him by the phone while he was over there living the college experience. She told me not to worry and that he would come back for me. Meanwhile I needed to think about where I was going to school and live my life.

Even though I promised to visit at least once a month, now I couldn't bring myself to even think about going. I haven't visited since he moved in. When he calls I talk to him but it's not the same. So his calls have become less and less. I guess this is called growing apart. Although at night all I think about is my first kiss, my second, and my third. I wished he would've let us have the afternoon maybe even the night before he said anything. Oh well you can't cry over what's already done.

****

"Chantel?" Cyrus knocked on my door, "are you decent?"

I had just gotten home from school a few minutes earlier. "Yeah," I said opening my door. "What's up?" I said sitting on my bed.

"How you feeling?" He asked

I exhaled, "I'm fine." Even though I wasn't. I've been dragging ever since that day with Derrick.

Cyrus sat next to me, "you wanna talk about it?"

"I already told you. He's out there in his college and I'm the little girl who was left behind. I just wish he wouldn't have said anything, and then I could live in denial for the next four years. Oh well, moving on." I looked at his face and he looked really upset. "What's wrong?"

"I saw our mother today." Then he exhaled. "I felt angry as soon as I saw her."

"Did you speak to her?" I asked rubbing his back.

He exhaled and inhaled. "I called out to her when I saw her. It was my knee jerk reaction you know. When she didn't respond happy to see me or like she was even concerned with anything about me or us. It hurt!"

"Did she say anything?"

He exhaled, "yeah. She said we could've said we were leaving. Then she said how they had to go to the apartment manager and ask for a smaller place just so they could afford to eat. No inquiry about how we were, or where we were. She doesn't care. She said our father was sick, and you know I looked at her like she was barking up the wrong tree." He stood up. "When she started going on and on about how he was doing, I walked away in the middle of her talking. I feel like seeing her has taken away my peace. You know what I mean?"

"I do," I said wiping tears away. "Cyrus, we don't need them! She has to answer for choosing him. What mother does that?" I said through tears.

"Still hurts," he said in a defeated tone.

"I know, believe me I know. The way she would look at me all the time was wrong! I'm her child, I was not competing with her for her husband's attention." Cyrus spaced out for a minute. By the way his jaw was tightening I imagined him remembering beating our father up. I stood up. "Cyrus!" I touched him to bring him back to me. He looked at me with pain in his eyes. "You are a wonderful son and brother! You're gonna make some lucky mother-in-law so happy one day." He nodded his head like he was fighting to come back to me. "You're a good man! You let your little sister have the bedroom." He exhaled. "Cyrus," I said waiting for him to look at me. When he looked at me I tilted my head back, "do I have a booger in my nose?"

Cyrus started laughing. "I like you, you're silly."

"I'm serious. I was crying, you know that can cause boogers."

He inspected my nose still laughing. "No, you're clean. I love you baby girl." He said giving me a hug.

"Love you big brother." I said hugging him back. "We should order dinner and watch a movie."

"How about I cook, we watch a movie, then when Caprice comes you can do your homework." He smiled.

"You need to burn off negative energy." I said rolling my eyes.

"We need a two bedroom."

"Yep! I almost have enough saved for a car. Then we can work towards the apartment."

"I told you, you didn't need all those clothes." He said

I sucked my teeth. "What would you know about it? I've never had real clothes in my closet before. It's my right as a girl to look nice whenever I feel like it."

Cyrus smiled, "I guess. With my quarterly bonus it should be enough so we can move."

"Thank goodness you signed a month to month lease."

****

"Don't you look pretty today!" Kevin said staring at me as he entered the office.

I smiled, "thank you, how can I help you today?"

"There's no chance that you've miraculously turned eighteen is there?"

"Nope, I'm only seventeen."

"Well that's a step in the right direction, I'll take it." He smiled, "I'm here to get Curtis' mail."

I hesitated, "but each person is supposed to get their own mail. I'll need to call him." I said reaching for the phone number.

"No it's ok. I was really trying to use him as an excuse to see you. He can get his own mail."

"Ok," I said putting my phone down. "So now you see me," I smiled.

He slightly grinned at me. "You're extremely innocent you know that right?"

"Is that a bad thing?"

"I love it!" He grinned

Ms. Laverne came out the bathroom. She was still rubbing her hands on a paper towel. She looked irritated taking one look at Kevin. "Why are you here?" There was no smile on her face.

"I came to say hi." He said trying to charm her.

"Hi, now get back to your assignment." She ordered.

"It's after hours. I was dropping by to say hi to Chantel." He said still trying.

"You don't need to come by here saying nothing to this under age girl! Don't make me not like you! If I don't like you, you'll never go on another assignment!" She said with her hand on her hip.

"Maybe I should've come to see you."

"Well you already chose wrong so keep it moving. Go on…" She said shooing him away.

He laughed, it sounded kind of forced. "Ok, ok. I'll go…" He said putting his hands up. "Good evening ladies," then he walked out. He smiled at me through the glass as he walked away.
Ms. Laverne was irritated; she picked up her phone and pounded each digit like she was trying to break the phone. Her cheeks were red, so she was pretty irritated. As she put the phone to her ear, I heard a phone ring and then Malcolm walked around the corner. He was looking at his phone, he looked at Ms. Laverne then he asked her what was wrong. She started fussing as she followed him to his office and they closed the door. When she came out she was still irritated. "I don't get a good vibe about him. Don't trust him you hear me!" She said like a mother would.
"Yes ma'am!"
"There are some guys who just slither around. He's one of them, you gotta protect yourself you hear me?"
"Yes ma'am." I watched her chest go up and down as she tried to catch her breath as if she had just been running. "Can I ask how you can tell he's not to be trusted?"
"For one what did that fool know about you when you first met him? He saw you and instantly went into cat daddy mode. He doesn't want anything respectable. If you go for that sort of thing when you're of age, I guess that's your business. I can't sit back and watch him prey on you while you're too young to understand."
"Ok" I said thinking about what she said. "And you don't put Derrick in the same category?"
"No honey, Derrick really likes you. He seems to think handling things this way is best. He's not doing it to hurt you. I also don't want you over here waiting on him. If the opportunity presents itself, take it. Enjoy your youth."

****

"This is Quesha, she's our new employee. Quesha this is Chantel she used to work here." Cadence said
We both said hello. I could see her sizing me up when she thought I wasn't looking. Cadence gave me a smoothie on the house. I was waiting for Pearla and Liz it was my day off and we were going to browse the stores and see if there was anything new we wanted. Plus I was keeping my eyes open for a few things for our new

apartment. We were moving next weekend. "So what's new?" I asked

Cadence was happy I asked. "I have a boyfriend." She said with a big smile as she watched my face for a reaction.

"Ok, that's great?" I was confused cause she was at my house the other day with Cyrus.

"Don't look at me like that. That was the last time, Cyrus knows that we won't be seeing each other anymore." She said with a smile.

"Congratulations." I said giving her a hug.

She looked past me. "Do you know him? I think he's waiting for you."

I turned around and there was Jaloni, a guy from school. Funny thing is that I had just noticed him the day before. He was a little taller than me, toasted almond complexion, and VERY cute. He looked like he was working on the courage to approach me. I smiled at him, he swallowed then he walked over. "Don't you work somewhere in this mall?" He said

"Yes" I said still smiling at him. He seemed like a little boy compared to Derrick. His emotions were too easy to read. "This is Cadence." I said

They both said hello. "Do you have to work now?" He asked

"I'm waiting for someone, what's up?" I asked thinking he was going to ask me to tutor him or something.

"I have to get back to work, I'll talk to you later." Cadence said walking away.

Jaloni motioned for me to follow him to a nearby table. He stood by my chair until I sat down then he sat across from me. "Are you waiting for your boyfriend?"

"I don't have a boyfriend." I said

He sighed a sigh of relief. "Good!" He said mustering up the courage.

"Good?" I asked

"I like you, I've liked you for a long time. Will you go out with me?"

My mouth literally fell open. I smiled really big. "Ok".

He looked relieved. He smiled real big, "can I have your phone number?"

"Of course!" I said now blushing myself. I opened my purse and pulled out a pen and he gave me a napkin.

I wrote my number down, I felt giggly. Then Pearla walked up to the table. "Cousin who's this?" She said eyeing Jaloni.
"This is Jaloni he goes to my school. This is Pearla." I said

"Her cousin Pearla," she said to him. Then she looked at me, "why you didn't tell him you're married?" She said wiggling her neck.
"Cause I'm not!" My eyes told her to cut it out. Pearla huffed while looking Jaloni up and down. "I'm gonna go, but call me ok." I said smiling at him. When I stood up Quesha was watching us. I didn't smile at her cause I didn't know what she was looking so hard for.

****

"Thanks for helping man, I appreciate it." Cyrus said to Jaloni. They shook hands.

Jaloni and I talk on the phone everyday. And even though it's only been a little over a week he eagerly volunteered to help Cyrus and I move. We had to rent a small truck to move all of our furniture. I felt so grown up having furniture to move. I decided to change our number since we were moving across the city. I wanted a fresh start with everything. Jaloni and a couple of Cyrus' friends from work helped us move. I made sure they had plenty of water during the move then I made sure they had plenty of pizza once they got everything moved in. Ms. Laverne suggested this apartment that was reasonably priced. It was small but big enough for us. It was a small building only three units. Our apartment was towards the back and it had an upstairs and downstairs. Upstairs there were two medium sized bedrooms, one on each side of the hallway. The bathroom was in the middle. I hoped that was enough space so that I wouldn't hear Cyrus and his company. There was a half bathroom downstairs a small kitchen. A small dining room, there was even a little backyard. The unit came with a one-car garage, and street parking. Cyrus told me to park my little car in the garage. He said even though the neighborhood was quiet, he would feel better about me parking in the garage on the nights I came home from work and he was still at work or something like that. Pearla and Liz helped me unpack and set stuff up as the men moved them in. By nightfall we were all moved in and unpacked. Jaloni stayed downstairs while Pearla and Liz helped me set up my room.
"We should plan what we're gonna do for our winter break. You gotta work?" Liz asked

"I asked Malcolm if I could work my summer hours during those two weeks and he told me no." I said

"No?" Liz asked

"He said he wanted me to take time off and relax." I said

"Aw! Isn't that nice." Liz said

"Yeah, but you know Malcolm. It sounded like he was mad when he said it. I had to think about it to realize he was being nice." I said

"That's Malcolm for ya. I think he owns this building." Pearla said

"What?" I said not completely surprised but I didn't want Cyrus to know.

"I think Drew and his momma used to live here when he was little. Some how this place is connected to Malcolm is all I know."

"I would thank him, but he doesn't seem receptive to thanks." I said

"Still say it though, Malcolm has that hard exterior but he bleeds like the rest of us."

"I guess so. Doesn't Malcolm seem like a super hero taking pity on the poor and over worked like me? What was his father like?" I asked

"Nobody really knows, my momma said it was between these three guys, but even then you don't really know. His Momma's dead though, I don't know how she died. Momma Shuga, his grandmother and my great" she shook her head. "My momma said she was a trip! My Momma's head still be all twisted up behind her."

"So Malcolm was kind of like an orphan like me an Cyrus?" I said taking everything she was saying in.

"I guess so," she said

"So that explains why he and Derrick don't smile much."

Liz smiled, "you don't know that Malcolm is his step-daddy?"

"WHAT?" I couldn't believe it. "You can't tell Derrick you know though. Neither one of them acknowledge it. Derrick and Darryl's last name is Mason. Andrew's last name is the same as his Momma's, he's a Wallace. Malcolm is a Latour like us." She said

"Where's Derrick's father?" I asked

They both shrugged. "Anyways! Before we got distracted, I was gonna suggest driving up to Tahoe for the day at least once during our vacation." Liz said

"What are we gonna do out there?" I asked

"We could have a day playing in the snow. Then we come home. Do you think your car could make the trip?" She asked Pearla.
"Yeah, I just need to get some new tires. Who's going, just the three of us?" Pearla asked
"I want Barry to go, so I say we invite as many people as possible." Liz said smiling at the thought.
"So I could invite Jaloni then?" I said
"I guess he seems cool enough. But if people need rides can we count on the other three seats in your car?" Liz said
"Of course! Are you guys going to get snowsuits? I've never been to the snow."
Then Jaloni knocked on the door as he opened it. "Hey" he said smiling at me.
"Hey yourself, Pearla and Liz wanna plan a day trip to Tahoe. Do you wanna go?" I asked excited.
"That's kind of far. I probably wouldn't be able to go." He said sounding disappointed by the idea.
I forgot that fast that we were only in high school. Since it was only me and Cyrus I didn't have to ask for permission to do anything. Until now I had nothing to do. Jaloni said he'd ask his parents anyways in hopes that they would say yes. Then we all took him home in my car. When I walked him to the door. He hugged me and then awkwardly went in for his kiss. It was a nice kiss, but I liked Derrick's more. Pearla and Liz were hooping and hollering in the car. We went back to my house and planned out our trip.

****

Cyrus ended up having the day off, and he wanted to go with us so I brought him. Part of me thinks he wanted to see if Pearla was actually calmer like I said she was. When we got to Pearla's house there were a lot of cars outside already and we were on time. There was a nice sized crowd of teenagers in her living room all waiting for us to arrive. Even though there was a ton of them Derrick and Darryl stood out in the crowd. I felt heat flash across my face when I saw Derrick, he was watching me. There were a good twenty cars all-full of people. Derrick asked Cyrus which one of us drove. Cyrus pointed at me; Derrick almost smiled and asked me for a ride. Pearla asked if Felecia could ride with us, and Darryl happily volunteered to take the last seat in my car. Cyrus insisted that Derrick ride in the front with me. We weren't even on the freeway good, "so I hear you got a boyfriend." Darryl said with a smile in his voice.

"Who told you that?" I said feeling my hands start to sweat.

"Oh a little birdie told me. But good for you Chantel! Good for you!" He said grabbing my shoulder and shaking it. Even though he was playful his light grip felt too strong. My insides shuddered at the idea of him grabbing me for real.

"Who is he?" Derrick asked not looking amused at all.

"A boy from my school." I said lowly.

"Yeah he's cool peoples, you'd like him." Cyrus said

"Would I?" Derrick lowly barked while cutting his eyes behind him at Cyrus.

"Yes you would, he's more her speed. Nice little square boy who's nervous about holding her hand." Cyrus said matching Derrick's tone.

"You went backwards? How could you go from D-Rick to a square? I will never understand women!" Darryl said throwing his hands up and smiling at Felecia.

"Derrick and I were never together." I said

Thanks to Darryl the topic of "Derrick and I" was an open and comical debate. Cyrus and I said that Derrick and I were never a couple, Darryl told Felecia she agreed with him and that we were a couple. Derrick as usual had nothing declarative to say on the matter. During our debate Derrick's cell phone rang, it was his brother Drew. His girlfriend made them run late but he caught up to our caravan on the freeway. Darryl got mad and quiet for a minute when Derrick said Drew had Toya with him. I've never seen Darryl angry and his silence was scary. It seemed like he was thinking then he snapped out of it and got everybody going again. Then out of nowhere he asked if we were going to have a snow fight. He had a wicked smile when he looked at Derrick and said Toya was having one whether she wanted to or not.

We stopped at a little shopping center along the road to the snow lodge. Our group bought one store's entire inventory of sleds, inner tubes, hats, gloves, etc. When I was in line to pay for my things Derrick took everything from me and when it was my turn he paid for it all. That was a nice change; Jaloni was always operating on his allowance.

Drew's girlfriend was gorgeous. It figures he would be with a girl who looks like that though. Darryl kept giving her evil eyes and bumping into her whenever he walked past her. Then I saw their cousin Lanie kick her hard. She didn't even try to act like it was an accident or anything. She booted her with her thick boots and then looked at her with no remorse in her face. Toya frowned at her and then she limped over to Drew. Darryl was cracking up which made Lanie laugh as well. Erica, Lanie's sister told her not to provoke a situation, she told her to let Toya create the situation cause they all knew she would. Then Lanie's brother EJ told her to cut it out, while Zoey high fived her. He reminded me of Derrick the most with his no nonsense approach to everything. Then he took his sister's items and his girlfriend's stuff and put it on the counter to buy. The storeowners were so happy with us as they looked around at their empty racks, they told us to come back whenever.

It seemed like as soon as we parked the snow fight began. We didn't even get far away from the cars before we were being ambushed. Felecia was screaming at the top of her lungs cause she was getting lit up. Derrick grabbed me and pulled me behind a dumpster. He told me to stay low, I begged him to help Felecia cause she was an easy and unfortunate target. He brought her with us, and eventually Drew and his girl made it over to us. When Darryl got to us his eyes turned evil. "She can't be on our team! She's gonna slow us down!" He told Drew

"Man! Chill out!" Drew said. Cyrus made it over to us and he couldn't stop laughing. He said everybody was against us. My heart sank cause it was a lot of people and I didn't want to get hit in the face with a snowball. The guys huddled, Drew pointed out a hill. They all agreed then they came back to us. "Here's the plan! We're gonna run together. I'll lead the front Darryl will bring up the rear. They're gonna be bombing us but it's ok, cause we're gonna run fast. Anybody who falls or separates from the group will be left behind!" Andrew said, Cyrus was making snowballs while Drew spoke.

"TOYA!" Darryl said irritated. "He's talking about you!"

"How you know he's not talking about one of them?" She said pointing at Felecia and I.

"Cause it's you! YOU KNOW WHAT YOU DO!" Darryl said giving her serious eyes.

"Focus!" Drew said, "ladies we're using the sleds as shields while we run. Keep up with us; once we get on the other side we're taking them out as they come over the hill. Got it? Stick with us! RUN! Ready! We don't have much time." Then he put his hand out, "SOLDIERS UNITE!" they all yelled. Andrew Ran out first and we moved very fast behind them. They were throwing snowballs at us and HARD! Toya and Felecia screamed the entire way. I couldn't stop watching Derrick throwing snowballs and hitting each one of his targets with a vengeance. Anyone who was close to us got hit, and they fell to the ground upon contact. We ran up the hill. Drew put his sled down and he pushed Toya down on it. He jumped on the back on his knees and they went down the hill. As they went down Drew turned them to face us so he could fire snowballs on anyone who was crazy enough to follow us. I was delighted to be on the sled with Derrick, Cyrus had Felecia but he didn't have fancy moves like the rest of the boys. He sled down and laughed all the way. Darryl's crazy behind stood on his sled and fired on people as he went down the hill. As soon as we hit bottom Drew told us to make more snowballs and they fired on anyone stupid enough to follow. The funny part was watching each one of them fall to the ground screaming talking about the boys threw too hard. Felecia and I took our assignment seriously, we were snowball-making machines. Toya complained that everyone was acting juvenile. She got on all of our nerves. The smart ones who went down stayed down. Anyone who got up was knocked back down. One guy called himself playing hero and sneaking around the other way. Derrick and I fired at him. The look on Derrick's face when our balls hit the guy right next to each other. He asked me if I threw that ball, and when I said yes he CHEESED real big! Once everybody said they surrendered, all of a sudden Toya started getting lit up with snowballs. She was screaming and even Drew was smiling. She screamed for Drew to help her, and he told Darryl to stop. Darryl said she was a victim of friendly fire. We had a good laugh at her expense. Darryl said he liked the way Felecia handled herself on the battle lines. She blushed and said thank you. Just about everybody had at least one bruise from a snowball except our team. Andrew shamed them for going against the soldiers; he told them they're always prepared. We ran up and down this hill for hours running up and sledding down. We eventually made our way to the actual lodge and then we played on that hill. Toya kept looking at me evil because Darryl clearly liked me. I know I thought she was pretty at first, now not so much. We were sitting at the cafe area and Toya was staring at me with an ugly look on her face. Derrick noticed it and proceeded to curse her out so badly in front of everybody. His voice was low and his eyes were evil. Drew didn't say anything, but he didn't seemed surprised either. Toya started giving Drew a hard time for not defending her. He told her she was wrong and she needed to apologize to me. When she scoffed at Drew and looked like she refused to budge Derrick looked like he was about to get up when Lanie, Pearla, Liz, and a bunch of other cousins came over looking crazy. Lanie asked Derrick what the problem was even though she was in motion towards Toya, and he pointed at her. Her face dropped looking at all those crazy girls. Drew reminded her that all she had to do was apologize, Toya threw her hands up and apologized in surrender. Lanie smiled and said Toya wasn't stupid. Drew looked irritated but he knew it was Toya's fault. Darryl of course was on the sideline instigating telling Lanie to get her

anyways cause he didn't like her. Lanie's brother told her to sit

down like he was her father. She looked like she wasn't going to do

it for a minute. She did as she was told but she didn't look happy about it. I had my hands in my lap, I was kind of speechless. Derrick grabbed my hand and held on to it under the table. Cyrus tried not to look impressed but I knew he was.

One of their friends a girl named Sherrell and Cyrus hit it off and they spent the rest of the afternoon talking. I sat on a log at the top of the hill catching my breath. Derrick came and sat next to me.

"So this boyfriend..." I smiled. "Is it serious?" He asked

"It's only been a couple of months, but I like him." I said

He shot me serious eyes, "I don't like it, but what can I say?"
"You have a girlfriend?" I asked feeling jealous.

"Not exactly. I don't want to talk about it though. It's dumb and something I'm going through right now." He took a deep breath. "Brace yourself I'm about to be selfish again." He paused for dramatic affect. "I miss you, I miss talking to you, I miss spending time with you. I love you so much and there's nobody out there like you. Where are you going to school?"

I was dumb founded, "YOU WHAT?" Feeling like I was gonna slide off the log.
"You heard me," he said looking around at the people coming up and sliding down.
"Derrick!" I said feeling frustrated.
"I know! I know!" Then he moved closer to me, grabbed my hair kissed me firmly and deeply. I expected all the snow around us to be melted and gone when I opened my eyes. "I love you Chantel. And like a good girl you're gonna stand by him right? But this is winter break, you belong to me for these two weeks and vice versa. We can go back to ordinary life when our vacation is over. Say yes!" He said with his arms still around me.
"Yes!" I said

Cyrus rode back to the Bay with Sherrell. I passed my car keys to Derrick and enjoyed watching him drive my car. Darryl convinced everyone that we needed to stop to eat. I called Pearla from Derrick's phone and told her we wanted to stop for food. She led the caravan to a diner once we hit interstate 80. A lot of our group had to keep moving to get home before their parents got upset. Our group size shrunk drastically but it was good. We were still about twenty deep when we went inside. I grabbed Derrick's hand as we walked. He tensed up and then he relaxed, Cyrus looked at our hands and shook his head at me. I smiled at him, he barely smiled back. Toya kept cutting her eyes at me. When I went to the bathroom she was at the sink washing her hands. "So, you're Derrick's latest conquest." She spit with as much venom as she could. "I could've sworn I just saw him with two gorgeous females. What would he want with you?"
I hadn't even said hi to this female or even been properly introduced for that matter. "What are you saying to me? You don't even know me!" I could feel myself getting angry.
"I'm just saying, you're not even on the right level. Very girl next door, and well Drew and his brothers only date females like me or better!"
"How are you the barometer as to what's acceptable?" I spit at her.
"The what?" She frowned
I smiled at her washed my hands and left her with that dumb look on her face. I tried to look unaffected when I went back to the table but Derrick still asked me what was wrong. I shot Toya daggers

with my eyes. "Drew! Man you gotta stop bringing her around!" Derrick said frustrated.

Drew was talking to someone and he stopped mid-conversation. "What happened?" He said looking at Derrick then me.

"I told her about Derrick's dates for the club opening." She said with as much attitude as she could muster sitting back in her chair.

"Why would you do that?" Drew asked her

Toya shrugged, "just thought she should know what she's up against." Then she put her hands up, "Girl Code!"

"There was no code to the way you were talking to me. You were insinuating that I wasn't pretty enough to be sitting here." My face was stinging.

"What? I don't know how she walked out the bathroom with all her teeth!" Pearla said sitting up in her chair.

"Why is it any of your business who's sitting next to me? You're just jealous because, with the exception of Drew, nobody else wants you here. And you see everybody loving Chantel. You do this every time!" Derrick got madder.

Toya faked surprise, "oops! Was that a secret?"

"It could've been, but hey if you're so fine; who's the chick Drew was smashing last night?" Darryl said

Drew smiled I couldn't tell if he was laughing or embarrassed. "He was with me last night at the club." Toya said matter of factly.

Darryl laughed hard, "I know! And yet he still felt the need to get it in with somebody else before going home with you! You are so stupid!"

Toya looked at Drew like she couldn't believe it. He smiled at her and shrugged, "oops!"

Toya stood up and fixed her mouth like she was gonna curse Drew out. "YOU BETTER NOT!" Pearla yelled, "You will NOT disrespect my cousin in front of me! If you value your pretty little face you better sit down and SHUT UP! You wish you had it going on like Chantel otherwise why would you go out of your way to try to hurt her. You are HECK OF UGLY! And you know it! You have nothing to offer a man other than a screw, and apparently that ain't even good if my cousin has to hook up with someone before going home with you. Sit down and shut up!" Toya huffed and walked out the cafe. "Or walk out the door, I guess I forgot to mention that option." Pearla said laughing. "She better be happy

Lanie had to go home!" Everyone laughed.

She and Darryl high-fived, "I like your style!" Darryl said
Derrick looked at my face then he told me to come with him. He took me to a booth away from the group. "I've been passing time with these two girls in my building. It's not deep or serious." He said watching my eyes.

I looked down at the table. "She said they're pretty."

He sucked his teeth. "You are beautiful, what do you care what she thinks they are?"

I was surprised, "you think I'm beautiful?" I watched his eyes looking for a put on or a sign that he was lying.

"Of course I do! Maybe you don't know who I am, but I have specific taste. Why do you think I follow you around like a lost puppy?" He said matter of factly.

"You don't." I said with a smile.

He almost smiled at me. "Yes I do. Why do you think we're out here right now? I didn't want to come to your place and your little boyfriend was there."

"You did all this for me?" I smiled even bigger.

"Of course!" He said then he kissed me.

"Can I ask you something?" Derrick nodded. "When I went to get my car, I saved up to get this little bucket, but when I went to get it the salesman convinced me to get the car outside, but he gave it to me for the same price as that beat up bucket. Did you have something to do with it?" I asked

"I couldn't have you driving that beat up jalopy, it would've broke down as soon as you drove it off the lot." He said

"What about the apartment?" I asked

"My mom owns it." He said matter of factly.

"That makes sense, the deal was so sweet, and we barely paid anything to move in. How did you get her to rent it to Cyrus and I?"

"I told her I needed it for a friend. She knows if I vouch for someone they're Golden."

"Is Malcolm nice to me because of you?"

"No!" He shook his head, "Malcolm yields to no one but my momma. If he's nice to you then you've done something to get on his nice side. You're a hard worker, and anything you have with Malcolm is because you've earned it."

"So... You're my vacation boyfriend?" I asked

"Is that what you want?" He asked

"No! But, if it's all you have to give right now, I guess I don't have a choice." I said

"Did you apply to my school?"

"No, there's no way I could afford that school, even with a scholarship."

He looked disappointed. "Try to transfer over. We can figure the rest out after you get in."

"I'm not good enough to go there." I said slouching.

He sucked his teeth. "At some point you gotta start believing in yourself. Stop doing that!" His irritation surprised me. "Every time I pay you a compliment you counter with something negative. Stop doing that!"

"I didn't realize I did that. I was just telling you the honest truth. I'm not a straight A student like you."

"Everybody there isn't either. Just think positive and apply." He said, "life would be better having you there with me." Then he kissed my hand.

When we went back to the table Drew was still sitting and talking. You could see Toya outside standing by the car waiting. It was cold out there, she didn't look happy, and Drew didn't seem concerned. Cyrus watched me until we made eye contact he asked me if I was ok, and I smiled and mouthed yes. When the check came Drew said he was paying since we all had to deal with Toya. No one complained or objected. As we walked out to the car Drew asked Derrick if we were coming over their cousin Jeff's house. He said JoJo and Sasha were out for the break. Derrick asked if he was bringing Toya, Drew laughed and said no. Then Derrick looked at me to ask if I wanted to go, and I was already shaking my head yes when he looked at me. He laughed, which always made me happy to hear his laugh. Darryl and Felecia turned the backseat of my car into a make out station; at least I hope that's all they were doing. Derrick turned up the radio and only looked out the side mirrors. I told him I needed to study his face so I stared at him. He literally smiled for a long time while he blushed. I loved every moment of it too. When we stopped for gas, the knuckleheads in the back were knocked out; completely exhausted they didn't wake up at all.

Derrick and I had our own kissing session while the gas was pumping. As we were arriving back into the Bay Felecia said she was spending the night at Pearla's so as long as it was ok with Pearla she wanted to hang with us. Darryl called Pearla and told her Felecia was spending the night with him and to cover for her. Then he called their mother and told her he was going over their cousin's house and then he'd spend the night there. You could hear her voice over the phone. She didn't sound convinced he wasn't trying to get over. He told us Malcolm was gonna show up at some point to verify his story.

When we got to the house Darryl got really excited when he saw his uncle's car outside. He hopped out the car so fast, he completely forgot about Felecia in the back seat. I was kind of nervous cause I didn't know what to expect when we went inside. The first person I saw was Tim and his face lit up when he saw me. He came over and gave me a huge grandfatherly hug. "How you doing sweetheart?"

"I'm good! How are you?" I said hugging him back.

"I'm good now that I see you. Lauren!" He called out with his arm still around me. A woman came out the kitchen, "this is the girl I was talking about. Doesn't she remind you of Annette?"

The woman's eyes watered up. "Yes she does!" She came over and hugged me. "How are you baby, I'm Auntie Lauren."

I introduced Tim and Auntie Lauren to Felecia. She looked just like me when Ms. Laverne told me he was Derrick's grandfather. Then we had a whole conversation about how they favored. With Derrick standing next to Tim once you got past color you could see that they favored. Darryl was talking to his Uncle Jeff, Uncle Malachi, Uncle Timothy, some cousins, and Uncle Frank; they all had serious faces like they were figuring something out. Tina, Erica, Lanie, Zoey, and Sasha said they were happy some more girls came. We were talking in the living room, Tina and Sasha didn't come to Tahoe with us. Felecia and I told all of them about the incident at the restaurant and Lanie told us about the fight Erica had with Toya. Erica seemed so sweet and calm, nothing like they were describing the fight to be like. Erica simply said that Toya messed with her brother and she wasn't going to stand for it. Lanie explained why she didn't like her, but it didn't sound like she liked too many people really. Her eyes looked crazy as she happily talked about the evil things she's done to Toya. Then she looked at me and said she was very protective over her family. I didn't care that she looked at me; I'd never hurt Derrick on purpose. I told her that it was good that they had someone looking out for them, Derrick watched us while talking to his grandfather. I smiled at him and then he smiled back. His grandfather stopped talking when he smiled. He told him he forgot Derrick had teeth and that he should smile more often.

I called Cyrus and told him I was with Derrick's family. He thanked me for calling and he was going to bed. Malcolm showed up around one-thirty in the morning, checking up on Darryl. We all started laughing when we saw him walk in. He walked through the house then he left. When I was ready to leave Derrick was already reading me. I asked him if he wanted me to take him to his car or if he wanted to hang out with me. Of course he said he wanted to hang with me. He told me that when he was a baby they lived in my apartment. I asked him why they moved, and he said they had a fire and the building burned down. He said they never came back. He got quiet for a minute like he was thinking about something. Then he snapped out of it. "So where did you learn how to throw like that?" He almost smiled.

"Cyrus taught me. He needed me to pitch to him so he could practice for baseball. First he had to teach me how to throw, and then he made me practice with him. He said I had to be good otherwise I couldn't help him."

"That was impressive." He said slightly smiling.

I yawned, "thank you." Then I smiled at him. "You wanna sleep down here or upstairs?"

"Where do you want me to sleep?"

My hands started sweating. "You can sleep upstairs if you want."

"Only if you want me to." He stared at me.

I put my finger up, "no hanky panky!"

He chuckled, "I make no guarantees."

I went in the bathroom and put a nightshirt on. When I came back in the room he was shirtless and his body looked like it was chiseled. I didn't mean to stare but I couldn't help it. He took off his pants. He folded his clothes neatly; I couldn't believe Derrick was in my bed. I couldn't believe I was almost naked laying next to him. He put his arm around me and I thought I was going to literally burst into flames. He kissed my forehead and said goodnight. I laid there thinking he was going to make a move and I'd FINALLY lose my virginity to the one person I had been dying to give it to. But his arm became like dead weight. He really went to sleep! I was so disappointed; I laid there blinking for thirty minutes making sure he was really sleep. I fell asleep disappointed.

Chapter 5

I woke to Cyrus knocking on my door gently as he opened it. I looked at him and he looked startled to see Derrick in my bed. He and Derrick exchanged stares. "I was coming to tell you Jaloni called you last night, but it looks like you don't care. I'm going to work I'll be back later." Then he shut my door.

I got up and brushed my teeth. Derrick used my toothbrush to brush his. At first I protested, but he said it wasn't different from kissing. The same plaque was exchanged. I didn't agree, I wasn't scrubbing his teeth with my tongue when we kissed, but I didn't really care so I dropped it. He took my hand and led me back into the bedroom. He gently laid me down, and we proceeded to have a long make out session. I always wondered what this was like, I would see it on TV all the time but I couldn't relate to the feeling. Every touch and every feeling was new. I thought we were building up to the big finish so I kept bracing myself for it. Then he asked me if I was hungry, I was so focused on him I didn't have an appetite, but he was hungry. I offered to make him breakfast; he wanted to go out to eat. We washed up and then we drove all the way to Richmond to this little cafe called Anna's Place. It was next door to an Italian food place and a Chinese food spot. It was a simple spot but the breakfast was delicious. I asked Derrick how he knew about this place all the way out here. His face got very serious as he said he comes out there from time to time. He looked off for a minute then he asked what I wanted to do. I wanted to say I wanted to go home and see what happens, but instead I told him to surprise me.

We went to Pearla's house to get Derrick's car. Her mother Renee and their cousin Bernadette told us we better come inside and say hello. A few minutes turned into hours and before we knew it the day was gone. We were having so much fun. We finally left close to eight. Derrick followed me to the apartment. He took his duffle bag out of the trunk of his car. Cyrus was home when we walked in the door. He looked at Derrick's bag, and then he shot me a look. I smiled at him cause I knew he wanted to say something, but really what could he say? He parades females in and out of our apartment constantly, how could he say anything when he knows how much I care for Derrick. "Jaloni called," he said walking upstairs.

I looked at Derrick, "I should call him huh?"

"For what?" He said walking up the stairs.

I didn't know what that meant, so I left the matter alone all together. Derrick said he wanted to take me out to dinner since the day escaped us. When I pulled a dress out of my closet he smiled at it. KILL ME! I love his smile just as much as I love his laugh. Neither one of these things are done too often so the fact that he's been smiling at me for the past couple of days makes my heart rejoice. When I came back in the room from my shower Derrick was on the phone, he looked at my robe like he was trying to make it come off by looking at it. When he got off the phone I gave him his towels and he got in the shower. I quickly lotioned up and dressed so that I wouldn't have to be embarrassed dressing in front of him. I thanked Pearla and Liz as I twirled in the mirror admiring myself. When we were at the store we were having a battle. They told me to get the dress, and I told them I'd never have anywhere to wear it to. I guess they knew better. My hair, I stood there not knowing what to do with it. In defeat I left it in the low bun that seemed to compliment my dress style anyways. I put on two different shoes then I walked across the hall and knocked on Cyrus' door. "Which one looks better?" I asked him smiling a mile wide.

He pulled me into his room. "I know I don't have the right, but…"

he looked me in my eyes. "What are you doing?"

"We're going out to dinner, did you want me to bring you back anything?" I said

"You know what I'm talking about, don't play dumb." He was irritated.

"We're just hanging out for the rest of the vacation together. Then we're going back to our normal lives." I said matter of factly.

"You're gonna hurt Jaloni, he really likes you."

"No I'm not. I like him, but I love Derrick. Come on you know the truth."

"Let me say this, just like I've never asked you to lie for me. I will not lie for you."

"Ok, but I don't see why you would have to." As if it was timed, the phone rang. He smiled at me. "Don't answer it!" I said grabbing his arm as he moved for the phone.

"It could be Caprice or Sherrell. I'm supposed to see Caprice tonight."

"What if it's Jaloni?" I said panicking.

Cyrus smiled and then he picked up the phone. "Hello?" My heart was pounding. "Hold on," then he put his hand over the receiver.

He pointed at my shoes, "the one on the left is fine. It's Caprice, have fun tonight." Then he went back to the phone.

Derrick was walking into my room with only a towel wrapped around his waist. I stared at the water beads dripping down the middle of his back. "You look nice!" I joked.

He chuckled, "you're beautiful. I like that dress." He said staring at me.

"Thanks, I'll be out of your way in one second. I just need to get the other shoe.' I said opening my closet.

"You don't have to leave this is your room." He said taking his towel off.

Even though we messed around earlier, I didn't see it. "Wow!" He almost smiled and put on lotion. I told him I wanted to lotion his back. It was my excuse to touch his naked body. I couldn't stop smiling as I got on the bed behind him and rubbed lotion on his back. There's nothing like touching a man's body. I kissed his back and he reacted, it surprised me and made my smile that much bigger. I kissed the back of his neck, his breathing got deeper. "If you keep this up, we won't leave." Then he kissed me, and got dressed.

"You're not embarrassed to be naked in front of me?" I asked as we drove.

"What's to be embarrassed about?"

"I don't know, me seeing your body. I don't know."

"Did you like what you saw?" He looked into my eyes.

"Yes!"

"Then there's no reason to be embarrassed. You're not gonna be embarrassed in front of me eventually. I loved what I saw earlier, but you're new to this so it'll take some time."

"How do you know I'm new to this?"

"You have innocence written all over your face."

"Everybody keeps saying that."

"Who's everybody?"

75

"This guy named Kevin, he works for Mitigated. He comes by from time to time, Ms. Laverne don't like him though." I sighed, "Any who he told me I looked innocent too."

"So he flirts with you?"

"Kind of, but Ms. Laverne shuts him down. She said he slithers." I laughed.

"What do you think of him?

"What do you mean?" I had no idea what he was talking about.

"You like him?" He glanced at me.

"I don't know, hadn't really thought about it. I guess he could be cute to somebody, but I never thought about it."

Derrick was quiet for a minute. "You can't date him."

"Not that I want to, but you can't tell me who I can and can't date. Especially when you're going back to the double mint twins." I said wiggling my neck and adjusting in my seat.

He smirked, "double mint twins." His low tone laugh was kind of scary. We pulled up to the light; he cut his eyes at me. "You heard what I said." His face was scary serious, I had never seen him look like that so I left it alone. I didn't know if that was jealousy or something else. When we pulled up to a building a valet person approached the car. He told them to wait. He looked at me.

"Chantel when do I tell you what to do?" I thought about it and he doesn't. "When I tell you something I may not explain it but trust that I'm not bullying you. When I bully you, you'll know the difference. Kevin isn't right. PLUS I don't want you talking to him." He smirked.

"Ok," I tried to act like I understood.

When we got out the car he told me he hoped I liked dinner. When we walked in the man at the door greeted Derrick by name. He told us to follow him to our table. The place was dimly lit. There was a stage and tables all around the floor with drippy candles, a very romantic scene. Our table was right in the front of the audience. Our waiter brought us menus; everything on the menu was really fancy. I didn't understand half the entrees on the menu. I asked Derrick what he was going to order. He said the filet mignon was delicious. I felt embarrassed asking him what filet mignon was. He smiled at me and told me to trust him, I watched him as he ordered for us. He knew exactly what he wanted and how he wanted it. I wondered if he was like that with everything. When the waiter brought us wine, my eyes got big. He gestured to me to be cool. Why he always gotta push the limit? Why couldn't we enjoy our meal without me feeling like we were going to get caught sneaking? "Well look at the love birds!" A familiar voice said. I turned around to see Tim, Malcolm, and Drew at the table behind us. "Hey you!" I said getting up to give him a hug, "how are you tonight?"

"I'm good, I'm glad to see you guys still hanging out." He said smiling at us.

I waved hello to Drew and Malcolm. They said polite hellos but both of them had serious faces; they were going over information in a binder. It kind of looked like they were meeting to discuss business and reporting to Tim. Then a short guy walked up to our table. He was smiling really big and he looked eager to talk to Derrick. "They told me you were out here. Please tell me you've come to jam with us." The man said kind of begging.

Derrick motioned towards me, "this is Chantel. If you can convince her to sing, I'll play one song." Derrick said smiling at me.

I felt like I lost my air, he did NOT just say that! The wicked smirk on his face and the guy's pleading eyes let me know I heard him right. "Please!" The guy pleaded. I shook my head no, "OH PLEASE! I'LL GIVE YOU ANYTHING YOU WANT!" I started to reply, but by the way Derrick tilted his head it was like he read my mind and he told me I better not say anything negative. I almost slapped myself when I heard myself agree to sing. I could tell my early surrender shocked Derrick as well. "YES!" He did a one-man celebration. "My name is Gus. After your meal, which is on the house by the way..."

"It better be!" Tim chimed in.

I didn't know he was listening. "Tim! I was so focused on your grandson, I didn't see you over there." Gus said as he walked over and shook his hand. Drew and Malcolm held the same annoyed expression as they waited for Tim and Gus to finish their conversation.

Derrick touched my hand, "what do you want to sing?"

I grabbed his hand, "I can't think!" My eyes glazed over as I did a nervous laugh. Derrick patted my hand and waited for me to get it together. Gus told Derrick they had a sax for him, or he could take over any of the other instruments. The band came out and played beautiful jazz melodies while we ate. I downed three glasses of wine and my nerves lightened a lot. Derrick kept watching me almost smiling. Looking at him made me feel like I could do this and there was no need to be scared. I thought of a song, he actually smiled when I told him. I could've died! That smile took away any nerves I thought I had. He told me to hang tight and then he went to go tell Gus. The band took a little break, Derrick told them he'd play a song with them and then he'd play during my song. A few of the band members kind of looked at me funny when he said I was going to sing. I hoped my voice didn't crack, or I messed up so badly that they look at Derrick funny. Apparently they all knew him and he was a pretty big deal around here. We ordered dessert, but Derrick gave our waiter specific instructions, he didn't want our dessert to come out until after we performed. Derrick went on stage with them when they came back from their break. The audience erupted in applause when they introduced Derrick. I didn't recognize the song they played. The rest of his band had music they were following. Derrick played from his heart. I glanced back at his father's table and they were all enjoying the music. Even though Malcolm was looking very stern, I detected a hint of pride in his demeanor. When the song was over an attendant brought a stool and a microphone and stand out for me. Derrick gestured for me to join him on the stage. I wanted to run in the opposite direction, but I took a seat on the stool. The attendant asked Derrick how close the microphone should be. Derrick looked at me like he was calculating something. He moved the microphone out a little further, then he winked at me. Then he told me when I said go they would play. Thank goodness it was so dim in this room, I could pretend like it was just Derrick and I. I imagined I was in concert and all these people came to see me. I couldn't disappoint. I took a deep breath and then I dropped my hand... the musical introduction was short but that was good. "I must've rehearsed my lines, a thousand times, until I had them memorized. But when I get up the nerve to tell you the words they never seem to come out right. OOOOHHHHHH IF!........." People in the audience screamed out as I sang. I focused on Derrick only though. My heart stopped pounding and the song flowed through me. When I finished everyone stood up and like thunder they were applauding and asking for more. I was so surprised, I didn't think anyone was gonna like my singing. Embarrassed I hurried back to our table; Tim gave me a hug and said my song was beautiful. Drew had a huge smile on his face, and Malcolm's eyes smiled but his face remained stern. I gave Derrick a HUGE hug, and he held onto me while I trembled. I didn't understand why I was trembling other than the fact that I never would've let anyone hear me sing outside of Cyrus, and now he had me doing things I never would've done. I LOVE this boy so much! He has no idea.

When we sat down Drew came over to our table bringing his chair. "That was amazing! I had no idea you could sing like that." He said smiling.

"Thank you, you really liked it?" I asked in disbelief.

Drew gave me a look like are you kidding? "Of course! You've got talent. And it appears that I might need you."

I frowned, "need me?"

"Yes, you! Did D-Rick tell you about my club?"

"I heard a little bit about it." I said thinking of Toya.

"My plan is to have local musicians come and play, or in your case sing there regularly. I'd love it if you were my first artist."

I looked at Derrick and I didn't see any objection on his face. "You think I'm good enough to sing in your club?"

"You're gonna be the next mega star. That is if you want to be. Elegant Affairs could just be your stop along the way." Then he got comfortable in his chair. "Chantel how come we've never talked?" I shrugged. "Do you want to be a celebrity? Our momma kind of works in the industry, between her and Malcolm you could be the next mega star. AGAIN! That's if that what you want. We have cousins who can sing, and they've promised to make guest appearances at the club. Unfortunately their school schedules and stuff like that interfere with what I have in mind."

I felt like he was talking too fast for me to comprehend although I knew that wasn't the case. "If Derrick wouldn't have caught me singing one day, I never would of sang for anyone. If Derrick thinks it's a good idea, I'll do it. I have no self esteem around this singing thing."

He nodded his head like he understood. "So I know D-Rick is gonna say yes." He smiled at Derrick, who blank stared back at him. "So I'll need you to come by the club and we'll discuss scheduling, promotion, and money."

"Money? You're gonna pay me?" I said in disbelief.

"Of course! Time is money. You're really helping me out by agreeing to do it." He said

Then our waiter brought our desserts to the table. Drew went back to his table and Derrick told me I sang BEAUTIFULLY! I felt like I was going to float away. His approval was the only one that really mattered to me.

****

It was our last Friday together, I was trying not to mope around feeling sorry for myself that he was leaving and that I'd have to go back to ordinary life but I couldn't help it. Derrick and I have spent everyday and night together. I got over being disappointed every night when he went to sleep. We'd make out in the morning and that was good. I wanted to experience more, but Derrick wasn't going any further. That was puzzling but I guess it was ok. Eventually Jaloni stopped calling everyday. I didn't know what to say to him so I left him hanging. I figured we'd break up when I got back to school. "When is your spring break?" Derrick asked "Beginning of April, why?"

"Talk to Pearla, let's plan a trip somewhere."

"What about work?"

"I'll talk Malcolm into giving you the time off." He said

"April does give me a chance to save up some money to go." I said calculating imaginary cost.

Derrick blank stared at me. "You don't pay when you're with me!"

"Did I offend you? I didn't mean to."

"When have you ever paid for anything with me?"

"Never! But I still didn't want to assume." I said still apologizing.

"When you're with me assume you're not paying for anything." He huffed

"Sorry! Geesh!" He was sensitive today.

"Can we spend today inside?"

"Why?" He said with a semi attitude.

"Prepare yourself I'm going into complete girl mode." I said, and he cut his eyes at me. I scooted into his lap and put my arms

around his neck. I looked into his beautiful brown eyes. "It's our last Friday together. I'm trying to keep it together but I just want you to hold me all day. I'm sad our time together has to end. I want Derrick love all day and I don't want to share with anybody." I said nuzzling my head into his chest. I could hear his heart pounding.

"You sure about that, I know I've been moody today. I'm liable to bite your head off." He said

"I don't mind your bite, I just want to be up under you today."

He exhaled and put his arms around me. "I wish you were coming to my school next year. April seems too far away to exist like this again. It's not like you come to visit me." He squeezed me a little tighter.

"What about the double mint twins? Won't they get mad about me coming around?" I looked at his face.

His face was stone, "you should ask me if I care. I'm just passing time with them. You should be honored that it takes two of them to get through until I see you again."

"I don't see that as a compliment, but whatever. I don't want to think about them right now." I said

"Good, and I won't think about your little boyfriend." He said squeezing me a little tighter. "But you know what I do want?" He looked at me, "a chocolate peanut butter smoothie."

"You never did tell me why you like that one." I said staring at him. "Pineapple peach is your general flavor, but when you're sentimental you like the strawberry banana. What's chocolate PB about?"

He looked at me, "you!"

I instantly started blushing, "what?"

"You were standing out in the mall handing out samples. You were sampling that flavor. I normally don't go for samples, but I thought you were cute so I took the sample. You stayed on my mind, so I would come back to the smoothie stand only when I saw you were there. At first I only ordered that one from you. Then I ventured out to the others. I started watching you, you were so focused on your job and working hard at it. I didn't think you noticed me at all."

I couldn't stop blushing. "But I knew your name."

"And fifty other regulars. You were good at what you did." he said matter of factly.

"I didn't think you were looking at me." I said

"I still am." He said looking at me, "you're beautiful!" Then he kissed me, "now let's go get my smoothie."

As we walked up to the smoothie stand Quesha had a very stuck look on her face. I figured she was reacting to Derrick like Shelly did, but then she said. "Derrick." and she had pain on her face "Quesha" he said with no emotion in his.

Her eyes glazed over, I knew that pained look. "Can I have a chocolate peanut butter and a pineapple peach?" I said wanting to change the unspoken subject.

"You never said goodbye, you just disappeared." She said ignoring me.

Derrick showed her no emotion as he looked at her. "Ok" I said wondering how long she was going to ignore that I was standing there.

"Derrick please!" she begged

I looked at him, and he rolled his eyes. "I don't do this! I came here for a smoothie. If you want some public scene you better find somebody else. We have nothing to talk about. Give Chantel her smoothies, and we won't have any problems." Shelly jumped when Derrick started talking, he wasn't happy. Quesha put her hand over her mouth as her eyes watered up. Quesha went to the back leaving Shelly to finish our order. Shelly nervously came over to input our order. Derrick handed her money without uttering a word. Shelly's hands were shaking she was so scared. Derrick didn't look friendly, but it made no sense to me for her to be so scared of him. I didn't say anything, and we walked back to the car in silence. When we got back to the apartment Cyrus was leaving, he told me Jaloni called. I sat on the couch staring at Derrick; he knew my question so I didn't see the point in saying anything. "There's nothing to talk about!" He said flatly.

"Yes there is, she was in tears Derrick."

"We went out a few times. She did nothing for me, I stopped calling. It's not deep, let it go." He barked

"Well say that, I don't wanna have to ask you. Just tell me Derrick."

"Ok" he said sitting next to me.

"You know, Malcolm's starting to look better. Did your parents make up?"

"I don't know what they're doing." He sounded irritated.

"Will I get to meet her soon?" I asked

"I guess so, she's been busy with work."

"Ok" I said feeling disappointed.

"Don't be like that!" He barked, "why wouldn't I introduce you to my mother? You've met everybody else who matters."

Ugh! The mood swings! "Seriously Derrick, I was only asking. When you react like that it makes me wonder if there's more and you're just not saying anything."

His whole body twitched, I could literally see him bouncing around on different reactions. His voice got real low and his face was irritated. "Timing is everything. If you know I'm irritated about that girl why would you ask me about my mother, especially linked to Malcolm? I'm still working through all that."

"If those feelings she had were only one sided why do you have a reaction at all?" I said getting irritated myself.

Derrick looked at me for about sixty seconds without saying anything. "I'll be back." Then he left.

I sat there stuck looking like, "did he really just leave?" My feelings were hurt, but I waited. I waited two hours, when the phone rang. I jumped at it thinking it was Derrick. "Hello?"

"Chantel, why haven't you called me?" Jaloni asked

"I'm sorry. I've been running the streets with my friends. How was your vacation?" I was trying to pull myself together.

"Horrible! I've been missing you!" He said sincerely.

"I'm sorry Jaloni. I didn't mean to ruin your vacation." I felt horrible.

We talked for an hour, before there was a knock on my door. Excited to see Derrick I got off the phone with Jaloni. I told him I would call him back tomorrow. I opened the door, and I felt disappointed to see my neighbor Rhea, a very religious but sweet woman. "How you doing darling?" She said with a smile.

"I'm fine and you?"

"Oh I'm good honey. I just wanted to let you know I was going to have some friends over tonight. If we are too loud for you or it gets to be too late, please feel free to let me know. I'll try to keep the noise down."

We chatted a few minutes, I told her not to worry about the noise. Then I looked at the clock. Derrick had been gone over three hours. He had to be crazy to think I would continue to sit here waiting on him. I grabbed my keys and got in my car. I had no idea

where I was going but I was leaving the house. I drove around for a little bit. In a defeated manner I decided to go home, but I stopped at the gas station to fill up first. "Chantel!"
I turned around to see Jaloni. He had on basketball shorts and a ball in his arm, he was all sweaty. "Hey! You need a ride home?"
"Sure!" He said with a big smile. He finished pumping my gas, and then he got in the passenger seat. When we pulled up to his house he invited me inside to have dinner with his family, but I declined. I told him I needed to go home. Then I got out the car and I talked with him for a little bit. "Can I see you tomorrow?"
"You know what I can't tomorrow. But I'll see you at school." I tried to let him down nicely.
"I haven't spent anytime with you this whole vacation, I miss you."

"I know, I'm sorry. It's been a crazy vacation." I said, knowing Derrick would never settle for such an sorry excuse for an explanation. Then I saw a car approaching real slow down the side street. It was Derrick's car, my insides SCREAMED! How in the world did he find me? "Jaloni, I gotta go. Go inside!"
"What's wrong? Who's that?" He said looking at the car.
Derrick got out of his car in the middle of the street, no hazard lights or anything. I wanted to run but Jaloni wasn't running and I didn't want to leave him there alone. "Jaloni, please go inside." I hurried to the driver side of my car.
"So this is your little boyfriend." Derrick said
"Jaloni this is my boss' son."
Jaloni looked surprised, "are you supposed to be at work?" He said moving backwards.
"Something like that." I said getting in my car hoping Jaloni would move faster.
Derrick was staring at me; I waited until Jaloni went inside then I stepped on the gas my car fishtailed as I drove away. I swear Derrick still had to walk back to his car but he caught up to me in no time flat. My heart was pounding out of my chest. I didn't know what to expect from Derrick when I got to the house. Obviously he went looking for me, how in the world did he know where Jaloni lived? I put my car in the garage and Derrick took his time walking from the street up to my apartment. Cyrus was in the kitchen, he called out that Caprice was coming over and he was making dinner. I said that was great then I ran up to my room. I took my shoes off and I climbed in the middle of my bed with my back

against the headboard. I waited for Derrick, my heart was pounding. I could hear him coming up the stairs, every step sent shock through my body. He opened my door and his face was very serious. He took his jacket off and laid it at the foot of my bed. He sat close to my feet and then he pulled me in to him. "Sometimes I forget you're only a little girl."

I didn't know how insulted to be by his statement. "What do you mean?"

"Exactly, you don't understand cause you're a little girl. Why would you interrupt our time to go be with him? He's going to be with you for the next three months. All we had was this two week vacation."

"You left me hanging without a word for three plus hours, you left mad. I didn't think you were coming back. I didn't go looking for him."

"Right, little girl answers." He was irritated; I turned my body away from him. I didn't know which way he was gonna go with this, but my feelings were really hurt. He got up and walked down stairs.

I heard him and Cyrus talking, they both got excited about something and got really loud. I went to the doorway and listened, they were talking about sports. I rolled my eyes and closed my door. I wanted him to go home or come and apologize then make me feel good like he has been doing. I turned on the new TV he bought me for my room and laid there watching it. What was I supposed to do, wait around here like a helpless puppy waiting for his return? Little girl answers? Seriously? I felt so small. Derrick came back upstairs, "the food is ready. Your brother can cook!" I didn't say anything I kept staring at the TV. "Are you hungry?" I didn't respond. He huffed and closed the door behind him. "I'm sorry. I left upset. I went to clear my head, and then I was trying to track my momma down. The time got away from me. I didn't do anything to your little square boyfriend." I still didn't respond. "I'm not mad anymore why are you upset?"

"I guess I'm too much of a little girl to understand your explanation!" I barked at him.

He huffed, "come on. Don't act like this, we don't have much time left together."

"Act like what? You're the one whose panties got all in a bunch because you saw your ex. I'm supposed to understand that when

you left here seemingly upset behind another female that you were coming back to me or whatever. You've never made me feel so small, and so insignificant. You really hurt my feelings. Maybe we've spent too much time together. Maybe you should leave."
"You want me to go?" His voice was low and stern.
"Yes! Please leave!"

Chapter 6

After Derrick left, Cyrus came upstairs to offer me dinner. When I told him what happened he told me he was proud of me for standing up for myself. I was scared Derrick would be done with me like Quesha. I didn't know what their story was, but I knew there had to be more to it than what he said. I told Cyrus how he had been moody all morning and then all that happened. He explained that guys are taught to suck it up, and he said Derrick was definitely a master at doing that. That kind of made me laugh. Then Drew called to make sure I was still coming to the club tonight. I had forgotten all about going. We were going to go over his proposal for me to perform and he wanted me to get a vibe for the club so that I could prepare songs, meet the band, stuff like that. I didn't feel great about going alone. But what could I do? Not knowing what to expect I didn't want to be in a dress, so I put on black pants that seem like they were made with me standing in them, and a halter-top. I put on high heels, and I moved my ponytail to a bun on the top of my head, which made my eyes pop, and I put on big earrings and bangles. When I slowly came down the stairs I could hear Cyrus and Caprice talking at the table. I was surprised to see Derrick standing by the door patiently waiting. I forgot I was mad at him and smiled, he looked really good in his cream-colored sweater and dark jeans. He almost smiled at me, his eyes ran over my clothes and then they settled on mine. He genuinely apologized for not looking at the big picture. He told me he was dreading going back to school and not being able to spend time with me like he was used to. I accepted his apology and I was relieved that I didn't have to explain why I asked him to leave or have another argument about why my asking him to leave was the right thing to do. Cyrus was watching us, and Caprice tried to pretend like she wasn't, Cyrus smiled at me to show his approval. Derrick opened his umbrella as we walked out; he put his arm around me as we walked to his car. His cologne was intoxicating. We arrived at Elegant Affairs at seven-thirty on the nose. Drew was already there and he was dancing in the middle of the dance floor like it was his own party. He told Derrick to join him, but Derrick declined. Drew danced really well. I knew Derrick could dance as well, but we mainly two stepped together. I've never seen him just go at it like Drew was doing. But I figure he could dance just as well if not better than Drew by the way Drew told him to come dance like they used to. Drew pointed to a booth in the VIP section and he told us that's where we'll be hanging out. He said since the club was still new police could show up at any time so we couldn't drink out on the floor. Then he took us up to his office; he had a few forms in the middle of the desk. He called them his Chantel papers. Derrick sat back and listened to Drew explain everything to me. Drew took his time explaining all aspects of the contract and he patiently answered my questions. He said we were starting with a six-month contract to get a feel for me as a performer and to make sure I would be a good fit. He said normally he would never sign such a long contract but he said I knocked him out with my voice and he had no doubt that I would deliver. He said they would hold auditions for backup singers, and then a photo-shoot for promotional photos. He said his cousin Gwen's company would handle all the promotions. He said there would be a budget for clothing. Then the money…. he broke down what he expected to take in at the door on the nights I performed and the revenue generated from the bar and kitchen. Then he showed me what he wanted to pay me per performance. My insides screamed then I looked at Derrick. Derrick didn't have a reaction; Drew smiled and asked me if I was haggling him for more money. I was speechless, he wanted to pay me a lot of money per performance, four performances a month at least, and I couldn't believe it. But then he said I twisted his arm, even though I hadn't said anything and he bumped it up an additional five hundred per performance, and an incentive kind of like a commission on holiday weekends if I packed the place out. He said I could sing some ballads, but my goal was to get people out of their seats and to put on a fun show. Then he told me not to discuss my contract terms with anyone outside of Derrick cause he would not be so generous with someone else. I sat there trying to imagine what I would do with all this money, on top of my job at Mitigated. He told me to come back Monday after school to help conduct the backup singer auditions. He said whomever we liked on Monday would be asked back on Wednesday and then we'd make the final selection then. I thanked him for working around my schedule at Mitigated. Drew said he would have new contracts for me to sign on Monday reflecting the correct amounts. Then he asked what I wanted to drink, I looked at Derrick and I told him to order for me. Since I had no idea of what to drink. So he ordered a whisky sour for me and he had jack and coke. We sat in Drew's office drinking and chatting. "Grand dad was right, she does kind of remind me of Grandmomma." Drew said looking at me with sad eyes.

"I hadn't thought of that until he said it, but I can see it now." Derrick said looking at me too.

"How do I remind you of her?"

"Your complexion for one. You've got that deep chocolate tone to your skin just like she had. I was little when she passed, but I remember her face mostly." Derrick said

"Grandmomma didn't take no mess though, our momma and Malcolm tell stories about her that make me wonder how our momma ever survived, or why grand momma liked Malcolm for that matter. But she was always so sweet and kind to us." Drew stuck out his chest; "I was the first grandchild so I had her to myself for awhile. All I had to do was hit her with my big brown eyes and I could almost have anything I wanted."

I smiled at their reminiscing over their grandmother. As far as I know mine are still alive but my parents didn't think it was a priority for us to know our family. So although our mother was an only child, our father had at least one sibling and possibly cousins etc. "Why do you guys call your father by his first name and your mother momma?"

"I think Malcolm would have a cow if we called him daddy." Drew said cracking up, "he's never been into the labels. I also think he'd lose it if he thought any of us even tried to call momma Amber." Drew said

"The name doesn't change who he is." Derrick said

"Subject change real quick." Drew said putting his hand up.

"Chantel we're letting you into the guy world by having you work here." I nodded my head not knowing what he was going to say next. "You're going to see something's happening around here. Derrick is vouching for you, but I feel the need to say what happens in this club stays in this club." He said pointing his finger at the desk.

"What do you mean?"

"If you see me hook up with somebody. You can't go running back to Toya or anybody else telling them what you saw." His face was serious.

"Ok."

"Or you might see the bouncers handling someone. There's no need to discuss that either."

"Ok," I said.

Then his face turned very serious, he looked a lot like Malcolm in this moment. "Also, our trust is very important. The fact that you have it so easily says a lot. HOWEVER, you have to always be smart!" He sat back in his chair taking a swig of his drink. His voice got deeper, "everything we do is legit. However, there are some people who would like to believe that the Wallace's and the Latour's are up to no good." My eyes got big, he was being scary. "Is this too much for you to handle?" He looked at me and then at Derrick.

"She's ok, go ahead." Derrick said reading me.

"There's a couple of detectives that don't like us. They swear we're up to something. They're always looking for the weak link in our chain. Unfortunately for them we are a family of loyal achievers. We're welcoming you into our family." He smiled

I smiled back, "Cyrus is the only family I have."

"Not anymore, now you got a family of Wallace's and Latour's. We stick together and we protect each other."

I raised my hand, "I know it's stupid but I have questions." Drew laughed at my hand. "Is Toya a part of this family? Cause if she is, I'm going to have to bow out."

Drew cracked up and Derrick chuckled. "NO! Toya is not a part of this family." Drew said still laughing. "I don't know why I gotta have her, but for right now I do."

"If Toya was a part of this family I wouldn't be!" Derrick said not laughing at all.

"We don't normally bring outsiders in too far. I mean there'll be limitations of course, but I want you to know that we're family; and from this point onward you have nothing to worry about. You will always be taken care of." His face was very serious and so was Derrick's.

"You know what she did?" Derrick said to Drew. Drew raised an eyebrow; "she kicked me out of her apartment!"

Drew looked surprised, he looked at me. "Yep! I like you already!"

****

We spent Sunday in my room; we ate, slept, and made out all day. It was wonderful! We talked about everything like we've always done. He told me about his classes, his school. He told me he understood if I didn't want to come to visit him regularly, but I had to come every once in a while. Looking at the calendar we picked a weekend where I'd come after work on Saturday and spend the night with him. I got butterflies in my stomach at the thought of it. I was excited; we'd be in his apartment alone for a whole day. Anything could happen since it hadn't happened now. I was still in tack, technically pure sort of speak. Although I was already sprung behind the things he did to me. I was ready, but Derrick is the master torture artist. He kept looking at me like he knew what he was doing to me; he'd smirk and fake surprise that I liked something. I couldn't even tell you what he was doing; I just know I wanted more. When it was time for him to leave I didn't care, I cried and wrapped my long legs around him. That gave him the excuse to make it seem like he was comforting me and not freaking out his own self. I never knew love could feel like this. All that time I spent feeling invisible was worth the wait to have Derrick in my life. I didn't want to walk him to the door. "I HATE COLLEGE!" I yelled
Derrick laughed at me, which was sweet pain and joy at the same time. "Try to get into my school."
We kissed our last kiss for the next however long and then I watched him drive away.

****

"This must be your little boyfriend, what's your name?" Drew said
"Little?" Jaloni said
"This is Jaloni, Jaloni this is Drew." Jaloni needed to calm down. I pointed to a chair over to the side. "Jaloni please sit."
We were on the second audition and we were making the final selection for my background singers. Most of the singers were

really good, and then…. then there were the ones I think Andrew

had there cause he wanted a closer look. Drew was full of smiles unlike his brother, Monday I watched him charm a couple of girls right out of their panties. Not my man, not my problem, but when Derrick and I are finally together I hope he never does me like Drew does these females. Most of them seemed like they were only here in hopes of getting closer to him. Which is why I was

leaning more towards the guys anyways. Drew had a whole scoring sheet, Monday anyone who got less than twenty points weren't invited back today. There was this one guy who was really good. I hoped Drew liked him as much as I did, but we'll see.
"All of you were asked to come back for a final audition. We only have three spots to fill and there are eight of you. So let me say

now... my apologies to those not chosen. For the chosen ones we will have a rehearsal right after auditions, your first performance will be Friday night. Are there any questions?"
The vixen raised her hand. "What about runner ups or alternates if for some reason one or more of your chosen can't perform, you'd have a backup." She tried to say as cutely as she could
Drew smiled, "your name?"
"Teresa," She smiled
He smiled, "Teresa. Thank you for the suggestion, but really I only need one background singer, two is great, and three is that emergency buffer. If I chose someone and they leave me hanging they're out of a job!" Then he smiled at me, "does anyone else think like Teresa?" He asked the group, no one said anything. "Just Teresa huh." Then he walked over to her and gently led her by the hand to the door. He opened it and said, "bye bye, only real dedicated singers need apply." Then he closed the door in her face. The bouncers in the corner started laughing. "We don't need

anybody who's already trying to think of loop holes. If you're gonna be here, be here. Do I make myself clear?" The group

nodded their heads. Drew clapped his hands, "Ok, let's get to it. Impress me!" He pointed at a singer, "Go!"
I shifted in my seat, I never seen this side of Drew. He seemed a lot like his dad today, minus the smiles and the flirting. The guy I liked stepped forward, he said his name was Jesse. I wrote it on the top of his scorecard. He had a wonderful voice; I gave him fives all the way down. I think Drew liked him but I couldn't tell. Next there was Stanley, he wasn't as good as Jesse, but he was good. I gave him a mix of fours and fives. Then Aleisha she was a little white girl with an amazing voice. She was a little powerhouse. I loved her too. Just because I didn't know how the other judges were scoring I picked one more alternate, Taj. I scored him slightly lower than Stanley but really he was a good alternate. The rest of them were girls and all I saw was stars in their eyes for Drew.

They didn't impress me. Drew took all the judges to his office, while he left the rest of them to sweat it out. He asked for our score sheets and I gave him my four. When he asked me about the other three I told him I didn't like them so there was no point in scoring them. He told me to do it anyways next time. Then he read off the scores, the girls I didn't like no one else liked them either. Drew smiled and said at least we all agreed on something. Stanley and Taj were neck and neck. It came down to splitting hairs. Taj was about the same height as Jesse, Gwen and Jenise said it would look better in pictures to have him instead of Stanley. As we were sitting there, I wondered if when we started practicing Drew would realize that the background singers were better than me. They had amazing voices, and until two weeks ago only two people had ever heard me sing. Drew delivered the boom without remorse, the three girls and Stanley were surprised they weren't chosen. Each of those girls thought for sure they were getting picked. Aleisha looked surprised to hear her name actually. What I liked about her off the bat was that her voice stood for its self. She wasn't trying to push up on Drew, and she wasn't dressed like some kind of vixen like the rest of the hoochie crew! Drew had the bouncers escort them out. The band greeted all of us. Drew's cousin Gwen was a feisty red head; she went into immediate promotion mode. She had a photographer snapping pictures of us rehearsing, as she consulted with Jenise on direction. Jenise kept giving the photographer direction on how to capture the pictures. Drew said he wasn't expecting perfection on Friday since we didn't have much of a chance to rehearse, but he expected professionalism. I gave the singers the songs for the night. My face started stinging as I stood in front of the microphone to rehearse. All of a sudden I felt like all eyes were on me. I closed my eyes and imagined that Derrick was standing in front of me. After a while I realized no one was singing and the band wasn't playing. Panic struck my heart as I thought they hated my singing and suddenly Drew realized he made a mistake. "Whoa!" Bruce the drummer said.
"What was it bad? I can do better?" I looked around nervously.
"YOU CAN DO BETTER THAN THAT??? Yo Drew she's amazing!" Bruce said
I don't even know where they came from but I erupted in tears. Jaloni and everyone else looked startled by my sudden outburst.
"Come on honey." Gwen said taking me by the hand. "Drew we'll

be back in five minutes." She said escorting me to the bathroom. In the bathroom she wet a paper towel and she wiped my eyes.
"Feeling better?"
"Yes thank you." I said taking the towel from her.
"You have an amazing voice."
"Thank you." I dried my eyes.
"Sometimes this will seem like a fairy tale, and other times it will seem like a nightmare. Hang in there for the fairy tale ok."
"Ok."

"Now let's go. Time is money." She said with a smile.

Jaloni asked me if I was ok when we walked back on the floor, he looked really concerned. I told him I was ok, and I took my place back on stage. Rehearsal went smoothly after that.
I talked to Derrick for a little bit Thursday night. I was all nerves; and he calmed me down a lot. I didn't ask him if he was coming my assumption was that he wouldn't miss it.
Cyrus was excited for me. He told me that our parents moved to the building across the street. He said he put the laminated flyer in her car door. I asked him why he did that, and he said she needed to know how wrong she was. But I knew he was secretly hoping that she would have a change of heart and actually care about us. I knew the truth even if he didn't. She didn't care and she never would. Jesse and I were the first singers there. Jesse asked me if I was nervous, and I told him I was terrified. So he rehearsed with me, which helped me loosen up. He gave me good pointers about engaging the audience. I took everything in like I was studying for a quiz. Gwen walked in with a garment bag and a couple of guys following her. She said they were there to do my hair and makeup. I told Gwen that I needed to feel like myself, so nothing over the top. The hair stylist braided up my hair and then he put extensions in. He made my weave a little longer than my hair then he put all kinds of heat on it. I was thankful that he didn't burn my hair out doing all that. He styled it just past my shoulders and very curly. I loved it. The hair stylist got started on Aleisha's hair. The makeup artist looked at the dress brought for me. He said he was going to give me a more naturally glamorous look. He said he wanted to highlight my eyes and show them off. He said my skin was

beautiful so I didn't need foundation, but he put something on my face to help minimize the shine. When he was done Gwen high fived him. The photographer got her camera ready and she started snapping as soon as they turned me to the mirror. I gasped for air when I saw my face. It was me, but just like he said he made my eyes stand out. I started to cry and he showed me how to dab my eyes and not mess up my makeup. We kicked everyone out and then we put on our dresses, etc. I wondered if this is what it felt like to be a celebrity. Jesse and Taj told us we looked beautiful. We spent the rest of the time back stage rehearsing. Jesse said his pregnant wife was going to be in the audience. Taj and Aleisha said they were unattached. They asked if Jaloni was coming and I told them he couldn't cause he was under age. When I told them that we're both 17 they couldn't believe it. They all agreed that I carried myself in a very mature manner. I thanked them. My heart started pounding when Gwen took them to the stage and she told me to wait in the room. I wished Derrick was there telling me it was going to be ok. What if I got out there and no one liked me? I told myself to suck it up! I told myself I was singing to Derrick and everything would be ok. We were singing an upbeat song first. We were doing three back to back. I was excited that people were already up and dancing when I came out. I got right into the song. I remembered what Jesse said about engaging the audience, so I gestured towards people while I sang. One girl got really excited when I did that and she danced harder. Everything he told me to do was working. After the three songs I introduced the band and the backup singers. Then we went into three more songs. The crowd loved us to my surprise and delight. When I told the audience I was going to sing two more songs and then we would be done people started yelling encore. I smiled really big; I thanked them for liking us. I sang both of the songs I sang for Derrick. People were standing up and cheering me on. Everyone's applause was overwhelming for me. When I stopped to gather myself, I guess they thought I was doing it for dramatic affect cause they got louder in their applause. When I finished everyone was going crazy. I thanked everyone and I made my way to the dressing room. Then I cried my eyes out, I was relieved, happy, confused, and proud, and did I say happy? I was happy it was over, etc. Drew came in the room first; he gave me a big hug. He said I did better than he thought I would. He gave each of us envelopes with checks for tonight's performance. Then he reminded me I couldn't drink just in case he got raided tonight he could lose everything if they could prove I was drinking under age. He put my arm around his and he led me back out to the floor. The dance floor was packed. Cyrus was waiting for me when we came out the room he gave me a big hug, he told me he was proud of me and that I did such a good job. Sherrell echoed his sentiments then they went back on the dance floor. A girl walked up to Drew she was pretty and all smiles. She asked him if he wanted to dance. He told her maybe later. Then she asked him to introduce her to me. I could tell he didn't want to but he did it anyways. "Chantel, this is Karen." I said hello. Then Drew told her he'd catch up with her later.

He took me to the VIP section and I recognized his uncles, Tim, Malcolm, and his cousins. At the next table he introduced me to his cousin Sophia, his cousin Ethan who's married to Jenise who I met earlier, his mother Amber, and then Darryl was there. I gave Darryl a funny look cause I know he's younger than me. Darryl smiled at me like he read my mind. "When you're tall they don't question as much."

I didn't see Derrick anywhere. Someone needed Drew for something, so he told me to have a seat and he'd be back. "You're really good." Amber said trying to talk over the music. Jenise gave me a thumb up, cause she knew how nervous I was earlier. "Thank you!" I smiled, she liked me.

Then Jesse came over with his wife, he introduced her and then he said they were going to go home. Darryl told me to come dance with him on the dance floor. Just as I was about to ask Darryl where Derrick was, he was coming towards us. Darryl started dancing with a random girl. I put my arms around Derrick's neck and I squeezed him tight as I kissed him. He told me I did a wonderful job. Then he told me I looked very pretty. We were slow dancing to a fast-paced song. I was enjoying my off scheduled moment in his arms suddenly the music stopped, and the lights came up. I saw Stanley going off and Drew looked pissed. He told one of the bouncers to get Stanley out. Stanley started yelling and saying he wasn't leaving then his backup stepped up and he smiled as if to say he had Drew cornered. Derrick told me to go back by his mother and he walked to the left. I did as I was told. I spotted Darryl on the right. I looked at Malcolm and all the uncles; they had un-amused looks on their faces. Drew told the guy standing closest to him to get everybody out. A lot of people ran out. When the crowd cleared, all the guys in black shirts and grey pants stood out. Stanley had about ten guys with him, but their were men everywhere. Drew said that it was too late for Stanley, but this was the last chance for the rest of them to leave. A few of the guys with Stanley ran out the club. Then Drew ordered for the rest of them to be taken out. Drew's men swarmed in like locust. Each of the guys tried to fight back, and each of them were being dragged out by at least three guys each. Malcolm told Drew he did too much talking. Drew shot back angry fire and then they stared at each other. Malcolm said now there's this big ole scene and people are gonna be wondering what happened, there will be questions. Drew was angry, his grandfather walked over to him. He put his arm around him and he talked him down. Amber and Sophia were focused on Drew, Amber's eyes were sad as she looked at her son talking to her father. As they were talking one of the bouncers asked Drew and his grandfather if they were going to reopen. Derrick's Uncle Frank told Drew to open the doors and let people back in. There were gonna be questions either way, he might as well make money while people had them. Drew and Tim hugged then Drew came back to our table while Tim went back to his. Drew was trying to calm down. They turned the music back on and people came back inside. I didn't know what happened to the sea of black and grey, but they were gone. I was looking for Derrick; I didn't see him or Darryl. Drew was telling his mother and cousin how Stanley auditioned but he wasn't chosen. I thought it was ridiculous that he would come back to start mess behind it, but I guess ignorant people are just ignorant.

Derrick came to the table and asked me if I rode with Cyrus, I told him I drove my own car. He told me he had to take care of business tonight but he'd come by the office tomorrow afternoon. Then he told me I needed to tell Cyrus to take me home. It wasn't a good idea for me to stay at the club. Amber was watching Derrick and I interact, she didn't say anything but I know she saw us.

****

"So I hear you knocked them out last night." Ms. Laverne said with a big smile

I blushed. "Everybody seemed like they liked the show."

"I feel so left out, how come you never sang for me?" She pouted

"It's a long story, but I lacked confidence to sing in front of

anybody until… " I thought about it, then I laughed. "Until Derrick made me."

"Can you sing for me right now before we open?" She said scooting up close to her desk looking eager to hear anything.

I blushed harder, "like what? I don't know what to sing."

"You can sing something you sang last night." When I finished singing my song she was out of her seat hugging me real tight. "OH MY GOODNESS! BABY! YOU CAN BLOW!" She said hugging me so tight I was losing my air as I laughed

"Thank you Ms. Laverne. When I was growing up my parents would always tell me to shut up, they told me I sounded like an animal dying. If I would start singing in the shower they'd throw cold water on me and tell me to shut up. When Derrick said he liked my voice after he accidentally caught me singing I really thought he was being nice."

"Honey, I don't know what the deal is with you and your parents, but they lied to you. I don't know why they would lie to you like that, but they did." She said

"They hated us," I shrugged. "It's no big deal."

Ms. Laverne eyed me, "no big deal?"

"Yeah," I said taking my seat with the mail bundle in front of me. I was creating piles for each employee. "You know Lamont's mail is piling up. When is he coming in to get it?"

"I think he's coming back from vacation soon. Just keep packing it in." She returned to her desk.

Then the phone rang, "Thank you for calling Mitigated Staffing Solutions how may I direct your call?"

"Hey sexy!" Derrick said

"Hey sexy!" I said with a big blushy smile.

Ms. Laverne chuckled and then she turned to her computer. "So I'm on my way to have breakfast with my momma, I'll come by afterwards. What you wanna do after you get off work?"

"I know it probably gets old to you, but can we hang out, watch a movie and stay in?" I said hoping he agreed with me.

"Whatever you wanna do is fine with me. I think my grandfather and Malcolm will be there too. Maybe we can hang out at my grandfather's since he seems to be so fond of you."

"I like him too, I never had grandparents of my own. I'm glad somebody's grandparent likes me." I said all smiles.

"Ok so I'll tell him we'll come hang out. My momma might be there, who am I kidding she'll be there. You guys will get a chance to interact. How does that suit you?"

If he could only see how much I was smiling. "That suits me very well." I said blushing.

"Ok, I'll see you in a little bit."

"I can't wait." I said, "later."

"Later"

I was all smiles when we got off the phone; Ms. Laverne looked at me and smiled. An hour later Jaloni walked into the office. I said hi with a slight smile on my face. Ms. Laverne looked confused when she saw my face. Jaloni was asking what I was doing later on this evening. I told him I had some stuff to do for the club so I couldn't meet him tonight, but we were still on for tomorrow. Jaloni looked disappointed, but he accepted my decline. I gave him a hug, and then I told him I'd talk to him later. When he walked out Ms. Laverne was mugging me. "What are you doing? That's a nice boy."

"I know," I said feeling guilty.

"I thought you were talking to him earlier. I know its none of my business, but Chantel you can't do this. That boy doesn't deserve to be hurt like this." She said

I couldn't look at her guilt was all over my face. "I know, I don't know what to do. I like Jaloni. He helped me get through the last

few months, but Derrick..."

She cut me off, "that was Derrick?"

"Yes ma'am." I said with my eyes still glued to the floor.

"Honey Derrick's not going anywhere. All you're doing is hurting that little boy for something that can't work right now."

"We've got a plan, I'm gonna go see him at the end of this month." I said in our defense.

"Oh yeah, once a month visits that's how you make a relationship

work. If that's what you guys plan to do to make your relationship work then do it. Don't keep that poor little boy hanging on by a string and you have no intentions of doing right by him. Spare the world of another man scorned. PLEASE!" She said irritated. I opened my mouth to defend us. "NO! Not huh! I don't wanna hear it. You know you're wrong! There's nothing you can say to change that. Do the right thing Chantel. I don't wanna discuss it." Then she started mumbling to herself as she scooted into her desk. "Then they wonder what's wrong with the world, all these greedy kids. They turn into greedy adults! Thinking its fun to play with people's emotions and stuff! BUT OH NO! NO! NOBODY BETTER BREAK THEY HEART! Why didn't anybody tell these kids what comes around, goes around? Be good to people and most people will be good to you." I decided to tune her out cause she made me feel bad enough. I wanted to crawl under a rock and hide. A couple hours later the phone rang and Ms. Laverne answered just before I did. "WHAT? WHAT HOSPITAL? OK! OK! We're on our way!" She slammed down the phone. "Baby shut down your computer! Help me close up." She said with tears streaming down her face. "What is it?" I felt like I couldn't breathe.

"Baby, Tim is in the hospital. He had a heart attack; they don't know much else yet. I gotta call Henry, can I ride with you to the hospital?"

"Of course!" I said running to turn off the coffee pot, fax and copy machines, etc. Ms. Laverne called her husband and told him to come to the hospital.

As we were locking the glass door Kevin strolled up. "Where's the fire?"

"Not now Kevin we don't have time for you! The office is closed." Ms. Laverne said then she walked fast pace with me.

Kevin stood there watching as we hurried away. I drove as fast as I could to the hospital. Ms. Laverne told the front desk we were there for Timothy Wallace. One guard fixed his mouth to say there were too many people up there already, but another guard stopped him and told us to go up. I saw Derrick's uncles standing outside the waiting room. They hugged us, they looked upset and helpless. Derrick was sitting in a chair with his head leaned against the wall with his eyes closed. He opened them slowly when he heard Ms. Laverne's voice. He barely moved as he looked at me. I came directly to him and I put my arms around him. He let me hold him, he wasn't crying but he was really upset. He was quieter than normal even for him. Darryl had no jokes to offer, he was quiet as well. Mr. Davide came and eventually convinced Ms. Laverne to go home when it got late. Derrick laid his head on my shoulder, he wasn't sleep. Drew came in the room looking real big. His hands were red like he had been fighting. Drew looked like a huge ball of emotions. I don't remember dozing off, but the sound of screams early in the morning and the staff running jarred me awake. Everyone rushed out the waiting room. Derrick's auntie was hysterical; they were trying to revive Tim. Derrick's face was evil but not even his tears wanted to disobey him. A couple of the nurses begged us to go back in the waiting room, especially since there were so many of us. Derrick's face said he knew it was all-bad. Everybody started crying even though the doctors and nurses were still working on him. I sat next to Derrick and I held his hand. He stared straight forward. Darryl was standing next to his momma rubbing her back. Drew was hugging Sophia and they were both crying. Tina and her brother Tim were crying holding on to each other. When the doctor walked in the room Derrick squeezed my hand and his eyes turned red. The doctor had sad eyes as explained to our large group that Tim went into cardiac arrest; they tried to revive him but they were unsuccessful. Derrick looked like he was in shock; everyone including Malcolm gave way to tears. Seeing Malcolm cry made him seem so human. I cried while rubbing Derrick's hand. Derrick thanked me for coming. Then he said he was going to go back to his mother's house. He told me he would call me later. I was kind of sad that he didn't want me to be there for him, but I went home. Sleeping in the hospital wasn't exactly comfortable.

When I walked in the door Cyrus was on his way out to work. He asked me how Tim was doing, and I broke down. Cyrus rushed to me and he held me while I cried my heart out. I didn't realize how much I was holding back to be strong for Derrick until I broke down myself. I told Cyrus how Derrick and I were going to hang out with Tim that night. He was the closest I've ever come to a grandparent. I went up to my room and laid down. I was sleep for a little bit when there was a knock at the door. I moved faster than my body was ready for and I almost fell down the stairs. Catching my balance I ran to the door expecting to see Derrick. When I opened the door Jaloni was standing there. I completely forgot about him. His smile dropped when he saw me. I was a mess, so his reaction was justified. "What's wrong?"

I stepped to the side so he could come in. "I was at the hospital all night. A family member passed away this morning. I forgot to call you to cancel. I said as tears streamed down my face.
"I'm sorry to hear that. Have you eaten?" He asked with very concerned eyes.
"No, but I'm not hungry. I just wanna lay down."
"Go lay down, I'll fix you something to eat. Let me be here for you." He said rubbing my back. I decided to lay on the couch instead. Jaloni bumped around my kitchen creating delicious smells. My mouth decided against my stomach that I was hungry. Jaloni happily served me, and tended to me like I was a princess. I fell asleep on his shoulder while we were watching TV. I was awaken by a knock at the door. Jaloni asked me if I was expecting anybody, but I knew who it was. Jaloni answered the door. "Oh hey man how you doing? I'm Jaloni I don't think we met." He said extending his hand.
I could hear the hesitation, "Derrick," then he came in.
I sat up and tried to fix my hair. I didn't want him thinking we were doing anything. "I thought you were going over your mother's."
"I did." He said taking a seat on the love seat.
Jaloni sat next to me on the couch. He put his arm around me. "Did you hear about her family member who passed away this morning?"
Derrick stared at his arm. "It was my grandfather." He exhaled
"His grandfather?" Jaloni looked at me.
"Yes, remember I told you Malcolm's family has taken me under their wing." I said matter of factly.
Jaloni got quiet, and he put his arm down. Derrick leaned back on the couch and looked at Jaloni. "How long you been here?"
"I got here a few hours ago."
"He made me breakfast," I volunteered.
Derrick sat up, "is there any left?" He said walking towards the kitchen.
"Help yourself." Jaloni looked at me and shook his head. "What?" I whispered.
"Why is he here?"
"His grandfather just died." I said like I didn't understand the question.
"So!" Jaloni said

I frowned at him. Derrick came out the kitchen with a plate. He was staring at Jaloni. "You got something to ask me?"

"Yeah, why are you here?" He said leaning forward.

"I was coming to grieve with Chantel, but if you got a problem with it. I'll settle for beating you down. Actually it would feel real good to hurt you right now." He put a fork full of food in his mouth. "So what's up? You feeling froggy?"

"Why would you want to fight me?" Jaloni asked

"Why are you questioning why I'm here? It's none of your business." Derrick looked at him like he expected him to say something. He chewed some more food. "This is really good. You gonna be a chef or something?" Derrick watched him waiting for a response.

I could tell Jaloni was trying to understand what Derrick just said to him. "Who is Chantel to you?"

"That's my woman!" He said plainly.

"WHAT?" Jaloni looked at me.

"What? Derrick!" My face started stinging.

"Let me break it down for the kiddies. I'm her **_MAN_**, that's my **_WOMAN_**! You're her _boyfriend_, you guys hold hands. But you'll never **hit it**!"

"What?" Jaloni looked at me. "You've been playing me this whole time?"

"No!"

"Then what?"

"I happened that's what!" Derrick said trying to provoke him.

"I'm not stupid. I know who you are. I'd be a fool to think I could fight you." Jaloni inhaled, then he looked at me. "That's what I get for thinking you were different!" He walked to the door.

"Alright then Jajuki! You're alright!" Derrick said throwing him the peace symbol.

Jaloni kept walking even though I know that made him mad. He closed the door behind him. "WHY DID YOU DO THAT?"

He got up walked over to me and kissed me then he sat down. "We were talking about me when he had his heart attack. My mom was going off about the quote unquote twins. I know it's not right to think that our conversation caused his demise, but I can't help the way I feel. I need to be mad at somebody, blame something. I wish your little friend would've at least put up a fight. I need to do something before I go crazy!"

"How's your mother?" I asked feeling horrible.

"She's devastated! Both of her parents are gone. What do you think?"

"Should we go back to her house? I can't imagine it being ok for her to be alone." I said ignoring his snap at me.

""She's fine, my brothers are there." He said

"I don't know how to help you with this Derrick, what do I do?"

"Just hold me."

So I did!

Chapter 7

Cyrus and I went to Tim's funeral. The place was packed out. Derrick had on shades the entire time and he looked spent. But they all did. I felt so helpless and I didn't know what to do to help him. When I looked at the pictures in Tim's obituary you could see how in love he was with his wife. I could see why he didn't want to move on, she was the love of his life. Drew introduced Lamont as Yussef to Cyrus. I didn't say anything but he saw the question mark on my face.

Derrick's Mom looked helpless and sad. His Aunt Jade was completely out of it. His Uncle Timothy and his Uncle Malachi stayed close to their women. All of his uncles, especially Uncle Jeff and Uncle Frank looked devastated. There was a lot of pain in this room. Derrick told me he was coming over later; I sucked in the stupid disappointment that I wasn't going to go hang out with him with his family. I chatted with Pearla, Paulette, and Liz for a while. Erica kept hugging her momma and crying with her.

Derrick's cousins Eric and Lanie were with Darryl and Ryder. Normally they were the ones to keep everyone laughing, but there was nothing funny about today. No matter who it was devastation and loss was on everyone's faces. Then I told Cyrus I was ready to go. I wanted to cry my own tears away from the crowd of people. On the way to the store I asked Cyrus if he thought our grandparents were still alive. He said he had no idea. Suddenly I felt like I needed to know, I just didn't know how I'd find out. I was standing on the ice cream aisle in the grocery store when someone was walking directly towards me. I looked up to see Kevin coming straight for me. I smiled hugged him and asked him if he lived nearby. He only replied no, and then he changed the subject by asking what I was studying in the freezer. I told him I was trying to decide if I wanted ice cream, sorbet, or pie a la mode. He stared at me for a minute then he asked how far away was eighteen? I told him it wouldn't happen until the end of summer. He said I was almost ripe; I gave him a polite smile cause I didn't know what he meant. Cyrus came over and he asked who Kevin was. I introduced them, and then I told Cyrus that Kevin worked for Mitigated. I could tell Cyrus didn't like Kevin. When we left the store Kevin walked out with us. Cyrus immediately said he didn't like Kevin when we got in the car. I asked him why he didn't like him; he said he couldn't put his finger on it.

Derrick came over around two o'clock in the morning. He looked like he wanted to cry, but he wouldn't let the tears fall. When I held him he finally fell asleep, when my alarms for school went off I turned them off and I rolled back over. When I woke up Derrick was staring at the ceiling. I kissed his cheek and said good morning. He didn't say anything he kept staring. I brushed my teeth then I went downstairs and made breakfast. Derrick came down and his eyes were red but he was extremely quiet. I knew that meant he was in a mood, but I could understand why. I fought the urge to fill the silence with words. Cyrus left for work after he thanked me for breakfast and ran out the door. Derrick sat next to me on the couch. He put his head on my chest. He looked at me, I smiled. Then he kissed me. He kissed me long and deep. He untied my robe, and then he took his T-shirt off. He took his pants and his boxers off and he laid me on the couch. When he kissed me again, I got excited! It was Finally going to happen, I was ready. My mind wondered where the condom was, but honestly I didn't care. He started pressing in on me and I held my breath. Then he looked me in my eyes exhaled and backed up. "What's wrong?"

He had his hands up on his head. "Can't do it!"

"Why? What's wrong?" I said closing my robe.

He kept rubbing his head like he was frustrated. He slapped his hands together and grabbed his shirt. He stomped up the stairs. I waited a minute then I followed him up the stairs. He had one shoe on and he was rubbing his head again. His curls moved with his hands. I sat on the bed waiting for him to talk. "I need to focus on school. I can't be worried about what you're doing over here."

"Why would you be worried about me?" I asked not understanding what he meant.

His eyes turned evil, "you're waiting for me aren't you?"

"Yes" I didn't understand.

"I break you in and then you'll start giving it away as soon as there's distance between us. I'm not going through that with you. I wanna wait until I know we're gonna be together."

"Is that what happened with that girl?"

"What girl?" He spit

"The one that moved away." He didn't say anything. "Derrick I love you! Why would I do that to you? If I was gonna do that I would've done it already."

"So you weren't rubbing against that square?" He said giving me a knowing look.

"Derrick please calm down."

"Exactly! I break you in and then you'll let everybody in. I already know how this goes." He stomped his other foot in his shoe.

"Nope! You wait!" He shook his head like he was convincing his self he was right.

"Derrick, please talk to me! I love you!"

"I know you do! But if I'm not here what will you do?"

"Derrick where are you going?"

"To school!"

"But you're only on the other side of the Bay. Some people commute further to work daily. It's not like you're moving out of state."

"When I'm studying I don't have time for this back and forth stuff."

"Fine! I'll take a year off and keep applying until I get in. I'll come be with you."

That stopped him, he thought about it long and hard. "Why would you do that?"

"I love you, and I wanna be with you! I'll do whatever it takes to make it work."

He looked surprised, "whatever it takes?"

"Yes! I'm not going anywhere!" I said rubbing his back.

He sat there thinking for a while. "You want to get married?" My eyes danced around the room. "I'm not talking about today. Later on, is that one of your life's goals?"

"Yes" I said real slowly.

"What about kids?" His eyes were deadly serious.

"I don't know about kids." I adjusted on the bed. "I don't wanna be like my parents. I don't have an example of how to be. I don't want to mess anybody up."

"You think you're messed up?"

"Yes! The only self-esteem I have about myself is the esteem you and Cyrus have given me. Who do you know who had a messed up mother and they turned out ok?"

"Malcolm" he said matter of factly. "His mother and grandmother were a mess. The Malcolm you know today is nothing like he was before he met my mom."

I opened my eyes real big, "he was worse?"

Derrick chuckled, "yes."

"So what are you saying?"

"Eventually I want a wife. Eventually I want kids. I want all that with someone who wants it too. There's no room for assumption when it comes to family. You have to know the person you're with wants what you want."

"What if I don't want kids?" I almost didn't want to know.

"Then we're together for now, but when I'm ready for a family I guess we go our separate ways."

"I guess I could have a baby." I never thought about being a mother.

His body flinched, and his eyes turned evil. "No! You don't agree to kids to make someone else happy. If you do that you will never be happy. Children don't have a choice in whether or not they're born. They deserve to be loved and appreciated when they arrive. If you can't give them that don't have them."

"Why are you getting mad, we're just talking."

He walked out the room, and then he came back. "You do know my last name is not Latour, or Wallace!"

"Yes, but you are a Wallace." I said

"His name was David Mason." He swallowed. "He didn't want me or Darryl for that matter. I know what it's like to see that look in your parent's eyes. Malcolm is not my biological father. He's my natural father. He's...." He swallowed. "He's never had that look in his eyes. David! I HATE HIM!" His voice cracked and he was about to lose it.

I stood up on the bed and I threw my arms around him. "We can wait Derrick! I'll wait forever for you!"

****

Ever since that day at my house I avoid Jaloni at school as much as possible. To my surprise he hasn't answered anybody's nosey questions about us, and neither have I. It's nobody's business, but I was prepared to go with whatever he said, I was the one in the wrong. I was focusing in computer class when Jaloni pulled the chair at the computer next to me directly next to my chair. "I need to talk to you."

My heart dropped into my toes. "Ok."

His voice was low, but I could hear the hurt. "So the entire time you were cheating on me?"

"No," I lowered my eyes.

"So winter break then?"

"Yes," I said real low.

"How long have you liked him?"

"Since I met him."

"And how long was that?" He asked

"It's been almost two years now." I felt guilty.

"Why didn't you tell me?"

"I didn't know how." I said

He smiled, "I cheated too. But! You were my number one."

Instantly I felt better. "Really?" I said with a smile.

He laughed at me, "You're the first female to be happy about something like that. "

"I'm just relieved that you aren't devastated like everyone said you would be."

"I am! You almost got me killed by one of those crazy Wallace's. Good girls can cost you your life too." Then he smiled. "But I'm ok. I haven't told anyone we broke up have you?" I shook my head no. "Would you mind pretending while we're here that we are together? I get a lot of side play behind it."

"That's fine."

"Thanks" we hugged then he went his way and I went mine. I felt like my conscience was now clean.

****

I got into San Francisco University. Although I was happy I knew it wasn't good enough. Derrick wanted me at Stanford with him. Ms. Laverne celebrated while I sat there wondering what to do next. Malcolm walked in the door asking what the celebration was for. She excitedly told him about me getting into SF with a full scholarship. Malcolm looked at me like he was reading me. He told me to come in his office. My heart started beating, even though I didn't think he was mad at me, I didn't know for sure. I sat in one of the chairs in front of his desk. Everything on his desk was extremely neat and organized. He hung his jacket on the coat rack. Malcolm has been even more focused on work these days since

Tim's passing. He has pictures of Amber everywhere, but I don't get the impression that things are going all that well between them. I could be wrong, but I don't think so. "So what's your plan?" He asked me. "You're going to take the scholarship aren't you."?

"Yes, I don't really have a choice." I said

"So what's the problem?"

"Derrick wants me to go to his school."

"Did you apply there?"

"It was a late application, an easy decline. But I'm going to resubmit."

He leaned forward. "So what's the problem?"

"I want to be with him now. I don't want to wait any longer."

"Derrick's not going anywhere. What's the hurry?"

"It's going to sound dumb."

His expression didn't change, "which is?"

"I love him and I don't want to wait any more. I want to be with him as much as I can be."

"What do your parents think about him?"

"Haven't seen or spoken to them since we moved out. They don't care." I said feeling wounded.

"You know when you put everything you have into another person it can back fire." He said watching my face.

"Are you telling me that I shouldn't love Derrick?" Now I was watching his face.

"I'm saying I remember how it is at your age. I especially know how it is when you love someone as if no one else exists. It didn't work out for me, and it normally doesn't work for anyone." He looked at me. "You've got a full plate. School, work, singing, and you're trying to squish Derrick in there." He shook his head. "You're gonna have to give something up whether you want to or not."

"Malcolm with all due respect, you have so many balls in the air. I don't know how you juggle them all. What did you have to give up?"

"A lot! I don't have what I want right now. Right now I have business and that's about it." Then he sighed. "Here's what we can do. Let me know what your schedule will be. You can work in the city office around your school schedule. I personally don't think it's a good idea for you two to go to school together, but you will have to make that decision on your own."

"Thank you Malcolm! Why don't you think it's a good idea?"
"You guys need space to have experiences outside of each other.
You don't even know who you are yet."
"Weren't you with their mother at my age?"
"And we're not together today. But you're too young to
understand." Then he took out a folder. "You sure you wanna
know all of this? Once you know you can't take it back."
"Is it bad?" I said reaching for the envelope.
"I don't know. It's information, how that information hits you is the
thing."
"Thank you for doing this for me. I appreciate it." I said standing
up. I walked back to my desk and I called Cyrus. I told him
Malcolm gave me the background information on our parents. He
asked me to wait until I got home to open it. I told him about my
scholarship to SF and he was excited for me.
When I got home Cyrus met me at the door. We opened the
envelope carefully like millions of precious secrets were gonna
spill out. Copies of our birth certificates were in the envelope. It
wasn't until I saw the certified changed birth certificate that I
realized originally there was another name listed as the father on
our birth certificates. Daniel Shaw was the original name listed for
our father. Daniel is married with three kids. His oldest is five
years younger than me. A copy of his recent driver's license picture
made my mouth drop open. I told Cyrus I never thought about us
not looking like Reggie. Daniel lives in Morgan Hill, a suburb of
San Jose. His mother Rosa Shaw lives in San Francisco, and his
father passed away a few years ago. My heart was beating as I
picked up the phone. Cyrus watched me, he looked scared. I dialed
her number; someone picked up on the first ring. I looked at Cyrus.
He was sitting on the edge of his seat. "Hello?" A woman said.
"I apologize for the hour." I said recognizing the sleep in her voice.
"May I speak with Rosa Shaw if she's available."
"Speaking. Who's this?"
"My name is Chantel ma'am. My brother Cyrus and I are...."
"Oh my God! Chantel?" She screamed into the phone.
I looked at Cyrus. "Yes!"
Cyrus smashed his face next to mine so he could hear. "Baby
where are you?"
"Cyrus and I live in a apartment in Oakland."

"How did you end up there? We thought you guys were up north somewhere." She sound upset.

"No ma'am we've been in Oakland for a long time."

"Your father is gonna flip out. He's been worried sick about you two." Then she sighed. "Oh dear, let me figure out how to use this call waiting thingy. Hold on sweetie." Cyrus rubbed his hands together. He was as nervous as I was. She came back on the line as the other line was ringing. "Are you there baby?"

"Yes" I said shyly.

A woman answered the phone, she sound wide-awake. "Maria is Daniel awake?" The woman said yes. "Please tell him I need to speak to him." The woman asked her if she was ok. "Yes, honey I'm fine, but it's urgent." The woman gave the phone to Daniel telling him his mother is on the phone.

"Mom? Que pasa (What's wrong)?" He said

"Daniel! Chantel is on the phone! She's with Cyrus!" She said real excited.

He was quiet for a minute. "My baby girl?"

"Yes! She called me out of nowhere. Chantel baby say hello."

"Hi" I said not knowing what else to say. My father started crying. Cyrus smiled real big. "You guys speak Spanish?"

"Yes, our family is from Cuba. Your mother didn't tell you?" Rosa said

"No, we just found out about you a few minutes ago. She doesn't know we found you." I said

"What do you mean found out?" Daniel said

Cyrus pulled the receiver closer to his face. "We didn't know about you. Our mother never told us that Reggie wasn't our father." He said

"Cyrus? Where are you guys? I don't care if she gets mad I'm coming right now!" He was angry. The woman in the background started speaking in Spanish. He barked back at her in Spanish. "Give me your address I'm coming." He reminded me of Cyrus already.

"We don't live with our mother."

"We'll explain it when you come." Cyrus said

"Daniel, make sure you bring them to see me!"

"Yes mom I will."

Cyrus gave him directions to our apartment. I changed my clothes four times; Cyrus cleaned the kitchen with nervous energy. I kept

looking at his driver's license picture and trying to imagine him.
An hour later there was a knock at the door. My heart started
beating so hard I couldn't hear any more. Cyrus opened the door
and our father rushed him with a tearful hug. Cyrus hugged him
back and I felt frozen not knowing what to do. Our father was
cocoa brown with black curly hair. A mustache, and thick
eyebrows. He was shorter than Cyrus, but taller than me. He
looked at me with red eyes as he held his arms out. His hug felt
like a daddy's hug should. Cyrus wouldn't let Reggie touch me.
My... My daddy told me I was beautiful, and I felt my insides light
up. We all sat on the couch as Cyrus told him how we found him.
My daddy was angry but he was so happy to see us again. Then the
ugly questions came. The things Cyrus and I never talk about were
on the table. We told him everything, about Reggie's inappropriate
behavior. How our mother told the police we were lying, then she
made us tell them it wasn't true. Our daddy asked Cyrus if he was
ok now. Cyrus said once we moved out he started sleeping
peacefully; he wasn't worried about Reggie trying to hurt me
anymore. Our daddy told Cyrus he was very proud of him for
protecting me and he was sorry he wasn't there to protect him. He
was looking for us under his name, no wonder he never found us.
Our daddy used to play and sing in a band. Cyrus smiled real big
and he gave him a laminated flyer from Elegant Affairs for my
performance. He looked so proud, I sang a song for him and he
beamed with pride, which made me cry. I told him how they
always told me to shut up. Cyrus was the only one until Derrick
who encouraged me to sing. He took a deep breath and asked me if
Derrick was my boyfriend. When I said yes he looked like he was
trying to handle that positively. He told me he wanted to come to
my next performance. I informed him it was later on that night, and
every Friday. He said he was coming. He showed us pictures of
our brothers and his wife. He told us so much about our family.
Our grandmother was from Cuba, and our grandfather was creole.
Daniel was the oldest, he had two sisters. He said he was the only
one still living in the Bay Area. Both of them moved out of state
with their families. Around five thirty in the morning Cyrus was
now angry. We got in his car and Cyrus drove across Oakland to
our mother's. Cyrus pointed out her car. He said she must've just
gotten home cause there was no frost on her car like the others.
Cyrus banged on her door, clearly he didn't care anymore. Our

mother peeked out the door when she saw Cyrus she took the chain off and opened the door all the way. She still had her uniform on and she looked tired. "What is it Cyrus, I have to go to bed so I can go to work." She said with her back turned to us as we walked in. "I'm real..." She gasped when she turned around and saw our daddy standing with us. "WHERE DID YOU FIND HIM?"
"Why wouldn't you tell us?" I asked her.
"What?" She looked at us with hate, "what did you tell him?"
"EVERYTHING!" Cyrus said
"Why would you do that?" She said to Cyrus. "It's all lies Daniel!"
"You lied to us! Why would you make us believe that monster was our father!"? Cyrus said
"He didn't want us!" She yelled
"I didn't want you! I wanted my kids!" My daddy said.
"And you see where that got you! You wanted to be taken care of slaved for, you used children as control!" Our mother barked back.
"But you didn't want us!" Cyrus yelled
"Stop being dramatic!" She yelled back.
"You let that monster come after us! You don't even care!" Cyrus yelled
"Cause you were lying, and your sister was fast!"
"Where would I get that stuff from?" Cyrus yelled
"I don't know, kids at school, anywhere! My man is not gay!"
"You kept them from me to put them through this?" Our daddy asked.
"If you really cared about what they were going through you would've done whatever it took to be where they were. You didn't care!" She said
"I do care! I never stopped looking for them. You changed their names."
"Boo who! They're grown now! Who cares! I have to go to bed! I have to go to work in a few hours. Maybe I should've let you be around a little bit, child support would've been nice, instead of working all these jobs!" Then she looked at him, "but who I am kidding? You wouldn't have been any help!"
With all my might I pushed her into the wall! Her body flew into the wall hard, she wasn't expecting me to touch her. Cyrus' eyes were wide. I know he wanted to tell me not to but he stayed silent!

"YOU ARE EVIL! HOW COULD YOU NOT EVEN CARE
HOW YOU RUINED OUR LIVES!"?

"YOU RUINED MINE FIRST!" She screamed back holding her
bloody nose.

Derrick's words came back to my mind. That look he was talking
about is the same one I saw in her eyes but I never put an
assignment to it. I guess cause I never saw anything different until
I looked into my daddy's eyes. I've never fought anyone but I
wanted to fight her. She went to her bathroom to fix her nose.

Cyrus opened her bedroom door. "Where's Reggie?" He asked

"I don't know!" She yelled

"Come on kids, she can't hurt you anymore. Lets go!" Our daddy
said taking my hand.

****

Derrick's face was evil but he didn't say anything, he waited for me
to finish. I told him how Reggie used to mess with my brother, and
then Cyrus beat him up. Then he turned his attention to me, but
again Cyrus beat him up before anything beyond him touching me
happened. Cyrus was afraid to sleep too heavily because he felt
like he had to be alert for when Reggie would come around. I
hurried through the ugly part to get to the good part about my
daddy. I told him that my daddy has come to my last two
performances and how he's so proud of me. We met our
grandmother Rosa and she's so sweet. I got my big eyes from her.
My little brothers were the sweetest. They knew about us, and they
were excited to finally meet us. This summer they want to take us
to visit both of our aunts who were so excited to talk to us over the
phone. Derrick rolled his eyes. "What?"

He huffed, "nothing. I'm just being selfish! I'm happy for you. I
didn't plan on sharing you this summer. My uncle's getting married
this summer and I wanted you to come with me. But now I feel
selfish for wanting you to come with me away from your family."

I got really excited! "Just tell me when and we can plan around the
wedding." I said grinning from ear to ear.

He almost smiled, "the wedding is in Hawaii."

I screamed and threw my arms around his neck. I kept kissing his
cheek. "I wanna go, just tell me when and we'll plan around it! I
promise!" I said still kissing his cheek.

"You'd have to graduate and literally get on the plane that night. That's ok with you? Don't you think your family will want to celebrate with you?"
I hadn't thought of that. I deflated a little bit. "I guess it would be selfish to ditch them that night, huh?" I was hoping he said no.
"Yes." He said deflating as well. "But!"
"I'm so happy you said but! What's the but?" I said excited again.
He chuckled, "You could miss the wedding, but come out and spend some time with me." He cut his eyes at me.
"Just me and you and a romantic setting?" I got butterflies. "Mister Derrick what do you have in mind?" I said putting my body on him, and giggling.
"Nothing. You'll be on your period."
"WHAT?" I stiffened, "how do you know?"
"I did the math."
"What math?"
"The period math." He said almost smiling.
"That's not funny. My period could change up." I made a mental note to call my doctor to have him switch over my birth control. I didn't tell Derrick I was taking it. But I figured it was a good idea since the last time we almost did it and he had no condom. I didn't want to take any chances, I fear getting pregnant more than I do catching anything with him. But I figured that time was an impulse move anyways. I doubt that when we actually make love he'd come unprepared. I want to be prepared on my end as well.
"It could, but not by that much." He was so sure.
"You still want me to go even if I'm unfit to fool around with?"
"I invited you to go didn't I?"
I put my arms around his neck. "I love you!" I said as I kissed him.
"I love you!"

****

"Chantel Denise Shaw!" I proudly walked across the stage as my family cheered me on. Malcolm told Cyrus and I what we needed to do to have our names changed back. I was happy it happened in time for my diploma. The principal handed me my diploma and my daddy was right there almost on the stage snapping away. Jaloni kept smiling at me. I dropped my smile when I saw Derrick looking at us. He raised an eyebrow at me, and I gave him a guilty smile. "I gave him a congratulatory smile that's all."

"Un huh! You must want him to die!" Derrick said in a joking tone, but I wasn't sure that he was so I kept moving

"Hey! Hey Jajuki!" Derrick said to Jaloni who was standing with all his family. Parents, grandparents, aunts and uncles. When Jaloni looked at him he flipped him off and stood there waiting for a response. Jaloni's father got angry and started to respond. Jaloni grabbed his father's arm and begged him not to. "Jajuki look at my woman one more time and see what I'll do!"

"Little BOY! His name is Ja-Lon-ni! Get it right!" His grandmother said with her hands on her hips and wiggling her neck. She looked so cute.

"My bad ma'am." Derrick said laughing.

"You know she didn't see what you did." I said to Derrick as he walked with me.

"Yeah, but she's cute." Then his tone flipped. "DON'T SMILE AT HIM!"

"I can't smile ever?" I asked sarcastically.

"You can smile, just not at him. I have half a mind to pistol whip him. He knew I was right there. He's flexing thinking I won't do anything cause he's around his little family. I don't care who he's with!"

"Whoa Derrick! I'm sorry! I won't do it again." I said trying to calm him down.

When we walked out of the main auditorium my family was eagerly waiting for us. They had us posing for so many pictures you would've sworn it was a wedding. "So you're taking my only daughter to Hawaii!" My daddy said putting his arm around Derrick's neck.

Derrick shot me a look like, "What is this?" I smiled and shrugged. I hoped he was nice about it. Derrick moved his shoulders to remove my daddy's arm and then he faced him. "Yes Sir, I am." My daddy stood up straight to match Derrick's stance. Cyrus bucked his eyes at me and smiled. "What are your intentions with my daughter?"

"Right here daddy? In front of everybody?" I said feeling completely embarrassed.

"Why not? I have nothing to hide." Derrick said while still staring my father in the eyes. "I love your daughter very much. My intentions are to love her and be there for her as long as she's willing to have me."

117

"AAW!" My stepmother Maria grabbed my shoulders and smiled really big. She was enjoying the scene.

"Do you plan to get married?" My daddy asked.

I thought I was going to pass out. I started fanning myself. "One day, but not until we're settled with school and whatever else we want to do after."

Daddy smiled, "Ok!" Then he dropped his smile. "I don't like you guys going away together alone, unchaperoned, and alone."

"You said alone twice." My little brother DJ said.

"I know what I said!" He said looking at DJ like he better be quiet. Derrick looked at him, but he didn't respond to that. My daddy sucked his teeth and walked away. Cyrus smiled real big at Derrick, but his face didn't change. He grabbed my hand, "you ready?"

"Can we ride with you?" DJ and Mario asked.

I looked at Derrick with a big smile on my face. He told them to come on, and they had smiles as big as mine. When we got in the car DJ and Mario were too excited. They tried to act like they were cool for Derrick. "You guys don't think Derrick is scary?" I asked them

"Nope!" DJ said

"No, he's heck of cool!" Mario said

I looked at Derrick and he almost smiled. "Heck of cool huh?" I asked

"Yeah! I want a car just like this when I can drive." DJ said taking the whole car in.

"My uncle and my grandfather built this whole car. In a few

months I gotta pass it on to my little brother, it's his turn to drive it." Derrick rubbed his finger on the steering wheel. I knew he was thinking about Tim.

"That is so cool! Do you know how to build a car?" DJ asked Derrick.

"I could do it, what you got in mind?"

DJ suddenly got nervous. "Would you build a car with me?"

"As long as that's ok with your dad. He might want to do that with just the two of you." Derrick said

DJ and Mario high-fived each other in the backseat. When we got to the restaurant my daddy made such a fuss over me. He kept saying how proud he was of Cyrus and I. He said for everything that we've been through we've accomplished so much. He got emotional quite a few times, but he pulled it together. Derrick didn't say anything but I could tell he was reading my daddy the entire time. At the end of dinner, Derrick said good night to everyone. He had a flight to catch. He almost smiled at me when he told me he would see me tomorrow. I kissed him and told him I couldn't wait. Little Adon waved bye from my stepmother's arms. Derrick gave my grandmother a kiss on the cheek, he waved bye to everyone then he left. My grandmother said she liked Derrick; he was a man even at a young age. I told her all his brothers were like that. I said the other two smiled more, especially Darryl, but they were all men. She told me that was nice and she was happy for me. Then she whispered and asked me if I had protection for my trip. I choked on my drink. She laughed at me, but she waited for an answer. I told her I put myself on the pill but I felt funny buying condoms. She told me to get over that. She told me to make him strap up!

I could barely sleep; Derrick was going to be so surprised when I told him I wasn't on my period. I didn't care what he said; I was TIRED of making out. I wanted the real thing and he was gonna give it to me even if it killed him. I tried to imagine what sex with Derrick was going to be like. I already knew it would be AMAZING, but I wasn't sure on what to expect. In the morning I rechecked my suitcase. Bikini? Check! Sexy Sarong, that Pearla said I had to have when I bought this bikini? Check! Silky brown nightgown? Check! Toothbrush, underwear, clothes, dresses for going out? Check! Check! Check! I needed a separate bag for my shoes and hair supplies. Cyrus looked at my bags and said I was such a girl. Cyrus has been so much happier since we found our daddy. They talk all the time, and he's cut back a lot on the overnight guests. Although I knew Sherrell was probably gonna be around the whole time I was gone. I just hoped Caprice didn't pop up.

I had extreme butterflies when Cyrus took me to the airport. This was my first flight anywhere, and Derrick bought a first class ticket for me. I was too excited! The flight attendants were really nice and attentive. They brought me a fluffy pillow and a blanket, and I knocked out for the entire duration of the flight, I was so sleepy. When I walked off the flight Derrick was waiting by the gate. He smiled at me and my heart melted. We got the rest of my luggage and then we took a car service back to the resort. We had a beautiful suite. I asked him if he stayed in this suite the night before and he said no. We ordered room service and he said in the morning he'd take me around the island. I asked how the wedding was. He said it was nice, everybody had a good time.

When it was time to go to bed. I told Derrick I wanted to wash the flight off of me. I could tell he didn't suspect anything and he just knew he was right about my period. I was excited and nervous all at the same time. I put on my nightgown and I tried not to feel dumb about the whole thing. I wrapped the box of condoms up like a present even with a little bow, and then I hid them behind my back as I came out the bathroom. Derrick was laying down like he was going to go to sleep. Then I cleared my throat. He did a double take. "What are you wearing?"

I shrugged, "We're in Hawaii shouldn't I want to sleep sexy?"

"Yeah, but you're sexy in your robe too." He said smiling at my nightgown.

"I have a present for you." I said walking over to the bed and sitting in front of him.

"And I have a graduation present for you. Open mine first." He smiled.

"Ok," I wanted to know what could possibly be in this rectangular handheld shaped box. The contents of the box sparkled at me before I got it opened all the way. It was a beautiful diamond tennis bracelet. "Oh my goodness Derrick! How did you do this?' I said as he clasped it around my wrist.

"I had a little money saved. Do you like it?"

"I LOVE it! Thank you so much! Now open mine." I said facing him as my heart beat a hundred miles a minute. He had a confused look on his face when he saw the box of condoms. "Let's!" I said as I kissed him.

He tried to back away from me but I wouldn't let him. "Wait a minute Chantel!" He said trying to catch his breath. I smiled at him waiting for him to spill it. "Are you saying you're not on your period?"

"Nope."

"How? Cause I know I calculated right." He was smiling.

"They have these things called birth control pills, that can regulate when you have a period. My doctor and I made my period come the week before."

Derrick's smile halfway dropped; "if you're on birth control why do I need these?" he said dropping the box.

"It hasn't been six months since you've had sex. Those nasty girls could've given you anything."

"I was always protected when dealing with them. I'm good."

"Do you have any idea how embarrassing it was buying those? You're wearing them even if only for a minute." He kissed me deliberately and passionately. I was excited! It was finally going to happen. Derrick made sure there was more than enough foreplay, so much that I thought he was going to try and skip out on the real thing at one point. I looked down; I wanted to watch him disappear. I held my breath as he pressed on me. "Ouch! Ouch! Ok wait!" He stopped pressing and started kissing me. When I was ready I told him to go some more. I felt very full once he was all the way in. Every movement he made I felt it. It didn't hurt, but the feeling was new. I felt frozen and dumb; I didn't know what to do next. He rolled us onto our side and he held my leg up. This position felt so much better and I lost myself. Then he rolled us back on my back and he came hard. I could feel him throbbing inside of me.

We spent the next morning in bed, playing getting to know each other. I learned another expression on his face; there was a new one for when he was going to lay me down. I loved that expression most. We went down to the beach and the newlyweds were there. I congratulated his uncle and new auntie on their marriage. To my surprise they invited us to hang out with them. Denise said they've been together for years but she was happy to finally be Mrs. Wallace. Derrick taught me how to swim. He couldn't help but laugh out loud at me in my dramatic attempts until I got it. Derrick was a really good teacher in the water and out. First time ever, I thought about what it would be like to have a family with him. One like my daddy had with Maria.

Chapter 8

OH MY GOODNESS I LOVE SEX! How I waited this long to have it I will never know! I know most of my sentiment is because it's Derrick, and I was already sprung. But I can't get enough of this man! I've been willingly late to work; I've blown off my family and friends to stay under Derrick. Even Derrick has said that I can't fall apart because of him. I try to explain it to him, but he tries to act like he doesn't get it. I know he can at least empathize with what I feel even if it isn't as deep on his end. It's like when I see him I get mad if he has clothes on. I immediately undress him; I have a royal fit whenever my period comes. I hate the three-day break in my rotation. Derrick says I act like I'm cracked out. I told him to stop pretending the feeling isn't mutual. Derrick tries to pretend he won't yield to me, but he always does. I get my way all the time. I have a gorgeous man who loves me, a family that loves me. Could life get any better than this?

Pearla says I've been neglecting her so we made plans to shop for my trip to Florida but not at the Oakland mall. I was sick of it. I work there and it seems like no matter what, I keep seeing that girl Quesha. Every time she sees me she starts looking like she's gonna cry. She probably does cry, but I leave. Shelly asks me where my boyfriend is when she sees me without Derrick then when he is there, she acts all scared and timid. She makes no sense to me.

Pearla kept eyeing me but she didn't say anything at first. Then she saw me look too long in the lingerie direction. "YOU FREAK!" She yelled as she gave me a hug.

"What?" I asked not knowing what she meant.

"You FINALLY gave Derrick some!" She gave me another hug.

"Why are you saying that?" I blushed.

"You're different."

"How?"

"You just are! How do you feel? How long ago did happen? Where you scared? Give me details, without giving me details. After all we are talking about my cousin." She said jumping around.

"We did it in Hawaii."

"You guys went to Hawaii without me?" She pretended like I hurt her.

"It was supposed to be for his uncle's wedding."

"Which uncle? Not Malachi! Oh lord please don't say Malachi?" I smiled at her. I was enjoying her emotional outburst. "He was supposed to marry me! What part of the game is that?" She said sounding defeated. "Do you think I still have a chance?"

"Are you serious?" I asked laughing.

"Very!" She looked angry.

"I think Denise won this battle. But there are plenty of other men."

"But I want that one!" She stomped her foot and whined.

"Pearla, come on baby it's gonna be ok. You're gonna find a man finer than him. Your man is gonna be so fine girls will throw their selves off buildings cause he will only have eyes for you."

"You promise?" She asked sarcastically.

"Of course I do!"

"Can you make sure he has a big package too? Short men need not apply." She said

"Of course!"

We laughed and then I bought a couple of gowns. We had a nice afternoon shopping, but I couldn't wait to go to Derrick's and wear my gown. When I got to his apartment the smell of dinner hit me in the nose. He hugged and kissed me at the door, Drew was sitting on the couch looking upset.

"Well Chantel's here so..." Derrick said to Drew who was so upset he missed the hint.

"Hey Chantel!" He said with his eyes to the floor rubbing his head like Derrick does when he's upset.

Derrick was waving his hands telling me no. "What's wrong Drew?" Derrick threw his hands up and walked in the kitchen.

"Toya broke up with me." He said

I raised an eyebrow, "why is that a bad thing?"

"I'm used to her."

"Ok, but good riddance. Maybe now you can finally meet someone nice."

"You seen them, all of them want a piece of Drew. Andrew needs love too. You guys sitting over here looking mighty comfortable. My boy Hubby gonna be getting married soon. What is it supposed to be me and Yussef kicking it until we old and grey?"

"Maybe if you left Toya alone you'd find somebody decent. Them girls at your club won't workout. Just try being Andrew for a minute. See how it works out for you." Derrick said from the kitchen.

"You supposed to be an expert? Just cause you got Chantel don't mean you know everything." He said irritated.

"You looking at her ain't you! You should be studying at my feet." Derrick said from the kitchen.

Drew looked irritated. "Forget you man! You don't know."

Derrick came back out the kitchen. "Look at you! You are a ball of emotion."

"Everybody can't be as cold blooded as you and Malcolm!" Drew said

He frowned, "Chantel am I cold blooded?"

"Lukewarm."

"See! Lukewarm ain't cold!" We all laughed. "Seriously, try being Andrew. Let Drew go with Toya, you might be amazed at what could happen for you."

He had a box in the middle of the floor and an old record player. "What's that?" I asked

Derrick and Andrew smiled at each other with knowing smiles.

"Well it's time for me to go!" Drew said standing up.

"You just came to that conclusion?" Derrick said shooting him a look.

"Alright then Chantel, I'll see you later." He gave me a quick brotherly hug. "When you gonna come to sing for us?"

"I don't know, kind of need the time off right now." I said blushing at Derrick.

"I guess! I'm gonna start having less of a presence there myself. I need a break too."

"Un huh!" Derrick said shooting Drew daggers with his eyes.

"Alright! Alright! I'm gone, you kids have fun." He smiled at me,

"I'm going over Eric's!"

"Bye Drew, I mean Andrew." I said waving goodbye.

He was barely out the door as Derrick was closing the door on him. Then he clapped his hands together, "you hungry?"

"Yes" I said following him to the kitchen. "What did you make?"

"Green beans, rosemary chicken, and roasted red potatoes." He said showing me the different dishes on the stove.

"Oh my goodness that looks delicious!" I said as my mouth watered.

"But it doesn't stop there, I made you...." he raised his eyebrows at me. He opened the oven slowly to reveal his creation, "peach cobbler!"

I started jumping up and down. "I CAN'T WAIT! I CAN'T WAIT!" He had mentioned that peach cobbler was his specialty, but I couldn't believe he made one for me.

"Wash your hands so we can eat." He said taking the food to the table. I was so excited.

When I came out the bathroom I looked at the box again. "You still didn't say what the box is for?"

"We'll get to that in a minute. Let's enjoy dinner first." He said, as he poured wine to go with our meal. Dinner was delicious, Derrick is an excellent cook. We talked about our kitchen failures and our successes. At least his mom taught him a few things in the kitchen. Everything I learned in the kitchen was self-taught. We decided to wait for dessert. He told me to join him in the middle of the living room floor. "I was at Malcolm's earlier looking through his records and this one stood out to me. When I played it I thought about you. I thought about finding it on CD, which I may still do, so I can listen to it when I want. But I had to play it for you on vinyl so you could experience it the way I did." He kissed me, "you ready?" I shook my head yes not knowing what was going to play. "'I've been so many places, I've seen so many things, But none quite as lovely as you, More beautiful than the Mona Lisa, Worth more than gold, And my eyes have the pleasure to behold...." We slow danced in the middle of his living room to the teddy bear's beautiful melody. Each word touched my heart and I've never felt so loved, appreciated, or beautiful than in that moment. This was that feeling I had been waiting my entire life to feel. I kept telling Derrick how much I loved him, but I didn't feel like it stretched far enough.

"Baby you can't ever leave me. I think I would die!" I said as I laid on the bed completely spent from our passionate session.

He shot an evil look, "leave you? Why would you think about that right now?"

"I'm just saying I feel so loved right now. I can't imagine not feeling this way for the rest of my life. I want everything as long as it's with you."

"What do you mean by everything?" He said listening to my words carefully.

"I was never that girl who fantasized about having babies and the whole family life. With you, I wanna have your baby. I want to be with you in every which way I can."

Derrick was quiet for a minute. "I hear what you're saying, but I think we should change the subject." He said rolling over.

I sat up, "did I say something wrong?"

"You're making me uneasy. You're changing."

"I'm changing? How?" I said feeling panicked.

He kissed me, "I love you. I don't want to fight. Let's drop this for now."

"I can't! I'll be wondering all night. We might as well have this out now, either way you're not getting any sleep." I said sitting up.

He sat up and put me in his arms. He kissed my forehead. "We're just talking don't freak out, ok?" He needed me to agree.

"You know me, I can't agree to not freaking out. Spill it!" I said bracing myself.

He shook his head, "this is a mistake." then he exhaled. "I try not to think like we should've waited to go here." I started to sit up and he tightened his grip. "Now we're both open and nothing has changed. This is fine for the summer, kind of. But what happens next year when school starts? You're still not going here. I'm gonna still need you when you can't be here for me." He said

"How am I changing?" I asked trying to swallow the lump in my throat.

He exhaled again. "Your work ethic is slipping. It's not your fault though. We've been lost in each other. You've been late to work. You're not working at the club. Now you're talking about babies. You didn't want a family before, now you wanna have my baby. I'm flattered, but don't do it for me. You gotta want a family for you. What if I died right after the baby? Would you still love the baby if I wasn't around to help?" He rubbed my back, "I'm just saying it's a lot. I should've thought this through."

"It feels like you're rejecting me again!" I said crying.

"Again? I didn't reject you the first time, that's the way you took it. I'm just saying we should've waited to get in this deep. I don't think either one of us can see straight right now." He said rubbing my back some more.

"I should take next year off from school huh?" I asked

"NO! NO! That's not the answer. You need to go to school. What if we don't work out? I'll be that guy you gave up school for. I can't let you do that. You need to go to school."

"College is not like high school, we won't have classes five days a week, eight plus hours a day. We can make time for each other." I said

"You could move in here, and quit your job with Malcolm." He said

My heart wanted to say yes, but my mind said. "He's not your husband. Keep your job." I exhaled, "I can't live off of you Derrick."

"Either way you are anyways. Where do you think my money comes from? It's all from the same source. I need you to have time for me. I want you to stay in school; you could even sing at EA if you want. The day to day with Malcolm, I feel like that should be our time."

"And what will you be giving up? You're asking me to do something I've never done."

"Which is?"

"Rely on someone else to take care of me."

"You rely on Cyrus."

"No I don't! Cyrus and I work together. We split the bills fifty-fifty. I relied on him to be eighteen and get the place."

"What's so hard about relying on me?" He said irritated.

"I've never relied on anyone. The thought of it makes me scared."

"How could you lay here and tell me you want a family with me, and then the first thing I say you can't even do? I'm your man! You have to rely on me, who cares if you never did it before. There's a first time for everything."

"And what will you be giving up for me?"

"My private space." He said

"Are you really this insecure?"

His body jerked and he released me. "What?" His eyes were evil.

"I would be here. Coming home to you, but still maintaining a measure of my independence. You're so afraid I'd leave you or cheat on you that you have to have me under you at all times?" I said as I sat up to look at him.

"You're flipping this on me?" He barked

"This whole time you've made it seem like you were doing this whole gentlemanly thing for me. And it's really because you can't handle it!" I barked back.

He got up, "I told you to let it go! I told you this was gonna happen!" He said pacing the floor.

"Come back to bed Derrick, let's drop it." I said scooting to lay down.

"YOU CAN'T WHINE ME UP AND THEN EXPECT ME TO TURN OFF THAT EASY! YOU CAN'T BE THAT DUMB! WHEN I TELL YOU TO LET IT GO! LET IT GO!" He was still pacing.

"Dumb? Dumb is to keep putting your past relationship whoa's off on me! That's not fair to me."

"That's because you don't have a past relationship to speak for. I'm your beginning and your ending. You have no idea what it's like out there. I tell you what I need; I'm honest with you. You don't know what you want. Or even how you want it unless I've given it to you."

"What are we arguing about? You want me to go out and get a boyfriend so I can come back and compare notes with you? This argument is dumb! You're just mad cause I read you! Mister read everybody and hide behind scary looks and deep voices. I'LL KILL YOU CAUSE I'M SCARY! Who cares?"

He stopped in his tracks looked at me with the weirdest look on his face. "You don't know who I am do you? You have no idea of what I'm capable of do you?" He said walking to the bed. He got in my face, "YOU DON'T KNOW ME!"

"Are you threatening me?"

"I'm only gonna say this once and we can drop this whole thing." He shook his head like he was agreeing with his-self. "If you EVER cheat on me!" He laughed a wickedly scary laugh. "I'm not responsible for what happens to you!" He stared into my eyes, "love is a scary thing and it can make you do crazy things. Go ahead stay at your school; keep your job all of that. But let me even kind of think something is going on with you and someone else...." He licked my lips, "I'll kill you! That's not a threat it's a promise!"

"Seriously Derrick? You're supposed to be scary now?" I said trying to mask my fear of him in this moment. He looked crazy and like he was making me a bonafide promise, not a threat.

"You should be scared!" He said then he laid down calmly as if we weren't just arguing. "I'm going to bed, you want the light on or off?" He asked. I didn't say anything; I laid on my side of the bed asking myself how did we end up here. I was declaring how much I loved him, and that turned into an argument. I watched the clock change from 12:32am to 3:05am. I hadn't slept a wink. I sat up to go to the bathroom. "Where are you going?" He said without a trace of sleep in his voice; I didn't say anything I went to the bathroom. I didn't need to be out here to go through this. When I walked out the bathroom he was sitting up wide-awake. I put my shoes on and I put my coat on. His eyes were evil as he watched me dress. I grabbed my purse and I walked out of the door. When I got in my car, and pulled out on the street the night was silent and still. Before I got on the freeway Derrick was right behind me. I huffed, was he really going to follow me all the way home? I didn't want to argue at home in front of Cyrus. I pulled off the 101 and looped back around and headed back to his apartment. He parked back in his stall, and then he met me on the sidewalk. "I apologize." He said before I said anything.

"For?" I said with attitude.

"Everything!" He said coming in for a kiss.

I backed away. "Ok," I said then I walked to his door. He opened the apartment door. I went in his room and shut the door. When I came out I handed him his pillow and a blanket.

He frowned, "what is that?"

"I don't want to sleep with you tonight." I said laying them on his couch.

He started laughing, "you've got to be out of your mind if you think you're putting me out of my bed."

****

"Daniel! She's BEAUTIFUL!" My Auntie Deborah said with eyes just like mine.

"Thank you!" I said blushing and looking at her in amazement. All my life I felt like I was different. That no one looked like me, and here I was standing in front of both of my aunts feeling like we were mirror images. I didn't look exactly like either one of them, but they were definitely my family. Their children favored Cyrus and I. Auntie Tania and I were the same deep chocolate complexion. Auntie Deborah's son Larry was chocolate too. It was weird they remembered us from when we were babies and it was the strangest thing to have no recollection of them at all. Of course everyone right away wanted to hear me sing. Cyrus was eager right along with everyone else. Since I was used to singing in front of people I sang a quick song and then my aunties and cousins all joined in the song. They even got my daddy and grandmother to join in. I had so much fun with my family; I had no question of whether I belonged with them. DJ and Mario spent the whole time asking me questions about Derrick. Whenever I talked to him they had to say hello as well. Derrick said he was happy for me out here getting to know my family, but he also said he missed me. He even sounded a little sad about it. I told him I missed him too and I couldn't wait to get back to him.

"So your dad says you sing in a club, are you going to take it any further?" Auntie Tania asked me as we sat in her hot tub, while Cyrus and all the kids played in the pool.

"I have some connections if I wanted to, but I haven't decided what I want to do yet. I figure once I get out of school I'll decide for sure."

"Why would you wait? The younger you start in the industry the better. It's hard to get out there once you're older." She said

"But twenty-two is a good age to get out there. It's still young, but I'll have some education behind me as a safety net in case it doesn't work out."

"You're gonna make it! You can go all the way, I can see it now." She said with stars in her eyes.

"My boyfriend's family has connections. However, he and I agreed that I need to make the most of the experience when it does happen. His mother and his father dabble in the industry, but they don't stay in the limelight. Matter of fact, do you know that singer Torrie?"

"Who doesn't know Torrie? I love her music!"

"My boyfriend's mother was her choreographer until more recent."
"Seriously? I love her videos!" She was thinking about it for a minute. "Wasn't she the one who was going with that rapper Comfort? I love his music too."
"I don't know, but I'm just saying I like how they still get their hands dirty even if they're not in the forefront. I might wanna fall back and have a family one-day. I'll need to know how to still make money even if I'm not standing in the front saying everybody look at me."
"Having a family doesn't mean you can't stay in the spotlight. I see glamour and glitz ahead for you. I think you should strike now while you can." She said
"I'm trying to look at the big picture. That whole industry is here today gone tomorrow. When I do strike out there even if I make it or not, I wanna have my foot in the door with a vice grip refusing to be moved."
"I get it." My Auntie Deborah said, "Tania everybody doesn't dream of being a star no matter what. Respect her approach."
"I just don't want her to wait too long and then it doesn't happen at all for her. Some of the most talented people never make it." She said sounding irritated, "just don't forget your family when you do make it big. We wanna cheer you on when you're on the journey."
RIGHT! I got the feeling she wanted something for herself through me. Yeah, I was happy to meet my aunts, but Tania was not my favorite for sure. She seem to approach everybody with a what's in it for me attitude. Talking about don't forget your family. Did she forget I just met her, she could easily be forgotten? When I talked to Derrick that night I was ready to come home and be in his arms. I hated that I still had another four days out here. I tried to stay around my grandmother as much as possible, even my daddy seemed a little different around his sisters. I still loved him very much, but it was like they looked at my voice as if it were a gold mine. Cyrus, my grandmother, and Maria were the only ones who stay consistent, them and the kids of course. To calm me Derrick played our song for me over the phone. The way he played that sax was like he was singing to me, "you're my greatest and latest inspiration…." I missed him like crazy! No matter when I called him, late at night or early in the morning. He always answered, I apologized for calling all over the place and he told me it was fine and that he missed me too.

On our last night out there we went to a restaurant where they had a karaoke setup. OF COURSE IT DID! I refused to go up right away. So of course Auntie Tania went up first. The whole restaurant cheered her on, and she ate it all up. DJ and Mario got up together. Mario had a powerful voice in his little body. I stood up cheering them on. Larry could sing too. My daddy and aunties sang a song together. I didn't feel like singing, but they kept bugging me about it. I felt like our family hogged the mic enough. I tried to find a song I could sing to satisfy that I sang without taking the evening too serious. I found it! The rest of the restaurant cheered me on with my lighthearted fun song, "I'm too sexy for

this shirt too sexy for this shirt so sexy it hurts...." My aunts and daddy were not amused. But Cyrus seems to know exactly why and he cheered me on. I love my brother, everyone should have one.

"Why would you sing that song? What if there was someone here who could give you your big break? And you just pissed it off trying to be funny!" Tania spit at me.

"I'm on vacation! I deserve to have fun as well! If I wanna sing a goofy song for the fun of it I CAN! This vacation is not my only chance. If I decide to go in that direction it won't be for another four years anyways."

"Stars are not made over night! How long do you think it would take to launch you once you're discovered? You seem to think you can just go in with all these demands and it just happens that way.

Somebody please tell her it's not that easy."

"Which is exactly why I need to go to school first. I may never make it, but I'll be making money one way or another. Singing isn't my only talent. I'm smart and a hard worker, if I give that up just to sing then yes I could see being as desperate as you are. But I'm not, so I'm NOT!"

Auntie Tania had fire in her eyes, I didn't care, she was on my nerves. When we got back to our hotel my daddy called himself trying to explain my auntie's point. I asked him if he understood mine. When he said yes, I asked him if there was anything else we needed to talk about. He didn't like me getting smart with him, but I was over it. I wanted to get back to Derrick and be done with this whole thing. I was so happy I had my period while I was out here. All I wanted to do was be under Derrick when I got home.

We barely stepped in the door at the house. I threw my unpacked suitcases on my bed. I kissed Cyrus on the cheek and waved bye to Sherrell who met us at the house and I went straight to Derrick's. He seemed a little surprised to see me so soon. He said he thought I would be too tired to come out tonight. I told him I had to see him and the sooner the better. I wrapped my legs around him at the door. We barely made it in. When he laid me on the couch female perfume hit my nose. I stopped kissing him and I eyed him, he gave me serious eyes back as he asked me what was wrong. I told him I smelled something, he frowned at me cause he didn't understand what I meant. I told him I smelled perfume, and he looked at me like I was crazy. I got up and stared at the couch, it looked normal but the smell was there. Derrick didn't say anything. He let me have my crazy moment. I sniffed the couch again and the smell got stronger in between the cushions. I stuck my hand in them; I glared at Derrick when my hand touched something. I pulled out a red lacy bra that was too small to be mine. I felt like I was going to be sick. "WHAT IS THIS?"

Derrick looked like he was analyzing the bra. "That has to be old. I think its Marisa or Chloe's."

"You think?" I was angry.

"Yeah" he said nonchalantly. "I'm not cheating on you."

We had never fooled around on this couch, nor had I ever laid on it before. I guess I had no reason not to believe him. Now the mood was killed. I stared at him feeling numb. "Throw it away." I said tossing the bra at him. He put it in the trash. "How are the twins?" I asked sarcastically, I was also checking to see if he talked to them. "They're fine. They should be back in a couple weeks."

"They're coming back to this building?"

"Yeah, they didn't give up their apartment, they just went home for the summer." He said walking to his room. He came back with a notepad and his sax. "I wrote a song for you."

My heart sped up, but I also wanted to tear into him about still communicating with them. He couldn't handle Jaloni smiling at me, but he still talked to his sex buddies. I didn't like it. He read the lyrics to me and it was beautiful! My irritation melted away. Then he played the melody for me on his sax. It was beautiful! Ok, ok! I was back in the mood.

Chapter 9

"Baby I'm gonna miss you, make sure you make us proud," Ms. Laverne said.

"Thank you, I'll call you regularly. And I'll try to get over here to see you when I can." I said packing up my box to send to the SF office.

"What are you gonna do in the city?"

"Pretty much the same thing there that I do here."

Ms. Laverne's face turned serious. "You're gonna see something's baby. Malcolm is a good man, never doubt that ok." She watched my face. "There's a lot of things you don't know, but that's ok. There are aspects to this company that you don't need to know about."

"Like why some applicants are treated differently than others." I said watching her face.

"Treated differently?"

"Kevin applied, and I didn't give him the normal paperwork. Some people who apply don't get the same processing. I keep seeing Kevin around and he says he's working or something but it doesn't seem like it."

She smiled, "something like that. Are you moving in with Derrick?"

"Not completely, he's been acting weird lately. I'll be there most of the time, but I still live with Cyrus for now."

"Love will do that to people." She said defending Derrick without knowing what he does.

He's still my sweet Derrick, and I love him. However, ever since that night, I think I finally see what scares the life out of Shelly about Derrick. He can be scary sometimes. "Yeah I guess."

"How's your family doing?"

"They're ok, all my daddy wants to do is talk about music. He calls me talking about music all the time. I know I shouldn't complain, but I wish he knew me like he knows music. I told him about the song Derrick wrote for me and I think he got jealous." I frowned, "are daddy's supposed to compete with your boyfriend?"

"Different dads do different things. Try to accept yours for who he is. If there's something that bothers you speak on it, but don't fall apart. Music is a big part of who your father is. I bet he's so happy to have that connection with you that it's all he sees. It's up to you to help him see more. You may come to like having music as your bond."

"It just feels like they want music to be my everything and it's not. They don't understand that the musical world is new to me. I didn't dream of being on stage or seeing my name in lights." I said feeling defeated. "I don't like the pressure they bring."
Ms. Laverne tried to smooth out the rough edges of my family, but I wasn't feeling it. I wasn't feeling them right now. If I could pull my little brothers, Maria, and grandma Rosa out the bunch I would. Daddy wasn't that bad it's just that he's constantly on me about singing at EA again. I go every once in awhile, but honestly between Aleisha and Jesse they do a pretty good job of keeping the club rocking.
We locked up the office and Ms. Laverne and I walked to the parking lot. The parking lot was practically empty but there was a car parked between our cars under the light post. We looked at the car and then each other. We stopped walking cause the scene didn't look right. I started walking backwards, so did Ms. Laverne. "Let's go call Malcolm." She said
Then Kevin got out of his car. Ms. Laverne hissed and told me not to tell him I'm switching offices. "Good evening ladies." He said standing in his doorway.
Then another car rolled up real slow. A guy I didn't recognize rolled down his window. "Kevin, what are you doing?" The guy said
Kevin looked like he didn't recognize the guy. "You got people watching me now?" He sounded angry.
"No, but should we?" The guy responded nonchalantly.
"I came to talk to Ms. Laverne and Chantel."
"Nope! Don't put my name in whatever you're up to. You can talk to me during normal business hours."
Kevin smiled, "you don't like me huh?"
"No I don't!" She said putting her hand on her hip.
"But I love you!" He laughed.
"Kevin! What are you doing?" Then the guy pointed at me. "That's Derrick's woman, I suggest you drive away."
Kevin looked like he was suspended in thought. "Is that right?" He thought about it for a minute.

"Who are you?" I asked the guy.

"Nobody," he said to me. "Kevin!" Kevin looked at him. "You need to go."

"I just wanna say hey." He said defensively.

The guy picked up a cell phone. "Hey, Kevin's here. Did you...." He took the phone off his ear. "It's for you."

Kevin huffed and walked to the phone.

Ms. Laverne looked at me and shook her head. Then she whispered, "go to Derrick's house don't stop until you get there."

"Ok," something didn't feel right. Although I said I was going home before. I didn't like the way this felt, I was going to do as I was told.

Kevin gave the phone back to the guy he was irritated. "You didn't have to call Curtis on me man. I'm cool!" He said walking back to his car. "Don't nobody trust nobody no more." He drove off as huffy as he sounded.

Ms. Laverne and I hadn't moved, the guy looked at us. "How you doing Ms. Laverne?"

"I'm good baby how are you?"

"I'll be better when I see you two drive off. You tell her what to do?" He asked Ms. Laverne.

"She has instruction."

"Now Chantel don't be alarmed. I'm gonna follow you until I know you're secure." He said calmly.

"What's going on?" I was starting to feel scared.

"It's not safe to be standing out here. Call her from the car." He was waiting for me to get back in my car.

"Derrick just bought me this thing. I don't really know how to work it yet." I said holding out my phone.

"So talk to her later, but I need you to get a move on it." He said rushing me.

I got in the car. Then Ms. Laverne told me how to put the phone on speaker so I could drive with it in my lap. "What was that?"

"Kevin is on suspension right now. That boy has a few screws loose. Malcolm is not gonna be happy when he hears about this."

"Why was he waiting for us?"

She laughed, "I highly doubt he was waiting for me. I wouldn't be surprised if he was doing a count down to eighteen for you. He was probably coming to stake his claim not knowing Derrick already claimed you."

"Ok, but the whole thing was random and weird. This nobody guy is following me. How do I know he's not some stalker or he won't hurt me?"

"He won't baby. He's just doing his job. You'll be fine."

"It's his job to follow me home?"

"Someone always makes sure we make it to our cars safely. Malcolm has it set up that way. He's following you today cause that scene earlier wasn't cool."

"Malcolm pays someone to make sure we get in our cars and drive away?" I said in disbelief.

"Yes honey. Stop worrying about it. I'm home, so I'm gonna talk to you later. Enjoy the rest of your weekend."

"Thanks you too." I said letting her hang up so I didn't have to look down too hard at the phone.

When I got to Derrick's place the building was humming with students moving into their units. Mr. Nobody blocked my car after I parked in the visitor parking and then he followed me up the stairs. Derrick was standing outside his door in jeans and no shirt when I walked around the corner. It was like he was waiting for me to round the corner. He looked at me then his eyes still searched, when Mister Nobody came around the corner, first thing out his mouth was not hi to me; but telling mister nobody that his timing was off. Mister nobody apologized and then he shook Derrick's hand. I went inside and then Derrick followed. Derrick looked at me, "you ok?"

"Who was that?"

"Nobody."

I blew air, "why are you walking around half naked?" I frowned at him.

He smiled, "I was waiting for you." Then he kissed me. My irritation melted away. As I was surrendering to the feeling, the front door opened and a female cleared her throat. I looked at a gorgeous female standing in the doorway. "Hello" she said

I looked at Derrick. "You know better than to walk in my door like that. What's wrong with you?" He barked

"Sorry, old habits die hard." She said still standing there.

"What do you want?" He snapped

"Why are you standing...."? The other girl appeared. "Oh, hello. I'm Chloe." She said coming to greet me.

"Oh yeah, I'm Marisa." The first girl said coming in the door and closing it behind her. I looked at Derrick, why were they walking inside like they thought this was that kind of party. "So Derrick you do kiss after all."

"What do you guys want?" He looked irritated.

Both of them frowned. "Why are you mad?" Chloe asked

"I didn't invite you in here."

"We need invitations now?" Marisa asked with attitude.

Derrick pointed at me, "This is my woman! Yes you do!"

"So what are we chopped liver?" Marisa asked

Derrick glared at them. "Do you want me to answer that?"

"Hold on you guys. We're adults we can talk this out." Chloe said trying to take charge. "Obviously this is not a good time. Derrick can we come back in the morning?"

"For what? I'm not sharing!" I said

Both of the girls blank stared at me. The fact that they were standing there irritated me. "You heard her, you don't have to go home; but you gotta get up out of here." He said shooing them out the door. "Sorry about that!"

"Since when do you leave your door unlocked?" I snapped at him.

"I used to leave it unlocked all the time. Temporary relapse." He said locking the door.

"That better be your only relapse!" I growled.

"What's that supposed to mean?"

"They're as pretty as Toya said they were!" I know I shouldn't have felt insecure about them. But looking at them made me feel ugly. Didn't matter that he appeared to put me above them who knows if he left the door unlocked because originally he was planning to welcome them back, and his plan was spoiled when mister nobody called to tell him I was coming.

"Why do you care what they look like? I'm with you!" He stared at me.

"I know, I didn't expect them to be that pretty." I said looking at the floor feeling stupid for showing my insecurity.

He lifted my chin, "Chantel. You're beautiful! They don't matter."

****

"Tiffany and Crystal this is Derrick's girlfriend Chantel. Chantel, these are our honorary little sisters Tiffany and Crystal, and the baby girl is their little sister Chelsea." Darryl said proudly.

"Nice to meet you." I said to all three of them, they were gorgeous teenagers.

"Derrick you were finally nice enough to a girl to have a girlfriend. I worried about you." Crystal said

"I guess so." Derrick said looking around, "your father's here isn't he?"

"Yeah, but he's with our little brothers and our mother." Tiffany said

"You guys didn't tell me the whole family was gonna be out here that's even better." Darryl said

"How you figure?" Derrick sounded irritated.

"Calm down, it just is." Darryl said waving Derrick off. "What you wanna ride first?"

"We gotta take Chelsea back to our parents first then we can ride everything." Crystal said excited.

Chelsea was the cutest little girl; she looked just like her big sisters. She looked disappointed about their resolve to get rid of her. Chelsea looked up at Derrick with big pleading eyes. Derrick exhaled and picked her up. "You wanna go see the puppets on ice show?" He asked her. Chelsea said an excited YES! Derrick looked at Darryl, "go ride one ride and then meet us back right here!" Darryl said ok, but Derrick eyed him like he knew Darryl wasn't coming back. "You going with them or coming with me?" He asked me.

"No! She go with them!" Chelsea said folding her arms.

"Ooh! She is trying to take your man." Tiffany laughed.

I looked at Derrick slightly amused and I do mean slightly. "What do you want me to do?"

"Go with them for at least this first ride; but meet me here." Then he walked away. Chelsea was too excited to have Derrick to herself. I told myself she was just a baby, let her have her moment.

When we were in line the girls started looking me up and down. Darryl smiled at them but he didn't say anything. "So you sweet on our big brother? Interesting." Tiffany said

"WHO ARE YOU?" I said sarcastically.

Darryl started laughing, "Do you know who Dwayne Reed is?"

Of course I know who he is. Only a fool wouldn't know who he is. He's all over TV and major eye candy. "Of course." I said

"They're his daughters." He said

As soon as he said it. I saw how they both looked like him. I was still lost, "ok. What does that have to do with you?" I asked not getting the connection.

"They're dad and my momma used to date. Just because they broke up doesn't mean we stopped being a family." Darryl explained

"Where's Drew?" Crystal asked

"His best friend is thinking about getting married soon. He had best man duties to tend to, or he's doing his job and talking some sense into him. He's gonna try to catch up with your dad before you guys leave." Darryl said

"Can you take us to see your mom before we leave?" Crystal asked

"Is that ok with your momma?" He asked

"She doesn't have a choice." Tiffany said with attitude. "It's her fault anyways."

Crystal gave her sister an irritated look, "don't start that! You make things harder than they have to be sometimes. That was a long time ago. Let it go!"

"She's doing it again, don't tell me you can't see the signs." Darryl shrugged at me. "What's she doing?"

"NOTHING!" Crystal gave her sister a look like she needed to shut up. "ANYWAYS! Are you and Derrick in love?"

"Yes," I said.

They smiled at me the same way. "That's beautiful! Crystal remember how daddy was when he was in love?" Tiffany said

"Cut it out!" Crystal snapped at Tiffany.

"It's just Darryl. We can be honest with him. She's an extension of Derrick. If we can't be honest with at least them I'm gonna explode!" Tiffany said

"Fine! Darryl, Chantel please don't judge us or tell anybody?" Crystal begged

Darryl and I leaned in. Tiffany went on a tangent about her parents.

Since I was unfamiliar with the story they explained their parent's previous divorce. Their father's relationship with Amber. All of them agreed that Dwayne was completely in love with Amber. It sounds like the girls were just as in love with the idea of her as their stepmother. Nobody knows why Amber and Dwayne broke up. They all said that both of them took it pretty hard. Darryl said his mother threw herself into work, and the girls said that's when their mother crept back in. They said their mother loves their father, but their father was still in love with Amber and everybody knew it. Tiffany was angry because their mother played too many games and Amber would've never happened if she would've been straight with their father. It was weird how no one faulted Dwayne for loving Amber or being broken up about losing her. I was amazed that a man that fine, second to my Derrick of course, could love someone that deeply. On TV you see playboys all over the place, but he never loves further than the one he's with. For him to have loved her, lost her, and still bleed for her was amazing.

Tiffany cried angry tears for her father. Darryl hugged her, rubbed her back. "I know it's hard, but your dad was a forty-niner, and we're Raiders! It was doomed from the beginning." He said with a smile.

Both of the girls erupted into laughter. "He's a Giant now!" Crystal said wiping her eyes.

"If it ain't Black and Silver it's doomed!" He said putting his foot down.

"Please! When they get divorced AGAIN! Cause we all know it's gonna happen, he's gonna marry your mom. Then we'll be a blended family, blue, black, red, and silver!" Crystal said

"All jokes aside, I don't think our parents will get back together. No matter what, we'll always be family though." His face was very serious which was unlike him.

"Why?" Tiffany asked through pained eyes.

"At the end of the day she's gonna get back with my dad." He said matter of factly.

"Are they together now?" Crystal asked

"Not exactly."

"So there's a chance!" Tiffany blurted

"Barely!" He exhaled, "but if that's what you need to be able to sleep at night." He shook his head.

"Don't you just love Amber!" Tiffany smiled big listening for my answer.

My face started stinging. I haven't interacted with her ever really. "She is lovely."

Darryl watched me like he was reading my face. "Who's riding with who?" He changed the subject.

We were almost to the front of the line. Crystal and I opted to ride together since Tiffany acted like it was gonna be life or death if she didn't ride with her big brother. I told myself not to focus on the fact that I haven't interacted with his mother all that much. If his mother was like mine I could understand. But he talks to his mother regularly, and he sees her on a regular basis. She's not far from me, why don't I know her? She's my stinking landlord for crying out loud. When we got off the ride everyone was all smiles Derrick and Chelsea were waiting by the exit. Chelsea had a multicolored snow cone that was too big for her little hands. She was determined to try to master it. Derrick was holding her trying to help her eat it. I could see him register my annoyance. "How was the ride?"

Everyone started talking at once, and I shook my head going along with them. "Let's find our parents so we can drop her off, then we can go crazy!" Crystal said excited.

Derrick grabbed my hand and then we walked to the kid section of the park. I was so happy that TV didn't exaggerate his size and make him bigger than he actually was. Dwayne had on shades and a hat. His hat was appropriate so it didn't look like he was trying to blend in even though he was. I smiled, but then I dropped my smile when Derrick looked at me. "I assumed they found you guys. How you doing?" He said shaking Darryl's hand then Derrick's.

"Somebody is a mess!" He said talking to Chelsea who was still working on her snow cone. She had red, blue, and green food coloring stains all over her face hands and clothes. But somehow Derrick's white wife-beater T-shirt was unaffected. Dwayne smiled at his baby girl, and then he looked at me. "Hello."

"Daddy! That's Derrick's girlfriend." Tiffany said with a smile. "You've been nice enough to her to make her your girlfriend?

Wow!" He chuckled. "I'm Dwayne," he said extending his hand to shake mine.

"Chantel" His hand was big and strong. I told myself don't melt Derrick is watching; but oh my goodness I can't believe Amber broke up with him.

"Beautiful name for a beautiful lady." He smiled while he shook my hand, my heart skipped a beat.

Derrick pulled my hand away, "stop trying to charm my girlfriend." His face was serious but I knew he was kind of joking. Dwayne laughed, "You haven't changed."

"Nope! Neither have you." Derrick said looking him in his eyes. Dwayne's face got serious and it looked like he instantly started hurting all over. "No I haven't."

Then a very pretty lady walked over with a stroller with two little boys in it. She gasped when she saw Chelsea, "Dwayne! What is she eating?" She said in a disapproving tone.

"Michelle you remember Derrick and Darryl? And this is Derrick's girlfriend Chantel."

She took Chelsea from Derrick. "Yes, I remember. How is everyone?" She said getting her diaper bag, and throwing away the cone.

Dwayne looked irritated by her lack of interest. Tiffany stared at her father's irritation. "WHY DO YOU ALWAYS HAVE TO ACT LIKE THIS? CAN YOU SAY A DECENT HELLO? WE'RE VERY HAPPY TO SEE THEM!" She screamed at her mother and then she stormed off.

Crystal and Dwayne sighed; Darryl put his hand up to tell them he was going after her. "Why does she think it's ok to talk to me like that?" Michelle said still going through the diaper bag.

"She's a teenage girl." Dwayne said

"That's no excuse!" She said

"Looks like she's a daddy's girl to me; both of them for that matter." Derrick said

"I'm a good mother!" Michelle was flustered wiping Chelsea's face and hands.

"That doesn't make you a bad mother." Derrick said

"You could've been nicer mom." Crystal said

"Come on, don't gang up on her. Your sister said a mouth full." Dwayne said

"This is not easy for me! How am I supposed to be?" She said as tears rolled down her face.

Derrick looked at Crystal and he told her to go hug her mother. Crystal raised her eyebrow at him like I've seen her dad do on TV. Derrick smiled and then pointed his eyes at her mother. Crystal huffed then she went over and hugged her mother. Tiffany and Darryl came back, and Tiffany gave a very forced apology. Then we left, Derrick grabbed my hand again and we walked behind Darryl and the girls. "So he's still in love with your mother."

"It looks that way." He wasn't interested in going in any further on the topic.

"The girls seem like they're rooting for your parents to get back together."

"Fairy tales! That's not gonna happen."

"Why do you say that?"

"My momma is in love with Malcolm, even if she's trying to act like it ain't so right now. Dwayne didn't completely suck, but he's not my dad."

"The girls asked me if I loved your mother as much as they do." He looked at me. "Why don't I know her? Why doesn't she want to know me?"

He exhaled, "don't go all crazy."

"Me go crazy?" I said sarcastically.

"She knows about you. She's been on my case too. It's my fault, she travels a lot. Then our schedules. It's been hard to pin it down to an occasion."

"It doesn't have to be perfect Derrick, I just want her to know who I am."

"I know," he looked away.

"I'm not gonna ask you again Derrick."

He eyed me for a minute then he kept walking. The girls excitedly shared stories about "the good old days" as they called them. Family vacations, and parties. The girls affectionately shared the story of when Amber taught them to swim. I started to understand why their mother was falling apart. Clearly her husband was still in love with another woman, but I can only imagine what it must feel like to know your children are in love with her too.

****

Derrick and I barely slept last night! He made Oysters Rockefeller on the grill on his balcony, amongst other things. Wine and good food equaled a night of ridiculous passion. He kept waking me up which I did not mind at all, but by round five I didn't see the point of sleeping just to wake up again. I told him oysters were restricted to the weekend. Neither one of us had early classes this morning, but we still slept longer than we were supposed to. So needless to say we're rushing over each other. I tried to kiss him quickly and make my way to the door, but mister all hands on deck decided one more go around was in order. Needless to say I didn't make my class; but I still had to go into the office. I re-showered and then I blew him a kiss as we hurried out. Stamina my baby has! I smiled all the way to work. I parked in my designated space in the Mitigated garage. Brandy was arriving at the same time. She looked at my goofy grin and rolled her eyes. "I need to get me a man so I can look goofy like that too." She teased.

"How are you?" I said walking with her towards the door to exit on to the street.

"I'm good..."

Somebody stepped out of the shadows of the dimly lit garage. We both screamed, and Brandy stepped in front of me ready to fight.

"Didn't mean to scare you."

"Kevin?" We said in unison.

He looked at Brandy with a question mark on his face. "Have we met?"

"Yes!" She said not relaxing.

"Goodness girl! What you gonna do, beat me down or something? Relax!"

"I have a bad feeling about this. Come on Chantel, he's up to no good."

Kevin sucked his teeth. "Whatever! Chantel can I talk to you for a minute?"

"No!" Brandy said still protecting me.

"I can't, I gotta go." This whole scene seemed creepy. I wanted out of this garage.

"I'll only take a second." He pleaded

I opened the door to the street. "You can walk with us." I said not wanting to be rude.

"I don't wanna walk with her." He pointed at Brandy.

"Sorry we always walk together."

"Yep! I'm always here!" Brandy spit at him.

"Fine!" He huffed holding the door open. "Why didn't you tell me you transferred out here? I've been stalking the Oakland office for months looking to talk to you."

"You heard him STALKER!" Brandy said in my ear, but loud enough for him to hear.

I smiled, "I didn't realize I needed to report that to you."

He stared at my face, "what happened to my innocence?" He huffed, "you done got with junior and he turned you out!" He sounded angry.

"Um Kevin, I don't know what you're getting at. And I don't think my personal life is any of your business." I walked a little faster.

"I wanna take you out."

"I can't. I have a boyfriend."

"You can't have friends?"

"I don't need friends."

"We all need friends. Friends make the world go round." He said, then Brandy laughed at him. He got mad, "who are you laughing at?"

"You! You're pathetic!" She said. Kevin started cursing and acting ugly. Brandy kept laughing as we walked into the building. As if he knew better he didn't enter the building, but he stood there looking pissed off. "He's not stable girl." She chuckled to herself.

"How can you tell?"

"Look at what just happened. Where did he come from? I'm good about watching my surroundings and I didn't see him coming."

"You are good about that. Where did you learn that?"

She sucked her tongue real loud, rolled her eyes, and put her hand on her hip. "I'm from Richmond! It's an acquired skill." We both laughed.

Brandy was my best friend at work. She was a little older than me, but a lot of fun. She's even hung out with Pearla, Liz, Erica, Zoey and I a few times. We share a cubical space, she's on one side and I'm on the other. Everyone in this office is really nice though. I know some of them wonder if I'm Malcolm's daughter cause I'm so young and he brought me in directly. I like the idea of it so I don't confirm or deny anything. Brandy has it bad for Lamont I mean Yussef. She just about loses it whenever he comes in the office. I can tell he knows she likes him. He comes and chats with me from time to time. Brandy gets real quiet and bashful whenever he's around. One time he came in with Drew and I honestly thought her head was gonna explode. It's hilarious to me.

My desk phone buzzed, "Chantel!" Malcolm's voice reached out and grabbed me. Brandy wasn't in her chair, I stood up. I saw Brandy and Yussef in Malcolm's office through the glass in his door. I walked in and everybody's faces were serious. Malcolm told me to sit. "Security tells me that someone was following you two this afternoon." He sat back in his chair. "Is this the first time he's popped up on you?"

Everybody looked at me. "No, he does it all the time this morning was the first time it was creepy. No I take that back, that night in Oakland was the first time it was creepy. Today is the first time I've seen him since then. Why? What's wrong?"

"He doesn't work for me anymore. There's no reason for him to be around here. And there's really no reason for him to be talking to you. Ms. Laverne has informed me about his little crush on you. Do you feel threatened?" He asked plainly.

"No, should I feel that way?"

"No, but I had to ask. From time to time you're gonna see Mitigated staff around your school and other places. I don't want you to be alarmed or feel scared. It's just a safety precaution."

"Precaution?"

"You're family remember." He said not looking at me. "Yussef I need the layout of the school, the plans from the city, etc."

"You're going to my school. How do you like it?" Yussef smiled "It's fine I guess. I don't understand, but I guess you guys got it all under control." I said, and then I looked at Brandy. "Why are you in here?"

"She makes sure you get to and from your car safely." Malcolm said still looking at his computer.

"Like you're security?" I couldn't believe it.

"Your girl is bad!" Yussef said looking at Malcolm's screen. Brandy blushed, "thank you."

"So you weren't exaggerating earlier when you were ready to take him out?"

"Nope!" She smiled again.

As we were talking the lights flickered, then the power went out and then the fire alarm went off. Everyone paused on the main floor, the speaker system made an announcement for everyone to evacuate the building. Malcolm opened his door. "Everybody take your laptops home. Go home, I'll tell you when to come back in the office!" Malcolm packed up his computer and some files. He looked irritated. "There's no fire." He said to Yussef.

Brandy and I grabbed our purses and laptops. "You gonna go home?" She asked

"Yeah, I'll go spend some time with Cyrus. Then I'll go to Derrick's, he's at school right now anyways."

"Sounds good."

We walked down all the flights of stairs and out onto the street. The entire building was outside and everybody was looking up. Brandy told me to come on and keep moving. Mitigated staff were in the garage getting in their cars. Brandy waved bye and I headed to Oakland. Cyrus wasn't home when I got there. I logged my computer in then I started working. Cyrus came home about an hour later. He was happy to see me. I told him about my morning and he looked real thoughtful. He said he didn't like Kevin either. "Guess who I saw at the airport this morning?" I looked at him, I didn't feel like guessing. "Your mother in-law."

That wasn't uncommon she flew around a lot. "Is that all?"

"She met some young girl there, and they looked all cozy."

"Was it Sasha?"

"I know who Sasha is. I don't know who the girl is, but they stood out is all I'm saying."

His words hung on the air. I called Derrick but he was in his class so he didn't answer. My stomach grumbled, "Let's go eat."

"Where we going?"

"You feel like Mexican?" I asked

Cyrus looked at me straight faced. "You wanna go to that place Derrick took you?"

"Of course!" I said smiling.

"GOOD! I don't go without you." He smiled real big.

"Why?"

"Whenever I'm with you they hook me up. Whenever I've gone without you my food have been standard portions."

We both laughed, I drove to Gonzalez's. Derrick and his family always come here. My heart slowed down when I saw Derrick's car in the parking lot. He was supposed to be in class. If he wasn't in class why didn't he answer my call? I started chewing the inside of my cheek. Cyrus asked me what was wrong, I told him nothing. I was truly hoping it was nothing. When we walked in the door Derrick was looking at me. He was sitting next to his mother who was all smiles and talking to a girl who had her back to us. The girl's hair was shoulder length and jet black, it moved with her movements. His mother said something to him and then looked to see who he was looking at. She had a question mark on her face. Derrick waved us over. Derrick told us to sit down. Cyrus sat next to the girl, and I sat next to Derrick. "How you doing?" Amber said to me.

"Momma you remember Chantel." He said even toned.

"Of course, you sang at EA for a while didn't you?" She said, and then she looked at the girl. "She has a beautiful voice!"

"Thank you," I said flashing Derrick a look. Is that all she knew me for?

"Momma this is Chantel my girlfriend." He said

The girl tensed up, "girlfriend?" She said

"Girlfriend?" I said looking at him. How did I get demoted to girlfriend from woman?

Amber looked angry but she didn't say anything. "And this is her brother Cyrus."

"You look familiar." Amber said

"I work at the airport. I see you all the time." He said

"Ok, nice to meet you." She said

"Chantel this is Brooklyn." Derrick said

"I'm sorry I didn't know." She said

I shot Derrick daggers with my eyes. His face didn't change. Cyrus ordered his food to go, while I sat there brewing. Everyone was silent; my mind was running fifty miles a minute. When Cyrus' food came I stood up. I told Amber it was good seeing her again, and I told Brooklyn it was nice to finally meet her. I wanted to spit at Derrick, but I walked away. Cyrus said bye and then he came with me.

I went in my room and shut the door. I expected Derrick to come knocking at any moment. After two hours I realized he wasn't coming. It took everything in me not to call him. Instead I called Pearla but she was on a double date with Liz and Walter. When midnight hit and not a word from Derrick I got angry and I got in my car. When I got to his apartment I tested the knob and the door was open. Derrick was sitting at the table doing homework. He rolled his eyes when he saw me. "I'm doing homework!" He said like he was warning me.

"What is that supposed to mean?" I asked feeling heat come out my ears.

"I'm not gonna do some emotional scene with you. I know today looked bad, but I'll fix it. Right now I gotta study."

"So…. you're gonna fix it how?"

"I'm gonna have my momma over more often so she can get to know you." He said nonchalantly. "Ain't no point in arguing about it."

Carey Anderson

"Oh! Just like that and it's fixed?" I said
"Yeah, you want her to know you right. We don't need a scene for
that. I'll just fix it."
I looked around the room. Clearly this fool thinks I DON'T
REMEMBER! "Oh Derrick you're the best boyfriend EVER!" I
said sarcastically.
He cut his eyes at me and he dropped his pen. "WHAT?"
"You're the best boyfriend ever!" I spit with venom.
"Boyfriend?"
"Well now I can't be demoted to girlfriend and you keep your
title." I said going in his room. I grabbed a plastic bag and I threw
all my stuff in the bag. Everything I could think of. I set the bag
next to the door.
He rolled his eyes, "why you gotta be so dramatic?"
"Dramatic?" I couldn't take it anymore. I cursed him as hard as I
could. Derrick sat there with no expression on his face. Like my
words had no affect on him. "You tell me how dramatic you would
be if the shoe were on the other foot?"
"You're overreacting. I told you I'm gonna fix it!" I could see him
trying to calm himself.
"I ask you about your mother. It takes you demoting me from your
woman to your girlfriend in front of your ex woman for you to
think its important!"
Then his face cracked! I guess he thought I didn't remember her
name because he only said it once. A woman does not forget
something like that. I have never seen so many emotions flash
across his face in my life. He got up so fast I didn't see him move.
He stopped me from opening the door. "Wait a minute! Who told
you that?"
"You did! Now move out the way. I don't want to be your
girlfriend anymore!" I said
"Wait a minute! I didn't tell you that."
"Yes you did!"
"No I didn't!" He said convinced he was right.
"Did you actually forget something? Wow! There's a first! Move
out the way!"
"No I didn't!"
I blew irritated air. "Go back in your mind. You were explaining
the difference between a girlfriend and a woman. Until today I was
your woman, and the only woman before me was Brooklyn!" He

had such a busted look on his face. "Now you remember that, don't you? Now move out of my way before I call the police on you."
He frowned, "I don't care about the police! They can't do nothing to me!"
"I'll call Malcolm!"
He mimicked my voice. "I'll call your daddy on you!" Then he got off the door. "So what Chantel! It was a slip of the tongue, not worth all this. You're just looking for a reason to leave any ways. I didn't touch that girl, I wasn't sitting next to her, and I didn't even deny you in front of her. One little slip of the tongue is worth you making the biggest mistake of your life, fine then. This is as good as it's gonna get. I don't do emotional outbursts! I'm not gonna beg you to come back. This isn't even worth all this!"
"You've changed. My ex couldn't even smile at me without you getting upset; but you can keep in contact with yours. You leave your door unlocked for them. Suddenly all their stuff keeps popping up all over the apartment unlike before. You tell me your mother wants to meet me, but today it looked like she didn't even know about me. Then you don't even mention that she's coming into town or that the marathon the night before was probably because you were excited to be seeing her! You don't get it and I thought you were smarter than this!" I opened the door grabbed my bag and walked out. He didn't come after me just like he said he wouldn't.

Chapter 10

"Just because you're one of those naturally thin heifers don't mean you don't need to workout! And I need a workout partner, and it looks like you're it!" Brandy commanded

"I'm going to ignore the fact that you called me a heifer, cause I know I need to workout just for the sake of being healthy." I said as I put another spoon full of pie in my mouth. Brandy rolled her eyes at me while she laughed.

Working out with her has been a wonderful distraction for me. I try to fill my down time with music, exercise, and more music. Brandy has been walking around looking amazing, while my body has toned up nicely as well. I've always been smaller, but now I got cuts. I got so excited when I saw the cuts in my stomach come in. That was all it took I was addicted to the gym. I started going even when Brandy couldn't make it. After my showers I do a daily inspection of my body. Everything looks so pretty, and then I remember how ripped Derrick's body was. I'd laugh at myself for wanting to show him the difference over a year can make. If nothing else my new body is my best-kept secret cause I don't show it off. I want to, but with Kevin popping up everywhere with his creepiness I don't want to. Yussef gave me mace for my keychain just in case there was a moment of indifferent timing. His words not mine. I hope I never need to know what he's talking about.

****

"I like your hair!" Mario said as he reached out to touch my braids. "Does it hurt?"

"It was sore at first, but its good now." I said allowing him to touch my hair. "Mario promise me something." His eyes got big. "You will always ask a woman before you touch her hair. Some women can be really offended by that." I warned

His eyes were big, "does it offend you?"

"Depends on who it is. But you can touch my hair."

My daddy came back in the room armed with his acoustic guitar. "Ok baby girl, now it's important to know timing and notes." He strummed his guitar.

My eyes filled with tears. "Yes daddy."

My daddy reached out and grabbed my hand. "He'll be back. I'm so proud of you for standing up for yourself. No matter who they are, you can't let people walk all over you cause they won't stop once you allow them to. He cares about you, he'll be back."

"Thank you dad

"I've always loved music. Your grandma would sing to all of us and she encouraged us to sing. My heart would get heavy and I'd turn to music. When your mother ran away with you guys I thought I was gonna die. She stole pieces of my soul. Music helped me through it. I'd sing songs for you guys all the time. I'd dedicate songs to you in my heart." He strummed his guitar; "I'd play a song for you like my life depended on it. I know I talk about music a little more than you'd like me to, but music is how I survive. Music can be love, it can be joy, and it can be pain. Music can save your life! When you feel something, write it down. Later on it could be a song or the bridge to a song." His passion for music was definitely there.

"I guess I didn't realize you wrote music too." I was taking everything he said in.

"Have you ever written poetry?" I nodded yes. "That's a song without a melody." He got excited. "Bring some of your writings, I bet you have a bunch of songs within them."

"Cyrus writes poetry, he's really good. He's been talking with this guy that we know about poetry. He's too shy to perform it like the guy we know does, but they're both really good."

"And you're good too, right?" He smiled.

"I guess so. My heart hurts." I said as tears fell.

"Your heart is getting stronger, preparing you for the future. No matter who it is, you stand up for you."

"Thank you daddy. I wonder who I'd be if I grew up with you."

A tear fell from his eye. I had no idea he felt emotional in this moment. "Me too! Even though we know it wasn't intentional she instilled independence in you guys. I don't have to worry about you two. I know that you will still stand if something happened to me. I hope your little brothers will be as responsible, only time will tell." Then he strummed his guitar. "This is the song I sang for you."

First he explained the difference in the chords, E, B, C# minor and A. My daddy played this song with so much passion but the song was mellow and sad. It made my heart speed up and then slow down. I had him play it over and over. As sad as this song was it made me feel better. Mario sang the song with us.

I had a new focus, my heart was bleeding, and I felt like I was drowning. Music was my only lifeline to keep me sane. I know Derrick said he wasn't gonna come after me, but I wished he would. Malcolm has been business as usual, he doesn't mention Derrick, but he never did before either. Sometimes I see Yussef at my school, or other people who look familiar but I focus on my classes. Pearla and Liz have their men, so we don't have as much time to spend together. After awhile I started to feel like I shouldn't be so involved with Derrick's family. Obviously he wasn't coming for me, and I didn't feel comfortable anymore.

"Can I talk to you?" I asked Malcolm.

He looked away from his computer, he gestured for me to come in and sit down. As usual his face was stern, with no readable emotion on it. "Shoot!" He waited for me to speak.

My insides screamed. "I think I need to put in my two week notice."

"Do you think that's necessary?"

"I think so."

Malcolm cocked his head to the side. "Why would you let emotion stop you from handling business?"

Malcolm is always intense, and I think this is his version of being nice. I wanted to run out screaming. "It's all mixing together for me these days. I feel like I'm losing myself."

"You will finish school, have your grades slipped?" He said staring me in my eyes.

"Yes, I will finish, and no they haven't." I said with my eyes to the floor.

"Derrick is stubborn and hardheaded. You gotta stand your ground with him, but he's reasonable to a measure. I know this is hard, but you're doing good."

Shock was all over my face. "Thank you."

"Take some time off, but I'll keep you on. You don't irritate me like my last assistant did. When you're ready to come back call me." Then he returned to his computer.

"Thank you Malcolm!" I said feeling like the President of the United States just paid me a compliment.

When I got home I told Cyrus what I did. He asked me what I was gonna do for money. I told him I had savings (thanks to my gig at

Elegant Affairs!) and if I needed to I could try my hand at singing for my supper. I told him Malcolm said I could come back. Once I told him that part he calmed down a lot.

******

Cyrus and Sherrell had a baby girl that they named her Roseanna after my grandmother, so all of us moved into a townhouse styled apartment in Jack London Square that has a security system at the front door and parking in the garage. Cyrus said he would feel better about the times when we were home alone with us living there. My daddy was so excited to be a granddad; I think he was more excited about the baby than Cyrus, who was pretty excited himself. They were such a cute family. I never thought I would be one of those girls who wondered if I would have a family. Being with Derrick made me want one, but now I don't see how it's possible. Whenever I try to date it never works for one reason or another. Most of these guys want to get physical too quick, and when I turn them down there goes the possibility of a relationship. The possibility to move on. Plus I keep hearing Derrick in my head talking about he breaks me in and then I go around with everyone else as soon as he can't be there. I guess I'm proving to myself that I am the faithful kind even if Derrick didn't give me credit for it. I feel like the guy should be worthy of me. And I have yet to find someone worthy. It gets hard at times, but oh well.

****

"How you doing?" Ms. Laverne met me to share my big hug with her.

"I'm good how are you?" I said

"Oh you know how it goes. I miss you."

"I miss you! I was on my way to the shoe store, but I had to pop by and say hi."

"I'm glad you did. I was about to go to lunch. You interested?" She asked

"Of course!" I said moving so she could lock the door. We went to the food court ate lunch and caught up. She was disappointed that Derrick hadn't come around yet, and I was tired of holding my breath. As I was pouring out my heart, I saw a familiar walk out the corner of my eye. My head whipped around so fast. I couldn't believe it was him. He had the nerve to try to dress young and look like a random guy. Ms. Laverne looked at my face and sighed. He

sat at the table with Quesha and held her hands. I COULDN'T
BELIEVE IT! Ms. Laverne patted my hand and told me to be
calm. I didn't know she knew who he was. I debated within myself
whether to say anything or not. I was going to walk away with Ms.
Laverne when I saw him touch her like he was trying to run game.
I stormed over to his table. "Reggie!" I yelled
He jumped and then he looked at me. "Chantel! Where have you
been?"
"Where's my mother?" I spit at him.
"Work I guess. What do you care?" He said, "When was the last
time you've spoken to her?"
"Chantel what's going on?" Quesha asked
"This is my mother's husband!" I yelled
"Father? You're married?"
"Only legally!" He said to Quesha, "what do you mean I'm not
your step daddy."
"You are not my father!"
"Don't start that junk. I am your daddy!"
"You are not my father. I found my real daddy. How do you let a
woman with two kids support you while you abuse her children?" I
yelled
Quesha's face turned green, "WHAT???"
"He's a low life, pathetic excuse for a man, child molester, down
low, GO GET YOURSELF TESTED! Our mother said you were
sick. What's wrong with you?" I continued yelling.
Quesha started crying, she walked away from the table. "WHY
ARE YOU LYING ON ME? YOU'VE ALWAYS HATED ME!
YOU AND YOUR BROTHER!"
"YES we hate you and you know why!" I rolled my eyes. "You can
keep lying to everybody if you want to, but I was there, and so
were you! You know I know and am telling the truth! I don't know
how you live with yourself!" Then I walked away.
Ms. Laverne hugged me and helped me to calm down as much as
she could. I told her I was going to indulge in some retail therapy. I
thanked her for calming me, and then I went to the shoe store.
"I have been looking for you everywhere!" Kevin said
I frowned at him as I put the shoes I was looking at back. "Why?"
"I never got a chance to talk to you. Get to know you, all that." He
said smiling.

"Right, so if you never got to know me why would you be looking for me? That makes no sense!" I was already in a bad mood and he wasn't helping my mood.

"Somebody's testy, I thought it would've been flattering to know that a guy who hasn't really had a chance to get to know you has been checking for you. You're making it seem, I don't know, different."

I leaned my head back and exhaled. "I'm not in the mood for this! I'm having a bad day!"

He put his hands up, "ok don't get all testy. My bad! Can I get your number so I can call you later?"

"NO!" I said

He frowned, "No?"

"I don't want this. You keep popping up at weird times out of weird places. I keep getting a creepy vibe when it comes to you. And THEN on the day when I can't take anything else you show up asking for my number. NO!"

"Oh! I see! Suddenly I'm not good enough for you no more!"

"Honestly Kevin, when were you ever good enough for me! I don't even understand why we're having this conversation. I said I wanted to be left alone and here you are still talking! I can't even buy shoes in peace!" Then I stormed past him.

Kevin grabbed my arm and it felt like a vice grip. "Who you think you're talking to? Didn't anybody ever teach you how you should talk to a man?"

I snatched my arm away. "I keep telling you nicely that I'm not interested and you don't seem to understand that. I guess this is the only way you understand that I'M NOT INTERESTED!" I was tired of the song and dance.

He doesn't show up at my school, thank goodness. Every time I think about going somewhere here he is. I was tired of this whole thing. If he went away maybe I wouldn't think about Derrick so much.

****

"What's up Chantel?" Darryl said walking towards me with his arms extended for a hug.

"Hey Darryl! How you been?" I hugged him back.

"Missing you. Where you been?" He smiled.

"School, home, singing for peanuts. How about you?"

"Singing for peanuts. Good one."

157

"What are you doing here?" I was at my hole in the wall mom and pop bistro. This place is off a residential street off of Shattuck. There was a big window and tons of coffee tables and even a few beanbags. Local artist come and perform for free. Local students come for coffee and pastries; some do homework, most vibe off the relaxed atmosphere and performances. Most people read poetry and some sing, I do both. My dad's been teaching me how to play his guitar, so this has been good practice for the things I learn.

"I came to see you, see how you're doing. Find out what's new." He said

"Aren't you sweet. I never thought you'd find me here. I thought this place was off the grid." He didn't respond to that he smiled.

"You're up next." Jamie said to me.

"Jamie this is Darryl, Darryl this is Jamie."

"Nice to meet you." Jamie smiled

If looks could kill! I patted Darryl's arm asking him to be cool. When the house saw me moving towards the front they erupted into applause. "Thank you, before I sing my new songs are there any requests?" People shouted out the three songs they always ask for. Two of them were written by my father. I loved the way the crowd swayed to my melody. I felt like I was really coming into my sound. Darryl's goofy behind jumped right in with everyone clapping, snapping, and swaying to the melody. Everyone was standing and demanding an Encore when I was done. So I sang one more song then I was done.

"Who would've thought you could get better?" Darryl said

"Thank you, music has been my best friend these days."

Then Jamie came and sat down. "Great set!" Then he kissed my cheek.

Darryl's face changed from angry to smiling all in three seconds. "Who are you?" He asked Jamie.

"I was gonna ask you the same thing." Jamie said looking him up and down.

"Darryl" I put my hands out hoping to calm him. "Jamie is just a friend." I said

"For now!" Jamie said staring at Darryl.

Darryl smiled at Jamie. Then he looked at me. "I'm gonna ignore him! He's gonna make me catch a case in front of all these people." He laughed an irritated laugh. "Anyways, I want you to come to my graduation."

"Isn't that like more than a year away?"

Darryl laughed, "Consider this advanced notice. I don't want any excuses. College graduations are just as important as high school."

"Un huh! Why are you really here?"

"Can't a nigga miss you? Do I need a reason?" He laughed

"I guess." I exhaled, "how's Derrick?"

"It's about time! Why it take you so long to get to the point?" Then he made his face mockingly serious. "He's ok, he's ok!" He said shaking his head.

I looked around, "is he here?"

Darryl blew air, "think about that question. If he was here your boy over there would've been picking 'em up."

"What's that supposed to mean?" Jamie said slightly raising his voice.

Darryl leaned in, "if you keep testing me! Just sit there, shut up, and be happy I'm not dropping you for your blatant disrespect! You better ask somebody who I am before I let you find out." Then Darryl smiled.

Darryl's tone didn't match his expression, clear indication of a crazy person in my book. "Darryl he doesn't know you or your family. Please be nice." I said mildly.

"Tell him to shut up!" He said leaning back in his chair.

"Jamie can you give us a minute?"

"Fine! I'll be back in a little bit!" He said giving Darryl the evil eye.

"Fine, I'll be back in a little bit." Darryl said mimicking him.

"Yeah! I gotta beat him. He did this to himself." Darryl said nonchalantly.

"Don't hurt him." I calmly pleaded.

Darryl smiled and patted my hand. "It's for the best!" Then he looked at me, "when are you going to call my brother? It's been years."

I sat back in my chair. "I'm not going to call him."

"What? Why not?" Darryl bounced in his chair like he was throwing a tantrum. A few people looked at him and he smiled at them and asked them how they were doing like they had a problem.

I started laughing. "You are too silly!" Then I exhaled again. "The more I think about it, the more I feel our time came and went. Derrick wasn't serious about me. I'm fine with that now."

Darryl's mouth was hanging open. "Who are you? I need the Chantel that was there during it all! What man goes out of his way for a random chick like Derrick did for you? He waited for you!

He don't let girl's spend the night, and he wanted you to move in with him. I could keep going. He don't kiss girls, but he was always kissing on you!"

"Did he send you?" I looked Darryl in his eyes.

"No! And if you tell him I came we gon' have problems! I am the peace keeper!" He said calmly. I frowned at him. "In my immediate family."

"Why didn't he tell your mother about me? If I was so *special* to him."

"You assume!" He shook his finger at me. "You assume that he didn't tell her. I know for a fact that he did."

"Why would she be all cozy with his ex if she knew about me?" I said feeling like it happened five minutes ago.

"Brooklyn was a part of our family for a long time. My momma liked her, unless your name is Toya, you're not automatically cut off with her. Derrick was in the wrong place at the wrong time. Derrick decided to visit momma at the last minute, he calls where you at? He goes; he didn't know she was there. A little after he gets there here you come." He said

"Un huh, he told you all this?"

"Please! Momma was upset, I heard them talking. Then when I didn't see you around after that, I've been asking. Slowly pulling the pieces together."

"This is all very sweet, but I'm not gonna call him. If I meant all that much to him why wouldn't he come after me?"

"Battle of the wills." Darryl said

"So why should I give in first?"

"Cause I can't take this no more. You guys are driving me *crazy*! Drew and that beast had a baby!"

"What beast?"

"Toya! But fortunately Andre seems to not have her beastly ways. He looks just like Drew actually." He showed me a picture in his phone. The little boy looked exactly like Drew.

"Aw! Look at him! He's so cute. Are they still together?" I asked giving Darryl back his phone.

Darryl frowned, "no! He's got a new girlfriend that he's sticking to. She's alright; I'm just tired of breaking in new people. Even though he says he's not, I know that fool is waiting on you."

My heart fluttered. "You think so?" I said trying to mask my excitement.

"You can't try to tell me that you would be content going from my brother to that joke." I smiled but I didn't respond. "I heard you're over there at Gus' singing."

"Singing for peanuts." I smiled

"Is that what you're going to do? Sing for peanuts. You know we can help you."

"I don't see how." I said

Darryl smiled, "you'll see; but first you gotta answer. Do you want to focus on music?"

"Yes, I gotta put my degrees to work somehow."

"I'm gonna take off. Don't be alarmed; I need to twist your friend's mouth up real quick. I won't kill him, but..." Then he winked at me.

I wanted to say, "no! Wait! Stop! Don't!" But Darryl had that crazy look in his eyes so I left it alone. I stayed a little longer then I went home. Jamie texted me a few days later telling me that he got in a fight with three *BIG* guys. He said his jaw was broken and now wired shut, but I should see the other guys. I laughed at the exaggeration; I knew that his jaw had Darryl written all over it.

****

Tonight felt special, I couldn't tell you why. But I held on to the feeling. "Which one should I wear tonight?" I asked Sherrell holding up my options that I narrowed down to two.

"What look are you going for?" She asked with her eyes bouncing between the two of them.

"I was thinking sultry, like Billie Holiday or close." I said

"Ooh! Then definitely the long black. Do you have a flower?"

I pointed to my vanity, "it's silk, but I think it will work."

She walked over to my big silk flower. "You made this barrette yourself?" She said inspecting the flower in amazement.

"I didn't like any of the ones they had at the mall and they were too expensive. I made that for less than five, the most expensive part was the flower."

"You gotta make some barrettes for baby Rosa."

"Of course! As soon as my baby gets some hair she's gonna have barrettes." I stepped inside my small walk in closet to put my dress on. "Can you zip me?" This dress hugged me just right. It was strapless and soft. "Do I look like a singer?"

"You most certainly do! You look fantastic!" Sherrell said grinning from ear to ear.

We tried for a while but we couldn't get the front of my hair like Billie's picture. So I opted to slick it all back and still wear my flower as my decoration. I put on my fake pearls, and my tennis bracelet that Derrick gave me. My earrings were small pearls, and my makeup was simple. When I stood up Sherrell gasped then she started snapping away, taking pictures.

When I got to The Place Where Jazz is Played, Gus was more excited than normal to see me. He was really animated and he told me I looked beautiful as usual. Everybody kept smiling at me like they knew something I didn't. The band Narration and I rehearsed and then I went back to my dressing room like I always do. The hostess Candice came in my room with big eyes. "GUESS WHO'S HERE! YOU WILL NEVER GUESS!" She didn't give me a chance to answer. "SHAMELESS!"

"The rapper?" I asked

"YES GIRL!!! AND HE'S SITTING AT THE FRONT TABLE!!" I got butterflies, after a few months when I didn't hear anything from Darryl I assumed he forgot about me. "That's nice, don't make me nervous. My nerves girl, my nerves!"

She did a happy dance, "I know I'm just so excited!"

Then there was a knock at the door. Candice opened it. It was Gus and he was wearing that huge smile. "Candy tell you who's in the house?"

"Yes, I just didn't expect a rapper." I said turning to my mirror. Gus frowned, "that's not who..."

I looked in the mirror as he walked in my door. It felt like I lost all of my air. I couldn't take my eyes off him; it had been too long since I'd seen him. "Chantel," he said flashing his dimples. I could've melted right out of my chair.

"Derrick," I said as calmly as I could.

We stared at each other for a minute neither one of us speaking then Derrick looked at Candice and Gus who forgot they were standing in the middle of the room ear hustling. "Oh! Yeah! Come on Candice!" Gus clumsily ordered.

When they left the room I watched Derrick but I didn't say anything. My heart was beating too fast. He actually looked nervous. "I didn't realize you were here." I deflated a little bit. He wasn't coming for me. "I... I'm caught off guard by all this." He didn't seem like his normal calm self.

"Have a seat." I said pointing to the couch.

"Ok," he said agreeing with me. "You look beautiful!"

I couldn't help it I smiled. "Thank you, you look good."

He pointed behind him with his thumb, "I'm here with somebody. But she's not really somebody. She's just who I'm with."

"Ok" I said getting a kick out of seeing him unglued.

"The point! I have a point! Did I tell you, you look beautiful?"

I smiled bigger, "you can tell me again. I don't mind."

He chuckled, sat back on the couch and exhaled. "I wanted to know if you wanna sing your song?" I didn't respond right away. "I brought the music if you forgot the words."

"I know the words. I'm trying to gauge my nerves right in this moment."

He flashed his dimples again. "Is that a yes?"

"Sure, you think Narration will be able to keep up?"

"Yes" then he stood up. "I guess saying we need to talk is an understatement huh?"

"You would know." I said trying to be cool.

"I missed you." Then he exhaled, "we're gonna talk." He stood up.

"I'm gonna play a song, then I'll invite you out."

"Ok," then I smiled at him.

He smiled then he walked out the room. I exhaled the most dramatic exhale. I checked my face and dress in the mirror. Who cares who was in the audience Derrick was here.

I walked backstage as Narration was finishing their opening song. Brady went out and introduced D-Rick and everyone went wild. Derrick glanced at me one last time before he provided the saxophone vocals to the song. It was almost as if he was singing. "Over time, I've been building my castle of love...." Gus put his arm around me and swayed with me. When the song was over the house gave him a standing ovation. But how could they not? He was magnificent! When he invited me out the house got loud again and that made me feel really good. I gave each member a hug; I was stalling to calm my nerves. When I got to Derrick he held me as tightly as I held him. The first time we touched in years and his body was warm. We let go at the same time. I took my mark on the stage and the music began. I sang the song Derrick wrote for me with all my heart. Everyone erupted into applause the stage rumbled from the sound of everyone's applause. We held onto each other as we bowed for the audience. Derrick and I walked off the stage together. I could tell he wanted to hug me again but he didn't. Derrick grabbed my hand and led me to the table. It wasn't hard to tell which one was there with Derrick they were all paired off. I smiled at Yussef as Derrick introduced everyone at the table. The girl with Shameless was Yussef's sister, Latia. They looked just a like, no question of whether they were related. Then he introduced me to Valerie. If looks could kill I would've been dead, I understood the feeling. "Should I leave?" I asked wanting to be respectful of his date.

"No, you stay." He said pulling up two extra chairs.

"I need to get with you. That song has to get out to main stream." Lewis said

Derrick had no noticeable reaction. "You think so?"

"I know so. Can I get your info from Latia?"

Derrick handed him a card. "Really Derrick? You're gonna have her sit at our table?" Valerie said like she couldn't take it any more.

Everybody looked at her with a sucks to be you look. "Derrick I'll leave." I said as I attempted to stand.

"Chantel sit! Valerie if you have a problem with my friend sitting here, then you leave. If you choose to stay, I don't want to hear another peep from you about it. Chantel is just as welcome here as you are, if not more." He said in a low rumble.

Valerie looked stuck and like she didn't know what to do. She looked at Latia like she was asking for advice. Latia didn't give her a reaction either. Then Valerie stood up. She gathered her purse and sweater, and then she left. Derrick didn't appear to be phased by her walkout at all. He pushed Valerie's chair away and pulled my chair next to him.

Then the table relaxed, and everyone started talking and enjoying the rest of Narration's set. When it was time I went back on the stage to perform. I sang a couple of my dad's songs, my songs, and then I closed with the song that Derrick dedicated to me. It was perfect that he was there and that I planned my music this way without knowing he'd be here. The house went crazy! Derrick

looked like he wanted to kiss me; he stayed in his seat almost smiling at me holding those dimples prisoner. Derrick hung around after closing waiting for me. "Valerie's not gonna be waiting for you?" I asked as we walked to my car.
"We weren't deep. She'd be a fool." He said staring at me.
I glanced at him and then I glanced away. "What are the odds that you'd show up here tonight?" I said
"I know! How have you been?" He asked still staring.
I shrugged, "ok I guess. How about you?"
He exhaled and looked at the ground. "Chantel I don't do emotional well. Showing feelings has never been my strength. I shut down when things get emotional." He exhaled again.
"You smiled more tonight than I've seen you smile in one setting before. You're making progress."
"That's because you're here. Are you seeing anybody? Anybody I need to kill?" He almost smiled.

"Is that a joke or are you serious?"

"It's only a joke if there's no one."

"Let me think of how to answer that." He stared at me. "There was this guy who was checking for me. Then he said he got into a fight with three guys, and his jaw got broken. Haven't talked to him since. I think he's still recovering, but he wasn't my man, just a friend."
"Sounds like he popped off at the mouth to the wrong person."
"I think he did."
"That's too bad." Derrick faked sympathy.

"So I hear you're an uncle?"

Derrick actually smiled releasing the dimples. "Yeah, he's nothing like his mother thank goodness! And you're an auntie too."
I smiled, "you talked to Cyrus?"
"No," he said staring.
"So what's the deal Derrick?"
"I want you back, but I have a feeling you're gonna be difficult."
He sucked his teeth.
"Tell me the truth...."
He cut me off, "I already know what one of your questions is gonna be. I was younger and dumber. My intention was not to hurt you."

"So you were cheating on me?" I stared at his eyes. His eyes hit the ground. "You kept saying it was gonna be me. Deflecting!"

"I know, you're right." He said

"Is that why you kept me away from your mother?"

"Her reaction was just as painful as yours. I wasn't ready."

"How do I know you're ready now?"

"I guess you'd have to trust me."

"You do know we have no foundation for trust."

"I know, which means I have to start from scratch. Can't you see it's killing me not to kiss you right now?"

"Derrick I haven't been with anyone else!" I felt my anger.

"I know!"

"You know?"

He looked in my eyes. "I know!"

"You hurt me and acted like I was overreacting."

"I know!"

"Why are you always testing me?"

"It's hard to trust someone outside of your family." He said

"I know, but I trusted you!"

He exhaled, "I know. Look, I don't expect this to all be ironed out tonight; but I won't stop until I have you back."

"Whatever Derrick!" I said walking to my car.

I unlocked the door, and then he pushed the door shut. He stood in my face. "Don't disregard me like that. I know I was wrong, but that doesn't stop me from getting angry about being disregarded."

I could feel the warmth from his breath and body. I wanted to kiss him, but I wasn't gonna do it. "Fine."

"You know it only makes you human if you let me kiss you right now."

"A weak human!"

"I won't tell if you won't."

That was the longest and most delicious kiss of my life.

Chapter 11

"Yo! Son! These lyrics…." Shameless was jumping around.

Derrick gave him a knowing look. "Let's go over it again!" Derrick said over the speaker.

Latia and I looked at each other and smiled. We had been in this studio for twelve plus hours working on Shameless' part of the song. "I'm hungry!" Latia called out

"I could eat!" I said, "Derrick are you hungry?"

"I guess so," he said preparing to go again.

"What do you want to eat? I don't know what's around here." Derrick took his cellphone out his pocket. He handed it to me. "Call my cousin Sasha, she lives out here. Ask her to suggest someplace."

I grabbed a pen and paper then Latia and I stepped out of the studio. I called Sasha, she answered on the first ring. "Hey D-Rick!" She sang

"Hi, this is Chantel. I'm not sure if you remember me, I'm Derrick's friend. He told me to call you cause we're down here at Malcolm's studio and we were hoping you could suggest somewhere good that we could get some take out or delivery."

I could hear a smile in her voice, "Which studio are you at?"

I told her which one and she told me she would bring food; she was leaving the office when I called. She got to the studio faster than I thought she would. She brought Thai food and it smelled delicious. We gladly took a food break. Derrick shared information about the song with Sasha and she said she liked it. Shameless said this song was greatness in the making. When he asked Derrick what inspired him to write and arrange such a beautiful song the room fell silent. Derrick looked at me for what seemed like forever, and then he replied "love." Everybody smiled, I couldn't stop blushing. "There was this little girl whose humility caught my eye. When everybody else was thinking they were too good to put in work, she seemed happy to do it. She was a hard worker, and never above anybody. That stood out to me. I started watching her, taking her in on a day-to-day basis without her knowing I was there. I would hear this melody like it was her theme music. Over time the words to express the song came too."

"Whoa! Look at you! Gushing with love all over you! Must be nice." Sasha said, "this is so unlike you!"

Derrick cut his eyes at her, "YOU BETTER NOT TELL NOBODY!" We all laughed he didn't.

"Let me give you my checking account number so you can make regular deposits. Black mail can get expensive." She teased, "Where are you guys staying and how long will you be out here?"

"I have a house out here, we're gonna roll that way in a little bit." Shameless said

"Chantel and I are staying until this track is ready. Lewis has a few days out here. Malcolm's engineer is gonna smooth everything out and then its going on his current project." Derrick said

"How long did contract negotiations take?" She asked

"Not long. My project is wrapping up any ways. My first release from it is on the radio now. I wanna perform this song live. It'll be good exposure for Chantel. We got a few more collaborations in the works. The world is gonna know who Chantel is." Shameless said

Sasha smiled, "are you ready? Your life is about to forever change."

"It makes me nervous, but I'm excited!" I said, talking about it made my stomach do flips. I made my daddy PROMISE not to tell his sisters about me being in the studio working on my own project. I could tell it was hard for him, but I was happy he chose me over telling them. I brought Grandma Rosa and my little brothers to the Studio in Oakland a few times. She told me she was so happy for me. Grandma Rosa and Malcolm hit it off immediately. I saw another side to him the first time they met. Malcolm was still very serious but his whole presence was endearing. He kept making sure grandma had any and everything she could want. Grandma said she liked him very much. The boys were all very quiet whenever he came around, they didn't test Malcolm like they always do with Cyrus. They all looked at him like they look at Derrick, like he was the coolest guy to walk the face of the planet. Adon especially took to Malcolm like he was a favorite uncle. My daddy thanked Malcolm for taking care of me. Malcolm didn't say much to my daddy; I couldn't tell if that was a good thing or bad. He kind of had the same look on his face like

Derrick would, like they tolerated him but they saw something I didn't see. Derrick would never say anything against my daddy, but he didn't say anything good other than he was a very talented musician.

Around midnight we decided to throw in our hats and get some rest. Sasha told me to call her when we had some down time this weekend so we could all hang out. On the ride over to Lewis's place Derrick pointed out the building where his parents shared a condo. He told me depending on how our schedule ran he hoped to be able to take me by there. I didn't know if that meant his mother was out here and we'd see her or what. I didn't question it; I just knew he wasn't getting back "in" until he properly introduced me to his mother. Which still hadn't happened yet. Honestly I was happy just to have him back in my life.

These last few months with him have been great. We talk on the phone all the time, which is good because we've both changed during our time apart. As if it was possible he's quieter now, and there's something in his facial expressions that is new. I haven't put my finger on it quite yet. He said that there have been some things going on in his family that has them all kind of scattered handling business. I know that Mitigated has really taken off and they're now across the country. It amazes me how that little boy from Oakland turned his temporary staffing company into a countrywide business. Malcolm has set up a presence in all the major cities; Derrick has become his right hand man in all his endeavors. If Malcolm or Juan can't make it Derrick goes in.

Mitigated is not Malcolm's only business. He has quite a few Drew's barbershop locations. I go to the Drew's in Richmond per Yussef's referral to this lady named Roz, his stepmom, who braids my hair. What I love about her is that she won't sit you in her chair and go after the money. She takes her time, even though she moves quickly, and does my hair right. She makes sure that my braids are done to where there's not a lot of tension on my hairline. With Roz braiding my hair it had grown so much and it's so healthy. I keep it braided to keep things simple.

Malcolm also owns a bunch of recording studios all over California. Derrick brought us down here to the one in LA cause he liked the equipment in this particular studio best. The one in Oakland that I go to is nice, but this one was a lot more LUSH and fabulous. That's just the ventures I know of. I know he owns property, etc. Malcolm is spread pretty thin all over the place.

When we pulled up to Shameless', or Lewis as Latia calls him, house I was surprised that it looked so normal. It was a nice house, but it didn't look like a rapper's house from outside. Latia told us to come in the kitchen for a nightcap. She played bartender, and she poured the men something brown. She called our drinks buttery nipples, and it was delicious. We sat at the table relaxing. This was definitely not Latia's first time here, she knew where everything was; and the way she took care of everything and Lewis they seemed like an old married couple more than "just friends" as she kept demanding. Lewis wouldn't argue with her, but he didn't look at her or treat her like they were just friends. "So you gonna be up to touring with me?" Lewis said as he took a drink.
"Yeah, I guess I'm nervous cause I don't know what to expect. What's it like traveling from city to city like that?"
"I think of it like I'm a traveling salesman. I go from city to city encouraging people to not only buy my newest product but to continue to support my old ones too. After the awards ceremony we're gonna be like peas and carrots." Then he took another drink. "Wait more like before, cause we're gonna have to shoot the video." Then he looked at Latia, "will you be my video vixen?" he smiled at her.
"NO! NO! ABSOLUTELY NOT!" She said smiling.
"One of these days I'm gonna get you to say yes to something." He smiled
"Keep dreaming." She said still smiling.
"When does your project release?" He asked me.
"I don't have a release date yet. I guess as soon as I'm done touring with you, my stuff will come out."
Lewis whistled, "sounds like the next two to three years of your life are gonna be hectic. You guys ready?"
"I guess so, how do you guys manage?" I asked
"We're not together!" Latia said, all three of us blank stared at her. She laughed, "what? We're not!" She said using our empty glasses as an excuse to get up and make more.

"That's how we manage, we don't," He said annoyed.

"Let's change the subject, this can get ugly." Latia said rolling her eyes.

Derrick was taking everything in, not saying too much. Latia showed us to the guest room. I tried not to show a reaction when she automatically put us in the same room. Derrick smiled releasing his dimples. "This is not funny." I said smiling.
"You want me to sleep on the floor?" He asked
"Yeah right, we both know you aren't gonna do that." I laughed
He laughed, "Dang Skippy I ain't sleeping on the floor. You want me to ask for a separate room?"
"You can stay as long as you don't feel on my booty." I said being funny.
"I can't make you any promises." He said staring at me.
"Whatever," I said laughing him off and taking my bag into the bathroom. I brushed my teeth then I put on my flannel pajama pants and tank shirt top. I put my scarf on my hair, brushed my teeth. When I came out the bathroom Derrick was staring at his phone. "Your turn!" I said happily.
He cocked his head to the side as he looked at my pajama pants. "Cute!" He said as he pulled at them when he walked past me into the bathroom. I got into the huge had to be a Cal King bed and tried my best to look sleep when he came out the bathroom. I peeked and I knew it! He was naked, I closed my eyes and I told my body to calm down cause we weren't getting ANY tonight. He got in the bed and he sat up, he didn't even look at my face. "So faking! You're not sleep." I tried to stop myself from laughing but it came bursting out anyways. His eyes were a little droopy from all the drinks. "What are we gonna do when you're on tour?"

"I don't know," I said sitting up.

"We need a plan." He said like he was trying to figure it out.
"I don't know if this is a good time to start for us. We both know how faithful you can be when I'm away." I smiled a painful smile.
He grabbed my hand, "I love you, but I don't want to lie to you and say I can do it."
"Should I do like Latia and deny that we're in a relationship?" Derrick sucked his teeth. "It seems to work for them." I said
"It doesn't work." He said cutting his eyes at me. "Surely you can see that. And if you can't you will when you're out there with him. It doesn't work. We have to have a plan."
"Well I can tell you I'm not gonna wait for you while you hump the whole world." I said with an attitude.

"You're my woman Chantel! No matter how far apart we are. I know I can't be there all the time. I've got business and family responsibilities. I will be with you as much as I can be."

"Is that the plan, that you'll be with me as much as you can be?" I asked

"I guess so. I need to think." He said hitting his head.

I laughed, "goodnight D-Rick!" I said laying down again.

"Seriously? You're gonna go to sleep? You've been singing to me, we drank. Now you're gonna go to sleep?"

"Yes, I'm going to sleep. We're going back to the studio tomorrow I need rest." I closed my eyes.

He kissed my cheek, he rubbed my back. "I miss you, I know you miss me."

I huffed, "I've gotten used to living a celibate life. There's lotion in the bathroom if you need help." I pulled the covers up to my neck. Even though I really wanted to give in, I knew I couldn't. Even more important, Derrick knew I couldn't either but boy was he testing me. When I didn't respond to him anymore he tried to act mad. He scooted to the edge of the bed on his side. So I sprawled out and proceeded to fall asleep hard. In the morning Derrick and I awoke to the sound of fools talking heck of loud for no reason. Derrick's red eye popped open as I was opening mine. He was up and pissed before I could reach out to him. In that moment I wished I would've gave him some cause then he'd be a lot calmer in this moment. "Where are you going?"

He was putting pants on. "They need to shut up!"

"Derrick this is not your house, you can't..." He walked out the door while I was talking. I ran to my suitcase and grabbed my sweatshirt. I ran down the hallway. Latia had her scarf still on and she was trying to pull Lewis back. I didn't realize the noise was stemming from an argument. Derrick had his hands in his pockets but he was still mad.

"You still owe me!" The big guy yelled in Lewis's face.

"I can't believe you brought this to my house! If you don't get out of here!" Lewis said

"I'm not leaving without my money!" The guy said folding his arms.

"Nigga this Beverly Hills! The police should be here before I dial! Get out!

The guy shook his head, "nope. And they ain't leaving either!" He gestured behind him at the equally big guys relaxing in the doorway.

"Can you guys hurry this up, I'm trying to sleep!" Derrick said unaffected by the scene.

The guy looked Derrick up and down. Derrick looked like a skinny shrimp compared to him. "Take your butt back to sleep! Ain't nobody talking to you no way!" He barked at Derrick like he was running things in this house. Then he turned his attention back to Lewis. "I'm not leaving here without my money!"

"This argument is between you, the studio, and the label. I'm not required to pay you anything! This is the last time I'm gonna say it nicely. Get out of my house!" Lewis commanded

"I'm not leaving and you need to have your tramp fix us something to..."

Derrick fired on him! The guy went down like a sack of potatoes. We were all caught off guard. The guys at the door jumped and straightened up. One guy came at Derrick and every strike Derrick made echoed in the hallway. That guy went down too, the last guy standing had his gun out. Derrick rolled his eyes at the guy and turned his back to him. "What is this about? I'm tired and you got fools yelling, and calling my cousin out her name. I want them gone and I want to go back to sleep!"

"Um! Excuse me! You don't turn your back on somebody who has a gun!" The guy in the doorway said.

Derrick waved him off and continued looking at Lewis.

"Raymond, you not gonna shoot nobody put the gun away! We'll tell them you went down fighting too." Lewis barked, Raymond lowered his gun. You could see fear in his face. "This is ridiculous! Baby go call security." He said to Latia.

The big guy started stirring on the floor. "Stan I know you're mad about your money. I don't blame you. You're in a different league and you gotta play the game differently. I don't owe you money. Get a lawyer and go handle your business; but don't EVER come to my house again! Just in case it's unclear for any reason let me say, we are not friends. If you EVER IN YOUR LIFE DISRESPECT MY WIFE AGAIN IT'S LIGHTS OUT FOR YOU!" Lewis said

The guy shook his head trying to get his bearings about himself. "What did you hit me with?" He asked still laying on his stomach.

"I barely touched you! Stop being dramatic!" Derrick barked with no sympathy. "Don't ever disrespect my cousin again you hear me!"

"Who's your cousin?" The guy said slowly getting on all fours. "She is!"

The guy got up slowly. The guy had a big knot and a small cut by his eye. The knot kept growing. He moved his face like it hurt. Then he cut his eyes at Derrick. "Nobody has ever hit me like that!"

"There's only one me and I'd like to go back to sleep if you don't mind. You can have your conversation and whatever. Don't disrespect my cousin, and don't wake me up! Got it!"

"Yeah nigga whatever!" The guy said.

Derrick cut his eyes at him. "But you heard me!"

"I heard you!" He said irritated.

"Latia come out of here, let them talk." Derrick commanded.

Latia did as she was told. She grabbed my hand and pulled me with her to the master suite on the second floor. She was breathing hard when she shut the door. "Is he always like that? He's almost as bad as Malcolm." She said a little jittery.

"He's a little pent up." I smiled

"Gees! Knocking people out."

"It was kind of cool huh!" I smiled a knowing smile.

"Yes! When people like that have your back, why would you fear anyone?"

"I know right." I said

"Are they gonna have you travel with someone?"

"I hadn't thought of it. I don't know." Now I was wondering.

"More than likely. Drew has my brother on his girl and she works a nine to five. You're about to be out there with a different caliber of people." Then she swallowed. "When Lewis is on the road, we are not together. I designed it that way."

"Ok."

"I don't want to know about it either. I can only imagine what you're gonna see."

Latia's words stayed on my mind all day. I asked why Lewis referred to her as his wife. She said he wants to get married, but she wasn't ready. He gave her the title already. Derrick had a car service come pick us up and take us to a hotel. Then the car took us to the studio. We worked for a few hours then Latia and Lewis had to go to the airport and go their separate ways. Derrick almost smiled at me, "you wanna keep working?"

"I'm kind of tired." Since he was giving me an option.

"Sasha's gonna come pick us up. Is it cool with you if we hang out with her?"

He was up to something. "Of course." I said eyeing him.

"Stop being so suspicious woman." He flashed dimples at me.

When Sasha came she seemed normal. She convinced Derrick that we needed to try this new restaurant after she made a stop. They seemed like they were both acting. I flashed Derrick another look from the front seat, and he winked at me. We pulled up to a guarded gate, Sasha gave them her name and which studio we were going to. This place was huge, and when we got out of the car all you heard was music when someone came out of the door of the studio we were going into. Derrick grabbed my hand and kind of led me. When we walked inside we walked down a long hallway with two bathrooms and dressing rooms on either side. When we walked out of the hallway I saw a group of guys and girls dancing. "AGAIN! 5, 6, 7, 8!" She commanded. My face completely lit up when I realized it was Amber. "That was better everybody, but when you hit that eight count you should be here!" She hit the move. The dancers were taking mental notes. She had her hair pulled back in a bun. She had stretchy pants on and a T-shirt that stopped at her stomach unintentionally showing off her rocking body. They were all covered in sweat. She looked up and smiled when she saw us. "Everybody take a ten minute water break. I'll be right back." She came over and kissed each of our cheeks. Does that mean she likes me? "How are you sweetheart long time no see." She said to me.

SHE REMEMBERS ME!!! "I'm good, how are you?" I tried to say as calmly as I could.

"I'm good." Then she turned to Derrick. "I need you!" She smiled.

"Me?" He didn't smile back.

"Yes, you!" She got excited. "I need to demonstrate a salsa routine I want them to duplicate. Sasha you too." She told them what she needed in what I assume is dancer language cause I didn't follow it. She told them how she wanted the dance to go. They both said they got it but they didn't rehearse at all.

Amber gave me a chair next to some other people on the sideline. Then she told everybody to watch the three of them. She counted

off, and they moved fluidly. Derrick spun one then the other. My mouth fell open watching my man move like that. I had no idea. Everyone stood up clapping when they were done. Then Amber told them to take their marks and then she counted off. They were definitely professional dancers; they picked up those amazing moves FAST. Sasha and Derrick sat by me and we all watched in amazement as Amber directed the dancers. I loved every minute of it. She reminded the dancers of the start time tomorrow and then she dismissed them. She talked with the director about marks for the dancers, etc. Then she asked where we were going to dinner. Derrick told her we were in the same hotel so we'd meet her in the lobby. Then she invited me to ride with her to the hotel. I smiled extra big as I released Derrick's hand without a second thought about him. I could hear Sasha laughing, but I didn't look back to check for him at all. I sat in the front seat of her rental car grinning from ear to ear. We made LOVELY small talk all the way to the hotel. I was so cheesy and giddy; I kept laughing which made her laugh too. She excused herself at the hotel to go cleanup and change. I smiled really big at Derrick, he almost smiled back. We had a couple cocktails at the bar. "Drinking on empty stomachs, who's supposed to drive?" Amber tisked.
Sasha smiled at Amber. "Auntie slash Cousin slash second Momma can you drive us?" She said batting her eyes.

Amber smiled, "no. Let's go!" She said ushering us towards the Lobby. There was a limo waiting for us. Sasha and I got really excited, Derrick was.... Derrick. Sasha told the driver where to take us. In the car we talked about everything. Sasha got a phone call on the way, she was giving someone instructions. Then she told Amber JoJo was coming too. The restaurant had a line out front that went half way down the block. Suddenly my jeans, heels, and blouse didn't feel dressy enough. Sasha led the way, she told the hostess to add another chair to our table. Then she went back outside to the limo. When she came back inside the hostess sat us down at our table. The atmosphere was really tranquil. The lighting was low, with candles on each table. There was enough space around each table where you weren't listening to each other's conversation unless you focus real hard. Whenever someone walked in most people's heads turned. So I assume some pretty big deal people come here. We ordered more cocktails and appetizers. Then Derrick's cousin JoJo walked in. He said hi to Derrick and me then he gave Amber and Sasha hugs and kisses. "When do you go back?" He asked Amber.

"Couple days" then she looked at me. "I like to be around for my grandson as much as possible."

"It's hard enough to take in that you are his mother." I said pointing at Derrick. "I can't imagine you as a grandmother. You look like you could be his sister not mother."

Amber blushed, "thanks sweetheart."

"So we're gonna have an actual celebrity in the family." JoJo said smiling at me.

"You remember me?" I was surprised. When I was at his house all those years ago, I thought I blended in pretty well.

"Of course, you've come to my house and you were singing at EA." He said

JoJo spoke just like Derrick and his brothers. Same mannerisms and everything. You could tell they were all close growing up. I imagine that they had a blast running around Oakland as there own little contained unit. JoJo picked up his drink and as he moved it to his mouth he asked Sasha who our audience was. I didn't realize how red Sasha's face was until he said that. Whoever it was they were behind me so I didn't turn around but I watched everyone else's reactions. Sasha said she was another jealous female. "She better turn away or she's gonna bring the Oakland out in me real fast!" She said

"Who is she?" Amber asked

"A insecure female who can't handle her man is all."

"What does her man have to do with you?" Amber asked

"I didn't know he was married. Instead of checking her man, she wanna be harassing me." Sasha said

Our waiter came to our table. "How's everything?"

"Can you do me a...." Sasha's Oakland accent came out. She took a deep breath. Said something to herself to calm herself. "The people at that table over there." She pointed at the table behind me.

"They're bugging me. Make them stop or kick them out."

"Right away!" He hurried away.

Then the restaurant manager appeared at the table behind us. Everyone was looking so I turned around. The woman looked like a Beverly Hills beauty, blonde and thin. Her eyes were evil and she looked angry. Her friends shot daggers our way as well. The manager spoke calmly with them and they spoke at the same time.

After a few minutes the woman flipped Sasha off and then she and her friends walked out. Sasha made a kissy face at the woman then she laughed to calm herself. JoJo looked irritated.

"Joseph you ok?" Amber asked

"Who wants to hear that their niece was fooling around with a married man!"

"Don't be a hypocrite!" Amber said

"Exactly! Thank you Amber! Yeah! Who are you to talk?" Sasha said full of attitude.

JoJo smiled real big, "oh yeah! But still! I'm your uncle!"

"JoJo you're barely two years older than me. Can you leave all that uncle crap on the table!"

"Does your momma know?" JoJo asked

"Does yours? What kind of a dumb question is that?" She shot back.

"Dumb? You need to calm yourself little girl. I'm not one of these punk white collar fools you be messing with out here." JoJo glared at her, he reminded me of Derrick.

Sasha huffed; the table was quiet for a minute. I looked at Derrick and he shrugged. Eventually conversation returned to our table and everyone relaxed. Derrick touched my leg under the table. I reached down to hold his hand and he moved my hand out the way. I kicked his foot, but he kept pulling at my top. I scooted my chair closer to Amber and away from him. He almost smiled then he excused himself from the table. Amber smiled the most endearing smile at me. I felt like I was going to float away.

When we got back to the hotel Amber hugged us goodnight. She said she had to be up early. Then she told me she was happy that we got a chance to interact. I couldn't stop smiling, that was all I wanted.

When we got into our room I went straight into the shower. I was excited to finally be with Derrick again. When I came out the bathroom he smiled at my nightgown then he got in the shower. I turned on the TV as I waited in the middle of the bed. Then I saw his condoms on the nightstand. I frowned at them cause we never used them, why did he need them. My body tensed up, I crossed my arms as I waited for an explanation. Derrick's smile dropped when he saw my face. "What?"

"Why do you have those?" I said angry.

He looked at the nightstand then he looked at me confused. "Condoms?"

"Yes!" I spit at him.

His confused look didn't go away. "I'm lost."

"We've never used them Derrick, why do you have them?"

"For your protection."

"You have something?" My stomach fluttered.

"No, but I also wasn't sitting at home milking my broken heart."

"You weren't a virgin when we got together. Why do we need them now when we didn't need them before?"

He rubbed my leg. "As a child I made that decision. It wasn't the smartest way to operate. I couldn't live with myself if I allowed my selfishness to hurt you."

"What's changed? Are you not strapping up? Did you have something?"

"Nothing worth all this. The condoms are for your protection." I started to say something else and he kissed me. We made out for a long time. He put the condom on and then he tried to go in, but he couldn't. He looked at me in disbelief. He told me to relax and I tried to relax, but he wasn't getting in no matter what. He backed up and looked at me. "What's wrong?"

"Nothing." I felt horrible.

"Obviously that's not true." He said trying not to look irritated. "You're so tense I can't even get a finger in there. These condoms bother you that much?"

"I guess so." I said putting my eyes on the bed. "Have we changed that much? Is there somebody at home that you don't use condoms with? And now I'm your side chick? I don't know Derrick maybe we're not ready to go here yet."

"No we're ready, but you need to live in the moment. This is a Derrick and Chantel moment and you're turning it into a what about everything else. Do you want me?" He asked staring into my eyes.

"Of course I do. I don't want anybody else. I guess it's hard knowing that you're out there and I've been waiting on you." I said deflating.

"Here we go, get it out." He said sitting up straight to take in what I was going to say.

"You accused me of going wild once we finally did it. I kind of made it a point to prove you wrong. And it sounds like you lost it.

We're not even saying we're going to be together cause you can't not be out there." I looked at him. "So you're out there and I'm out there. What if we meet people we develop feelings for? We're gonna agree to keep it moving?"

"There's only one me." He said

"Same here, but you can't wait for me?"

"I can lie and say yes I will wait. I'm honestly telling you, I don't think I can do that." I blew air. "If you want me to lie to you, I can but; that would be hard because I've always been honest with you. I'm not worried about catching feelings for someone else. No one will ever mean to me what you do."

"What do I mean to you?" I asked

"I love you! You're my heart! Nobody knows me or will ever know me like you do." He said staring me in my eyes.

I felt my body relax a little. "Are you just saying that cause you want some?"

He smiled flashing his dimples. "What does your heart say?"

"Tell me you love me again." I smiled

****

"We don't know how this song fits in with the tone of the rest of your project." The female executive said.

"This song is the icing on the cake. I'm not under contract. You guys can keep this project. I'll make another one!" Lewis said standing up.

Juan looked at Derrick and I. We were in the conference room, in the San Francisco office on a video conference with Shameless and his label. "Hold on Lewis, lets discuss this." The guy said, "I actually like the song and I see exactly how it relates. The question is, will your audience follow it?"

"We shoot the video next week. After the awards performance, the video will go live and people are going to be into it. Trust me!" The guy said, "It won't hurt the project to leave this song in but, my concern is how you have this contract written up." The guy gestured towards me. "You're barely collecting royalties on this song. Almost everything goes to them. Why would you be ok with that? You're pushing it out there to mainstream."

"Play it again!" Lewis ordered the guy in the corner. "Close your eyes and listen!" They played the entire song. "You're vibing with your significant other and then this song comes on. Do you know how many babies are gonna be made to this song! This is his song," he said pointing to Derrick. "I'm just honored that he's letting me push it for him. I don't have all day. Either you're agreeing to my terms or you're not."

My heart was beating, I didn't understand why he was doing all this he could've dropped it and kept moving. The executives and Lewis continued talking for a while. When they finally gave in I wanted to scream. Lewis looked at the camera and he told us, "and this is how history was made! I'll see you next week."

Juan turned off the volume on the microphone but we could still see into their conference room. He had paperwork in a folder. "Ok Chantel," he exhaled. "We know Lewis, we don't feel there's any real threat with him. If something changes you let us know immediately!" He flipped through pages. "Brandy is going to be with you while you travel. We're gonna put one more person with you. My thoughts are...." He drummed his fingers on the table. "If you're traveling with females no one will question it."

"Why do I need anyone?" I asked

"Safety. You're gonna be around a bunch of guy's day in and day out. Someone might start feeling their-self while you're out there." "Why two?" I asked

"One may have to leave for whatever reason. This way all our bases are covered."

Even though it was my career Malcolm was overseeing everything. Malcolm had Ryan Wallace and Sonny Derrick's cousin and uncle handle all my contract negotiations for Shameless' single.

When we walked out the office, I went to Brandy's cubical. "So I hear we're going on vacation together." I whispered.

Brandy smiled and hugged me, "we're gonna have so much fun!" She whispered back. "Are you traveling as Derrick's girlfriend?" She asked

I thought it was an interesting question. "No."

"Even better!" She got excited.

"Why is that better?"

"Cause you'll be able to mingle. Meet new people." She said

Derrick was waiting for me by the door. "I gotta go but we'll talk." I said hugging her and then walking out with Derrick.

When we got to the lobby Derrick exhaled. "I want you to meet someone." I looked at him with a question mark. I wasn't aware that there was anyone else to meet. "Let's get in the car." We walked to the garage and got in his black SUV. He put his keys in the ignition. "I love you!" Then he started the car. We drove to Richmond; I thought he was taking me to the cafe again. This time we drove into the heart of the city. We pulled up to a two-story house. The house looked like it had been there since the fifties. The yard was neatly trimmed; everything about the house was neat. It stood out in the neighborhood. Derrick exhaled and then he told me to come on. I got out of the car and waited for him. He grabbed my hand firmly, I looked at him and his face was very serious. He knocked on the door and a woman answered. She was very excited to see him. She gave him a big hug and invited us in. "Auntie Lorraine this is my woman Chantel." He said introducing us. This woman looked at me smiled and hugged me. She was black so I was a little confused. I had gotten used to meeting his other family who were mostly all white. "It's nice to meet you." She said "It's nice to meet you too."

"How's she doing today?" He asked her.

"She's so so, but you guys can go up." She said walking back to her study room.

Derrick grabbed my hand again. He led me up the stairs and down the hall. We stopped at the second door, and then he knocked lightly. "Come in" someone said. When he opened the door there was a woman sitting on the bed looking out the window. She looked at Derrick and smiled. "David! I was beginning to think you forgot about your momma!" She said really happy to see him. Derrick squeezed my hand, and instantly the room got hot. "I want you to meet somebody." He said

"I already know Patricia. How are you doing baby." She said giving me a hug

"Grandma this is Chantel." He said

She looked at him for a long time. "Derrick?" He shook his head yes. She looked like reality settled over her. She half smiled, "how you doing baby?"

He almost smiled, "I'm good. I wanted you to meet Chantel."

"Hello" she said looking me over. "How's Amber? How are your brothers?" She asked

"They're doing good. How are you?" He asked with sad eyes.

"I'm ok most days. I miss my baby though. I can't believe he's gone." She said rubbing her stomach like there was a void.

I assumed she was talking about Derrick's biological father. He talked to her very gently, and he waited for her to respond. After awhile his Auntie came up to the room. She stood in the doorway smiling at Derrick interacting with his grandmother. Then she motioned for me to follow her out the room. "Would you like something to drink? Lemonade, water, kool-aide?"

"Lemonade if it's not too much trouble." I said following her down the stairs.

"How's Amber?" She asked smiling.

"She's good."

"I don't know how she manages everything. She works so hard." She said. Then she kind of stared at me. "How long have you and Derrick known each other?"

"Since I was sixteen." I said

"Does he talk about his father's family?" She asked

"Derrick talk?" I smiled

"He's always been a different kind of child. I've never really known a baby who barely cried or laughed as little as he did." She exhaled

"Even as a little kid he was like this?" I asked sitting on the stool at the counter and sipping my lemonade.

"Yep. When I came to see him for the first time, he stared at me. No cry or anything. His eyes moved around looking at everybody. It was like he studied your face. He didn't startle easy or anything, he was always a different child. How is he with you?"

"Fine I guess. We talk, he's an amazing man!"

"Amazing?" She raised an eyebrow.

"I've never met anyone like him. He's the smartest person I know.

It's like he's a human computer almost, he rarely forgets anything.

He doesn't mind explaining things so I understand them, I love that. It seems like the world knows not to mess with him, but he's always my gentle giant."

She smiled, "that's good to hear. How's Andrew doing? He used to drop by all the time. I barely see him anymore."

"I guess he's busy, I haven't seen him much lately either. You know how it goes." I said not wanting to say he has a new

girlfriend in case it's not public knowledge.

Then I heard slow foot steps, Derrick was walking with his grandmother. She had tears pouring down her face. "Dionne what's wrong?"

"David doesn't remember our song!" Then she put her hands on his face. "How could you forget baby? It was all we had sometimes. When your dad would leave we'd sing it, how come you don't remember?" She started crying out loud

Derrick looked so hurt; I leaped off the stool and hugged him. I didn't know what else to do. "Tell me how the song goes again." Auntie Lorraine said

"It goes…" She was trying to remember, "it goes…" She looked up at the ceiling and then down at the floor. "OH MY GOODNESS DAVID! I FORGOT TOO!" Then she started laughing. "Guess it wasn't that memorable if neither one of us remembers." Then she patted my arm, "Patricia you've always been a nice girl. Thank you for being good to my baby."

I looked at Derrick, "who's Patricia?" I whispered. Derrick shrugged.

"David remember when we used to go to the city and play at the beach? You were so cute running around. Make sure you take your babies out there. The fresh air will do them good." Derrick didn't say anything; he stared at his grandmother with sad eyes.

We stayed for a little while longer then Derrick looked like he couldn't take anymore. So I looked at my watch and told him we needed to get moving. I hugged his aunt and grandmother goodbye, and then we got in the car. Derrick was real quiet, and I didn't know what to say so I waited for him to say something. When he pulled up to the garage gate, he entered a code and the door opened. I stared at him, cause I didn't give him my code. He parked in visitor parking. We took the elevator to the fifth floor. This was the top floor, and all the apartments up here were three bedroom and two level. I had the Master suit on the first floor and Cyrus and Sherrell occupied the bedrooms on the upper level. When we walked in the door Sherrell was pacing. She exhaled big when she saw me. "CHANTEL I NEED YOU! I need to go to work, and Cyrus has mandatory last minute overtime. I didn't want to call you, but since you're here would you mind keeping baby Rosa until Cyrus comes home?"

"Of course where is she?"

Sherrell grabbed her things, "she's in the crib." Then she ran out the door.

Derrick beat me to baby Rosa's room. She was standing in her crib holding on to the railing. She smiled the prettiest smile when she saw Derrick. Derrick picked her up and he had the same look on his face when he was holding Dwayne's little girl. She kept smiling at him and watching his face. Sherrell called from the car to tell me that the baby had just eaten and had her diaper changed. Derrick brought the baby in the living room. "She's so pretty." He said looking at her.

I eyed him, "you look mighty comfortable holding that baby."

"Babies really do calm your soul when you're aching huh."

"That was pretty heavy huh. What happened to her?" I asked

"My momma said she was in a bad relationship with my grandfather. I guess some people weren't built strong enough to deal with foolishness."

"Where's your father?"

"Malcolm is probably at home." He cut his eyes at me.

"Derrick please talk to me. You know all about my family. You had to have taken me there for a reason."

"Now you know all of me. It's too much to talk about. Right now anyways. I wanted you to see, so you'd know. Just hold on to it." He said returning his attention back to baby Rosa.

I watched them for a little while. Baby Rosa wasn't afraid of Derrick either. "Do you want one?"

He frowned, "not any time soon. What about you? Did you change your mind?" He said looking at the baby.

"Only if it's with you." I said watching his reaction.

He smirked, "yeah, we'll see."

"You don't believe me?"

"I guess we'll have to see. Your world is about to be turned upside down. We'll see how much time you have to even think about me." I moved closer to him, "you don't think I'm gonna think about you?"

"You'll be too busy."

I kissed the side of his face. "I'll never be too busy for you."
                              ****

Brandy and I walked into the studio. It was just after eight in the morning and Amber was already sweating the dancers out. I got so excited when I saw that she was the choreographer for this video. She stopped dancing to come over and hug me. I introduced her to

Brandy. She told me to watch the dancers and that we would have time later where she could work with me individually. I wasn't a professional dancer so I welcomed the idea. At lunch break Lewis came on the set, he was talking to the director and a little to Amber. He was very focused and not very social. I heard the director tell him they wouldn't need him until tomorrow. Amber told me a lot of my portion was gonna be in front of a blue screen. She explained the storyboard for the video, since I wasn't considered the main artist I wasn't a part of any of the planning. So basically Shameless was gonna be pursuing a girl the whole video, while I was singing. The song would be his theme music to get this girl. So they had to shoot me in all these different looks to piece them together to tell the story. The dancers had corresponding costumes to mine and they would have to do their routine in each costume perfectly. I did the stuff Amber showed me but I felt stupid. She had the director record me so I could see how stiff I looked. She laughed and leveled with me. "It's gonna feel stupid at first, but once you get the hang of it, I promise it will translate well on screen." After her little pep talk I did the stuff she told me to do. I still felt stupid, but when they played them back even I was amazed. Amber smiled real big at me. It was after two in the morning when we finally left the set. We were coming back in five hours. Brandy and I dove under our covers. I screamed at the alarm when it went off. I begged Brandy to get in the shower first so I could get the last few drops of sleep in before it was time to go. We were holding each other up when we met Amber down in the lobby. She told us she needed coffee pronto, and we drug our tired bones to the coffee shop on site. I asked for a double cappuccino. Brandy asked for the same. Amber ordered some fancy huge drink, and then we climbed into her rental car and made our way to the studio. Some of the dancers had the nerve to be energized and ready to go. While I was in hair and makeup Amber worked with the dancers. As soon as I was ready they started shooting my parts. I didn't know how to pretend like I was singing so I had to sing for real. I pretended like I was singing to Derrick, then everything felt normal. When I watched the play back I couldn't believe I was watching myself. I told my father to make sure he encouraged everyone to watch the awards ceremony and then they could all be surprised together.

Three days later my parts of the scenes were done. Shameless had a little more shooting to do, but none of his was choreography. So we flew back to the Bay with Amber. She was so much fun, I had to keep reminding myself that she was Derrick's mother. I thanked Brandy for coming with me and I told her I'd see her again in a couple of months.

****

Sound check went great. I couldn't believe in a few hours this auditorium was going to be full of people. Then millions of people were going to be listening to me sing. I was so nervous I couldn't see straight. Lewis said we were going to some club after the show to celebrate. He told Brandy and I to stay close by. Since I wasn't somebody there wouldn't be a costume change for the performance. I was fine with it cause I really liked the way my dress hugged my body. Celebrities started arriving and I did my best not to be star struck. A lot of people were going crazy backstage when the singer Torrie arrived. She wasn't anything like they portrayed her on TV. They made her seem so nice and sweet, and she was a horrible diva. I took notes on how not to be. Brandy and I talked with the dancers as we watched the show from the green room. When it was our time the announcers announced that Chantel featuring Shameless would be up next. Lewis smiled at me, "You're name first." I couldn't believe he did that. We took our marks on the stage. This was it! My moment to shine, this would make me or break me. I closed my eyes and thought about Derrick. How this was all his fault! If he would've left well enough alone I could be at home on the couch with him right now, admiring others for their talents and never thinking about my own. When we came back from commercial the announcers announced my song, my heartbeat was so loud I could barely hear anything else. I couldn't believe I was doing this. I opened my mouth and I sang my heart out. The audience was swaying to my groove; I took that as a good sign. We weren't half way through the song and people were up already. People started screaming like they couldn't take it. By the time Lewis came people were already gone digging my groove. I have never heard the sound of that many people applauding all at once, it sounds like thunder. When the song was over the announcers were sitting there speechless. "When somebody tells Shameless to bring his A game, he brings his A game! I'm sure that won't be the last time we hear that song." One announcer said.

187

"Can somebody bring me some cold water, I need to cool down!" The other announcer said.

Back stage the dancers and I screamed, while we jumped around cheering. Then I ran to the bathroom and threw up, I was too excited! Brandy asked me if I was ok. I told her it was my nerves. Lewis gave me the biggest hug! He kept saying we did it! His cellphone rang which reminded me that I needed to get to mine. Even though the show was technically live there was a ten-minute delay incase there were any editing emergencies. I picked up my phone just as they cut the camera to me. It was like I wasn't looking at myself. I didn't know who that woman was, and her voice was amazing. I couldn't believe I actually sound like that. How wrong could my mother and Reggie have been? It made me sad that I thought about them in the happiest moment of my life. My phone lit up and it was Derrick. I was crying so hard I could barely say hello. He was immediately alarmed, I spoke in between sobs. "They said I sound like a animal dying! They did everything to shut me up! Are you seeing this? I'm not what they said I was! Thank you! This is all your fault!" I laughed through my tears. He was quiet for a long time. "Are you there? Did I drop you?"

"Turn around!" His voice echoed.

I screamed and I jumped on him. "I need you so much right now!" I kept kissing his cheek. Brandy smiled and walked out the room, she closed the door behind her. "I know I should be happy." My phone started ringing. It was my dad and everyone else. "I know I should be grateful! But in this moment all I can think about is how wrong they were and how right you are!' I gave him a wet kiss. "I love you so much! Thank you for everything! Thank you for seeing me when I couldn't see myself."

Chapter 12

"If it isn't little miss I wanna be a star!" Kevin said walking up on me.

"Hello" I said trying to be nice.

"It's real funny how now you're too good for me. Once upon a time you were digging me too."

"Depends on how you define digging. Why are you here?" I asked looking up at him.

"I wanna take you out. Show you a good time like I always intended to. I get why you said the last few times we saw each other it was creepy. I'm not a jerk or anything like that. I like you, always have." He said

"Thank you Kevin, but I'm not in a position to go out with you. You gotta know that."

"Just because I'm not the boss' son?"

"I didn't plan it, it just happened."

"You better never step out of line. You've got some underlying freak ways in you. I can see it, if you show it against that family you gonna end up like every other person they tire of." I didn't say anything, I blank stared at him. "Ask your father-in-law what happened to Charles!"

"Who's Charles?"

"My cousin!" He said staring into my eyes.

"Where's he?"

"I'm saying you should think twice about the people you show so much loyalty to. I like you, and I think you're making a huge mistake passing up on me." Then he smiled. "When their little reign over Oakland comes to an end don't worry, I'll still want you." Then he patted my arm and walked away.

As if it was timed Pearla came back to the table. She looked at my face. "What's wrong?"

"Kevin is or was here."

"Is he still pushing up on you? Some people can't take a hint." She said shaking her head.

"Who's Charles?"

She frowned, "Charles?"

"He said he's Charles' cousin and that when you get tired of me you'll do me like you did him."

"I don't know who Charles is, and obviously he's trying to start some mess. He's trying to get you one way or another." She said dismissing the whole thing.

I wanted to dismiss it too, but the seed had been planted.

****

"Daddy this is not my tour. As soon as it's my project I will make sure you're involved." I said reassuringly to him.

"It was like a dream come true seeing you up there on that stage. Have you talked to your aunties?"

"Deborah, I don't have time for Tania right now. Everybody is coming out of the wood works. Poor Cyrus can't go to the store without being harassed."

"Chantel that's your aunt, please call her." He pleaded

I huffed, "Derrick's here I gotta go. I'll call before I take off. Love you talk to you soon."

"I love you, and I will talk to you soon."

I jumped on Derrick wrapping my legs around him. "You ready?" He asked me.

"Yes," my heart was pounding. Tomorrow night I was stepping on a plane to meet up with Lewis's entourage to begin his tour. It seemed like I was doing a bit much for one song, but Lewis kept putting emphasis on the exposure I would get.

"We're gonna head out to my Uncle Frank's then we can go out to dinner." Derrick said grabbing my bags.

I stared at Derrick while he drove us. I think he's so used to me staring at him he doesn't even notice it anymore. "Are you gonna miss me?"

He cut his eyes at me. "What do you think?"

"That's not an answer Derrick."

He sighed, "of course. Do we have to do this right now?"

"Do what?"

"All this sappy sentimental junk. We'll get to it, but right now I'd rather enjoy our time together." He tried not to bark at me.

"I'll accept that cause I know you're trying your best to suck it up right now. But I wanna hear it all. How much you're gonna miss me. How sad you'll be while I'm gone. And I want you to tell me without copping an attitude."

"Attitude?"

"You know how you do whenever I'm leaving. You're always heck of short with me, and you act like you're mad at me. I would like to leave for once without having that experience. Thank you very much sir."

"Maybe you should stop leaving me so much." He snapped

"I'm leaving you! YOU...." I took a deep breath, and I calmed myself when I saw the almost smile on his face. "Why do you do that?"

"You're the one who falls for it. Don't act like I'm the only one over here feeling some kind of way about you leaving. Let's talk about something else." He said

"Like?"

"When you get back."

"Ok?"

"Shouldn't you stay with me?"

I let the question sink in. I had a bunch of emotions dance all over me and they rendered me unresponsive. "What do you mean?"

"Move in with me." He said matter of factly.

"I wanna say yes, but I need to think about it."

He cut his eyes at me. "What's to think about?"

"Everything! Living with someone is major, we can't move in and think everything will work out. I need to think about it."

He shook his head. "Fine!"

"What?"

He looked mad, "nothing!"

"D-Boogie don't be mad!"

The name caught him off guard and he chuckled. "What did you call me?"

"D-Boogie" I said smiling. "I've been calling you that since that time we were in LA you didn't notice?"

"Honestly I didn't know what you were saying, it's not like I was gonna stop to ask you. As long as you weren't calling out some other guy's name I'm not questioning it."

"I like when you smile"

He dropped his smile and went back to his serious face. "Whatever."

"Why don't you smile? Why do you always have to look mad, or mean?"

"I don't, that's just the way my face looks. I was born this way."

"So I hear."

"From whom?"

"Aunt Lorraine said as a newborn you were this exact same way. That's amazing."

"Outside of Darryl what man in my family walks around smiling all the time?"

"Darryl doesn't smile all the time." I defended him.

"Darryl is always laughing about or at something. Unless he's extremely pissed off he's laughing."

"Its not a weakness for him to be that way."

"I didn't say it was. I'm just saying he's the only one in my family to that extreme. That must come from his father's family."

"I don't know, your mother and some cousins can be pretty silly at times. I love that about them. Especially Amber, she makes me laugh all the time. I'm happy to know her." I smiled real big. "Still didn't answer my question."

"I told you I was born this way. It's just my face."

"Can you try to smile more around me?"

He frowned, "NO!"

"No?"

"What you think I'm supposed to be some grinning fool just because I love you? It doesn't work that way."

"Can you smile for me right now?"

"Nope"

"Why not?"

"Because you asked me to." He almost smiled. He was in a mood so it didn't matter what I said this is where we were going to end up fussing until we ended up wrapped up in each other. Outside of the downtown area of Walnut Creek I had never really been out here. Uncle Frank lived in the hills; there was a gate at the bottom of the hill that he lived on. There were surveillance cameras everywhere and high fences. Derrick entered a code to open the gates and we drove in. Immediately I noticed all the dogs roaming freely on the property. None of them barked but they seemed to watch the car. There were lots of trees and guys stationed every so often. I figured Uncle Frank was a big deal just driving up to his house. His house was HUGE! When we parked Derrick told me to let him open my door. I remembered the dogs so I wasn't moving.

And sure enough when he got out the car, a BIG beastly looking dog approached Derrick while the others were waiting for instructions. Derrick said something to the dog and it became like a puppy and the rest of the now gentle giants came over for some love. Derrick took his time petting them and then he told them to sit and they all did. When he opened my door, I didn't want to get out. He told me to go on. All of the dogs watched me. Derrick told the leader to say hello and he came and sniffed me. Derrick looked me in my eyes, "NO FEAR!". I made my hand as firm as possible when I petted the dog. The others came sniffing and I petted them too. Then Derrick told them to go, and they left us.
"You command even the dogs!" I said smiling at him.
He made a funny face, "that turns you on?"
"Your power always does!"
He shook his head, "Women!" His uncle was standing in the doorway.
"Derrick, Chantel." He said with the same serious face that Derrick always has. He let us in then we followed him to a beautiful room where the walls were made of glass and it over looked his property, which was massive, and the city below. It was breath taking. There were three other men in the room, they all had drinks in their hands and they greeted Derrick with the same serious faces. "What would you like to drink?" Uncle Frank asked pointing to someone who was waiting to mix our drinks.
"Single malt, and give her something girly with a kick." Derrick said to the person.
The person nodded and brought Derrick and Uncle Frank their straight drinks and then he brought me a pretty glassed drink and he set the second one in front of me. Then he left the room. I tasted it and it was delicious. Then Uncle Frank introduced me to his sons, Franky, Fernando, and Ethan. I asked if Franky and Ethan were twins cause they looked an awful lot a like. They said no, and explained that the three of them were very close in age. "So you're going on tour tomorrow, you excited?" Uncle Frank asked.
"Yes, very!"
"Malcolm says that you have your own project in the works." He kept his eyes on me like he was reading me the whole time.
"I have quite a few songs recorded and ready. I guess when I actually have a record deal I'll decide which ones to put out, if any of them go out right away."

"Outside of Malcolm's Studios and Amber's jobs we haven't dabbled too much in the music industry. There's a lot of moving parts over there. It's a different game." He took a drink. "I want you to remember while you're out there that you're still a part of this family. You don't fear anyone or any of their idle threats. This family's arms are long and there's nowhere we can't stretch them."

"What does that mean?" I asked

"You're gonna meet some bullies. Corporate bullies even, point them out, and we'll handle them. All you have to do is your job don't worry about the rest. And since this is new to all of us there's gonna be a slight learning curve." Ethan said

Suddenly Kevin's words started hitting me like a ton of bricks.

"What?" Derrick said watching my face.

"What if you and I fall out? Will I be out there on my own again?" Uncle Frank looked at Derrick, "you guys fell out?"

"We were doing our own things for a minute." He said to his uncle.

"Nothing changed, you weren't alone. And you never will be."

"Could you ever tire of me, and then you guys just leave me out to dry?"

"Only way something like that would happen is if you turned on the family." Uncle Frank said

"Where is this question coming from?" Derrick asked watching me.

"I was out with Pearla and Kevin approached me. He was saying that when you guys were tired of his cousin Charles, something happened to him. Pearla didn't know who he was talking about. Brandy didn't either."

"Charles?" Uncle Frank asked Derrick.

"Sophia's husband," Derrick said calmly even though his eyes turned evil.

"There it is!" Franky said to Derrick and everyone like the light bulb turned on.

"Right! He needs a visit!" Derrick said

"To say the least!" Then Ethan looked at me, "how long ago was this?"

"A few weeks ago." I said looking at Derrick.

"Why didn't you say anything right away?" Fernando asked.

"Pearla said he was trying to get in my head. I understood that, so I kind of dismissed it."

"Let's be clear," Uncle Frank leaned in. "Whenever he breathes in your direction tell someone. We've been trying to put his malfunction to something. That was the detail we were missing. If you see him let us know. We need to have a special visit with him."

"What does that mean?"

"Less is more Chantel. He's trying to divide and conquer." Uncle Frank said.

We talked for a little while longer. I finished both of my drinks. Once I realized Uncle Frank and his sons were more mature versions of Derrick I relaxed tremendously. I had them smiling by the time we left. Uncle Frank wished me well on the tour. He told me to let him know if I needed anything no matter how small it was. I hugged him and he stood frozen when I did it. He turned a little red, and then he hugged me back a little. Derrick didn't look mad, but he shook his head smiling like I was a mess or something. We decided to have dinner at a place in downtown Oakland before heading to the hotel; we parked in a garage in the corner by the stairs. Dinner was delicious and I could see Derrick's sentimental side wash over him. He told me he was going to miss me, and he'd pop up out there as much as he could. He had my itinerary, so he should know wherever I was and wherever I was going to be. When we were walking slowly holding hands back to the car, I noticed that there was no one around and barely any cars parked by us anymore. I was in love with the sentimental moment I was having with Derrick. When we were about ten steps from the car I heard footsteps, it sound like running in our direction. Before I realized what was going on Derrick pushed me behind him and he had his gun pulled on a guy who was trying to run up on us. The guy also had a gun in his hand but he froze when he saw Derrick's. His pause was a sign of weakness I guess. Derrick hit him with his left and the guy dropped his gun. Derrick put his gun back in his waist so quick his hands moved quickly and proceeded to beat this kid down. "Next time pay attention to who you're running up on! You better ask somebody who I am!" Derrick kept going until the kid was down and unresponsive. Then he told me to call a number that he rattled off the top of his head. He stood over the guy like he dared him to move. A female answered the phone, "This is Seaver!"

"Hello? This is Chantel." She listened, "Derrick told me to call you."

"Where are you?"

"In the parking garage on Broadway. A guy tried to mug us."

"Is he down?"

"He's on the ground."

"Is he dead?"

"No, he had a gun. He's unconscious."

"Call 911, I'm on my way." She said

I hung up and Derrick looked at me. "Be hysterical!"

I nodded, and then I dialed the number. "911 what's your emergency?"

"A guy tried to mug my boyfriend and I." Derrick frowned at my choice of words.

"Where is he?" The operator said.

"My man beat him down." Derrick smirked at me. I blew him kisses.

"We have a unit in the area. They should be there in less than one minute. Are either of you hurt?"

"No! We're ok, but the guy is down."

Then we saw flashing lights pulling up the driveway, a police car pulled up. A female officer got out of the car, she looked familiar but I couldn't place her. "Chuck?" She said looking down at the assailant. "YOU'S A STUPID SOMEBODY!" Then she kicked him.

"His gun is over there." Derrick pointed at it.

She smiled at Derrick, "you know you didn't have to beat him this badly."

My blood started to boil a little bit, who was this woman. "What's up Chantel? How you been?" She said like she recognized me.

I went over my mental Rolodex. Derrick was actually smiling at me like he was reading my mind. "Hey."

She looked at me, realizing I didn't recognize her she smiled at me then at Derrick. She called over the radio for ambulance assistance. She took our statements for what happened then another car pulled up. The guy got out and he talked to officer Seaver. Derrick kept smiling at me. It was driving me CRAZY who is this female? They took pictures of everything. They took our statements; an ambulance came and took our assailant away. The female officer gave Derrick a hug and all I could see was RED! She came over to me with a smirk on her face. "Alright then Chantel, it was good seeing you again." She said walking up on me as if she was going to hug me. She stopped right in front of my face so I could take a good look at her.

"Tanisha?"

She smiled, "officer Seaver here at your service."

I grabbed her and hugged her tight. I was so relieved! "Hi Tanisha! How are you? Why didn't you say anything? OH MY GOODNESS!"

Derrick was in an all out belly laugh. Tanisha was cracking up too.

"Its ok, it's been a few years."

"I'm so sorry!" I said feeling horrible.

"It's all good." She said patting my back.

Derrick had those dimples out pointing out at me. When we got in the car, neither one of us said anything. He was smiling and I was stirring in my juices. I loved seeing Derrick break any man down. It was effortless on his part, and it was over before it began for them. We checked into the hotel and the bellhop brought my bags up to the room. Derrick tipped him and I ran around the room screaming because it was beautiful. When the door shut Derrick picked me up, "so you were jealous!" He smiled again.

"You've been turning me on all day!" I kissed him.

"I like to see that you care!" He kissed me deeply. I wiggled my way down then I pushed him on the bed. He smiled, "what are you doing?"

"Ssshhh!" I said, I took off my jacket. I turned on the clock radio. I took off his clothes and stripped him down to nothing. Then I took off my clothes and tried not to feel dumb standing there in front of him. He sat there smiling at me taking me in. He sat up and kissed my stomach. "You are powerful! I love your power!" I said gripping his curls. I pulled his head back and I made him kiss me. I was the boss that night; he did whatever I told him and only when I told him. It was GREAT! In the morning… I was convinced he was trying to blow my back out. My eyes couldn't roll any further, I couldn't scream any louder! I didn't have any more sweat to render! I couldn't feel my legs. When we couldn't go anymore he kept holding me and squeezing me.

"I don't want you to go!" He said above a whisper. When I tried to look at him he wouldn't let me see his face. "Everything's gonna change. You were my personal treasure! You belonged to me alone! Now you're gonna blow up. Everyone is gonna love the same things about you that I do. You won't belong to just me. I'm happy for you! You're gonna be successful, you work too hard not to be. I want you to go out there and give it your all. I want you to make my sacrifice mean something. Don't let me down." He said grabbing my thigh. "I don't want you to go! But you better go!"

"Derrick," I said. I tried to pull his face up so he would look at me but he refused. "Baby, can you please wait for me?"

His body stiffened, "I'll do my best. But I can't make you any promises." He cleared his throat. "I'm not gonna make you any promises. I'm not even gonna tell you that you have to wait for me."

I gasped, "who are you and what did you do with my Derrick?" I said sarcastically.

"I'm not going to do you like my father did my mother. She's spent her life waiting for him. I've seen it all, their highs and their lows. I don't think he could ever bounce back. I don't want that to be us. If we end up together I don't want you waiting your whole life for me. I don't wanna see sadness in your eyes like I see in my mother's."

"Derrick, I don't want anybody else. You're all I've ever wanted. We can make this work. Ride with me on this." I pleaded.

"No, I can't!" He said above a whisper.

"Why?"

"I can't! I can't wait around waiting for you. Waiting for you to remember me. Waiting for you to notice me. I know it's not the same thing, but it brings up all those feelings."

"What feelings?"

He exhaled, "he'd come over excited about Drew. Panting over my momma, but he never paid me more attention than he had to. Malcolm always included me. If he's ever felt anything about me not being his biological son I've never known it. My momma, my brothers, Malcolm. They never treated me like there was

something I needed to wait for with them. But him…. he couldn't even see me. I'm better off without him. Waiting for you would rehash all those feelings about him. And no one deserves to go through that."

"Maybe you guys can reconcile while I'm gone. Malcolm could find him for you."

His body stiffened again. Then he got up and went in the bathroom, he turned on the shower. I went in the bathroom, got in the shower, and he was letting the water beat him in the face. He was breathing slowly; I got in the shower with him and I held on to him. We stood under the water for a long time. Then we took a nap or at least I did. I awoke to room service bringing lunch. Derrick's eyes were red, but I acted like I didn't see them. We talked about all kinds of things. I told him I wanted to pay for Cyrus' student loans, but I needed to make the money to make it happen. So Derrick and I concocted the plan. We'd have his job make it like they're reimbursing him to go to school. Derrick said he would work out the details for me. But he told me to act surprised when Cyrus told me about it. I told Derrick it was important that Cyrus thought the opportunity was generating through his job and not through him or Malcolm. He said he understood and he wouldn't let on that it was any different. The later it got, the quieter Derrick got. I didn't say anything and about an hour before it was time for me to leave tears streamed out of my eyes but I didn't say anything. I called my daddy and he didn't help me. He made me more emotional by telling me how proud he was of me.

When we got to the airport Derrick got a ticket to walk me to the gate. Brandy and Caprice were waiting for me at the gate. They smiled but gave us space to say goodbye. Derrick's face was probably the most serious that I've ever seen it. When it was time to board Derrick gave me a long and deep kiss. I reminded him that he said he would come see me along the way. It didn't go unnoticed that he didn't respond to that. He watched me walk down the ramp. When I sat down Brandy rubbed my hand.

****

We landed at JFK airport early in the morning. We all agreed that we were hungry and food needed to be our first stop. When we got to baggage claim there was a young guy with a white paper that said Chantel Shaw. He was smiling at me as soon as I saw him. He had luggage carts on standby. We pointed out our bags and he loaded them on the carts. He moved very fast but we followed him without incident. He led us to a black SUV with tinted windows. Instantly I thought about Derrick, but this car had big flashy wheels. I asked Caprice to sit in the front, while Brandy and I climbed in the back. I wanted to call Derrick but the kid had

Shameless' music pouring out the customized sound system. He drove super fast, I watched as all the New York drivers bullied their way around the highway. We pulled up to a really fancy hotel. We were trying to name all the movies we saw this hotel in. The bellhop took our luggage and the guy gave his keys to the valet. He told the bellhop which room to take our luggage to. We followed him to the nineteenth floor. The guy opened the double doors to room nineteen-twelve. It was beautiful. The guy pointed to a room in the suite with two double beds. "This is you guys room." The bellhop put our bags down. The guy attempted to send the bellhop away without tipping him. This kid put a bad taste in my mouth. I gave the bellhop a twenty, I figured it was the least I could do.

We moved our bags around then we heard someone at the door. The young guy opened the door and told them they had perfect timing. We saw staff walking in and we could hear carts. The smell of food hit our noses. I told them to go ahead and that I wanted to call Derrick. He answered on the first ring. I told him which hotel we were at and I gave him the room number. He told me he loved me and got off the phone a lot faster than I wanted him to. In the dining room there were a bunch of guys and amongst the guys I saw my girls. I wondered how I was supposed to be comfortable in this situation if I was here by myself. I didn't see Lewis anywhere. Everyone was getting food like they were starving. Brandy pulled me into the procession with her. She gave me a fork and plate. It was standard hot breakfast, but we were starving so you know it seemed better than it actually was. The guys had all the couches and chairs, so we sat on the floor in the corner eating. When we

were almost done Lewis and a guy walked in the door. Lewis' eyes immediately went to us sitting on the floor in the corner. Lewis put his hand up to the guy talking and he walked into the room. He looked around at everyone. They were engaged in their own conversations etc. Then he asked why we were sitting on the floor. I told him because there was nowhere else to sit. His eyes turned

angry. "Listen up!" His voice boomed. "How all y'all niggas gonna let these ladies eat on the floor while you sitting comfortably on the couches and chairs?"

"My bad Lewis!" One guy said.

"These are our little sisters during this haul. I'ma let this time go, but let me see some junk like this again, you're all fired!" Then he told us to come with him and this other guy. We followed him to the master suite. It was really nice in there. "This is my manager Wade. Wade this is Chantel."

"Hello, this is Brandy and this is Caprice."

Wade smiled at us and said hello. "Your first concert is tomorrow night. In the morning we'll go to the arena and check everything out. Tonight you guys are going to club Twilight. It will be good for people to see you guys out together."

I frowned, "what do you mean together?"

Lewis laughed, "Rumors might start flying about us. We'll maintain that you're my little sister. Trust it will die down."

"You got a boyfriend at home or something?" Wade asked me. Brandy bumped me knowing I was going to say a quick yes. "It's complicated."

He smiled, "this lifestyle puts a strain on any relationship. You might as well cut your losses now."

"You mean you don't have anybody at home waiting for you?" Caprice asked with a smile.

He smiled, "I'm not the artist. I can have a life."

"Do you guys have something to wear tonight?" Lewis asked

"I brought clothes for the concerts, and travel." I said

"Wade, take the girls shopping."

"Now?" I asked wanting to get back in the bed. It was six in the morning back home.

"Yes! The day is gonna get away from you if you don't go now." Wade said, "be ready in five minutes."

"Meanwhile, I'm gonna have to explain to these knuckle heads how they're gonna conduct their selves on this tour. You would think certain things wouldn't have to be said." Lewis said

We grabbed our purses. "What do you think of Wade?" Caprice asked me.

"I don't." I said tossing attitude.

"Give her some time, they just broke up." Brandy said

"Who broke up? We didn't break up!" I said highly defensive.

"What are you calling it then?" Brandy asked

"We're.... We...." I got frustrated because now that she said it, it felt like we broke up. "We're on a break right now." We all laughed.

"Wade is cute!" Caprice said

"Whatever!" I shrugged

We took a cab to some boutique looking store. There were quite a few of them on this street. "So ladies, you can't be looking busted talking about you're with us. I like that your hair is braided," he said to me. "We can send you back for touch ups when we need. I'm not dropping money every stop for you two to get your hair done. So you better do whatever females do to make it work. Seven outfits that includes shoes and all your accessories. Pick out everything, I'll pay. I don't want you looking like hookers, but I don't think we have to worry about any of you looking like church girls." He smiled

"But we could look like hookers?" I rolled my eyes.

"Not what I said but ok, poor choice of words. My bad, I apologize." I rolled my eyes again. He laughed at me. "I've got paperwork to do. Call me when it's time to pay." He handed his business card to Brandy.

"How much time do we have?" Brandy asked

"Please tell me you can get this done in three hours?"

"Hhhmmm! I guess we can try." Caprice said as we walked away. Wade stood there watching for a few minutes. Then he shook his head and sat down at an outside table at the cafe.

I was getting frustrated with my girls they kept thumbs downing to the things I liked. Yes they were a little on the conservative side; but so what. In defeat I sat down while Brandy and Caprice gathered stuff for me to try on. After awhile I loosened up and had to admit the stuff they picked out was cute. The shoes they paired with these outfit were down right evil! The heels seemed sky high, and I was already tall enough. But these heels made me heck of tall! My feet were definitely going to die! Brandy called Wade when we were ready. I stopped looking after awhile when the tally in my mind reached two thousand and was still climbing I couldn't take it. Wade took us out to lunch we had a whole "getting to know you" session. He asked how I knew my girls. Caprice told him she met me at my old job in the mall. She kind of "dated" my brother for a while, I laughed at her quote unquote specification. And then Brandy and I had been tight since we worked in the city. Wade said he met Shameless while he was in school. He said they've been tight to a point since then. He said they didn't get into each other's personal lives too much. Caprice asked him again if he had a girlfriend or wife, and again he talked around the question.

I finally got to knockout for a few hours. My nap was glorious! I woke up feeling refreshed and ready for anything. Lewis was in his room with the door open. While everyone else clowned around in the living room. They were having a group debate about something and Caprice was on one opinion and some of the guys were on another. I knocked on Lewis's door; he had a notepad and a pen.

"Come in." He smiled when he saw me. "I'm over here trying to be like you and D-Rick."

"What do you mean?"

"I wanna drop a few verses for Latia."

"Aw!" I got all-sentimental for him while he blushed. "I'm sure she loves everything you do for her."

"Yeah!" He said still blushing. He showed me what he had. It was really nice, softer than I expected to see him go. He said he was thinking about collaborating with the rapper Comfort for this one. The song did seem like it was more Comfort's speed than his. Comfort was always rapping about loving a good woman. His style definitely had some major dignity assigned to it. Shameless on the other hand rapped about everything, and that included hoes. The way his voice sat on a chord though, it was pure artistry. I brought in my notepad that I used to write all my poetic scribbles. On the plane before I fell asleep I wrote about four poems for Derrick, he always seemed to be my muse. I showed the poem I had in mind that seemed to fit with his words. Lewis got excited! "Yes! Yes!" He said clapping his hands together. People looked at us in the room. Lewis ignored them. "You sing this hook for me tonight.

Let's see what type of response we get."

"We're performing tonight?"

Wade walked in the front door dressed for the night. "How come nobody's ready?" Then he came in Lewis's room. "You two are really the only ones who matter and you're not dressed!" He growled.

Lewis motioned for him to come over. "Check this out!" He said handing him the notepad.

Wade was frowning at first then he started reading. His frown melted away and then he awkwardly bobbed to an imaginary beat. "Nice! You wrote this right now?"

"We did." Lewis said smiling. "The hook is hers."

Wade peeked at me. "She can sing and write? Alright, alright! Now go get dressed!" He barked at Lewis. "I'm tired of you always running on CPT!"

I took that as my queue to get moving as well. We locked our door and took turns in the shower. I called Cyrus while I waited; we talked for a few minutes. Then we brought my daddy in on three-way. He was so excited to hear from me. When we were all dressed and ready to go we opened the door. The guys got quiet as they all stared at us. Wade came back up, he was clapping his hands. "Good! Everybody's dressed! Now let's go! The car is downstairs." He knocked on Lewis's door. He went in then he came out. "Chantel! Lewis wants you."

Lewis didn't have a shirt on yet so I put my eyes to the floor and refused to look at him again. All I saw was a six-pack and I knew looking any harder was disrespectful. "I just wanna make sure we're clear. I don't know if Latia told you how things go when I'm on the road..."

I interrupted, "she maintains that you guys are not together. She's already told me she doesn't wanna know."

He stopped in his tracks probably looking at me. "Isn't that messed up? How would that make you feel?"

"Feel?"

"Yeah!"

"I know, and she knows you love her. She's not ready. She's not asking you to sit on your hands waiting for her." He sucked his teeth. "You could wait for her anyways. Maybe that would help."

"I guess! I called you in here so that you wouldn't be giving me the stank face all night."

"Understood."

"And try to not be all star struck. A few of my friends are gonna be at the club tonight."

In the stretch limo Wade pointed out the six bodyguards to us. They looked like goofy guys to me. They were not like the Mitigated staff I was used to. Lewis' main bodyguard looked like he was about business though. Brandy whispered to me that she

wanted to bite him. I laughed cause he was cute. He was just a tad bit taller than average height. He was Husky with honey kissed skin and brown eyes, low fade and nicely trimmed beard. I didn't think he was paying us any attention until I caught him staring at Brandy's butt. When I told her she got excited. They put us at a booth next to Lewis' in the VIP section. Caprice told Brandy to go ahead and drink and that she would be on point for the night. Brandy said I needed to relax, so we took a few shots. Pretty soon the guys in Lewis' booth started looking familiar. I definitely recognized Dwayne Reed and Comfort right away. Pretty soon their booth looked like the celebrity booth. We danced on the dance floor almost all night. I wondered when we were supposed to perform, then I realized that Lewis was tore up. He was barely putting coherent words together in a sentence. Wade told us we were leaving. We walked out of the club with Lewis and some girl. On the way back to the hotel Brandy and the bodyguard were exchanging looks. In the lobby Lewis' entourage decided they wanted to go find another party. Wade left, and the six of us rode the elevator together. This girl was all over Lewis. "OH SHAMELESS! OH SHAMELESS!" She kept moaning, but he wasn't touching her. She was all over him and he was letting her be. We barely got in the door and she was hiking up her skirt. Lewis walked in the room, sat on the bed, he took out a condom. I didn't mean to look but we were all kind of standing there with our mouths open. The girl took off her top and fell to her knees. The bodyguard closed the door. All three of us looked dumb, I couldn't believe I was watching that. And I couldn't believe that this girl was doing all that. "Ladies would you like to have a drink over by the bar?"
I pushed Brandy forward, "what's your name?"
"Paul"
"Caprice and I are gonna knock out. Brandy you were thirsty right?" I gave her an evil grin.
I called Derrick and we talked for a little bit. He said my constant yawning was making him tired too.
Caprice covered her head, "does she have to be loud? I bet you she's doing all the work and trying to make it seem like she's the best he's ever had! This is gonna get old real fast!" She barked
"You're just jealous!" I laughed

"I am! Maybe I should call your brother and have him get me off verbally like he normally does."

I frowned, "he has a family."

Caprice looked at me. "You do know that me and your brother still see each other?"

"What?" I said feeling horrible for Sherrell.

"Did you think all of a sudden we stopped seeing each other? Cyrus always comes back to me. He has this thing about letting people go. He still gets down with Cadence from time to time too. But don't worry I'm not gonna mess up his family. If I'm not seeing anybody I hit up Cyrus for a tune up. It's not a big deal."

"Do you think Sherrell knows?" I asked feeling depressed

"She'd be a fool not to." Caprice looked at me. "Chantel it's ok. I do love your brother if it makes a difference. I wasn't ready to be domesticated like he needed me to be. I left the door open for the cleanup woman. That could've been me laid up in your spot fat with a baby."

"Sherrell IS NOT FAT!"

Caprice put her hands out. "Whoa! Calm down! She hasn't lost all her baby weight yet. It's not like it matters. Cyrus loves her more for it." She rolled her eyes, "I shouldn't have gotten rid of mine is all I'm saying."

"You were pregnant?" I couldn't believe it.

"I was on assignment I couldn't up and leave. Plus, the whole idea of it scared me. Cyrus begged me not to do it, but my mind was made up. He didn't talk to me for a long time after that. He won't touch me without a condom now. And that's when he's in the mood to deal with me. It's my fault, I knew he was a good guy." Then she put the pillow back over her head.

That was a lot of reality to take in. I cracked the door. "Is it safe to come out?" I called out.

Brandy laughed, "of course!" Paul said

They were sitting at the table talking. Both of them were grinning from ear to ear. I made a quick drink, drank it, and then I went to bed.

"WALK OF SHAME! WALK OF SHAME! *WALK OF SHAME!*" The guys were shouting in the living room. We popped up and ran to our door. We opened it just in time to see skanker's-remorse on her face. The Goons weren't making it any better. They were loud and embarrassing, I had a feeling this wouldn't be the last incident we'd see like this.

We went to the gym and pounded out our frustrations in the gym. When we got cleaned up, Wade took us to the concert location. He went over the set with us and how it was going to function. He explained what the stage would look like for the opening act. Wade really knows his stuff and he took his time explaining things and answering my questions. I rehearsed a little with my headset microphone. We had fun on the stage clowning around. When Lewis and Paul arrived, Lewis was focused and not friendly at all. He was about business, but I really feel like he was embarrassed about last night. So I didn't say anything, I rolled with him.

As the opening act was coming to a close my nerves started setting in. I kept pacing back and forth waving my hands around. I kept breathing and telling myself I could do it. How did I get through this last time? I thought about Derrick. Yes! That's what I'll do. I could feel the tears welling up in my eyes. I put my head up to the ceiling I blew air I can do this. "Stop acting like you scared!" I screamed as tears ran down my face. "How are you doing this to me again?" I threw my arms around Derrick's neck. Now I could do it! This was just enough to get me through my first appearance. "Ok! Ok!" I shook my hands again. "I can do this!" I smiled at Derrick, "thank you for coming. I needed you here."

Derrick smiled. He hugged me, and then he told me to go out there. We walked to the side stage. Lewis had the house rocking and the audience sounded massive. I grabbed Derrick's hand cause my nerves had my stomach in knots. Shameless asked the crowd if they were ready to have his little sister join him. Some of the people applauded. When the music changed the audience got louder. I looked at Derrick with tears in my eyes. He flashed his dimples at me. The stage director checked my microphone one more time. Then he told me to go. The music dropped and Derrick smiled at me. It was go time. I opened my mouth and the song came out. The sound of the crowd felt louder than the music. I don't know where the dancers came from, but they were behind me executing Amber's moves from the video. I used Jesse's pointers and moved around the stage like I owned it. Shameless was on the other side of the stage changing his shirt and smiling at me the whole time. I got a glance of myself on the huge screens on either sides of the stage. It didn't even seem like I was looking at myself.

The woman on the screen seemed confident, nothing like me. I couldn't believe how many people liked our song. The crowd looked like a sea of colors. The reds and oranges stood out to me most. When the song was over I looked at Derrick and he flashed his dimples at me. Shameless told the crowd to give it up for me. I could feel the energy from the crowd blast at me. I stumbled backwards a couple steps. I tearfully thanked everyone for the love. When I walked off the stage Derrick picked me up, and I kissed him again. Then Shameless called me back out on stage. I shook my head no. He smiled and told the crowd I needed convincing. He told them to sing my chorus to me. Derrick rubbed my back while I was in his arms, I couldn't help it, I cried on his neck. I got down then I slowly walked on the stage. "New York!

Let's show my little sister some love!" The crowd went wild again.

Shameless had me sing along while his band played whatever melody he chose. I had to watch him and listen for the pitch of the song. My heart wouldn't slow down it was beating so hard. The crowd loved it! When I left the stage this time I pulled Derrick away from the sideline. I was afraid he was gonna pull me back out there.

Chapter 13

"Why can't you tell me when you're gonna pop up? Why do you keep popping up out of nowhere?" I said snuggling into his chest. "I don't want to promise to be here, and then not be able to make it. I can't be here with you as often as I plan to be." Derrick said, "so...."

"So?"

"I'm not letting it go. You moving in with me when you come home?" He asked

"Clearly," I huffed. "I kind of have reservations about shacking up with you where other females have spread their legs."

He sat up, "something that petty stands between you being with me?" He moved his body away from me. "You're out here with all these niggas! I see the way they look at you. I'm taking it on the chin. How often you gonna be home anyways? You gonna be there regardless, why not just stay?"

Derrick was emotional and I wasn't used to seeing this from him. Then again how often do I tell him no? "Maybe it's a girl thing. I can't consider your place home knowing that when I'm not there other females are."

"Why does it matter?"

"Cause it does!" I said holding my ground. "You said I'm free to do whatever, but you randomly pop up. It doesn't feel like I'm free. If I'm not free then let's just be official! You and me! AND HOW ARE WE GONNA BE UNOFFICIAL AND LIVING TOGETHER???? Matter of fact let's stick to that point! You get everything and I get nothing. That doesn't work for me!"

"Fine! I won't come see you then." He said snatching up his clothes.

"Why would you pull not coming to see me from what I just said? Why won't you wait for me?"

"I told you, I can't!"

"Then I can't, but I don't understand why you're leaving?"

"Cause you get on my nerves!" He barked

I stood up on the bed, "you can't stand to hear no! Derrick get it together! You can't possibly think I'll always do what you want me to just because you said it."

He walked back to the bed. "My asking you to move in with me is a big deal. You don't seem to understand that. You're dismissing it because you're not getting your way on one thing."

I put my arms around his neck. "Darryl said you don't let girls spend the night." I kissed him. "I get it. And I've never been with anyone else. I think that makes us even."

He put his arms around me. "It really doesn't."

"I want to be your only, you want me to move in. Neither one of us gets everything we want." I kissed him again. "We can celebrate the moments we have together."

"I hate you!" He said kissing me.

"You love me!"

He picked me up and laid me down. "I love you!"

"I know you do! I know it's a big deal that you're dang near demanding me to live with you. I get it." I said rubbing his head. "How you doing on money?"

"I'm out of cash on hand, but I still have your credit card if I really need something. Lewis has been footing the bill for everything so it's not a big deal."

He shook his head, "no. You're supposed to tell me. If I didn't ask, you weren't going to say anything?"

"I've got some money of my own. It's not that serious."

"What did we talk about?"

I huffed, "you're my *man*. If I need something just ask." Only my man when it comes to money. I tried not to think about it.

He put his hand to his ear, "did you do that?"

I huffed again, "no."

"You know what that means." I looked at him with a question mark on my face. "You're getting a *whooping*." He smiled. I sat up and clapped my hands excitedly. He took the little bit of clothes he still had on off. He effortlessly flipped me, and then I got my *whooping*. SMILES!

"I'm gonna ride with Derrick, I'll see you guys at the club."

"Ok, I'll tell Wade." Brandy said, and then we hung up.

Derrick came back in the room, "whoa!"

I did a quick turn, "you like?" When I bought this dress I bought it with Derrick in mind. It was black and short. It had a deep v-neckline in the front and back. I put on a silver belt and accessories.

"You're wearing my colors! You must be trying to stay in tonight."

"Does that mean you like what you see?"

"I love it!" He said, he looked at my shoes. "I like those shoes! You're almost as tall as me in them."

"They're gonna be killing me! But they complete the look."

Derrick took a deep breath then we walked to the lobby. The Goons and Wade were down there waiting for Lewis, Paul, and my girls. I noticed that Wade stayed to the back and only said what he had to, to Derrick. I knew Derrick noticed it, whether or not he spoke on it was a different story. I shook my head at Wade like he was messing up. He knows Derrick is my man. I don't get why he acts weird whenever Derrick is around. The rest of the time he's normal mostly. Acting like that makes him look guilty or like

something is going on between us and it's not. Derrick gave the valet his ticket then he stood there listening to the different conversations. The limo pulled in front of Derrick's rental car.

"What's that about?" Derrick said pointing at Brandy and Paul. They were walking normally.

"What? Everyone's getting in."

He sucked his teeth and looked at me. "You're smarter than that. You know what I'm asking you, are they hooking up?"

"How can you see that from them walking?" Derrick stared at me. "No they haven't, but they're digging each other."

"Do I need to remind her that she's here on assignment? She can get laid on her time." He barked, "I'd expect something like this from Caprice!"

"Derrick she hasn't done anything. She's been very professional. Both of them have. Caprice even turned down this one guy she said she would've normally went for when we were in Houston. They're taking their assignment very seriously."

"Un huh!" He said eyeing me

We walked in the club behind Lewis' entourage. As usual we weren't at the table with Lewis and his people, but we were right next to him. I still caught Derrick talking to Brandy. He was talking she was listening. Lewis pulled me to the stage area and he

told the crowd like he did in every city, that we were working on something and we needed their opinion on it. We performed the song we wrote the first night. I kept my eyes locked on Derrick and he was listening to everything. As usual the crowd loved it then I came back to the table. "Do you like it?" I asked Derrick.
"That's alright. Ours is better." He said leaning back.
"I know that, but the hook is mine." I smiled real big.
He gave me a kiss, "you did good." Then he sat back observing.
"So what's the deal with you and him?" He nodded towards Wade.

"Nothing" I said matter of factly. "That's Lewis's Manager."

"I know who he is. I'm asking what's the deal." He looked me in my eyes.
I frowned, "nothing."
"He likes you." Derrick watched my face for a reaction.
"No he doesn't." I frowned at the foreign thought.
Derrick shrugged, "suit yourself. I'm a man and I think I can recognize when another man is looking at my woman, but if you wanna play dumb until you're in a quote unquote situation, that's on you. Don't get that boy killed."
"Don't even joke like that it's not funny."
His face was serious, "I'm not joking."
"You're not even capable of something like that." I said brushing him off.
Derrick stared at me with no emotion. "Guess you don't know me."
Caprice and Brandy were trying to look like they weren't listening.
"Everyone at this table except you has killed more than twice." He stared at my eyes. I blinked my eyes at Brandy and Caprice. They both had guilty stares as they pretended like they weren't listening.
"I'm a Wallace, and don't even get me started on the Latour side!"
"Just because that's your family name doesn't mean that you are capable of something like that." I said rubbing my hands together.
"If I ask you a question just tell me the truth. The day I find out you lied to me we're gonna have problems."
"I didn't lie to you."
"Do you like him?"
"I don't know." I said staring at the table.
"Let me know when you know then." Derrick leaned back in his seat observing everyone. I didn't know what to do. So I sat there staring at the table. My heart dropped when I saw him calling

someone over. I hoped it wasn't... Wade. "Have a seat." Derrick said

"I was on my way that way. What do you need?" Wade asked

"I noticed that you have a fascination for looking in this direction. Is there something I can help you with?" Derrick said with his face like stone.

"It's my job to make sure everyone has what they need. I'm making sure they're covered." Wade said not cowering at Derrick.

"Seems to me you keep looking at my woman though. I haven't seen you glance in the other two's direction yet."

"That's because Chantel don't ask for help until she has to have it. Otherwise she tries to do everything on her own. Knowing this about her, I keep an eye out for her." Wade said directly.

Derrick looked at me. "See! I told you, you don't be paying attention. This nigga over here catching feelings."

Wade didn't say anything to that. "This is news to me. Derrick I didn't know." I said, my girls nodded their heads to cosign my ignorance.

"My personal feelings are none of your business." Wade said to Derrick.

Lewis stood up at his table. He held out his hands like he was asking what was up. "Anything concerning this woman IS my business!" Derrick shot back.

"Oh crap! MOVE!" Lewis said moving a groupie out the way. "Whoa! Whoa! Wade! I thought you were handling bottle service?"

"Yeah go *fetch* **BOY**!"

Wade cut his eyes at Derrick then he walked away. "Derrick!" Derrick stared at Lewis not saying a word. "Come talk to me."

"Ladies you go dance, have a seat Lewis." Brandy and Caprice got up. "You too!" Derrick pointed his eyes at me.

I didn't want to go, but I didn't dare stay. "Oh my God girl! Derrick is about to tear down this club!" Brandy said

"Wade has no idea who he's talking to. He needs to stand down." Caprice said

"You guys have killed people?" I asked with a lump in my throat. They danced closer to me. "Please don't freak out. It's not like we roll around hurting people. The situations were bad. We can talk about it more later if you want." Brandy said

"Are you guys really my friends? Or is this just an assignment?"

Brandy stopped dancing and her eyes filled up with tears. "I'm your friend! I love you very much!" We hugged.

"We are friends, I'm in love with your brother remember? They were going to send someone else and I begged Malcolm to send me. I had to promise heaven and earth just to be here with you. I'm your friend." Then we hugged, "but this is also an assignment for me. So I have to report everything."

"Everything?"

"Everything." She said shaking her head.

Derrick joined us on the dance floor. I kept frowning at him even though I was trying not to. Derrick took my hand and told the girls to enjoy the night off.

I didn't say anything the whole car ride. We went up to his room. "Take your clothes off!" He demanded, and then he went to the bathroom I could hear him peeing. I stood there debating whether to listen or not. He washed his hands and stopped in the doorway when he saw me standing there. "You heard me!" He leaned his head to the side while he stared in my eyes.

"Derrick, I..." I didn't know what to say next I thought he would stop me but he stood there listening. "I didn't know."

"You didn't have proof, but to lie to me and say you were completely clueless is wrong. Is that what you're fixing your mouth to say?"

"No, but why am I in trouble for what he feels?"

"Who says you are?"

I relaxed some. "I thought you were mad at me."

He started taking his clothes off. "Nope, not mad at you, but I'm about to blow your back out!" He said matter of factly.

"I'm kind of tired, and not in the mood."

"You will be." Then he took my clothes off. There was no smile in his face or eyes. He picked me up and carried me to the bed. He grabbed the lotion off the dresser. He gently laid me on the bed. The magic is in the hands. By the time he finished massaging, rubbing, licking, and sucking on me I was begging him to go in. Derrick is the master torture artist! He kept flipping me, dipping me, had me hollering! And then he gave me more. "Whose pussy is this?"

"D-Boogie!" I called myself being funny.

I was on the verge of another orgasm when he started laughing which vibrated through my body. He kept me going dang near all night. The sun came up and he was still working me over. He was making sure I knew nobody else could make me feel this way. He told me he loved me, and then he told me he wasn't coming out anymore. I cried, I told him I needed him. He said he'd be in the Bay when I needed him and when I came home. Six more months to go.

****

"Chantel why can't we get along?"

"Cause I can't stand you! I hate your name! Do you really have to live up to it? You get on my flipping nerves!" I said with as much attitude as I could.

"Whatever girl ain't nobody worried about what you feel! This is Shameless' show! Didn't nobody pay no money to come hear you sing." He shot back.

"And yet when I walk off the stage they're screaming for more. You need to get away from me with all this negativity and hatred! I can't stand you!" I yelled

"Or else wha…." Before Reggie could get to the "t" Caprice knocked the stuffing out of him. He took one too many steps in my direction. So he's been bugging me the whole tour, and then when I found out his name was Reggie too. It seemed to fit. He was annoying as all get out and one of the stupider Goons. The rest of the Goons were on their feet! Caprice knocked him down and he sat on the ground for a minute like he didn't know what just hit him. She was focused on him, waiting for him to get up.

"She wasn't messing with you! You need to learn how to leave people alone. You play too much Reggie!" Brandy said

"Thank you Caprice lets go. " I said stepping over Reggie and pulling my girls by the hands away. The rest of the Goons were still hooping and hollering because of what just happened. We went back on the bus to wait for Lewis, Paul, and Wade. "How's your hand?" I asked Caprice.

"Now it's throbbing probably because you asked." She laughed,

"but it's gonna be alright. He had more blubber around his face then probably anywhere else on his body."

The car pulled up, the three of them got out of the car followed by the cameraman. "Paul, can you ask the camera man to hold on one minute?" Brandy said all sweet and kind to him. Paul told the guy to wait then he closed the bus doors.

"What's up?" Lewis asked as his eyes bounced from each one of us.

"Reggie got in my face again!" I said

Lewis started to walk backwards. "BUT! Caprice laid him out in front of everybody!" Brandy said

All three of them burst out into laughter. They were belly laughing. Wade and Lewis had tears coming out of their eyes they were laughing so hard. "He got laid out by a girl? Priceless!" Lewis said

We blank stared at them. "Why is that so funny?" Caprice asked

"You're almost a dainty little thing. You think you could take a real man?" Lewis said sure of himself.

"You wanna find out?" She said

"Challenge... ACCEPTED!" Lewis said trying to be funny. "Wade next stop find us a gym where we can box it out."

"Alright Lewis. Don't run away crying, you did this to yourself." She said

"Bring the camera man on." Lewis was still almost laughing. "This girl, who doesn't want to be directly on camera has challenged me to a boxing match. I normally don't hit girls, but this one gave me permission to knock her out. This is the kind of dumb fun we have."

When the Goons started telling Lewis how it happened he wasn't laughing as much anymore, but he was still smiling! When we got to the hotel Wade and Reggie argued outside for a long time. It looked pretty heated. The Goons said Wade was telling Reggie that he was responsible for every mishap on our tour and Reggie needed to tone his attitude down. Reggie was a bully and he thought he'd bully us around; he got his hat handed to him by a girl in the process. That night the Goons kept teasing Reggie and he got really mad. He stormed out of the hotel. We couldn't find him when it was time to go out. Wade kept calling his cellphone, but he got no answer. Eventually it went straight to voicemail. The next morning still no word from Reggie. That afternoon police came to our hotel. Wade called the police cause it was unlike him to be gone this long. He explained we had to leave soon, and he was worried about him. Reggie was a hot head, but he never stayed gone like this. The police told him they'd contact him if anything turned up.

Next city, as promised Wade had everything set up. First Lewis
had to take pictures with the owners of the gym and stuff like that.
Once all that was out the way they changed clothes and got in the
ring. Wade and I were the judges. I pretended to humor Wade as
he explained how scoring was going to go. I knew my girl and this
wouldn't go past one round. They danced around for a while, and
one, two, one, two, BOOM! Lewis was down. He looked up at
Caprice in disbelief. She kept telling him to get up, and he shook
his head no, while he cracked up laughing cause he couldn't
believe she knocked him down. The Goons were having a field day
with the fact that Caprice had knocked down two men. Caprice
took off her gloves and offered to help him up and then he got up
dramatically. Then he told the camera that a girl knocked him
down with padded gloves on. We couldn't stop laughing.

After tonight's performance we're heading to Oregon. We were
going to be there for a week, so this time we we're staying in a
house. The Goons were already formulating a plan to try to
manipulate us into cooking. We fell for it the first time and we put
out a whole spread. They accused us of not knowing how to cook.
I made a few roasts with all the potatoes and veggies, Caprice
hooked up the green bean casserole, and Brandy made big fluffy
buttermilk biscuits from scratch. Everyone except Reggie was
appreciative, and then they started acting like big brothers and
protective as all get out. I told them I wasn't cooking for them no
more if they let Reggie get in my face one more time. They agreed
unanimously to keep him off of me. The girls and I went over a
menu on the plane. The Goons were coming by bus, so we'd have
almost two days without all the noise. The house was beautiful and
huge. There was an upstairs, downstairs, and a basement. The
upstairs was one huge bedroom with its own bathroom. Then there
were two bedrooms on the main level they each had two double
sized beds. Normally Wade stayed in a hotel but this time he
decided to bunk with Paul. Our first night we went out to dinner, it
was nice cause we were out with Lewis and not his alter ego. He
kept telling Caprice he couldn't believe she knocked him down.
She told him that's what he got for underestimating her power
based on her size. Pretty soon everyone was telling fight stories. I
didn't really have any unless you count making my mother bust her

nose against the wall a fight. Cyrus was always there to protect me. In that moment I missed my brother so much. "You're not much of a fighter I take it?" Wade asked while everyone else was involved in their side conversations.

"I have the best big brother, I didn't have to."

"And now you have your boyfriend." He said

I looked at him, but I didn't say anything. I didn't understand if he was asking or what. I looked at Lewis and Caprice. They were into their conversation, neither one of them had any type of look that said they were doing anything other than talking. I still had that "oh crap they're talking" feeling.

Dinner was good and our cocktails were nice. Brandy and Paul looked like they were going to burst; they hadn't made that connection yet. "How about we do this." Lewis said to our group. "Let's go to the store and get stuff for cocktails at home. Then we can kick back and chill."

Everybody was ok with the idea, but I was watching Lewis getting comfortable with Caprice. In my opinion if he drinks heavily he'll make a move on her. It's not my business, but he doesn't seem to go through with anything with anyone without alcohol. Wade was watching me while I took everything in. "Penny for your thoughts."

"A penny doesn't pay this fare. I'll keep it to myself."

He laughed, "Say that again."

I smiled and took another drink. I started looking at the whole set up. Did they do this on purpose? Caprice some how ended up by Lewis, and I'm over here by Wade. I guess it could've happened that way but man, it felt like a setup. In the SUV in the grocery parking lot Lewis says to the car group, "would everyone agree that tonight is a night off for all of us?" Everyone except me agreed but no one seemed to notice. "Anything that happens tonight stays between us. No need to share with the goons the camera or any of that. Deal?" Everyone quickly agreed, and that was my confirmation that this was a setup. Not that anyone cared, but it wasn't ideal for me.

We stood in the liquor section confused. There was plenty of wine and beer, but nothing else. One of the workers asked if we needed help. When we asked where's the rest of the liquor, he explained that we'd have to go to an actual liquor store for that. He pointed us to the nearest one. Lewis bought so much liquor they gave them boxes to put in the back of our car. I volunteered to be bartender, Wade volunteered to be my assistant. Sure enough Lewis started tossing drinks backwards. Caprice followed his lead. Paul and Brandy babysat their drinks, but they disappeared after a little bit. My ears perked up when I heard Caprice talking about my brother. She was telling Lewis how much she loves Cyrus, and how she messed everything up. Lewis looked sympathetic under his drunken stooper. He told her he had a good woman, but they had their drama, like it took the longest time for her to trust him a little bit. She wasn't putting out for a long time. Then he admitted that he liked that, he knew she wasn't a hoe. That sealed it for me, they were gonna disappear next. I stopped listening to their drunken rambles. I HOPE WADE DOESN'T GET ANY IDEAS! I watched Wade toss a couple drinks himself. Caprice said she had to pee but she went upstairs. Lewis followed two minutes later. Since Wade was tipsy himself he didn't notice that I didn't really drink, or so I thought. He sat on the couch and invited me to sit with him.

"How'd you learn to sing like that?" He said smiling.

"I open my mouth and it comes out." I said being smart.

He smiled, "how come your man stopped meeting up with us?"

"How come your woman never comes out?" I shot back.

"She... She... I'm working. They would slow me down."

"They?"

"My kids." He said looking at the floor.

"How many? How old?"

"Three, 9, 13, and 14."

"How are you out here on the road like this with teenagers who need you?"

His face looked sad, "doing this allows me to provide for them a lot better than if I was there. I get paid very well to do all this."

"Do you have to be here like this? You're his manager not his assistant."

He exhaled, "there's more but I don't want to talk about it. "You want kids?"

"Only if they're with Derrick. Otherwise no!"

He frowned, "why? I got money."

"What does that mean?"

"I know girls want money to take care of the baby. I got that."

"What does that have to do with me though? What does your money have to do with me?"

"You could have my baby." He smiled
"You're drunk!"
He smiled bigger, "maybe. Why are you waiting for that fake gangster?"
"What makes you think he's fake? And why he gotta be a gangster?"
"Gangster cause he's the only fool crazy enough to come at me like that. He must not know who I am. And fake because he didn't follow through when he had a chance. He talks a good game, but he lacks follow through."
"Clearly you don't know my man. He's lacking in nothing." I said irritated.
"Clearly you don't know me!" He said still smiling.
"What does that mean?"
"When is he coming back?"
"I don't know. I never know when he's coming."
He started to say something and then we heard laughter. Lewis and Caprice came falling down the stairs laughing their behinds off. Lewis was shirtless and Caprice lost her skirt, Caprice sat next to me on the couch. Lewis sat at the table laughing and pounding on the table. "What's so funny?" Wade asked
"She is so stupid!" Lewis said, "talking about no lazy sex! I only give my love the goods. Everybody else only gets a taste." Lewis said cracking up.
"Why is that funny?" I asked
"Cause who says that?" Lewis said still laughing.
"She's been saying that every time you hook up with a groupie."
"If I wanted to have lazy sex, I could get that anywhere." Caprice said
"You're looking for someone else to fill a void." Wade said to her.
"If I'm gonna do it, it might as well be good. Shoot, I could wait until we get home if it's not going to be good." She said
I looked at her cause I knew she was talking about Cyrus. Even though I know Lewis has been strapping up. I feel the need to warn my brother about this whole scene even though they said what happens here tonight stays here, I'm telling.
"You've got an interview in the morning, you should go to bed." Wade said talking to me.
"Him too!" I said pointing to Lewis.

"He can wear shades and none will be the wiser. You've gotta show your face. You need to look refreshed. Besides you're the only one not drunk right now. You can't be having any fun."

"It's too much going on right now. Caprice you coming to bed with me?"

Caprice was quiet for a minute; it looked like she was thinking. "You need me to go with you?" She looked like a little girl, with pain in her face.

"YES! PLEASE! Please come with me." I pleaded.

"Ok" She said getting up to come with me.

"So we're just friends?" Lewis said still chuckling.

She walked over to the table, "Friends." She said kissing him on the lips.

"I like that. I need friends." Lewis said

"What about me?" Wade asked throwing his hands up. "I need a friend."

Caprice looked at him. "You know what Wade you are really cute. You're smart, a hard worker, you've got a little playboy in you, but there's something about you that's just wrong. I don't know what it is yet."

Wade smiled at her, "you don't know what it is?"

"You've got a bad temper, but that's not what it is. I'm waiting." Caprice said

"How do you know I got a bad temper?" He said smiling.

"All me and Brandy have time to do is watch. Anyone stupid enough to argue with you seems to somehow change their minds and see things your way. Your powers of negotiation are amazing."

Wade's smile dropped, "what are you saying?"

I looked at Caprice and I begged her to stop talking with my eyes.

"I don't know! I'm drunk! Who knows what I'm saying."

"Un huh," Wade said looking at her like he was sobering up by the second.

I grabbed Caprice's hand, "good night gentlemen." I said as we walked to my room.

When we got in the room Caprice's face was completely sober. "I don't trust Wade!"

"What do you mean?"

"He's sneaky, the way he set up tonight. The whole thing."

"You're not drunk?" I asked looking at her completely lucid face.

"Girl Naw! I had to go along with everything though. Wade's gonna try to separate us. I had to lay Reggie out though. Crap!" She yelled above a whisper.

"I thought you were really digging Lewis." I said sounding relieved.

"He's sweet, but no." She said, "Wade is watching us, so we've got to be careful."

****

"So where did you grow up?" The female interviewing Shameless asked me.

"I grew up all over Northern California, but I've spent the most time in Oakland. That's where I currently live." I said

"What does your mother think of all of this?"

I immediately felt irritated, but it wasn't her fault. She thought she was asking a good question. "I don't talk to her, but my daddy is extremely proud. If he could've been here right beside me he would've been."

"So what's your relationship to Shameless?"

"Shameless is my big brother. He's showing me the ropes."

"Is there someone special in your life?" She asked

"There is."

She leaned in, "do we know him?"

"No, no one knows him like I know him." I smiled

"You're not gonna give us a name?" She begged

"Not yet."

"Fair enough. Everybody give it up for Chantel Shaw!" The audience went wild. "Like I said earlier. She's out here performing with Shameless. She dazzled you at the awards show. She'll entertain you tonight. She's got mad talent, she's gonna be around for a while. Chantel I have a special request." She smiled at me. "Would you perform an impromptu song for us?"

I smiled, "I didn't have anything prepared."

"The sign of a true artist is that they're always prepared." She said sarcastically.

I wanted to punch her in her face. "Chantel is always prepared." Lewis smiled at me.

"I need an acoustic guitar. Do you have one?" I looked around.

"Of course we do. We'll get one for you while we go to commercial. We'll be right back with Shameless and Chantel Shaw."

As soon as the cameraman yelled clear. Lewis erupted. "WHAT WAS THAT? A PERFORMANCE WAS NOT PART OF THE DEAL!"

She pointed at the booth, "They told me to stretch!" Then she walked away

Wade and a suit guy came out. "The projected ratings are high for this episode, we moved the segment around. We need Chantel to perform." The guy said matter of factly.

"What are you paying her?" Lewis said

"Paying?" The guy scoffed.

"You better write it up before we come back from commercial or we walk." He smiled.

Someone from the back handed me a guitar. They gave me a stool and a microphone. Lewis, Wade, and the guy continued talking. A guy walked over with paper work. I saw dollar signs on the paper. Lewis smiled and gave me a thumbs up. We came back from commercial, the woman introduced me. Instantly I was back in my little cafe. I sang my song for Derrick. The audience was swaying and clapping along just like my cafe audience would. Lewis and the host were bopping to my song. "I could go all day, but I guess I gotta stop." I said when my song was over. The crowd stood up and the applause was loud.

"You wanna see more?" Lewis asked the crowd, they screamed yes. "Come to the show tonight!" The audience was loud.

Then we walked off the stage. When the behind the scenes people tried to talk to Lewis he refused to stop. He put his arm around my neck and made sure we walked out the door without stopping.

Caprice and Paul were with us, Wade followed a few minutes later. He said it never fails to be an adventure.

When we arrived to the arena we were rehearsing. Two guys came and flashed badges. They took Lewis and Wade to the side. All of their faces were serious. Caprice and Brandy stood next to me. The men kept looking at me. Caprice said to tell them I needed a lawyer if they start asking a bunch of questions. I didn't understand what she meant until they started heading in my direction.

"Chantel Shaw?" One guy said.

"Yes?"

"We have some questions about the incident in Michigan." He said

"Ok"

Lewis walked over in earshot. "When was the last time your boyfriend has visited you?"

I frowned, "why?"

"We have reason to believe he may be involved with the disappearance of Reggie."

Fire burned in my stomach. "WHAT?"

"WAIT A MINUTE! That's not what you just said to us! Where is this coming from?" Lewis said angry.

I shot Brandy a look then I held two fingers by my thigh until she nodded. Then I did the same with each digit of Derrick's number. When Derrick answered Brandy walked away with the phone on her ear. Caprice was watching like a hawk. The officers told Lewis they didn't have to disclose everything to him. Lewis was angry and Wade told Lewis to let me cooperate so they could get to the bottom of everything. Caprice looked away when Wade looked her way. Every time the officers opened their mouths to say something to me Lewis got mad and argued with them, he wouldn't let me answer anything. Wade and the officers got irritated. I stared at Wade until he looked at me. I asked him why this was happening. With guilty eyes he said they're turning over every stone. He said Reggie's family is losing it cause they haven't heard from him. Lewis got in Wade's face and said none of this has anything to do with Derrick or me. Wade got visibly angry when he said that. He told Lewis he needed to calm down and cooperate with the police. Lewis said we don't answer questions without lawyers and the officers needed to leave. Wade was trying to tell him that wasn't a good idea, but Lewis wasn't budging. Lewis grabbed my hand and pulled me to the bus. When Caprice and Paul followed he told them to wait outside. Lewis spent the next five minutes cursing. He said he didn't need this drama, he was pissed. He told me to call Derrick immediately and tell him everything. I asked him if he knew what happened to Reggie and he said he didn't. He said we just so happened to all have been in the suite together when Reggie stormed out. He said he couldn't remember anyone leaving, neither could I, we were in the room getting ready for the show while the Goons were still reliving Caprice's knock down.

Chapter 14

"So who do you have here with you today?" My male interviewer asked.

I exhaled slowly, "that's my daddy and mom" my daddy and Maria waved at the camera. "My brother Cyrus and his family" Cyrus and Sherrell waved. "My grandmother and my little brothers, my aunts and cousins."

"Wow! Your family's pretty diverse. That's your mother?"

"Technically my stepmother, but she's my mother."

The interviewer looked at my family. "You're Latina?"

I smiled an embarrassed smile. "I don't see why that matters, but yes."

"You just get more and more interesting. Every interview with you we learn more and more about you. You said while growing up, that you didn't believe you could sing? How is that possible?"

"My brother has always believed in me and supported me. We were separated from our father for some time. My brother was the only one who has always supported me." Cyrus smiled and sat taller. "When only one person tells you that you can, and you have others who tell you; you can't. You tend to believe the negative before you accept the positive. Or at least in my case."

"I'm sure there's an interesting story there. But we're out of time. I guess we'll have to have you on again. Chantel Shaw everybody." The audience applauded. "Her debut album drops in November. And here's her new video from that album. Thank you for coming again Chantel." I smiled, then as soon as the camera cut away, "Chantel unless you're ashamed about your heritage never say something 'like why does it matter'. Especially while you're new. People wanna put labels on you and figure out where you belong. Even if you're comfortable with who you are embrace it."

"I'm not ashamed of who I am. But, why are you talking like my background determines where you put me? I'm a talented artist; my background doesn't determine how talented I am. When I said it didn't matter that was because either you like me or you don't. I want people to like me because I resonate with them not because I was put in a category!" Then the audience started clapping. I forgot we were talking in front of people.

"Ok well I guess I misunderstood what you meant. If I misunderstood you, you gotta know others will too. That's all I'm saying." Then he stood up and shook my hand.

When I walked off the stage my PR agent was right there. He was talking rapid fire, he said he was going to the editing booth and they'd fix that conversation. He told me he set up the tour for my family and our guide was in the lobby with them. When I stepped into the lobby a few fans were waiting for me. It was so weird signing autographs, people looking at me like I was somebody. Everybody in my family looked happy except for Auntie Tania. I rolled my eyes cause I knew what she was gonna be huffy about. The only reason she is here is because of my daddy. I had no plans on inviting her. Our tour guide approached us, "hello my name is Lindsay. I'll be your city guide today. Please step this way." She led us to a limo bus. "Are you guys hungry?" Everyone said yes. The kids said pizza, and my aunties turned their noses up at the thought, they wanted to eat somewhere nice and where they could see celebrities. Lindsay looked at me for approval. I asked where she could take them and I'd go with the kids to get Chicago styled pizza. Lindsay asked how many we're going in each direction. Both of my aunts and daddy were going to the restaurant and the rest of us were going for pizza. Lindsay put them on the list at a restaurant and gave them vouchers for their food and drinks. As soon as we dropped them off I texted Lewis and told him which pizza spot we were going to. While we were standing waiting to order our pizza's Lewis, Paul, and Ramell walked in the spot.

Mario recognized them first. I asked Lindsay to take my father and aunts on a really good tour of the city, because the rest of us were going to hang out with Lewis and Ramell. Ramell immediately gravitated to my grandmother. They had a car for us and they asked what we wanted to do. My grandmother asked if she could see the studio they were working out of. Lewis told us he and Ramell were working on the song he and I wrote when I texted. Grandma Rosa thanked Lewis for letting me take a break from our tour to spend the day with my family. Then she thanked him for sending for all of them and putting them up in such a nice hotel. "I am so embarrassed, I had something to do with the break, but I didn't have anything to do with your travel arrangements."
"Oh I'm sorry, Chantel baby who am I thanking?"
"Derrick paid for you guys to come out." I blushed.

My grandmother rubbed my arm, "he's a good man sweetheart."
I blushed again, "thanks."
Everyone's eyes got extremely big when we stepped inside the
studio. Lewis played for me what he and Ramell laid down. Then
he said we should have some fun. So he sent each person in the
booth like they were a recording star to record one minute of
whatever they wanted. DJ was up first and he decided to rap. He
was actually pretty good. Mario sang of course, and his voice as
usual was amazing. Little Adon sang twinkle, twinkle little star.
Cyrus recited one of his poems, Sherrell and Maria were overly
silly and had us all laughing as they pretended to be me and sang
all off key. They were hilarious. My cousin Larry sang with an
amazing voice as well. My other cousins sang little songs and were
real cute. Then Grandma Rosa sang, Ramell couldn't believe her
voice. Her voice was smooth like velvet, no cracking or shaking
like she was an old woman. We were having our fun when Brandy
and Wade came into the studio. Brandy said hello to Cyrus,
Sherrell, baby Rosa, Maria, and my Grandma. Then I introduced
her to everyone else. As usual Wade was on the sideline watching
us. We played around for a little longer then Lewis and Ramell had
to get going. I called Lindsey and asked her to pick us up from the
pizza place. On the way to the pizza place Grandma Rosa asked
what the deal was with Wade. I shrugged cause I really didn't
know. She gave me a knowing look. I blushed and told her that he
liked me, but with everything that's been happening lately, the
feeling was not mutual. She said *UN HUH*! and eyed me like I was
holding back from her. That made me laugh cause I was
embarrassed, I told her I'd tell her if there was something to tell.
Then Lewis called me and asked me if I wanted to bring my family
back to the hotel. I told him I didn't think that was a good idea. I
told him I would explain later. Caprice was at the hotel, and I
didn't think it would be in good taste to bring her around them
intentionally. When I told her my family was coming she got
excited, then I saw the light bulb turn on as she confirmed that my
family included Sherrell. She was moody for the rest of the day,
but I understood why so I gave her space.
As the limo bus pulled up I told Cyrus I wanted to spend time with
him if it was ok with Sherrell. I've never been away from my
brother this long in my life. I was going through big brother
withdrawals. He smiled at me and said he wanted to spend time

with me too but he understood I was working so he was happy to be there. When we got on the bus my daddy and aunts were feeling pretty good about their lunch until the kids told them about ours. Again my Auntie Tania was visibly upset but I ignored her. Lindsey took us to tourist spot after tourist spot. I whispered and asked Sherrell if it was ok with her if I took my brother away for a little brother sister time. I could tell she felt left out even though she agreed. I felt bad for her cause I wouldn't want to be stuck with my aunts nor my dad when he's with his sisters. I asked Grandma Rosa if she would keep baby Rosa for us. She agreed before I could finish. I told Cyrus and Sherrell together that Sherrell was coming with us. Sherrell was excited Cyrus wasn't but he sucked it up. When we got to their hotel everyone went upstairs to change for dinner. I sat at the bar talking to Derrick telling him how much I missed him and how I wished he would change his mind about coming out. He wasn't budging, and then he reminded me that JoJo was going to meet up with us in Louisiana. I deflated; I thanked him again for sending my family out. He asked how things were going and I told him they were fine I guess. He asked if I needed pocket change. I told him I was good, and that he was paying for our dinner tonight. Talking to him was making me sad. Before I got off the phone I told him I needed him. Cyrus and Sherrell snuck down like they were sneaking out of detention. We laughed hysterically as we waited for a cab. Then I saw Wally, one of the Goons trying to blend in with the people in the lobby. I waved him out. I introduced him to my brother and his girl then I asked what he was doing here. He said Wade told him to keep an eye on me. Cyrus frowned, I asked why. He said he was making sure I was safe. I texted Brandy and asked where she was. She said she was in the lobby looking at me fussing at Wally. I laughed cause I didn't think I was fussing and I couldn't spot her. I asked her to come join us since Sherrell was with us. She said she'd join us at the restaurant so it would be less obvious. I told Wally to tell Wade we were fine and he could go back to the hotel or wherever. As we walked up to the restaurant Brandy was right behind us. The four of us sat down to a lovely dinner. Cyrus and I kept getting caught up in our own conversations. He told me he was almost finished with school, his happiness shined through and through. I told him I wanted him to be apart of my experience. I told him JoJo was going to be my acting manager until he was ready to take over, if he wanted the job of course. He told me of course he wanted the job. Then he looked me in my eyes and asked how Caprice was doing. Even though Sherrell was talking to Brandy I didn't feel right getting into that with him right on the spot. I gave him evil eyes and I told him she was fine. Cyrus knew by my face she told me and he gave me sad eyes. He kept saying none of this was planned. I told him I liked Sherrell and she was family. He said Sherrell was family and nothing could change that. Then he paused, his eyes had tears in them but nothing dropped. He told me Caprice broke his heart, he still loves her, but they could never be like they were. I excused us from the table and Cyrus and I went outside.

"Her job was more important than me, than us I guess. I wanted to marry her, everything! She couldn't commit to me! Sherrell knows about everything so it's not like this is some secret."

"She knows she has you by default?"

"She knows everything! I was too messed up for her not to know." I crossed my arms. "How in the world!"

"I was with Caprice."

I interrupted, "and Cadence!"

"And Cadence. Cadence moved on. It was just Caprice and I for a while. The only reason Sherrell happened is because she told me I was getting too serious. She calmed down when Sherrell came on the scene."

"Why didn't you say anything?"

"What was I supposed to say? Caprice doesn't love me back? Come on now."

"You have a family with Sherrell why do you still need to see Caprice?" Cyrus didn't have an answer for my question.

"I find it interesting how she can take all this time off work to be out here with you. She didn't have time for a baby though." Cyrus shook his head.

There was a disconnect, he didn't know she was working with me; that made me quiet. I didn't say anything to that. I was going to change the subject, but seeing Wade changed it for me. "How come you guys are outside?" Wade asked with Wally in tow.

"We were having a private conversation." Cyrus said glaring at Wade.

Wade put his hands up, "didn't mean to intrude." Then they walked inside.

"What's his deal?" Cyrus asked. Brandy was watching the interaction. Then Wade walked to our table, Brandy shot me a look. "Did you invite him?"

"No, but if he sits down he's paying." I smiled at Cyrus.
We watched as Wade had our waiter bring two more chairs. I didn't like how he barged in on our dinner, but whatever. Cyrus and I continued our conversation for a while longer. I told him about the guy Reggie coming up missing, and how the police wanted to question Derrick about it. Derrick had a lawyer call on his behalf and that seemed to squash the noise for now, but it didn't feel like the situation was over. No one has heard from Reggie yet, his family is beyond worried. I would be lying if I said I wasn't feeling a little worried about him too, even if he is a jerk. Cyrus told me that he saw our mother at the grocery store. He said he was with Sherrell and the baby, and she didn't even acknowledge them. He said she wanted to know if what Reggie told her was true that I was out singing for tricks. My blood boiled when he repeated it, he was angry as he told me. I asked him why he didn't defend me. He said he was caught off guard by how much she didn't care. I told him she cared enough to speak on it; she's never done that before. My poor brother is still waiting and hoping she will come around, it's not in her to come around. "There's one more thing." He said taking breaths like he was trying to find his words. "I love our father, so don't take this the wrong way." I searched his face, "I think he has a gambling problem."

"Why do you think that?"

"He keeps hitting me up for money. Promising that he's gonna pay me back. Then one day he comes with all the money I've ever given him and then some. He's spending real big, and really feeling himself. When I saw that I knew it was only a matter of time before he came back. Sure enough here he comes. Maria has him on an allowance and she's the breadwinner in their house." My heart sank.

"He has an addiction?" I said wide-eyed, feeling so disappointed.
"I hope I'm wrong, I really like Maria. I don't wish that type of situation on any woman, especially a good one." He exhaled "Didn't it seem great when we found our father who had been looking for us? Crying for us, every orphan's dream right? Then reality sets in and your parents aren't perfect no matter how hard

you try to only see them that way." I exhaled too, "you're the only dependable one in my life. Well you and Derrick, when he's not being a mule!" I yelled.

Cyrus laughed, "battle of the wills I see?"

"If that's what you wanna call it. I didn't know Wade liked me until Derrick told me."

"And what about now? Do you like Wade?" He eyed me.

"How could you ask me that!" I said acting insulted.

"Because I know you. You love Derrick, but when he's not around you tend to go in the direction of whomever's paying you attention."

I frowned at him, "I do not!"

He laughed, "Yes you do. That boy in high school. What's the name of that guy who followed you around at the coffee shop?" I knew, but I wasn't gonna volunteer to make his point. "Whatever, you know who I'm talking about. There's nothing wrong with wanting and needing attention. You just can't indulge every person who wants to give it to you. There's some pretty twisted people in this world." He said

"Like Kevin?"

He looked like a light bulb went off. "Yeah like Kevin." He started thinking real hard.

"What?"

"Nothing for now, let me chew on it for a minute." Then he took his phone out his pocket. "I need to call Derrick. I'll be inside with you guys in a minute." He said kind of walking away from me.

OF COURSE! Wade was watching, I rolled my eyes. "Who says we wanted to have dinner with you!" I said full of attitude, Brandy and Sherrell looked surprised.

"I figured since we're all here, we might as well eat together."

Wally was sitting there with a goofy grin. I rolled my eyes and sat down. "Is everything ok?" Wade asked all concerned.

"Fine!" I said, but I wasn't. The thought of my daddy having an addiction was bugging me.

"Where's Caprice?" Wade asked

"She's laying down," then Brandy leaned forward. "Female problems," she whispered.

Wally and Wade made disgusted faces, and we laughed at them.

Cyrus came to the table he was quiet and thoughtful. He wasn't paying Wade too much attention. Wade engaged him in a little bit of conversation, but Cyrus kept looking at him like he was reading him, while Wade was doing the same to Cyrus. We decided to catch up to the family and have dessert with them. Lindsey was taking them to a fancy bakery slash lounge restaurant place. This place was known for its gourmet desserts. We got there just before the family got there, and of course Auntie Tania was now hopping mad. "We flew all the way up here to be with you and you can't have lunch or dinner with us! You're too famous to have time for your family already?" She spit at me.

The only person coming to my defense was Cyrus and I told him to hold on. "First of all, we could've had lunch together but YOU chose to go somewhere fancy instead of staying with the group. You didn't have your panties in a bunch about it until you found out that we were actually with someone noteworthy. As far as dinner goes, I wanted to spend time with my brother! If you weren't on such a narcissistic mission you'd understand that."

"A what?" She was angry that she didn't understand what I meant.

"She's calling you self-centered and selfish momma!" Larry said giving me apologetic eyes.

"I'm selfish! I'm selfish! How you gonna fly us across the country not to spend any time with us. Why even have us here for all that?"

"I didn't want you to come, you can thank your brother for bringing you out here! He begged me to send for you as well. You're not here because I wanted you here!" My auntie looked shocked and surprised. I felt satisfied that she shut up! When we got to the table everybody was quiet for a long time. My Auntie Deborah started talking to lighten the mood at the table. She was being silly and eventually everyone started to relax. Everyone except Auntie Tania and I that is, she kept shooting me daggers with her eyes, and I kept rolling my eyes at her. She was just mad that I told her the truth. Everyone's eyes were big as their HUGE desserts were set in front of them. I ordered this apple streusel cheesecake cupcake. The description sounded divine, and the cupcake was HUGE. Cyrus and I tasted each other's desserts; he had red velvet cake with a vanilla milkshake. I had a coffee milkshake with mine. Everyone looked at us like we were crazy when we ordered. Brandy and Sherrell split a carrot cake cupcake.

I saw Wade and my Auntie Tania down there talking and I didn't like it one bit. I knew she was down there badmouthing me. So I started whispering to Cyrus talking about our dessert but looking at her the whole time so she could see how it felt. She got madder and madder until she exploded. "te desenvuelves mis nervios (you get on my nerves!)"

"What?" I said smiling at her.

"Tania Dejar de actuar como este! (Tania, stop acting like this!)" Grandma Rosa said, "es su sobrina (that is your niece)"

"Ella es un poco malariado (she's a spoiled little brat)" my aunt said.

"Si usted siente de esta manera por que llegaste? (If you feel this way why did you come?)" Grandma Rosa asked

"I guess I was hoping she'd prove me wrong, but you're just like your mother!"

Her comment sent fire through me and it was like I was outside of myself. I went flying through the air all the way across our long table and I was pushing her in her chair before she had a chance to stand up. She almost fell backwards but my dad caught her chair. In one quick motion she was out of her seat and I felt the warmth of her hand imprint on my face. I tried to hit her back but she blocked my hit and slapped me again. That's when I remembered I wasn't a fighter, but it appeared my auntie was and she was ready to mop the floor with me. I picked up a fork off the table to stab her with but my dad pulled her back and Cyrus was moving me back. "DON'T YOU EVER COME AROUND ME AGAIN? YOU ARE DEAD TO ME!" I screamed at her.

"Oh, does being a whore like your mother bother you? At least I know where your weakness is." She smiled

"You're just jealous because you're old and washed up. No matter what, you will never be me! Your opportunity has come and gone! You're jealous!" I yelled

She tried to lunge at me and Cyrus pushed her back. "You are out of line! We've had enough, you can go now!" Cyrus said standing in front of me like a wall.

"Is that how you're going to talk to your auntie Cyrus! You see how she did us!"

"I saw everything and like I said you are out of line! And it's time for you to go!"

"We rode together how am I supposed to get back to the hotel?" She said snatching her jacket off the chair.

"I hope you brought some money cause you're not riding with us!" Cyrus said

"Cyrus!" Our father said.

"Don't Cyrus me! You saw how she's been acting this whole time and you say nothing. You even go along with it. I don't understand why you would let her talk to your ONLY daughter like this! My name is the last name you should be calling right now. You should've checked your sister a long time ago, and none of this would be happening now."

Anger flashed across my father's face. "So it's supposed to make you a man talking to me like this! We can step outside and handle this right now!" My father said putting his arms up.

"Lead the way old man!" Cyrus said not backing down.

"ENOUGH!" Grandma Rosa yelled! People were snapping pictures of our table and looking in aw! "Tania apologize to Chantel right now!"

"But Mom!" Auntie Tania said.

"APOLOGIZE!"

"Sorry!" She spit.

"LIKE YOU MEAN IT!" Grandma Rosa said through clinched teeth and lips.

Auntie Tania huffed, "Sorry Chantel!" She said rolling her eyes.

"That's the best you can do? Remember you have no way home."

"Sorry Chantel for calling you a whore."

"Tania you are so jealous you can't see straight! What kind of an Auntie provokes her niece to want to fight her? You need to grow up! Next you'll be complaining about how she treated you like you deserve to be here. You don't have to be here. We are here because her man brought us out to support her, and look how you act. You don't have to wonder when the next time you'll be out here will be. And Daniel really? You are forever defending Tania even when you know she's wrong! Apologize to Cyrus! He's defending his sister just like you are."

Daddy looked at Cyrus and then my younger brothers. He blew air and folded his arms. "You must have me confused with somebody else!"

Grandma Rosa marched over to Daddy and grabbed his ear, "WHAT DID I SAY?"

"OUCH MOMMA! DANG! OK! OK!" She let go of his ear.
"Sorry Cyrus!"
"You kids don't let these goofy adults stand as examples on how to be when you grow up. You don't defend anyone to a fault. Tania you're always starting stuff!" Grandma Rosa said sitting down to finish eating.
I walked over to Grandma Rosa, "Next time I know who to invite and who not to. I'm tired, I'm going to head out to my hotel." I said giving her a hug. Then I hugged Maria, and my Auntie Deborah even though I wondered if she felt like Tania and just didn't say anything. I hugged my brothers, Sherrell, and the sleeping baby Rosa. Cyrus walked Brandy, Wally, Wade, and I outside. Wade

told Lindsey to put the tab on his card. I told Cyrus I didn't want to see them for a long time. He told me he understood and that he'd call me later. In the cab I put my head on Brandy's shoulder. She patted my head. Wade said my family was pretty typical. I wanted to be offended, but what could I say to that? I didn't respond I looked away and kept my head on Brandy's shoulder. I was over the day and I wanted it all over. When we got to the suite Brandy and I went to the room. Caprice had the door locked. We told her it was us and she opened the door in her robe kind of bent over for dramatic effect. Of course Wade was watching as we walked in. We locked the door and Caprice sat on the edge of the bed listening to how the day went. With pleading eyes she asked to see a picture of baby Rosa. She cried a little while she stared at the picture. You'd swear she was looking for traces of herself in baby Rosa's face. I asked Caprice what Cyrus thought she did for Mitigated. She said office temp work, I asked her why she didn't tell him everything and she said it was easier this way. Then there was a knock at the door. Caprice hurried under the covers on the other bed. Then Brandy answered the door. Wade was standing there his face was very serious. "Can you guys come out."
"One minute" then she closed the door. "There's police you guys." Caprice grabbed her phone and they both called numbers and then put their phones in their pockets. I wondered if I should call Derrick but Wade was knocking again. We stepped out the room just outside the doorway.
Lewis was sitting in a chair at the table now facing the police. "We have notified the next of kin and we regret to inform you that we

found Reginald Flowers' body. We will need statements from each of you." One officer said.

The other pointed to the camera man who's been following us around, "I'm gonna need all of your footage."

"Why do you need his footage? You need to find the person responsible for this. We could all be in danger!" Wade said completely irritated.

"More than likely this homicide occurred within your group rather than outside. Everyone and everything needs to be reviewed." The officer responded calmly.

"We have engagements to meet how long is this going to take?" He asked

"The sooner we get started the sooner we will be done."

"We need lawyers! We can't just sit here and set ourselves up like that." Wade yelled, "We don't have time for this!"

"We will need to make arrangements for legal representation, but how can we speed this along?" Lewis said calmly.

"I suggest everyone get on the phone with their lawyers and come up with something brilliant. We'll be back in the morning, but we'll take your footage tonight."

"YOU CAN'T DO THAT WITHOUT..."

The officer cut Wade off. "I've got the paperwork." He said handing Wade documents. Then he looked at Phillip the camera guy. "Sir!" He said opening a bag.

Phillip put his cartridges in the bag. The officer made him put the one in the camera in the bag as well. They took everyone's names and wrote info from each ID. As soon as they left I called Derrick in tears. The three of us were in the room. I asked Derrick what to do. He told me to calm down and they already had lawyers in route to us. He said all three of us would be represented. Then I told him about my aunt and how she acted. He listened then he told me to be prepared for things to probably get uglier before they got better.

In the morning the phones were ringing to our suite. One of the Goons pounded on the door and told me to pick up the phone.

"This is Ryan Wallace, I'm in the lobby. Please bring Caprice and Brandy down so we can discuss business."

I popped up and the girls looked at me.

I told him we would be down as soon as we brushed our teeth. We ran in the bathroom brushing our teeth and putting decent clothing on to go downstairs. When we got down to the lobby I was happy to see JoJo and whom I assumed was Ryan. "What's up Chantel?" JoJo said giving me a hug.

"This is Brandy and Caprice."

"This is my cousin Ryan. He's gonna be your legal representation." JoJo said

"I thought you weren't coming until Louisiana?" I asked

"That's what I thought too. Oh well right. You guys hungry?" He held a room card key, "let's order room service I'm starving." He said

Caprice smiled at me and then I noticed Brandy, they both had goofy grins. "Who's the white boy?" She whispered.

"Derrick's cousin, they both are."

"How?" Brandy asked

"I'll go over the family tree later."

"He's not like any white boy I've ever seen." Caprice said

Ryan and JoJo had a two-bedroom suite just like ours. Ryan set his laptop on the table and then he set up his little shop. JoJo ordered breakfast and told the person over the phone they'd get an even better tip if they hurried. Twenty minutes later we were eating. It was nice not fighting for our food with the always-starving Goons. JoJo was reminding me so much of Derrick I missed him more. Ryan video conferenced Malcolm on his laptop. I smiled so big when I saw him, I didn't realize how much I missed him. Malcolm's face was serious as usual; first he asked how things were going. I told him everything I knew. Malcolm listened while Ryan took notes. Malcolm asked what was on the videos. I said nothing other than us messing around. I told him the camera wasn't there when Caprice laid Reggie out. Then Brandy said the footage also showed Wade on the phone a lot, and him leaving to go look for Reggie. I was surprised she knew that so I asked her how she knew. Malcolm told me she's doing her job. Then Caprice chimed in that she had Wade's phone records, and that he spends a lot of time on the phone with the West Coast. Caprice said someone was visiting that night, but neither one of them could get a good look at the guy without looking suspicious. I sat back listening to my girls reporting in, and I couldn't believe it. JoJo watched my eyes like Derrick would. "Why did Reggie dislike you so much?" Ryan asked

"Probably because I didn't like him."

"He felt she thought too much of herself." Caprice said

"How do you know?" I asked

"He told me." Caprice said

I frowned, "Chantel don't be mad. They're doing what they're supposed to." JoJo said

"Clearly." I said feeling like the only person not in the loop. Listening to the way Brandy and Caprice described that night made me feel like I don't observe anything. They were so detailed in everything. Malcolm was quiet for a minute; as he thought about what they were telling him. When he stared at Caprice, she swallowed then he turned his attention to Brandy. "What's happening with Paul?"

Brandy shifted in her seat, "everything is going as it should. Lewis is clean."

I couldn't help it! I got up, "WHAT IS GOING ON?" Everybody looked at me like I was overreacting. "Do you even really like Paul?"

"Yes." Brandy said blank staring at me.

"But you're using him to get to Lewis?"

"Not to get to him, but I am keeping an eye on him. Making sure that the way he presents himself is the way he actually is." She said matter of factly.

"What about Paul? He really likes you!"

"I love him too, but this is business. Chantel please calm down." She said gently.

"Chantel, my number one priority while you're out there is to make sure you're safe. I sent my most capable girls to make sure you stay that way. Can you handle hearing this or do you feel like ignorance is bliss?" Malcolm asked in as gentle a tone as he could, but it felt like he was telling me to shut up and suck it up.

My mind kept sticking to his statement, that I was a priority in the world of Malcolm. With everything he has going on in his life, he actually cares whether I'm safe or not? My daddy didn't even ask how safe I was while I was out here. He was concerned with being seen and living good. Now I felt stupid, and everybody was looking at me. "No, I'm fine." I said quietly.

"So what's your plan?" Malcolm asked Ryan. Ryan was super sharp; he asked questions about things I think none of us had thought of. Malcolm shot back some section code something or another laws and bylaws. Ryan answered back in the same manner, we looked at each other. And for once I was happy to not be the only person who didn't know what they were talking about. We sat there watching, as they talked for a long time in a language none of us understood. Then my cellphone started going off it was Wade. I sent him to voicemail and he called right back.

Malcolm told me to answer it and to put him on speaker. "Hello Wade, I'm in the middle of something can I call you back?"

"Are you ok? No one knows where you are and the girls are not here either." He said sounding real concerned.

"I'm fine, we're talking to my manager and our lawyer right now. Did you need something?"

I could hear the question before he spoke, "your manager is out here? I thought he wasn't coming until Louisiana?"

"Did I tell you that?" I looked at the girls.

"I overheard you telling Brandy." He confessed.

"Wade you are one of the nosiest people I know. We are being taken care of. I guess we'll see you at the station."

"You're not going to ride with us?"

Even through the screen Malcolm's impatience was clearly visible. "No Wade we're fine. Thank you for everything."

When I hung up Malcolm opened his mouth. "I already know. You guys are not staying with them anymore. I guess I'm hanging around the rest of the duration of the tour." JoJo said nonchalantly.

"What?" I asked

"He's too possessive Chantel. He always has tabs on everything you do. He manages Shameless not you. You'd swear you were his woman the way he's all over you. You're sweet so you don't notice it. But he's too overbearing." Brandy said

"This is gonna cause friction when we follow her." Caprice said

"Chantel, talk to Lewis he's reasonable. Or you can have Derrick call him if you prefer." Malcolm said

"I can talk to him, that's not a problem."

For my benefit Ryan went over what to say and what not to say when we went down to the police station. Then JoJo walked us

down to Lewis' suite. The Goons were all spread out all over the place and I could hear Lewis and Wade talking. When we walked in the door the Goons stopped talking and stared at us in disbelief.

"Alright Caprice where did you find this white boy?" Someone yelled out and they all started laughing.

"See if I cook for you guys next stop." They started straightening up and apologizing. "This is Joseph and he's my manager." I said, Lewis and Wade came out the room. I introduced JoJo; Lewis shook JoJo's hand. Wade looked upset. "Lewis, can I talk to you for a minute?" When we went in the room Wade acted like he was coming in the room with us. I put my hand up and told Lewis I wanted to talk to him alone. Lewis frowned at Wade for trying to follow. "What's his deal?"

Lewis smiled while shaking his head. "He's good at business. I had no idea you would be his undoing."

"Me? How?" I said putting my hands on my hips.

"Never mind what's up?"

"We're gonna bunk out with Joseph for the rest of the duration of the tour. I hope you don't mind one more plus one when we go out."

"He's white!" He said smiling while he frowned.

"Only by his skin!" I said, Lewis started cracking up. "Joseph is one of the coolest people I know."

"Caprice likes him doesn't she?" Lewis asked

"Who doesn't she like?" I blew air.

He laughed again. "Well I hope he doesn't give her lazy sex." He said laughing again.

"So it's cool?"

"Of course! Doesn't matter to me." He said, "I can't wait for this tour to be over. I'm not even trying to think about an international tour right now!" He said throwing himself on the bed.

"They want you to tour overseas?" My eyes were big.

"Yeah, and its good money too. I just…" he shook his head…

"You're missing her aren't you?"

He rubbed his chest, "terribly! I don't know what to do."

"I wish I knew what to tell you."

He stared at the floor for a minute then he shrugged, "oh well right? Let's go talk to the police."

"Ok we'll meet you down there." I said, when I opened the door. Wade walked in closing the door behind him. "What are you doing?"

"I thought you didn't have a manager?"

"I do now, why is that a big deal?"

"Why didn't you consider me?"

"You've got your hands full with Shameless. I wanted someone who would have time for me."

"I've never even heard of this guy. He can't do a better job than I can."

"You are really possessive aren't you?" He frowned at me; "I wanna work with Joseph for now. If I feel like he's in over his head, I know where to find you Wade. What's the big deal?"

"Chantel you are talented, you could go pretty far. I'd hate to see your talent get wasted behind a manager who doesn't know what he's doing. This move right here could kill your career before it begins."

"If I have to look forward to hotel living, clubbing, and entourage deaths on the regular I'll pass. I'm gonna try it this way for a minute with Joseph. If it turns out to be a wrong decision then I'll move on! Now move I gotta get going." I said pushing past him.

"Leave her alone Wade. You really don't know how to take No for an answer do you?" Lewis said glaring at him.

We packed up our room real fast and moved our things up to JoJo's room. The five of us went to the police department in a cab. We were in first. Ryan let us answer most of the questions the police had, they were acting on behalf of the police in Michigan where the crime took place. They let us go relatively fast. Ryan and the detectives exchanged information, and then we were done with our portion. We waited for Lewis and then we went to the Arena for our sound check.

****

"Ok so, you're gonna have a nice little agenda when you get home. The label wants to finalize everything and then you'll be in full promo mode. Unfortunately your marketing budget isn't big enough to afford Amber just yet." JoJo winked at me. "But I was able to book you some studio time at North Star for rehearsals. That way you'll only have to be in LA at the studios a couple of days to shoot the next video. He showed me a calendar for the first month after the tour, and I was going to be working hard promoting my album. I exhaled, I was trying to envision down time with Derrick in there somehow. My phone rang again and the ringtone told me it was my daddy calling again.

"Why don't you want to talk to him?"

"I'm disappointed." JoJo sat down to hear me out. "Derrick told you how we grew up?"

241

He looked like he was trying to remember, "Refresh my memory."
"Cold blooded mother! She never acted like she cared about us.
Led us to believe that her man, was our father. Changed our last
names to his and everything. All Cyrus and I ever really had was
each other. Then when Derrick's grandfather passed suddenly, I
wanted to know my own grandparents, so I asked Ms. Laverne
how I could find them. She told Malcolm and he told me he could
do a background check on my parents and find out for me. That's
when we found my Grandmother and my real daddy. It was music
to our ears to hear that not only did we have a real daddy but that
he loved and cared for us. He had been looking for us all that time
and we didn't even know it. He taught me a lot about music, and

my musical gene actually comes from him. Now it's like they're
pushing me towards music to benefit them. My Auntie Tania is the
worse, but the way she says stuff and then my other aunt and

daddy go along with her. It's like she's the only one rude enough to
say what they're thinking. Instead of defending me my daddy
defends her, makes me think he thinks like she does. It hurts! You
know?"
"I hear you, but you gotta remember your parents are human. They
mess up just like we do."
"Your parents are perfect, what would you know?" I teased.
"Jeff and Lauren are far from perfect. My momma is crazy! Make
her mad and you better hope she only comes after you with a knife.

And my dad..." He laughed, "Jeff and I were coming into our man
strength and we were feeling ourselves. Call ourselves banding
together. United we stand, and united we got our hats handed to us.
I can still hear Uncle Tim laughing as our dad beat us down." I
started laughing. "You gotta understand we were a pretty big deal
at the time. We thought we were invincible too, and it was the two
of us. Well we thought Drew would stand with us, but
he wasn't stupid. I remember thinking is this what it feels like to
get beat up? I wasn't trying to let him win either. My dad is crazy,
although I hate it, he's the only person who can get away with
calling me boy." He said still laughing
"I still don't get the connection of how this relates to my story." I
said
"Parents make mistakes and they mess up. The older we get the
more human they become."

'O…k…." I said still not getting it.

"Oh and he messed up beating us up like that. Cause when our momma got home! He was running for his life." He said cracking up.

"How badly were you beaten?"

"Two black eyes, busted nose, busted mouth, knots upside my head, bruises all over my chest, permanent size twelve footprint on my butt! You should've seen my brother he was worse." Then he laughed, "after that he commends us for sticking together." He shrugged, "parents are crazy!"

"Yeah." I sighed

"Let that man apologize. Set your boundaries and enforce them. He's not perfect, but he's your father." He said

"Derrick tell you to say all this?" I eyed him.

"Right!" He winked

Then Caprice came out of the room. She looked good in her dress; it left nothing to the imagination as she strutted around the room.

"I'm ready!" She said modeling for us.

"Yeah, but the question is… for what?" JoJo joked, "I'm just kidding. Although your dress is showing everything you look nice."

"How are we kissing tonight, tongue or no tongue?"

He made a tired sound, "if we have to kiss at all. It's your show, you drive. Although, I would like to hook up with somebody tonight."

"Like having me on your arm is gonna stop that." Caprice rolled her eyes.

"True." He nodded his head.

"Ready?" Brandy said putting on lipstick as she walked out the room.

"Paul's a lucky man!" JoJo said

"Thank you! Thank you!" Brandy said twirling for us. "Looking good yourself Joseph."

"Thanks, let's have fun tonight cause you've got four shows over the next four days."

We met the Goons in the lobby. They were drooling over Caprice, as she smiled, she acted like she was surprised by their responses. Wade and Lewis came down and immediately Wade started talking JoJo's ear off about business. The whole car ride over you could hear Wade flapping his gums. When we got to the club as soon as we sat down an old school jam came on. JoJo grabbed my hand and said we had to dance to this song. The first time we went out dancing I had no idea of what to expect. I stood there looking stupid as JoJo broke it down to the floor and then picked it up. He was an excellent dancer, and I was convinced that dancing runs in their family. All of them know how to, and really well. Now that I'm used to it I can kind of see how he dances like Derrick. When we went back to the table the Goons were shouting out their approvals. Brandy asked him where he learned to dance like that. He gave her a dumb look and asked her like what? She tried to clean it up. He told us initially his sister and Amber taught them, but they all took dance classes at The Center in Richmond and then at Amber's school. Then Caprice pulled JoJo back out to the dance floor. If I didn't know better, I would've told them how cute they looked together. At the booth next to us, I could hear the guys going off about Caprice being with JoJo. A couple of the Goons, Kirk and Ray, went over to the table, they had some choice words with the guys. Then there was evil silence from that booth. GREAT! Just what we need. Then Wade came over with an acoustic guitar, and asked me if I would play a song before Lewis and I performed our song. JoJo and Caprice came back to the table. JoJo's face was very serious. "What's this?"

"I thought it would be a good idea to have her play a song before their song together." Wade said matter of factly.

"Wade when are you gonna learn to discuss these things with me first?" JoJo said glaring.

"My bad I'll remember next time."

"Dang Skippy you'll remember because she's not doing it tonight." JoJo said

"How you think you can just say no? This whole night has been prearranged, you can't just up and change our agenda."

"I'm sure your agreement is for Shameless to perform. Chantel is not under contract with you, so you cannot legally bind her to any agreements. Maybe you didn't know my name before, but I bet you won't forget it now." JoJo glared at Wade.

"Here's the thing, I'm not the person you want to make an enemy out of." Wade said stepping into JoJo's face.

JoJo smiled, "your problem is that you underestimate a stranger. You have no idea who I am!"
I looked at Brandy and Caprice, they almost looked unaffected, and they were calm. Lewis came over, "What's going on?" Wade explained the situation and how JoJo was being unreasonable.

Lewis was quiet for a minute, "if Chantel performs it's free publicity for her. It won't make or break the shows they're all sold out. You should've gone to Joseph; you know he's her representation. I bet if the shoe was on the other foot you would've had me marching out of here." Then he looked at me and then at JoJo. "I get it. Business is business! Whatever you guys come up with I'll roll with it. You need to decide soon though cause we're up in five." Then Lewis looked at Wade, "civilly!"
Wade blew air, "come on Chantel!" He reached out to grab my arm.
JoJo's face turned to stone, "Touch her and I will break your hand!" I moved my arm to avoid his reach. I sat down and moved close to Caprice. "We're leaving!" JoJo said
"This is not the stance you wanna take with me!" Wade threatened. "I'm not one of your Goons! You can argue like a female all you want by yourself we're out of here." JoJo said taking my hand.
My hand was sweaty when I gave it to JoJo, the whole scene made me nervous. When we got to the hotel and the three of them were busy. JoJo got on the phone and Brandy and Caprice got on their computers. I sat there nerved up feeling like I didn't know what to do with myself. JoJo told me to get some sleep cause we had radio interviews in the morning. I took a shower, but my mind was racing. I wanted to call Derrick, but I kind of felt like it was pointless. I wanted to see him and be with him, but
he wasn't coming back no matter how much I begged. Lewis called me a few hours later and told me it was a good thing we left when we did. He said a fight broke out in the club with those guys in the booth next to us. He said Kirk and Ray were fine and they got out in time. I actually liked Kirk and Ray, they were the Goons sent in to replace Reggie and another guy. I don't remember his name, but the other guy had a family situation so he had to go home. Kirk and Ray were not as goofy as the rest, and they were about business. When I walked out the room to tell everybody what Lewis told me Brandy was gone. JoJo's shirt was open; I saw

his six-pack and turned my eyes. Caprice still had her dress on and she looked relaxed. "What's going on?" I asked

"Night cap, you want a drink?" JoJo said walking over to the fridge.

"Where's Brandy?"

"Paul." Caprice said

"Were you guys about to hook up?" I asked

Caprice made a face, "I thought about it. But I'll wait!

We're almost done. I have specific taste," she said nonchalantly.

"Good thing I wasn't interested." JoJo shot back, "I have specific taste as well."

"JoJo do you date black girls?" Caprice asked

He looked at Caprice's dress. "Are we talking about dating or hooking up?" He handed me a drink and then went to sit back on the couch. He patted the seat next to him for me to sit down.

"Dating." Caprice said

"I date everybody, if I'm attracted to you I'll date you. Hooking up is just hooking up."

"So you've dated a black girl before?" She asked

He looked at me with a blank expression. "Didn't I just say that?"

"So why don't I meet your specifications?"

"For one you work for my cousin! That's mixing business with pleasure. Two, you're in love with her brother! That's drama waiting to happen. Three, you couldn't handle someone like me. You're used to the average guy. Nothing about me is average! I use my powers for good." Then he smiled.

Caprice looked at the floor. She looked like she was debating on how to respond to that. "You can tell?"

"Of course! And I read your reports. This is business, you and Brandy getting caught up. You've been working too long. You gotta switch assignments, but you came in this one all twisted up so go figure."

"I don't see the point in taking time off now. He's got a family." Caprice said sounding defeated.

"How many reports have you written in the past year? You sound love struck even now?"

Caprice waved her hands; "I don't wanna talk about this anymore. I'm too depressed."

Caprice's face was long and she was on the verge of tears. I felt
bad for her, and I tried to imagine myself in her shoes. I couldn't
imagine breathing if Derrick was living like a happy family with
someone else. If I had to stay away from him it would tear me up. I
comforted my friend in our room. She cried her eyes out on my
shoulder. She told me she does love Cyrus no matter what. She
was crying so hard I brought the roll of tissue from our bathroom
to her. Then I had her get in the other bed. I put the covers over
her, and I rubbed her head like Cyrus would rub mine when I was
upset. I even cried a little with her.

****

"The label is pushing back your release date. They don't like the
cover picture you have. Did you like it?" JoJo asked
My picture was pretty basic, but I didn't want to stress about it. I
sighed, "That's fine." Then a light bulb went off. "Does this mean I
have time to add another song to the project?"
"I think so, I'll have to check. I wanna pull in Gwen for your photo
session. I liked the pictures she got of you for EA."
"Can we afford her?" I asked with big eyes. I loved the pictures
they had for me at Elegant Affairs. Looking at those pictures made
me actually feel pretty.
"I'll work it out with her."
"I want to ask Lewis to work with me on this song."
"Another song?" He said shaking his head.
"All those other songs are for his project. It shouldn't be a problem.
I'll call him." I called him and asked him to come to our suite.
Paul came with Lewis. I went over what I had for him and I tapped
the count out to the melody. Lewis smiled real big he said he liked
the concept. Then he told JoJo that he and Wade would have to
work out the paperwork. He told me he was in but he knew Wade
would try to be difficult. JoJo smiled wide and said Wade would
be on board. "I'm surprised he didn't come with you." I said
Lewis smiled, "he's with his kids."
"His what?" Caprice said coming out the room and sitting next to
me.
"His kids."
"You know where they are?" I asked
"Yeah" he said watching me get my shoes. "What are you doing?"
"When my family came he was all in our business. What goes
around comes around." I said standing.

"Seriously Chantel?" Lewis said

"Oh! I'm so serious." I said grabbing my purse. "Let's go."
Everybody came with me. We walked a few blocks down the street
to a park. There were kids playing all over the park. On a bench
over to the side Wade was facing three kids. They didn't look
happy to see him, more like they were being lectured. When we
got close Wade spun around suddenly. He scanned our group then
he shook his head. "It's Shameless!" The boy said, all of their eyes
got big.

"What are you guys doing here?" He said not happy to see us.

"We just wanted to say hello to the family." Lewis said

Then a woman walked in our direction. She didn't look happy to be
there either. She had on a long strapless dress that didn't fit her. It
looked like it was supposed to be soft and flowing but instead it
almost clung to her body. It looked like she moved up a dress size
or two, but she was in denial. I guess she was dressed up, but yuck!
She lit up when she saw Lewis. "It's about time! I kept telling him
I didn't believe he worked with Shameless cause we never see you.
How you doing I'm Karquisha!" She said with the ghetto'est tone.

"I'm good." Lewis said, none of us spoke cause she didn't
acknowledge that we were there.

"Ooh! Ooh! Let me get a picture!" She said pointing her camera
phone at their faces as she came in for the picture.

"Ok..." Lewis said as she snapped.

"Shameless! Can I come to your show tonight?" The little boy said.

"Ooh! Me too!" Both of the girls said at the same time.

"You gotta ask your dad." He said nodding to Wade.

All three of them deflated, and put their eyes to the ground. "Well
what about me! I don't need his permission to do nothing! Shoot!
He owes me a night out! It's the least you could do!" She said like
she deserved a hook up.

"KEKE SHUT UP! YOU'RE NOT GOING TO THE SHOW!
NOW SIT DOWN AND SHUT UP! YOU NEED TO BE
WORRIED ABOUT WHY OUR DAUGHTER IS RUNNING
AROUND LIKE A LITTLE WHORE!" Wade barked

"YOU SHUT UP! SHE RUNNING AROUND LOOKING FOR
HER DADDY WHO'S NEVER HERE!"

Wade got in her face. "SHE'S RUNNING AROUND HERE
ACTING LIKE HER MOTHER!"

The woman slapped him, Paul grabbed Wade's arm before he retaliated. My heart sunk he was about to hit her like she was a man. Now I felt bad for coming, the woman was screaming at Wade calling him all kinds of names. She made sure she wasn't in arm's reach while she ran her mouth screaming all his business. Only one of the three kids was hers, I assumed it was the oldest behind the things they were saying. I wondered where the other mothers were, and the way she spoke she was the sanest one. Paul told Wade he understood, but he could not let Wade put his hands on a female. Then she looked at Brandy and asked her if she was there for Wade. Brandy looked at her like she was crazy but she didn't say anything. Karquisha got mad and started cursing Brandy from the top of her head to the bottom of her feet. Then she looked at Caprice and I, and asked the same question. When the girl started to come at us Paul couldn't block Wade. When she saw Wade got around Paul she took off running in her dress and out of her shoes towards the parking lot, with Wade right behind her. The kids looked at us with evil eyes. I tugged at JoJo's arm to leave, I regretted coming. You could hear yelling and screaming, they were arguing and I had no intentions of following them. We slowly walked away while the kids stared at all of us with hatred in their eyes. We stopped a block away at a cafe. "That was intense!" Paul said

"You see how unaffected those kids were? If that's what I had waiting at home for me, I'd stay gone too!" Lewis said

"How come you've never met any of them?" I asked

"We're not best friends or family. It's not like he's met my love. He can't even handle meeting you!"

"What is that supposed to mean?"

"If you saw the same scene I just saw it should be self explanatory. You're a good person and you're talented. If it wasn't for that I think he'd be all over Caprice." He smiled

"I'm second choice?" She said like she was offended.

"Admit it, you thought he was cute at first." Lewis said

"You surely do be concerned with who I'm interested in." She said rolling her eyes.

Our waitress came over and as she took our orders she realized who Lewis was. She got so excited. Lewis asked her to calm down but she was screaming and carrying on. When she took out her phone Lewis told us to go. We all moved double speed out of there. The girl was walking behind us screaming and on the phone. When we got outside Lewis yelled, "RUN!" With my girls in front and JoJo behind me we ran back to the hotel. Looking like big ole kids we went back up to our suite. Room service it was gonna be! That night at the show that girl Karquisha was there looking a Hot Mess! Her dress was too tight and too short. It didn't compliment her at all, but she knew she was too cute. Her hair was so ghetto I couldn't look directly at it for fear of my eyes crossing. I went on stage with Lewis who had the house rocking as usual. Even though my normal nerves had kicked in I knew I could feel her ghetto presence staring me down while I was on stage. We performed my song and then Lewis kept me on stage even longer than normal. The crowd was loving it so it wasn't like I had a problem with it. When I finally exited the stage left, Ghetto queen was still staring me down. Brandy and Caprice were right there making sure I walked with them to the dressing room. Brandy said I needed to learn how to fight. We all started laughing; she said I need to know self-defense or something. "What are you going to do when I'm not here?"

Caprice and I looked at her. "Where are you going?" Caprice asked

She smiled sheepishly, "Paul and I wanna get married."

"WHAT????" We screamed.

"How is this gonna work, with his schedule and everything?" I asked

"We're gonna work out the details, but we want to start a family right away. So I won't be traveling with you." She said

In that moment my stomach felt so empty. I missed Derrick like crazy, and I wouldn't mind a family with him. I couldn't wait for this tour to be over. I wanted to kiss him, and hold him, and feel his love all over me. I looked at Caprice and she had an "I'm happy for you, but this makes me feel bad about my life" look on her face. "I'm so happy for you Brandy. Let us know as soon as he pops the question. We'll plan your shower." I said happily while holding Caprice's hand that was now trembling.

With eyes full of tears Caprice said, "I'm happy for you too, it just hurts like hell!" Then they hugged.

Chapter 15

"Good now remember to hold your thumb like this. Otherwise you're gonna break it the first time you hit someone." Caprice said showing me how to hold my fist.

We were in the gym working it out all three of us were motivated for different reasons. JoJo was there for the release; Wade had been being so difficult it was ridiculous. JoJo would seem so calm and unaffected while dealing with him. As soon as Wade was gone JoJo would need to do something to release the tension. I keep thanking him for doing all this on my behalf. He tells me not to worry about it and that we're family so I shouldn't sweat it. The final leg of our tour was in California. I couldn't wait to get back to what I knew. Stores that made sense to me, accents that were understandable. For someone who's never been anywhere, I can now say that I've been all over this country. What I will miss about the south is the food. Ooh! Everything was so good!

Wade came barging in on our workout with Wally in tow. "Lewis is my client! You don't discuss anything with him without coming through me first!"

JoJo smiled he was mid-run on the treadmill. He stopped the machine and grabbed his towel. He was catching his breath as he stepped off the machine. "Chantel and Lewis discussed the project. I sent you paperwork, sign off on it and let's be done. Or, do you need to have a dramatic scene first?" JoJo said looking at Wade.

"He's not doing the song!" Wade barked

JoJo smiled again, "you're mad cause he told you he's going to and you don't want him to just to spite me."

"Do you have any idea who I am?" Wade growled.

"Nope, don't care." JoJo said nonchalantly almost laughing.

"I guess you'll find out the hard way."

As soon as Wade said that Wally reached over Wade and swung at JoJo. JoJo pushed Wally's fist away and countered with a left. You heard the hit connect with his face. Wally spit out blood while JoJo squared off. Wade walked by the door, he looked mad. Wally kept trying to come at JoJo, but JoJo was ready for everything he came with. JoJo had Wally on the ground, he told him to stop being stupid. "Alright! Alright! Uncle!" Wally yelled.

Caprice and Brandy started laughing. "If you're stupid enough to want to fight me, send yourself! How many others gotta get beat down before you learn there are other ways to handle things?" JoJo said

"Man! Let him up!" Wade said angry.

"I think you broke my nose!" Wally said as he slowly got up.

"Next time let that man fight his own battles. He sent you in here to see how I handle myself. Don't be this stupid again."

"Whatever man!"

"But you heard me!" JoJo said, "When do you ask, why he keeps sending you?"

You could see the question register as Wally walked out slowly holding his busted nose. JoJo got back on the treadmill and finished his run like nothing just happened. He reminded me of Derrick so much.

I was so over this city mainly because it was my last major stop on my way home. With the exception of this moment Wade has been extremely sweet to all of us. Caprice said it's because we saw his other side, now he's trying to make up for it.

As I walked off the stage Wade was waiting with a huge floral arrangement. When I walked past him he told me he guessed I didn't want them. I stopped in my tracks; I asked him who they were from. He said he didn't know. Then I asked how he knew they were for me. He said there was a card. I opened the card it said "Congratulations! I always knew you could do it! I'm sorry for the way I acted." That was it no signature. I looked at the card then back at Wade. He asked me if there was trouble in paradise and I frowned at him. "You need to be worried about Car-ke-ke or whatever her name was and get out of my business." I said taking the flowers and going with my girls to the room. JoJo told me if I was ready we could go. We didn't have to sit around and wait for Lewis to get drunk, pick a girl, and then watch him do the "I hate this dance" with some girl he regretted as soon as he picked her. I was so ready to go back to the hotel pack up my things and then sleep until it was time to fly to San Diego. As we gathered our things to leave the Goons asked where we were going. We told them back to the hotel. They started hemming and hawing cause they were tired too. They were the road crew, so it was part of their job to make sure the equipment was packed up properly etc.

When I got to my room I sat on the bed, I took a deep breath then I called my father. He was so happy to hear from me, we talked for about an hour before I thanked him for the flowers. He said he didn't send any flowers, we talked a little longer. Then I asked him as we got off the phone if he gave Auntie Tania my itinerary. He said no, I asked him if the flowers came from her. And he said she lived paycheck to paycheck he doubted that the flowers came from her but he'd ask. He texted me a little later and said she didn't send them. I called Derrick, he said he was in a meeting and he'd call me back. So I asked real quickly if he sent me flowers, and he said no. I knew it was a long shot calling Derrick I couldn't think of anything he needed to apologize to me for. I called Cyrus completely perplexed. I told him about the flowers and the card. He said he thought Wade was lying and that was his way of making sure I took the flowers from him. I gave up; it wasn't like I could take the flowers with me. So in the morning I took a picture of them and then I left them in the suite.

We were like little kids at the airport; we were so excited to be going to our home state. Lewis was signing autographs and we were on one side of the waiting area at our gate and Wade was on the other side on the phone. I know a major part of his job was being on the phone. I saw how much JoJo was on the phone, but I wondered about the other times. I remembered Caprice saying he was talking to someone on the West Coast a lot, and that someone was there the night Reggie disappeared. I wondered why the police didn't arrest him. Not that I really thought he would randomly kill someone, but I hated how up in the air everything was. In the end I just wanted to be with my man. Although it was good, he NEVER has to break me off like he did last time ever again. I was still sore a week after that, and it took forever for me to start craving him. I wanted the companionship more than I wanted the physical. That was probably his plan the whole time. I couldn't be mad at it cause it worked. At least I wasn't all pent up and frustrated like Caprice, she was so hard up she seemed like she was going to explode. With every guy she'd play the role like maybe she'd give it up, and then reject him. In my opinion she was comparing them to my brother. And yeah Cyrus is the bomb she wasn't gonna find anyone like Cyrus again. I think she knew it, which was driving her crazy. I felt really sorry for her, I kept thinking if I was her I'd distance myself from the whole thing, even though I know I'd feel like I wanted to

die. But I'm not her and I can't tell her how to run her life. I wanted
to get in Cyrus' ear about the whole thing. I wanted to tell him if
they couldn't move forward, which I didn't want him to do because
he has a family with Sherrell, that he needed to let her go.
Knowing how hard Cyrus holds on to the idea that one day our
wicked mother would come around I somehow don't see him
letting go of Caprice.
When we checked into our hotel in San Diego, I realized that
Derrick never called me back last night. That wasn't like him, nor
had he called all morning. When I called him I went to voicemail. I
figured he must be really busy, but it hurt my feelings a little.
Wade was being really sweet, to the point the guys were looking at
him like he was a traitor or something. He paid for spa treatments
for us in our room and then we all went out to a fancy dinner that
he paid for. JoJo was not impressed, he told us not to fall for it, and
that the nice put on was all game. I did my best to listen, but it felt
nice to be taken care of and at least paid attention to. When I went
to bed that night I laid there in disbelief when I realized Derrick
did not call me back. For a minute I wondered if he forgot to pay
my cellphone bill. I had Brandy call my phone to make sure it was
working. She was annoyed and tired but she called it for me. When
it rang she put her phone down and proceeded to fall asleep. I
buried my face in my pillow and cried myself to sleep, I know it
was a bit dramatic but it is how I felt.

****

"So, is your man coming to the show since we're in your home
state?" Wade asked in the limo ride from the radio station.
JoJo kept his eyes out the window but I saw his jaw lock. "Why
does it matter Wade, my man will show up when he shows."
"I'm just saying, I'm sure you'll be excited to see him. I was
wondering when you're going to be M.I.A."
Even though Lewis had shades on his irritation was clear. "Don't
worry about it." I didn't know how to answer especially since

Derrick hasn't called me back yet and it's been days. "When is Car-
Ke-Coke-Ca-Let coming out?"
Everybody fell out laughing, except Wade. "Why you gotta make
fun of her? She's a good woman. She takes care of all of my kids.
She takes care of me whenever I dip in."
"I'm sure you do dip in. You're always in everybody else's
business, why don't you share some of your business?"

"There's nothing to share. Karquisha and I... she does her things I do mine. We come back together when we need to. She gets on my nerves, but we get a long when we need to."

"So is that the woman at home you wouldn't talk about?"

"What do you mean?" He looked confused.

"Whenever we would ask you if you had a woman you'd wiggle your way out of answering the question. So that's her?"

"I guess." The way his voice carried everyone looked at him. "Is there someone else?"

"There's always someone else. Could've been you too if you weren't so sprung off that wanna be."

JoJo inhaled deeply and looked at me like he was about to blow. "That's disgusting! Why would I want to be one of your many?"

"What difference does it make if you're one of my many or one of Derrick's many? You're not the only one either way."

My stomach turned, and the Southern California heat seemed to stick to me. "Derrick loves me!"

"For how long? Out of sight out of mind. Eventually both of you will move on. Long distance relationships don't last. He got you out here on the road for months on end. He doesn't come for tune up anymore. He don't know what you're doing out here. Even if you tell him you've been faithful it's not like he's gonna believe you."

"My man trusts me, and I've never lied to him."

"What you need to concern yourself with is how Shameless' business affairs are going. Chantel will not be your next payday. And just so we're clear, as long as I'm around." JoJo gestured with his hands as if he was circling my body. "All of this is off limits to you. Don't even breathe in her direction!"

"Or else what?" Wade glared at JoJo.

"Wade, you're out of line. I couldn't let you fight Joseph." Paul said "Your job is to protect him." He pointed at Lewis.

"Yeah well new clause to my job description includes all of them." Paul motioned to all of us, Brandy smiled

"Her pussy that good, that you got it all twisted up?" Wade barked.

JoJo pushed Paul backwards; Paul was about to charge at him in this little limo. "What's the deal with you? You seem even bolder than normal."

Wade smiled, "what?"

"Who's waiting for you? You have to have some kind of backup out here. You're too froggy."

Wade sat back in his seat smiling at JoJo but he didn't speak. When we got to the arena Wade started handling business, and Lewis and I went through our sound check. "I'm getting tired of him. This tour has been even more ridiculous than normal. What's your contract like with Joseph?"

"Derrick set it up for me, but as you see Joseph's good. When is your contract up with Wade?"

"It ends in a couple of months. I don't think I want to renew."

"Why, you said he was good at business?"

"Yeah good at business, but it's stuff like the tour overseas. I've done it before, but right now I'm not feeling going so far away. I really wanna focus on some acting opportunities things that will keep me over here. My boy Dwayne has been in some movies and he tells me all the time about opportunities, but Wade's not trying to hear me. I'm the client, he's supposed to manage my interest."

Lewis shook his head. "He doesn't wanna hear me. He got that one-track mindset; he's not trying to move my brand forward. This business is here today and gone tomorrow. I'm starting to feel like it's time for us to go our separate ways. Then we got police checking for us. I don't need this kind of drama around me."

"What really happened with Reggie?" I asked

"I don't know."

"Is he trying to set Derrick up?"

"I don't know, but it seems like it huh. He recognizes that you're a gold mine, I wouldn't doubt that he's trying to make you his new client."

"He definitely doesn't know how to come at me. He doesn't know whether he wants to come at me professional or otherwise. He told me I could have his baby."

Lewis frowned, "when did he say that?"

"The night of *no lazy sex*." I smiled at him; he gave me a guilty smile back. "Please thank Paul for having Joseph's back this morning. He didn't have to do that."

"No problem, I didn't tell him to do it. Right is right isn't it?"

"It is." I said

'This conversation…."

I cut him off, "didn't happen."

"I was gonna say stays between us but your version works too."
The next three days and shows seem to fly by, but only because I
spent them wondering what was going on with Derrick. JoJo and I
went over my schedule in LA it was pretty jammed pack. It
seemed like the closer I got to home the busier I got. The good
thing is that the four of us were going to stay with Sasha instead of
a hotel. A real kitchen and hopefully real food.

As soon as my part was done in the show JoJo loaded us into a car
service and then we drove to Sasha's. Her house was beautiful and
kind of huge for just two people. She said the four extra bedrooms
came in handy when out of town guest came by, her man was out
of town so she was happy to have the company. We chatted for a
little bit and then we all passed out. It was nice to have my own
room for the first time. I woke up to a light knock on the door. I
told the person to come in and the cutest little ginger girl came in
my room with a huge smile. I sat up in my bed and JoJo walked in
behind her. I said hi to the little girl, she had to be related to Gwen
she looked just like her. JoJo introduced Paige; she was so sweet
and precious. He said Gwen was downstairs and I needed to get
going. When I came out the bathroom after my shower Paige was
waiting outside my bedroom door. She smiled at me again but said
nothing. Once I was dressed, very casually I opened my door so
she could come in. I held my new best friend's hand and we went
downstairs. Gwen took pictures of us with her phone. We hugged
and then she told me we had to get going. The car service took us
to a photo studio. Gwen introduced me to Brandon who was the
stylist. Brandon twirled me around and in the most dramatic
fashion shamed me for covering up my body in my baggy clothes.
He pulled multiple looks and told me to try them on. This one
dress was soft and billowy with long splits on either sides. When I
came out in the dress he put his hands on his forehead and stomped
his feet dramatically. "WHY DOES SHE COVER UP THIS
AMAZING BODY! WHY? Chantel! Those legs were meant to be
seen! Show them!" I smiled an embarrassed smile. Brandon now
armed with my body type in mind went back to his racks. He took
everything in my dressing room out. I looked at the stuff he gave
me and he shooed me away and told me not to come back until I
was fabulous. When I came out the room in the burgundy dress

everyone reacted to it. I asked my new best friend if she liked my dress. She shook her head very enthusiastically to show her approval of my dress. Brandon threw his body into Gwen, "OH MY GOODNESS! I'M SO GOOD I SHOULD SLAP MYSELF!" Brandon said, "Now to get you GLAM ready!" He took my hand, "MAKE-UP!" He said leading me to the chair. Then Blair came to do my makeup. I couldn't tell if Blair was a woman or a man, but Blair's makeup was fantastic. Blair explained that when I looked in the mirror my makeup would look a little heavy, but it would translate beautifully on camera. When I looked in the mirror I sat there in shock.

JoJo was trying to read my face. "Very beautiful!" He smiled at me and told me to get a move on it.

Brandon announced my arrival to the people standing around in the studio area. Gwen was directing someone around the props. The photographer stood there almost staring at me. His green eyes seemed like they were piercing through me. I stood there waiting for direction, after a minute he leaned his head to the side and he smiled at me. I got butterflies in my stomach. "Hi" he said. I smiled, he showed me where he wanted me and then he started snapping he hadn't said anything to me yet so I felt stupid having him snapping away at me candidly. Then he smiled at me again. "Ok, ok!" Is he flirting with me? I couldn't figure it out so I let it go. As I looked at him he didn't seem like someone who would be matched with me. Without these heels on I was probably still a little taller than him. His t-shirt was sleeveless and his cinnamon brown arms weren't chiseled like Derrick's. But he had a slight muscle tone. His hair had that cotton I could be curly if he would moisturize me look. His appearance screamed artist, he had on ripped jeans and he was barefoot. He was almost the complete opposite of Derrick and yet, he had my attention. When he was adjusting the lighting and measuring something he stood in my face. He was so close I could smell the orange juice on his breath. When he walked away I looked at Caprice who was looking like she was about to burst. She was giddy with excitement and she mouthed at me that I needed to get him. I looked for JoJo but I could hear him on the phone but he wasn't in the room, which meant he wasn't watching. Gwen was busy with next steps so she wasn't completely paying attention either. Then he told me to come over to the screen to see what he's captured so far and to tell him which ones I liked. Brandon and Gwen were discussing next looks and costumes. I stood at the screen looking at the monitor. His pictures were amazing, I felt like I was looking at someone else. I thanked him and I told him the pictures were beautiful, and then I told him he was very talented. He smiled at me and said he only captured the moment and that I did all the work. "What's your name?" I asked

"Gerard"

"I don't know how they're affording you, but I'm so thankful."

"So you're a singer?"

"Yep"

"Have I heard your work?"

"Have you heard 'Respectfully'?"

His eyes got big, "that's you? How does that much sound come out of you?" He smiled

I smiled, "just does I guess."

"Which ones do you like?" He said pointing at the screen. I pointed out my favs. "I like this one." He said staring at the picture. "Look at your eyes. They look like pools of chocolate gems. Cognac diamonds. Your lips," he inhaled. "Your skin!" Then he looked at me, "Chantel you are beautiful!"

I glanced at Caprice, she looked like she was foaming at the mouth. I told her to come over. I introduced her to Gerard. She said a respectful hello then he asked her which pictures she liked. We talked about the pictures, but he kept focusing his attention on me. I thought for sure he hadn't seen Caprice, but I guess he had. Brandy walked over when Brandon stole Gerard away for a minute. Caprice squealed into my shoulder. She said our little flirt session was too cute. I told her I thought she liked him. She said he was very yummy but he barely looked at her. She said if he licked his lips one more time at me, she was gonna bite him for me. I watched him talk to Brandon, even Brandon looked like he wished Gerard would look in his direction. Gerard was fine, but he was no Derrick. Thinking about Derrick released the butterflies from my stomach. I changed my clothes into more casual attire, washed my face to put more makeup back on, and they restyled my braids. This setting was like a park and they asked my best friend Paige to pose with me. We sat on the fake grass barefoot talking, playing hand games, and being silly. For the last look, Brandon dressed me in a strapless dress, they washed off my makeup and then gave me a barely there look, and my braids fell wherever they wanted. Gerard took pictures of my face mostly. Then he told Blair to stand facing me. He told me to look down and I did. Then he told me to slowly look up, and when I did he wanted me to think about love. So of course I thought about Derrick while he snapped away. Why hasn't Derrick called me back? We never go this long without touching base. Brandon broke my concentration by screaming that my eyes were too intense. Everybody started laughing. Gwen said there was no doubt of who I was thinking of. JoJo stepped in the room and said we needed to be leaving in forty-five minutes. Gwen asked Gerard when he'd have proofs for us to view. He said he'd work on it immediately and he'd call her to meet up with us to review.

I happily put on my jeans and baggy shirt. Those clothes were cute but not all that comfortable. Paige waved bye to Gerard while he stared at me with those monster eyes.

We went to Malcolm's studio; I tried not to look sad as I thought about being here with Derrick. I sat with the engineer and he crafted my melody according to my taps. What he came up with was a raw baseline; Derrick said he'd do the music for the song. So I needed the basic to record to. Once we had the music I went in the booth. I was getting frustrated the song wasn't coming out like I wanted it nor like I knew it could. No one seemed to know what I was talking about, but I knew. It wasn't working. I asked my best friend Paige to come sing with me. I had gone over it so much it was no surprise that she knew the lyrics. She was so cute, and her little girl freshness helped me relax. Then I had her sit on the stool and hold my hand while I sang. Then I could feel the song. When I finished I heard strong clapping over my headphones I looked up and Darryl was standing there with a HUGE grin on his face. Paige and I ran out the booth. Darryl hugged me and he picked up Paige and gave her a hug and kiss. Darryl said he came to hang out with us, but something told me there was more to the story. His cousin Eric was there too, I gave him a hug and then he said he liked the song. Darryl told him he should go sing the second verse. Eric smiled at him and said no. Darryl assured him that I didn't mind even though he didn't ask me. When I told him to go, he exhaled and went into the booth. Eric's voice was velvety smooth, and a little bit heavy. It was perfect. I went back in the booth and we changed the entire direction of my song. Now I didn't just like my song I loved it. I asked Eric if it was ok with him to use him on my song. He said it was fine, but he didn't want to be in the video if we

shot one. I didn't understand why, but I was happy he agreed to let me use his voice.

When we got to the restaurant the hostess led us to a banquet room to the side of the restaurant. Gwen's husband Martin, son Perry, and other daughter Peyton were waiting for us. I was hoping Derrick would be inside surprising me like he normally likes to do. I was disappointed when he wasn't there, but Darryl as usual had us in stitches. Shameless, Paul, and Wade showed up. Gerard entered the room right after them. He had a laptop in his backpack. He set up his laptop on a table to the side. As he pulled up my pictures Gwen kept gushing over them. They told me to come over; Gerard pulled a chair next to him. I exhaled and then walked over. The pictures looked even better than when I looked at them earlier. The picture that he took of Blair, and me he swapped Blair out with a faceless man. He made the picture sepia colored, and he made my eyes glow. It was amazing! The pictures of Paige and I playing were amazing. He captured my smile and if I didn't know any better I would've thought I was outside, alone and smiling at the world. The burgundy pictures were by far my favorites. Eventually everyone was admiring the pictures with us. I asked Gerard what he did to the pictures so I could understand how he retouched them. He brought up the originals and set them next to the retouched. The colors where sharper, the lines were crisp; he was good at what he does. Of course Wade was watching our interactions, but I didn't care about his watching eyes anymore. I told Lewis that I laid down my part to the song today. He smiled at Wade and then he told me he was going to the studio right after dinner. I asked JoJo if they got the contract settled. JoJo smiled real big and then he looked Wade in his face and said "Oh yeah!" Like he was the Kool-Aid guy. Everybody kind of chuckled except Wade.

When dinner was served we sat at the table like a big family. Gwen invited Gerard to stay for dinner. Sasha and her friend Ava sashayed in just as we were sitting down to eat. Wade sat there like he was trying to connect the dots. He was trying to figure out who each person was without asking.

So finally Darryl said, "who are you?" to Wade.

"I manage Shameless." He said

"He's your only client huh?" Darryl said sitting back in his chair like he's already figured Wade out.

"At the moment, but that will change." Wade said sitting back.

"Aw so, you have a business plan?" Wade nodded, "so your plan includes Chantel?"

Everybody stopped eating and looked at Wade. He looked at everyone and then back at Darryl. "Yes" he said point blank.

Darryl shook his head. "I guess I can help you with that. Nope, it's not gonna happen." Darryl said cracking a slight grin.

"Who are you?" Wade asked

"I'm her family." He said pointing at me. I took a deep breath; I could never get tired of hearing him say that. "Matter of fact with the exception of maybe four of you in this room, we're all connected. Chantel works with family."

Wade looked at Darryl real good. "You're Derrick's brother aren't you?"

"It took you long enough to figure that out. Not too bright is he?" Darryl gave a little chuckle.

Wade wasn't amused, "Chantel will want to trade up in the near future. I'll be here." He said

"Joseph has been doing a wonderful job, I'm not going nowhere!" I said

"Thank you cousin." JoJo said then he smiled at Wade.

Wade squinted his eyes, "cousin?"

No one said anything they let him sit there and work it out. Lewis had a mile wide smile on his face. "I didn't realize you were family either, my bad." He said reaching out to shake JoJo's hand.

"That's your sister?" Wade asked pointing his head towards Sasha.

"I don't know him, why are you giving him any information?" Sasha said full of attitude.

"That's my niece, but I can tell you're going in the wrong direction. We're all blood related." JoJo said

"JoJo!" Sasha said through clinched teeth.

Wade started looking from person to person slowly. Wade was quiet and not doing his normal "he's the head nigga in charge pose." He was taking everybody in. Conversation resumed at the table, Caprice kept sneaking me little smirks every so often. Gerard didn't look phased by anything happening at the table. Then again I only met him earlier that day so how phased was he supposed to be? After dinner Lewis, Paul, and most importantly Wade left. They were heading over to the studio. When they left everybody seemed to relax more.

****

This is the hardest I've worked in between shows yet. Interviews, meetings at the label, etc. Lewis laid his buttery vocals on the track. JoJo sent the track to Derrick in Oakland. He remastered it and tweaked it in one day. JoJo sent it to him Tuesday morning; we had it back late Wednesday afternoon. When I heard it, it sounded BEAUTIFUL! Derrick made sure the baseline definitely stood out. He pretty much changed all the music but the melody remained the same. I found myself bobbing to it when I heard it. The label loved it and agreed that it had to go on the debut album. They loved my new pictures. Gwen gave the negatives to Jenise, who designed the most eye catching and beautiful album cover and album photos. When we gave them the photographer's name no one had heard of him. The final blessing was given to my project and I instantly felt scared. What if no one liked it? Everybody loved Derrick's song, I was just the voice. My project had quite a few songs written by me on it. What if nobody likes me? Or they kind of like me, but not enough to spend their money to listen to me. What if people think I'm ugly like my mother always told me that I was? And then, they don't want to listen to my music because of it? What if everybody

says I'm too skinny, or too black, or too... or too…. too much of a loser to really do this? I exhaled and started to fall deeper into my pity party when there was a knock at the door. I told the person to come in, as soon as I saw Cyrus' face I jumped out of the chair and I ran to him. I gave him the biggest hug. "THANK YOU FOR COMING! THANK YOU FOR COMING!"

"I gotta see you on that stage." Cyrus said happy for me.

"Sherrell let you come?" I asked sitting down.

He frowned, "let me?"

"You know what I mean."

"She knows I came to see you perform."

"She knows Caprice is out here?"

He gave me an irritated look. "Yes, I told you I don't lie to her. She's not happy about me being here, but she knows."

"Ok," I said wanting to change the subject.

JoJo knocked on the door, "you're on in five."

263

Cyrus walked with me to the side of the stage. He gave me another hug and then I got ready to walk out. Cyrus' eyes got big as he looked out at the massive crowd. His eyes said exactly how I felt. I was always nervous whenever I went out, I always wondered if this was going to be the crowd that didn't like me, but truthfully my job was the easy part. They were already jamming with Shameless and into his groove, I slid out did my thing and slid back off. Unless he had the crowd call me back out.

That night we dropped Cyrus and Caprice off at a hotel, they were too excited. They barely let the car stop before they were opening the door and getting out. Brandy said Paul was coming to get her after the show. I wondered if that meant that Derrick was secretly coming. The only time they've left my side is when Derrick was around. Maybe Darryl came as a decoy to throw me off. I kinda didn't want Gerard to come to the Saturday show with Derrick there. There was no way Derrick wouldn't notice him. He notices everybody, and he would instantly take offense to anything Gerard did. I was dying to see Derrick so honestly I'd take what I could get. Sasha was unwinding with a glass of wine when we walked in. She asked how the show went and JoJo told her I killed it as usual. She smiled and congratulated me. She offered me wine, but I wanted to shower so that whenever Derrick popped up I would be ready. I just got off my period so I was READY! By the time I finally laid my head on the pillow I was cursing myself for setting myself up like that. The girls could leave because JoJo and Darryl were here. I picked up the phone and I stared at Gerard's card. What would I be calling him for at the booty call hour at that? I put his card back in my purse and I laid down.

JoJo was knocking telling me it was time to get up. I couldn't believe I was still disappointed when Derrick still wasn't there, hadn't called or anything. I was quiet the entire car ride to the gym. I put my headphones on and did my workout. I had some choice words for Derrick when I finally laid eyes on him. How dare he leave me hanging like this? The angrier I got the faster I moved, I was on the row machine working it out. My thighs started throbbing and I looked up in the mirror when I saw the reflection of sudden movement. It was Darryl falling all over JoJo while they held each other up while they laughed, Eric was on the bike laughing just as hard. I knew it was at me. I took my headphones off and they were hollering. "What are you mad about?" JoJo said "You were going, and then you thought about something and you kept moving faster and faster. We're looking at you like what's going on, and your face turned evil and you started going faster and faster. That poor machine was begging for you to take it easy and you just kept going and going. Goodness girl!" Darryl said cracking up.

I wanted to laugh with them, but then again I was too mad. So I rolled my eyes at them. "There's the girl from Oakland. Why girls always gotta roll their eyes?" Darryl was trying to make me laugh and I wasn't going for it. When I was done I sat over to the side pouting waiting for them to finish. When they were done, Darryl threw his musty arm around me. I frowned and tried to get away from him. He told me he wasn't letting me go until I spilled it. His arm was heavy and strong, it was pointless to fight. So I told him how Derrick said he was going to call me back and he hadn't. I told him every time I called he didn't answer. I told him I wasn't talking to Derrick when he did call me. Darryl smiled at me and started teasing me for being in love with his brother. Something so childish shouldn't have made me laugh, but it did. When I finally stopped laughing I told him I was still mad at his brother no matter how much he made me laugh.

Cyrus and Caprice didn't come up for air until the show that night. I was so jealous! So what if Caprice had held out longer than me, I missed my man! As I was talking to Caprice and Cyrus, we noticed a guy was sitting in a chair over to the side watching us. I asked Caprice if she knew him and she said no. He looked familiar, but the look on his face wasn't friendly so I took them in my dressing room and shut the door. Caprice stuck her phone out, took a picture of him and then sent it off. When Cyrus asked her what she was doing, she smiled and said she was taking a picture in case he turned out to be a stalker or something. When Brandy came in the room she told Caprice that he was a friend of Wade's. The two of them stood there comparing notes like I've seen them do for the entire duration of this trip. Cyrus frowned; I forgot he didn't know about this aspect of Caprice's job. I didn't say anything for fear I would make it worse. Cyrus started to say something after Brandy walked out the door, and I interrupted him. "ONE MORE SHOW AND THEN I GET TO GO HOME! SLEEP IN MY BED

BEFORE MY NEXT AND LAST SHOW!!!" I bounced around
excited. Cyrus smiled at me and Caprice thanked me for the
distraction. They walked me out and the guy was still there. I went
on stage, did my thing. I was barely off the stage when JoJo told
me I did a good job and that we were leaving. JoJo was talking to
Brandy and Caprice about the guy. Cyrus was taking it all in, but
he wasn't saying anything.

****

I had butterflies all day. This was it, after tonight's show we
perform in Sacramento. Then San Jose, and last but certainly not
least Oakland. I was going home for longer than a pit stop YES!
After the last Oakland show we were going to have a big party to
celebrate. I was excited to be sleeping in my bed. And getting back
to normal eating in my kitchen. My plane didn't leave until
tomorrow afternoon, but I had everything packed up and ready.
Sasha came flying in the door with Ava in tow. She said they
would meet us there cause she still had to get ready. Everyone
from the photo shoot was there when we arrived. My eyes
immediately landed on Gerard. He was talking to Blair and
Brandon. They had red cups in their hands and there was a whole
liquor spread. I put my garment bag and purse in my dressing room
and then I helped myself to a drink. Gerard came over and we
chatted about the normal niceties. His eyes kept scanning me, and
if I wasn't paying attention I might've missed him checking me out.
JoJo came over and told me to stick to the one drink until I went
on. Cyrus came over to meet Gerard. He was in protective big
brother mode. Gerard appeared as if he didn't notice. Eventually he
and Cyrus were chatting. The opening act was finishing up when I
had to excuse myself from Sasha and Gwen and run to get dressed.
Blair told me I did a good job while touching up my makeup.
When I came out the dressing room my eyes landed on the evil
guy. Wade gave me another bouquet and it had the same wording
on the card. I frowned at Cyrus cause I had no idea who was
sending them. He took the flowers from me and he told me not to
worry about it. Darryl and JoJo were talking when I approached
the stage. I heard Darryl say something wasn't right, which wasn't
helping my nerves. Then he locked his eyes on me and told me not
to worry cause he was there. I didn't know what he meant but I said
ok. I went out and sang my song. Shameless had the whole
audience swaying and he had me still on stage when you heard a

distinct pop. I jumped and looked at Lewis. He told the house to bring up the lights. Then there were two more pops as people in the crowd started screaming and running in every direction away from the pop. A guy had a gun and security was on their way. The guy turned towards the stage and Lewis leaped towards me and slammed me on the ground. I hit my head really hard. Immediately security and the Goons were all over the stage. Kirk picked me up like I was a child and moved quickly off the stage. There were more pops; I kept trying to focus my eyes. A bullet flew towards the off stage, everyone was leaving faster. Kirk stood me up and asked me if I was ok. I said yes, Gerard grabbed my hand. While Brandy barked out commands to everyone to get moving. Darryl told me to keep moving and not to stop for anything. I didn't see Sasha but Gwen and her husband got in the car ahead of me. Blair was screaming at me and telling me to get in. So I did, but I was worried cause none of my people were with me and I didn't have my purse or cellphone. Gerard shut the door and Blair took off. Brandon screamed at Blair to slow down, but Blair was moving. When we had been driving for a minute and the ability to think hit us. We realized no one had a phone on them. My purse was in the dressing room. Blair and Brandon left their things in my dressing room and Blair had keys to the car only because she took them out of her purse to get something from the car just before the madness. Gerard had just plugged up his phone to charge a little. I didn't know where we were or how to get to Sasha's house. Plus Cyrus had just changed his cell phone number so I didn't know it by heart. Blair took us to her house. She emailed Gwen cause we couldn't think of any other way to contact any of them. Blair's hands were still shaking. She went to the kitchen and made drinks for all of us. It wasn't until I reached for my glass that I saw my own nerves. Blair turned on the news and they were reporting that no one has touched base with Shameless personally, but there were a few injuries but no reported fatalities. Brandon's boyfriend came and picked him up. He said he knew where to find him. Blair played host-making drink after drink. I kept running to the computer cause I thought I heard a ding from Blair's email account. When I came back in the living room Blair was knocked out. I sat on the floor in front of the love seat. Gerard was across the floor in front of the couch.

"So Derrick is your boyfriend?"

"Yes"

"Where is he?"

"I don't know."

"It's complicated?"

"Yeah" I said in defeat.

"So complicated that I can't kiss you?"

"What?" I said sitting up straight and trying to find clarity.

"I want to kiss you, but only if its ok with you. I won't tell if you don't."

"I don't think that's a good idea." I heard applause in my head for giving the right answer even though I wasn't feeling it.

Gerard smiled a knowing smile at me and said ok. Blair woke up, she put the remotes in my hand and then she went in her room and shut the door. I got up and went to the computer. It was after two and no response from Gwen. When I walked back in the room Gerard was standing in the space to walk between the couches. My heart was pounding as I said excuse me. He grabbed my face and kissed me, and it was a good kiss. My knees buckled and he held me up as he continued to kiss me. Before I realized it, we were on the couch and my shirt was off. There were voices in my head arguing with me. One said don't do this, and the other said Derrick was doing who knows what with whomever he chooses. He's stopped calling me altogether, maybe he's fallen in love with someone else and he's regretting the fact that I'm coming home. I could tell this situation was not new for Gerard. He knew what to do and how to do it. When he pulled out a condom my insides screamed. He was trying to put the condom on real fast but I told him to hold on. When he backed up I looked at him at attention. I frowned, "where was the rest of it?" Maybe he wasn't completely hard. I didn't know how to ask so I took a minute to collect my thoughts. My head was spinning. It was hard to think, Blair's mixers had me slurring and outside myself. Gerard kissed me again and then he asked me if it was ok. I heard myself say yes. I felt him but barely and it was over not too long after it began. Immediately I understood why Lewis had to be drunk to do this. The guilt that washes over you is more painful than anything else. I went to the bathroom and washed my face I felt horrible. And then of course as if it was planned I heard the ding on Blair's computer. I ran to the computer, Gwen said they were on their way to get me. It was four in the morning. I knocked on Blair's door, and told her they were coming. Gerard was already dressed and sitting on the couch like nothing just happened. I couldn't look at him. I sat on the couch tipsy and disappointed in myself. When Blair went in the bathroom, Gerard came over and kissed me. He told me he'd deny anything ever happened. I made him pinky swear, and then he went back to his couch.

****

As we approached the curb a black SUV limo was waiting. The driver took our things. "Chantel why you so quiet?" Darryl asked "I guess I'm still shook up. That experience was crazy. I never wanna go through that again. It's got me rethinking this whole thing."

Everybody stared at me. I felt so self-conscious. Darryl put his arm around me. "You're so innocent, but that's a good thing."

His words stabbed me. I put my eyes on the floor. After awhile I looked up cause we should've been to my house a long time ago. We pulled up to a park in Hayward. There was a banner that said welcome home Chantel and a small crowd of people. "What is this?" I said feeling frozen.

Everyone was smiling at me. "There's a reason why I couldn't get an earlier flight." JoJo smiled, and I sunk into my seat.

When I stepped out of the limo everyone cheered and I cried. All these people genuinely happy to see me and I feel so dirty.

Everyone came in for hugs and I was looking for Derrick. When I found him, he was already reading me. He didn't smile, but he gave me a hug and kiss. Everyone had questions about touring. Lewis looked like he was trying to squeeze the life out of Latia. She was enjoying the attention. Everybody kept surrounding me, and I kept my eyes on Derrick who kept looking at me. Everyone was making a big fuss over me being back. My daddy and the boys were there with my Grandma Rosa. Maria had to work, but she was going to be at my last performance in Oakland. Sherrell and baby Rosa weren't there. Everybody was laughing and having a good time, I know I kept looking at Derrick like the guilty slut that I felt I was. Eventually he stopped looking at me. Everyone started leaving as the caterers started cleaning up. Derrick looked at me and told me I was riding with him as if he heard my thought to run away. As we walked to the car, I could feel the sweat appear on my nose. As soon as I sat in his front seat I got a napkin out of the glove compartment and I wiped my whole face. He got in the car, put his key in the ignition, and then he sat back in his seat. He looked straight ahead, "what's so hard about six months? We didn't talk for years, and some how six months without you seems like the hardest thing to do." He looked at me, "so this is your career?"

"I guess for now."

He inhaled and exhaled, "I guess? You guess? What do you know?"

"I know I'm waiting for you to call me back!" I spit.

He reached in his pocket, took out his cellphone, pressed a number then he put his phone to his ear. When my phone started ringing I looked at him but he rolled his eyes and didn't look at me. When I answered he said, "hello? Yeah! I'm looking for my woman! This nervous little girl in my car may have fooled them. I know better, my woman isn't scared of me." He almost smiled.

"But she is mad at you!" I said while laughing.

"Tell her that I apologize for upsetting her, but that last stretch was giving me too much anxiety. I couldn't take talking to her when I missed her like that. Tell her I love her!"

That stabbed me. "I thought you might've met someone else you like better."

"Who's better than you?" He said looking at me.

I hung up my phone. "Then why can't you wait for me?"

Derrick eyed me, "I love you!" Then he started his car to drive. When we got to my house little Rosa ran to me. She seemed so much bigger than the last time I saw her. I hugged her up real good. Then I unloaded all the stuff I brought for my brothers and little Rosa. I brought Sherrell every funky kind of earring I came across. She loved them all and was so appreciative. She didn't think I brought her anything. My dad looked a little disappointed when I didn't have anything for him. He wasn't on my favorite person list when I thought to get something for my brothers and Maria. So oh well. My dad stayed until Cyrus came home, he packed my grandma and everyone and left. Sherrell kept looking Cyrus in his face and he would give her a blank expression. He gave her a hug and kiss when he came in the door, but it looked like she was hoping to see something more than he had to give her. Little Rosa did not want me to put her down and she cried horribly at her parents when they'd try to take her away from me. She'd only go to Derrick if she thought he was going to stay near me. As soon as he walked like he was going towards her parents or her room she cried. So he gave her back to me in defeat. She fell asleep with her head on my chest and her little fist clinging to me. I felt so loved and so missed. I waited until she was dead weight and then I carefully gave her to her father who said goodnight and took her upstairs.

I looked at Derrick; I thought I would want to jump his bones. Now I feel awkward and unsure if I should tell him. He did say I was free to do what I wanted, but I also knew he'd flip out if he knew. I walked into my room and inhaled the smell of home. Derrick sat on the bed taking off his shirt. I stared at his beautiful body with so much appreciation. "Baby can I ask you something?"

"Shoot" He said taking his socks off.

"What.." I tried to think of a way to phrase my question. "Do you see yourself with me five years from now?"

"I can say I see it, but I don't know if I do."

His answer caught me off guard. "Please explain, and don't take a long time cause I'm about to freak out!" I said waving my hands. Derrick actually chuckled at me. "You are so silly." He composed himself. "I don't know if I can do this whole long distance thing regularly. It would piss me off if you held back from becoming the person you were meant to be just to hang around with me. A lot has been happening around here; I can't exactly go flying around the country to follow you around. I can see the distance wearing on both of us. I'll always love you, but I don't know where we'll be in the future."

"I HATE THAT I ASKED YOU THAT! Can't you ever give me the fairy tale? Goodness!" I said throwing my pillow at him.

"Chantel, no one will ever mean more to me than you do."

"Even Brooklyn?" I gave him an evil knowing look.

A wide range of emotions went over his face in sixty of the longest seconds. "What made you mention her?"

I got a lump in my throat; I sat on the bed and stared at his face. "You were seeing her while I was gone?"

He looked at me and didn't say anything right away. "I don't love anyone more than I love you. I don't know what made you bring her up though."

"Are we gonna do the whole compare notes things? Do I need to know? Do you?"

Derrick looked at me, "you have notes?"

"I didn't say that. I'm asking if that's how this goes? We share, or leave things unspoken."

His face turned evil, "you have notes?"

"Derrick I didn't say that. Please calm down."

His eyes were piercing me, "I'm calm. You just need to explain yourself."

"Should I ask who you were sleeping with while I was gone? Technically I'm not your woman when I'm gone. And you sure in heck are not my man when you're giving it to someone else."

"What did you do?" He stared at me.

"I didn't say I did anything, I'm asking. We both know you did."

"What did you do?"

"You can keep asking me all you want. I find it funny how you brought me here and didn't take me to your house."

He squinted his eyes at me, "you're purposely picking a fight. You're trying to deflect what's really bothering you. I'm not going for it."

"Derrick, when have I ever been ok with you being with someone else? You would have a fit if you thought I was with someone else. Why can't I be entitled to the same emotions?"

His face dropped, "you were with someone else?" His voice did a Derrick version of cracking.

"I didn't say that!"

"I know what you're saying Chantel! I know how to read between your lines." He was getting angry with every second that passed.

"I didn't say that! I was just asking." I said trying to throw attitude in hopes he would believe me.

He stood up and walked into my face. I wanted to run! "Why? Because I didn't call you back the last few weeks of your tour? You could lose faith in me that easily?" I didn't say anything, his

eyes were on fire. "I can't…" He started looking around, "I can't do this with you!"

I felt like he was stabbing me. "Derrick you're assuming I did something. I didn't say anything."

"Yes you did! You said it all!" He walked away looking for his socks.

"Derrick! Where are you going?" I said feeling a little panicked.

"AWAY FROM YOU!"

"So let me get this straight, you can have whomever you want whenever you want, but the moment that you THINK I did something you can't even be around me?"

"I know you Chantel!"

I started crying, "This isn't fair! GET OUT THEN LEAVE! YOU'RE NOT THE ONLY ONE WITH ABANDONMENT ISSUES! I NEED SECURITY TOO! YOU CAN'T CUT ME OFF AND EXPECT ME TO UNDERSTAND THAT EVERYTHING IS EVERYTHING! ESPECIALLY WHEN YOU'VE NEVER DONE THIS TO ME BEFORE! Fine! Whatever! I knew it was only a matter of time before you left me anyways." Every insecurity I tried to pull back came spilling out. "I never said I was cut out for this anyways. You were the one assigning something greater to me than I even thought of myself. Just so you know for your next chick. You can't build someone up and then leave them hanging. It doesn't work. I told myself to give you credit this time, and not to freak out. Even though you cheated on me because I didn't go to your school???? I waited for you, didn't hold none of that against you. DERRICK NEEDS! DERRICK NEEDS! WHAT ABOUT WHAT CHANTEL NEEDS? I NEED TO BE FIRST AND THE ONLY! I..." Derrick was reaching for his jacket. There was no point in talking anymore, so I stopped. I walked in my bathroom, I got in the shower. I heard my bedroom door close.

Chapter 16

I cried in the shower for a long time. I didn't see the point of
getting out. What kind of a life is worth living without Derrick in
it? I sat on my bed putting lotion on. Then I stared at the wall, it
wasn't even worth it. The best part of the whole experience with
Gerard was the kissing and foreplay. I could barely feel him and it
was over before I realized what was happening. It wasn't worth not
having Derrick in my life no matter how justified I felt cause we
both know he wasn't twirling his thumbs waiting for me. He didn't
say it wasn't Brooklyn either. I cried myself to sleep. I was
awakened to my phone ringing. It was Derrick's ring tone. I laid
there watching my phone ring. I looked at the clock it said 4:47am.
I couldn't move, he called again. I didn't answer. Then I heard the
doorbell. Cyrus called me; I told him it was Derrick. He asked me
if I wanted him to answer. I said yes cause if he was here he wasn't
going away. I didn't have it in me to move. I heard Derrick and
Cyrus talking. I knew he was mad by the extra deepness in his
voice. He walked in my room and turned on the light. "Get up!" He
commanded me. I laid there with my eyes closed, and tears seeping
out. He pulled my covers back and threw my feet towards the
floor, he made me sit up. I didn't open my eyes cause I didn't want
to see how angry he was. "Where's your jacket?" I pointed towards
my closet. He threw my jacket at my face. He tossed my shoes
across the floor then he waited by the door. I put on my jacket and
shoes then I followed him. He wasn't even parked in a legitimate
parking space. The doors were open and it looked crazy. I stood
there debating whether to get in or not. "If you don't get in, I'll
throw you in!" He barked at me.
"I'm not going anywhere if you're going to threaten me."
Derrick growled. Then he said, "Get in!"
So I slowly got in the truck. He slammed the door after I got in. As
he violently turned his car around I asked, "Where are we going?"
"I'm so MAD at you!" He growled, I sunk in my seat. He got on
the 880 freeway, over to 980, then to 580 south. When we got off
the freeway he made a left and started driving up the hill. "I went
to Malcolm's, I wanted to break your neck!" He adjusted in his

seat. "Why?" I shook my head. We pulled up to the top of the hill where new homes were being constructed.

"Were you sitting at home waiting for me?"

He exhaled, "not at first. But after that last night. I was spent for a long time. Then the closer it got to you coming home I was asking myself why. I started remembering my last conversation with my grandfather. Why am I spinning my wheels? I thought about what you said, and honestly I couldn't blame you for not wanting to live with me there. So I came here. I talked to the developer, my uncle; I put money down on the best lot in this phase, over looking the Bay. I was gonna let you run wild and put every customization and upgrade your heart desired in our home." He shook his head like he was trying to avoid the emotions he felt.

"Derrick, so you brought me up here to tell me you're done with me? Why are you telling me this?" I felt like my heart was going to explode, as I cried.

"BECAUSE IM MAD AT YOU! AM I SUPPOSED TO MAKE THIS EASY ON YOU? YOU LEFT ME FOR YEARS BECAUSE YOU WALKED IN ON ME SITTING AT THE SAME TABLE WITH MY MOTHER AND MY EX! I WAS DYING WITHOUT YOU! YOU COME BACK TO PUT ME THROUGH THIS?"

"What are you saying? Should I walk home? You said we were free to do whatever, but now I see you meant only you were free. Take me home I'm tired of crying."

"Was it worth it?"

I gave him a dumb expression, "what kind of a question is that?"

"Well?"

"I could ask you the same thing. It's a dumb question."

"Malcolm says I made this happen. That I should've been learning from his mistakes. I guess if I put you in my momma's shoes I can see all the plays in this situation." He exhaled hard, "I'm still mad at you! But I think we can get past this. What do you think?"

"Fine! Then I'm mad at you too! It's a given that you were out there and that's fine. But for me the world comes to an end. You bout to cry and everything."

My speaking on his teary eyes caught him off guard. He started laughing. "True, but I'm still mad at you."

"Well so what! I'm mad at you!"

"I'm mad at you!" He mimicked me. "So what!"

"SO WHAT TO YOU TOO!"

"DO YOU LIKE THE LOCATION?"

"What?"

"The house!"

"Where exactly?"

We got out the truck and he told me to look out for nails before I stepped. He said they were still working out the zoning but we'd have one of the biggest lots in the development. He said we could come back later to look at the plans. We stood in our would be driveway and watched the sun come up. On the way back to my place I asked him if he slept at all last night. He gave me a what do you think look.

****

Fortunately only Shameless had to meet with his Public Relations folks about the concert in LA. The concert in Sacramento was on extra lock down. They had extra security, metal detectors, everything to make us feel secure about performing out here. Wade seemed happy to see Derrick, but I knew there was something under handed in that smile. When it was time for me to go on stage Derrick assured me it was ok. Lewis could tell by my face that I was terrified. He told the band to stop the music. Then he introduced me to the audience, everyone clapped for me. He asked how many people liked my song. The crowd applauded, then he told them they could do better than that. They went wild! He made them sing my song to me. They knew the words and even my personal touches on the song. He had the crowd assure me that we were safe and that we were with family. As I stood there crying then he cued the music again. I sung my heart out which made the crowd get louder than they already were. Shameless had me stay out on the stage for the rest of the show, we killed it! Two more cities and this would be over! I couldn't wait, when I walked off the stage Ray was waiting with another bouquet. Derrick gave Ray evil eyes as he handed everything to me. Ray stared him back down. I was afraid of what Derrick might do so I introduced them. Derrick and Ray watched as I read the card. It said the same exact thing. Flustered I gave the card and bouquet to Derrick. Derrick put the flowers in the garbage but he held on to the card.

When we got in his car to leave I asked him what he was gonna do with the card. "I'm gonna find out who's sending it." He said simply. "Before I forget, Yussef's grandmother is getting married. They invited us to the wedding do you want to go?"

I smiled, "of course! I need to know when to have JoJo put it on my schedule." Then I got tickled. "His grandmother is getting married?"

"Yep, a widow and a widower found love."

I was quiet for a minute. "I'm gonna ask you again." I took a deep breath.

"Goodness gracious! Chantel please don't ask me while I'm still mad at you."

"Let's switch gears then. How long you gonna stay mad at me? That will determine how long I'm mad at you."

He chuckled, "what you gonna try to stay mad longer?"

"Yep one day longer than you. I should be mad longer."

"How you figure?"

"It's my right as a woman, and you were out of line!"

"So if I stopped being mad two days ago?"

"Then I stopped yesterday." I said

"Meaning we could do it tonight?"

"Do it?" I laughed, "You sound twelve!"

"That's not an answer." He glanced at me.

"No."

"No?"

"If we're not making love I don't wanna do it."

He blew air, "I guess I'm waiting."

"DANG SKIPPY YOU'RE WAITING! YOU MAY NEVER TOUCH ME AGAIN!" I said full of attitude.

He smiled, "that's cute."

"Cute?"

"You actually think you could resist me. It's so cute!" He chuckled. His statement made me mad. "FORGET YOU DERRICK! I could resist you if I wanted to."

"D-Boogie always wins!"

I laughed, "Not tonight he don't!"

"That's fine, I don't want none tonight anyways."

"What?" I laughed, "the fact that you think you could resist me is even more hilarious."

"Come on, we can go back and forth like this all night. Either we are or we aren't make up your mind."

"I'm kind of tired. You?"

"Still haven't recovered from my all-niter I could use some sleep." He said.

By the time we got to my house his phone had rung six times and each time he sent the person to voicemail. He had no expression on his face, and if it was business he would've answered. I went to bed not wanting to discuss it.

****

"You are really excited!" I said smiling at Lewis.

"Are you kidding? My love is coming to my show! She's always a pick me up!" He said kissing Latia's neck.

I smiled, "that is so sweet. You guys are too cute together."

"Thanks girl, I figure I might as well since everyone will be here." We looked at Derrick and Yussef as they stared at Yussef's laptop. I could see the cards on the table but I didn't know what they were doing. Derrick seemed irritated when another bouquet came in San Jose and then the first night here in Oakland. I know he wanted to ask if they were from my episode, but as long as his phone kept ringing I almost dared him to ask. So I guess this was the other route. Yussef clapped his hands, which sounded like thunder. Derrick's expression didn't change. I frowned at them then I looked at the happy couple. "So, what are you wearing to the wedding? I'm trying to figure out what I should wear."

"Wedding?"

Latia shot me a look then she turned her face to Lewis's. "Yeah I told you Yussef's grandma is getting married next weekend. You forgot?"

He gave her a look, "I guess so. Am I invited? Can I go?"

"You're my plus one." She kissed his cheek. Then she turned her attention back to me. "I'm in the wedding so my outfit is already picked out. I think you should show off those long legs." She smiled.

"Isn't your grandma religious? I don't want to be disrespectful."

"Very! You don't have to dress like a nun. I know you'll be fabulous."

When I looked back at Derrick he had his version of sad eyes, and Yussef was concentrating on the screen. Neither one of them looked happy or energized. Yussef glanced at me and then back at his computer. I put my hands out to Derrick asking him what was going on. He shook his head and told me he'd tell me later.

Then Wade came out to the stage going off. He was in Lewis' face asking why Philip was back. "First of all you need to remember who you're talking to. I'm not one of your flunkies that you can talk to any way you please. Check your tone!"

Wade was now boiling! "If you're gonna make ridiculous decisions like this I will address you in the manner that suits your actions!"

"Ridiculous? Wade you are overstepping your boundaries. Get out of my face and remember who signs your paychecks!"

Wade was angry Derrick, Yussef, and JoJo watched intently like they were devoting the scene to memory. "I thought you shelved the movie idea."

"No."

"No?"

"Why don't you want the cameras around? What are you hiding?"

Wade got even angrier and he stormed away. I gave Derrick a worried look. I didn't understand what was going on. I kind of figured since Latia was here that meant the worst was over, but now I didn't feel so sure. Derrick called Lewis over and the four of them spoke in low voices. Wade was fussing at Wally about something and the rest of the Goons sat back and watched everything.

During our sound check my cellphone rang it was my daddy. He said they were having a hard time getting through security. Derrick left to go get them; he came back with my family, Pearla, Liz, and Paulette. Lewis explained that they decided to beef up security. He said Wade had been acting too weird lately and after the show he was going to lay low until his contract with Wade was up. "Lewis is it safe for us to be here?" Latia asked, she was speaking my thoughts.

"I would never put you in harm's way intentionally. You're always safe with me." He told her.

My Braider Roz came and she took down my braids. As usual she did it so fast; during this tour each time we met up to touch up my braids I would allow a lot more time than we actually needed. My hair was completely down in minutes; she had a mixture she put on my hair that basically detangled it. She washed and deep conditioned my hair super fast. Then the stylist took over. My head felt so light without all those heavy braids. They braided my hair up and weaved it. I loved the look when they were done. Caprice came in the room she plopped down on the couch. I peeked my eyes at her while the makeup artist worked on me. "What's wrong?"

"Your brother is here with his girlfriend."

I felt bad for her, "why don't you tell him about your job?"

"It'll raise too many questions and I'd rather not." She sighed

"So what are you going to do?"

"Put my game face on and get through it." She said with the fakest smile.

"I'm sorry" I didn't know what else to say.

"It's my fault. Hind site is always twenty-twenty. You look amazing by the way."

The opening act was out there tearing up the stage. Back stage wasn't nearly as crowded as it normally was. Every time Philip pointed the camera anywhere near Wade he got an attitude and moved. Philip got a lot of footage of my little brothers, Pearla, and Paulette having a good time. Yussef told the cameraman not to shoot him. Philip made sure he did not capture Yussef at all. Yussef's face was unusually serious, he was calm but his eyes were watching everything and everyone. When Darryl, Jeff, and Drew walked in Wade seemed even more upset. I didn't get why Wade was so nerved up. I gave them hugs and I asked Drew where his fiancé was, I wanted to meet her. He said their little one wasn't feeling well, Amber was out of town so Tracy stayed home. Then he whispered that he didn't tell her she was missing this and for me to please not mention it. I laughed and told him his secret was safe with me.

Shameless had the crowd rocking! As if it was possible he was more confident on stage than normal, he kept looking back at Latia the whole time. When I stepped on the stage Lewis said, "GIVE IT UP FOR YOUR OWN OAKLAND NATIVE CHANTEL SHAW!" Everybody went crazy! The vibration from the crowd rumbled the stage. I swallowed my nerves and then we went at it. There's nothing like the energy from the Bay Area. At one point I looked up and Yussef was above the stage looking down at me. I didn't know anyone could even get up there or how he was up there. He smiled while he moved to our music. Goons were all around the stage; I stayed out until the end of the show.

I saw one of the Goons hand Derrick another bouquet as we walked off the stage. Everyone was fired up and telling us how good we were. They had our stuff packed up and ready to go as we stepped off the stage. We got in limos and then we went to Elegant Affairs. The people at the club went wild when we walked in. We took over the previously empty VIP section. Drew made sure we were squared away with bottles upon bottles of the good stuff, and then he went home.

Aleisha had the house rocking, I was happy to see her confidently doing her thing. She definitely had stage presence, and I'm sorry a white girl on the stage of a predominately black club killing it! Definitely gave her street credit in my opinion. Caprice sat next to Latia and I, while Cyrus and Sherrell sat a couple booths behind us with Pearla, Paulette, and Liz. Lewis and JoJo were discussing next steps.

Wade came in an hour after we were there with four big guys. The mean looking guy from LA and three others. Wade marched right up to our booth. "How come no one told me the after party venue changed?" No one said anything; I kind of assumed that he would understand that meant he wasn't invited, but I guess not. "I need to talk to you about my contract."

Lewis smiled, "my office hours are from?"

Darryl started cracking up, "dang he better look out for the balcony!"

"Shut up chump!" One of the guys said from behind Wade. Everybody's heads whipped to Darryl, he was still smiling. "Who says chump? How old are you? Definitely too old to be up in here using language like that. Somebody find this fool's walker and get him out of here." Darryl said waving him off.

"Lewis!" Wade growled.

"This is what you've been building to? You gonna act like a thug everywhere we go? I have no business to discuss with you."

"My contract!"

"Expires in a few months and will not be renewed. If you would like to sit down like businessmen we can do that tomorrow. If you gotta be all thugged out, just know this is the wrong place to go there."

"Oh I think this is the right place."

Lewis, Darryl, Derrick, JoJo, Jeff, Paul, Ray, Cyrus, and Kirk stood up. Then Yussef tapped the microphone, "Good evening ladies and gentlemen, EA is now closed. Please gather your belongings and exit the building immediately."

As the crowd left I didn't know what to do, I looked at Sherrell in the other booth and she looked as nervous as I did, Latia and I held hands. As the crowd dissipated the black tops and grey pants stood out. Wade and his men looked around at all the guys surrounding them. "Wade you're fired!" Then Lewis pointed, "You're the reason Stan came to my house all fired up."

"That's the fool you knocked out?" Darryl said to Derrick laughing.

The light bulb went off! Stan was the guy from Lewis' house that

morning, it's been too long since I've seen him I didn't recognize him. Was he planning on shooting my baby in LA? My heart jumped into my toes.

Wade started to say something then the police came in the club. "Wade Lucas, Detective Dartnell" she flashed her badge. "You're under arrest for the murder of Reginald Flowers!"

"WHAT?" Wade yelled looking a little crazy.

"You should really think about the company you keep. These Wallace's are on my list. I check out all their friends."

"The who?" Wade said looking confused.

The officer looked around. "Shoot! It looks like if I would've waited five more minutes I could've taken those four too!" She said pointing in our direction. Then she looked around, "where are your fathers?" No one answered her. She snapped her fingers, "next time! Cuff him and let's go. Did anybody wanna go with him?" She looked around. "Nobody? Fine!"

"You guys might wanna leave with her." Derrick said to the guys who stood with Wade. Then Derrick said out loud. "Got 'em?" Then random voices yelled. "Got 'em!" From every direction in the club. I didn't know what they were talking about.

"Which one of you wants to be my new best friend and tell me what's going on in here?" The woman said as they walked out.

"Caprice! You and Brandy take the girls back to the hotel." Derrick commanded, handing her something.

Paul and Cyrus had the same confused faces. Brandy kissed Paul and then she told Sherrell to come on. When we got in the limo Sherrell and Caprice kept looking at each other and looking away. They weren't mugging each other but they were checking each other out. Brandy was directing the driver and we pulled up to Derrick's place. "Wait a minute Derrick said the hotel." Sherrell said.

Pearla looked at Sherrell, "it's ok. Come on."

When we got to the gate Caprice found the key to open it. Then she opened his door and we spread out inside. Some sat on the couch and some sat at the table. I turned on the TV, and we started to try to relax. "I like your dress." Sherrell said to Caprice.
"Thank you," Caprice sighed. "Your daughter looks just like you! She's really pretty."
Pearla looked at Sherrell's demeanor, she wasn't her normal out going self. She kept looking back and forth between the two of them like she was trying to figure something out. Then Sherrell shot her a look like they were having a wordless conversation.
"WAIT A MINUTE! HOLD UP! This is the girl?" Pearla said to Sherrell.
"Yes" Sherrell said not taking her eyes off Caprice.
"Interesting" Pearla, said with a smile.
Caprice squinted her eyes, "interesting?"
"How could you be comfortable being the other woman?" Pearla asked
Caprice pointed to her chest, "I'm the other woman?" Then she looked at Sherrell, "you need to tell the story right!"
Sherrell looked away, I could see Pearla getting mad on behalf of her friend. "Wait a minute there's a whole story to this situation." I said pleading.
Pearla was starting to look a little crazy, "what do you mean Chantel?"
"I'm just saying it's not that simple, like who's the other woman or any of that. It's a complicated situation."
"Chantel, I know that's your brother so you wanna defend him, but he is so wrong. He's got a family with my girl, why is he still seeing her?"
I felt horrible, but of course I'm gonna defend my brother. OF COURSE! "Relationships are sticky like that. A better question is why is Sherrell staying in a situation like that? Pearla we gotta stay out of it. I love both of them, Caprice is my girl, and Sherrell you know I love you! We gotta stay out of it, they need to figure out how they wanna handle things." I said feeling good about my statement.
Caprice opened her mouth to say something when the buzzer for the door went off. Brandy said it was a girl as she looked at the monitor. My heart dropped cause I had a feeling I knew who it

was. Pearla and Caprice went to the door. "Who's this?" Caprice said as the buzzer went off again.

Pearla looked at me, "it's Brooklyn."

I looked at the clock, it was after three in the morning. "Buzz her in." I said

"So what were you saying about relationships?" Pearla said giving me mean eyes.

Everybody was looking at me; I took a deep breath and told them to move as I cracked the door open. Brooklyn looked upset and then startled when she saw all of us looking at her. "Where's Derrick?"

"What do you want?" I tried to take as much attitude out of my voice as I could.

"I need to talk to him." She said as she looked around the room. "Hey Liz, Pearla, Paulette," then she looked at me. "Chantel."

"Hi," I said fast. "You can't talk to Derrick but you can talk to me, would you like to step in the bedroom?" My heart was racing, I wanted to scream and act a fool. My mind kept telling me to hear her out first.

Brooklyn nodded as if to say ok, and then she led the way to his bedroom. I tried not to get mad that she obviously was no stranger to his place. "Cousin, I'm right here if you need me." Pearla said

I shut the door behind us after we walked in the room. She set her purse on the dresser and then she sat on the bed. I wanted to scream at her to get off my man's bed. I took a deep breath instead then I stood there waiting for her to speak. "I really need to speak to Derrick, when will he be home?"

"What do you want Brooklyn?" I said sitting on the dresser.

"I think I'm pregnant."

Everything went silent; I closed my eyes cause the room spun. Then I looked at her; I could feel sweat popping up on my nose. "How far a long are you?"

"I'm not sure yet, but I wanted to talk to him about it first." She said watching me for a reaction.

"Either you are or you aren't. Why would you come here unless you knew for sure?" I said watching her face.

Tears formed in her eyes, "I just needed to talk to him. I don't know what to do. He's not answering my phone calls! What am I supposed to do?"

"I know he had to have told you I was coming back. Why would you think he would answer your calls once I'm here?"

"What do you have to do with me? I know he likes you, and with you being on stage now; I know that adds another seasoning to who you are. Derrick has been in love with me since he was a little boy. He can't drop me out of the blue."

I smiled, "but he did. You are no longer his woman. I am! I can't believe you resorted to getting pregnant to try and hold on to him. You saw what happened to Toya; Drew is engaged to somebody else raising their son like a happy little family. I guess this story ends the same way." I sighed

"I'm not Toya, I wouldn't hand my child over to you or any other female."

"So if you are pregnant, you're keeping it?" I asked, I was sweating uncontrollably.

"OF COURSE!" She said looking at me like I asked the stupidest question ever.

"Take a test tonight. Let's end this now. I can ask somebody to go to the store."

"Do you know what time it is? Is there a store even open?" She said again like I made a stupid suggestion.

Fire turned in my stomach. "Look! You came over my man's house in the middle of the night, talking about a baby you're not even sure is there. What do you think Derrick would tell you when you told him? Were you hoping that some how your fall from number one would be restored because you told him he planted a seed? Derrick is smarter than that and in love with me. If you are pregnant, my man and I will handle it. You should already know, I'm not going anywhere!"

"Derrick is in love with me! He's loved me since he was a child!" She started crying.

"You're not pregnant! I don't believe you!" I eyed her.

"I think I am!" She said through tears.

"No, you're wishing you were. You're desperate to hold on to him. I get it, I wouldn't go this route, but I understand the desperation. You and Derrick are over! He's not gonna touch you ever again. Let it go!"

"He's in love with me." She said through tears.

"Do you even realize that you are in my man's place talking to me? It's over! Let it go! If there was something to you guys, the situation would be in reverse; only I wouldn't sink to such a low scheme to hold on to any man. Having a baby doesn't trap a man, it traps you! They will move on with their lives and you will be stuck for the rest of your life with a reminder of what used to be."

"Are you threatening me?" Her face turned evil.

"I don't know how you could take what I just said as a threat, but if that's what you want. Fine! Whatever! I got a living room full of crazy females just outside that door. Do you really wanna test me?

The question of whether or not you're pregnant could be fixed for you right now." Then I stood up. "Now that was a threat!"

"What kind of a female are you? Who threatens a pregnant woman?"

"YOU'RE NOT PREGNANT!" I yelled, "You're wishing you were, but you aren't."

"I think I am!"

I opened the door. "Pearla, could you please come here for a minute?" I tried to make my voice sound sugary sweet but I was livid.

"What's up cousin?" Pearla said stepping into the room.

"Brooklyn thinks she's pregnant."

Pearla laughed, "Derrick is not Drew!"

"I know right! She needs to take a test."

"I'm not doing anything until I talk to Derrick!" She said crossing her arms.

Pearla looked at her giggled, and then walked over to her. Her hand went up so fast I almost didn't see it. You could hear the slap across the Bay. I cringed, Brooklyn screamed. "You need to stop playing right now. I used to like you! Don't make me hate you! You're gonna pee on the stick that's it, that's all. Give me your car keys!" Brooklyn's hands were shaking as she gave Pearla her car keys. "Thank you, I'll be right back." Then she looked at me. "Liz will be here in case she feels froggy, which even I don't suggest." She looked at Brooklyn, "Liz is the crazy one!" Then she left.

Brooklyn's face was red where Pearla slapped her. I felt sorry for her, to a point. I went to the bathroom and I put cold water on a face towel. I gave it to Brooklyn to put on her face. Then I sat back on the dresser. Brooklyn is pretty, a completely different pretty than me. She's brown, not a dark brown like me but brown. She wasn't as pretty as Toya but she was definitely pretty. She has pretty brown eyes, but not as pretty as mine. A pretty mouth, but not as beautiful as my beautiful full lips. It was like she had everything I had but on a lower scale. High cheekbones, but mine stood out more. She was average height and I was tall, my breast and butt were bigger than hers. Her hair was shoulder length and permed. I've been wearing my hair braided and weaved up so long it has to be to the middle of my back at least. Even though I know she's smart, tonight was no evidence of that. Brooklyn and I kept looking at each other. "I hope we can find a way to get along for the baby's sake." She said holding the towel on her face.

I didn't say anything; cause I wanted to hit her for even uttering the words. The phone rang and I answered it. "Hello."

"We're on our way." Derrick said

"You have a visitor."

Derrick was quiet for a minute, "what does she want?"

"She thinks she's pregnant."

I could tell Derrick dropped the phone, he was cursing and swearing in the background. Then he put the phone back to his ear,

"I DON'T HAVE TIME FOR THIS NONSENSE!"

"Pearla and Paulette went to get a test for her. They should be back any minute now."

"Chantel, I promise you I stayed strapped up! I didn't kiss her, I…"

I cut him off, "it's ok Derrick just come home."

I could tell my reaction surprised him, "I'm on my way!"

Minutes later Pearla came in the room with four different kinds of test. "Why so many?"

Pearla laughed a nervous laugh. "I couldn't decide which brand was more effective. If it were me or my man, I'd want to know beyond a shadow of a doubt so I decided to lean on the side of the most accuracy."

Derrick walked in as I was hugging Pearla, "thank you cousin." I said

"She hit me!" Brooklyn said pointing to Pearla.

"Snitch!" Pearla said

Derrick looked at all three of us. "Why?"

"Does it matter? She hit me! You gonna let her get away with that." Pearla and I looked at Derrick.

"Pearla, can you excuse us!" Derrick said, he looked angry. Pearla walked out the room quickly and shut the door. "Brooklyn what are you doing?"

"Derrick!" She started crying, "You haven't answered any of my calls. How could you cut me off like this?"

"I told you Chantel was coming back."

"What about me? What about us? I took this job out here to be closer to you. I always told you I was coming back. Why would you put her before me?"

"We were kids. When you started calling me again way back when I told you things would never be the same. Once upon a time you were the woman in my life. That died the moment you treated me like I was beneath you. Like I couldn't comprehend what love is. You're not pregnant." Derrick's voice was strong but it didn't hold its normal point blank sound. My stomach turned hearing him speak to her from his heart. I wanted them to stop talking and I wanted her to go anywhere but here.

"I think I am!" She held on to her thought like her life depended on it.

"Even if you were and I know you're not, it changes nothing. I'm with Chantel and like I told you I will never touch you again. You should've never come here."

"She needs to know! She needs to know who I am! That you love me! That you're coming back to me! She needs to know."

"Chantel knows who you are, and she knows how much I love her. You and I will never be together again. This little stunt is not ok! Don't ever come to my place again!"

"Derrick!" She stood up, "YOU LOVE ME!"

His eyes were sad, "I used to."

"YOU STILL DO! STOP LYING!" She pleaded.

I could literally see Derrick's anger boil to the top. "YOU LEFT ME! I NEEDED YOU AND YOU LEFT! YOU SHOW UP WHEN IT'S CONVENIENT FOR YOU! YOU BRING MY MOTHER INTO YOUR STUNTS! ONE DAY YOU WILL MAKE SOMEONE A GOOD WOMAN BUT YOU ARE NOT THE WOMAN FOR ME! I DON'T LOVE YOU LIKE THAT ANYMORE! AND THIS RIGHT HERE SEALED IT FOR ME! YOU DON'T LISTEN! YOU'RE REMINDING ME SO MUCH

OF TOYA IN THIS SPACE! AND WE ALL KNOW HOW
MUCH I LOVE HER! HOW COULD YOU BRING THIS
DRAMA TO MY WOMAN!"

"I'm your woman!" She said through tears.

Derrick literally caught himself from flying across the room.
"Brooklyn you need to leave, you're making me come apart. I don't
want to hurt you! Leave and don't ever come back. Forget my
name!" He put his hands in his pockets, and then I saw it. A tear
left his eye.

I lost it! "GET OUT!" I grabbed her by her hair and I drug her out
the room. I didn't even know I was that strong. I drug her out the
room opened the door with one hand and kicked her out. Derrick
had her purse in his hand and I took it from him and I threw it out
the door cursing and screaming the whole time. I slammed the door
then I pushed Derrick back in his room, and slammed that door.

"FOR HER! FOR HER YOU ACTUALLY LET A TEAR DROP!
THAT TRICK!"

Derrick stood there like a wall trying to pull back his emotions.
"Chantel!"

"You had unprotected sex with her?"

"No!"

"Then what are you crying for? How dare you let her provoke any
kind of emotion from you! She thinks she still has you!"

"Stop Chantel!" He sounded tired.

"She thinks it's only a matter of time before you're back!"

"Stop Chantel!"

"She thinks…"

Derrick threw me on the bed. "SHUT UP! SHUT UP! SHUT UP!"
He yelled at me! "I am hanging on by a very thin thread right now
and you're not making it easy."

I got up off the bed and got in his face. "DON'T YOU EVER IN

LIFE TOUCH ME LIKE THAT…"

"OR ELSE WHAT?" He squinted his eyes at me.

I didn't know or else what. "Or else… Or else…." I shook my

head. "YOU DON'T WANNA KNOW MY 'WHAT'! YOU

CAN'T HANDLE MY WHAT!"

"NO YOU'RE BAD NOW! TELL ME 'WHAT'! TELL ME!"

I thought I could push him down if I moved quickly. He felt like a wall. Seriously! He smiled at my realization. "I'll go home that's what." I said feeling defeated.

"And then I'll follow you or send Caprice to screw your brother like I always have." He looked at me with evil eyes.

"What?" I knew I didn't hear him right.

"I needed to be sure you were who you said you were. It's a big coincidence how they hooked up huh."

"WHAT?" I opened the door. "CAPRICE!" She slowly walked in the room like she already knew; she closed the door behind herself. Derrick crossed his arms. "You've been on assignment all these years?"

She looked at the floor. "Yes" she said lowly.

"We're not friends?" I plopped on the bed.

"Yes we are friends, but I have to do my job first. Cyrus wasn't supposed to happen."

"You used my brother! You NEVER cared about him!" I started crying.

"I do love him! Everything I've told you has been the truth."

"Derrick I didn't sign up for this! You got people to be my friends!" I pushed through tears, "does Pearla even like me? Is this whole thing some kind of ruse you do for kicks?"

Derrick grabbed me by my shoulders. "I LOVE YOU AND I WAS NOT GOING THROUGH HEARTBREAK AGAIN! I HAD TO BE SURE!"

Cyrus opened the door. "Chantel are you ok?"

Caprice pleaded with her eyes. "Come in and shut the door." I told him.

Caprice cried harder, "No Chantel! Please! No!"

Cyrus came in the door, shut it and sat next to me on the bed. He put his arms around me and rocked me, while rubbing my head and back. "Do I want to know?" I shook my head no. "I think I've kind of figured it out tonight." He kissed my head. "It's ok."

"Cyrus.." Caprice said through tears.

"You work for Mitigated's personal security division." He said to Caprice, "Tell me the truth. Did you ever love me or were you playing the roll?"

"Cyrus I'm in love with you!" She said

"But your job comes first?" He spit at her.

"What if you didn't love me back? I would've been broken hearted and BROKE!"

"When I'm begging you not to kill our child, you were unsure of my love for you?" He roared.

Caprice looked at Derrick with a busted look on her face. "I didn't know what to do! I chose wrong!"

"Hell yeah, you chose wrong!" He rubbed my back some more. "Now you're second string, when I have time I will deal with you! But my family comes first!" Then he patted my back. "You ready? I think we've seen enough for one night."

I shook my head yes, and I stood up to leave with Cyrus. Cyrus and Derrick looked at each other without speaking words, and then we walked out. Everybody was standing around looking. Lewis was holding Latia's hand standing by the door when we walked out the room. Everybody was looking at each other. Darryl wasn't smiling or looking like he was about to crack a joke at all. Cyrus grabbed Sherrell's hand and told her to come on. Pearla smiled then she looked at Derrick, and her smile dropped. Cyrus asked Lewis if we could ride with him. He agreed and we left, in the limo Cyrus held on to me rubbing my back and telling me it was ok, and that he was ok. How in the world could I not go off? He was showing emotion to some girl he deemed not worthy of being with. When does Derrick show emotion? Besides he would have a fit if Gerard showed up here declaring his undying love and for me. Shoot, or if he showed up period. When the limo pulled up to our place there was a woman leaning against the building it was odd because the police were pretty good about making sure there was no loitering in this part of the city. We thanked Lewis for the ride and then I took out my keys to open the gate. I didn't pay the woman any attention. "Chantel?" The woman said

"Seriously? Tonight! You come around to night?" Cyrus said

"I want to talk to you guys." She said

"Tonight is not a good night." I said

"Please! I need to talk to you two."

"Where's Reggie?" I spit at her.

"He's gone. Please let me in."

"It's been a long night. I'm tired, and I don't feel like talking to you." Then I looked at Cyrus. "Don't be weak for her just because she's our mother." Looking at his face I already know he was weak.

"Is it important?" He asked

Then Derrick pulled up to the driveway in his truck. He looked at us, and then he went in the garage. I was happy he came even though I still wanted to scream at him. "I'm tired Cyrus." I sighed cause I knew he was letting her in.

"Just a few minutes Chantel. She had to have been waiting all night for us."

I rolled my eyes and walked through the gate. Derrick was standing on the other side of the gate. "Your mother has been sending the flowers."

I stood still, "what?"

I searched Derrick's eyes as if he would lie about something like that. "We found out today."

"Why?" I thought I was cried out, and yet there were more tears. "Why now?"

"Talk to her." He said with sad eyes.

"You know don't you?" He didn't respond, he just looked at me. Then he took my hand and we walked ahead to the elevator. I could hear Cyrus introducing our mother to Sherrell as the elevator door closed. I turned on the lights in the living room. Derrick went in my room. "No! Please stay out here. I need you."

He took a deep breath then he sat on the bar stool next to me. I held his hand as they walked in the door. She looked around the room with a big smile on her face. "Your place is nice."

"Have a seat." Cyrus told her.

She sat on the couch. "This is a really nice couch, we never had one this nice. You guys are doing really well."

I shot Cyrus a look. He grabbed Sherrell's hand before she walked away. Then he looked at my mother. "What do you need?"

"I know it doesn't fix anything but I am so sorry for everything. I can never undo all that I've done to you guys, but I needed you guys to hear me say the words from my mouth."

"Ok, we heard you. Leave!" I said not wanting to look at her any longer than I had to.

Cyrus rolled his eyes at me. "This is Chantel's boyfriend Derrick."

"Nice to meet you." She said to him, and then she started looking around. "Didn't you have a baby? What did you have?"

"Wait a minute!" I stood up. "It's not like we have friends in common. How do you know anything about us?" Derrick almost smiled at me to show I asked the right question. "Lets get down to the reason you're here. You need money or something? Your ex has us tapped out. What do you want?"

She squirmed in her chair. "Reggie left me."

"We should feel something about that because?"

She got irritated. "Do you have to be so difficult? I'm on my knees here!"

"I don't care what you're on. You couldn't possibly think you send flowers and come with that weak apology and then all of a sudden we'd be a happy family. You are EVIL! You think I'm sorry is gonna fix that? WHAT DO YOU WANT? I DON'T TRUST YOU TO DO ANYTHING ON YOUR OWN INITIATIVE! WHAT DO YOU WANT?"

"ALRIGHT CHANTEL! ALRIGHT! DANG!" Now she sounds like the mother I grew up with. "Reggie left me," then she started crying. "I was looking for him. After two weeks I filled out a missing person's report. After a few days the police called me and told me that they had a body in the mortuary that fit my description and they needed me to come and ID the body." She started screaming, "HE'S DEAD! HE'S DEAD!"

I looked at Cyrus who was getting caught up in her emotional display. "STOP THAT! WHO CARES!" I screamed at Cyrus.

"YOU DON'T SHED TEARS FOR THAT MONSTER! HE TERRORIZED YOUR CHILDREN AND YOU COME HERE LIKE WE SHOULD CARE! GET TO THE IMPORTANT PART!" Derrick's eyes were wide while he looked at me screaming. Ok so maybe I was being a little loud and rude, but it was making me mad that she was coming in here acting like I was supposed to be emotional about a monster. I guess it's sad that he's gone, but he hurt us. He never felt any remorse for how he hurt us. She let him hurt us, so that makes her just as guilty as far as I'm concerned. I'm not gonna shed a tear for him or her. If the fire inside me turns into tears it is for my brother. He has to be mixed up to feel anything for that monster.

"I loved him!" She cried

"More than your children! You designed it so that you were all we had, and then you turned your back on us! I don't know why you would ever come here! I will not let you manipulate my brother.

He has a weakness for you! BUT I DON'T! We don't care about

who you loved, who left you, and that he's dead. That's just one less person I have to worry about running into when I go out. PLEASE tell us why you're here. FOR THE LOVE OF EVERYTHING PLEASE TELL US WHY!"

"I'M DYING!" She screamed, I didn't know how to feel about that. Cyrus fell on the other end of the couch; Sherrell put her arms around him. "Apparently I've been sick for a long time and I didn't know it."

"And so now before you die you wanna try to put your soul to rest in peace?" I spit at her.

"CHANTEL!" Cyrus yelled

"CYRUS COME ON! YOU KNOW! YOU WERE THERE!"

It looked like it took all of his strength to stand up. "Yes, I was there for everything. And it will never leave me, but you're adding to the problem. NO REGRETS CHANTEL! One day you're gonna look back and realize how messed up she is. It doesn't excuse what she put us through. NOTHING will excuse that. I'm gonna walk that much taller cause I did my best to love her even when she didn't deserve it. I won't have regrets."

I clapped my hands. "I've been up for twenty four hours. I'm going to bed! You can sit out here and feel sorry for her if you want to. You can die knowing how much you forever affected my life! You will not get forgiveness from me!" I yawned and looked at Derrick, "are you ready? I'm sleepy!" Derrick looked at Cyrus and then my mother, and then back at me. "Oh! How did you find us?"

"Your friend." She said through tears.

"What friend?"

"Kevin."

Derrick stiffened, "Kevin?"

"Yeah, he gave me your schedule and arranged for me to send you the flowers. Is there something wrong with him?"

I looked at Derrick, he looked at my mother. "Call him right now." He got up walked towards my mother. She took out her phone; she called him and handed the phone to Derrick. "Your days are numbered!" Then he gave her, her phone back.

Chapter 17

He put his arm around me. I scooted away from him. He scooted in closer, I scooted away again. He scooted closer, and I fell off the bed trying to get away. Derrick's early morning laughter sounded like thunder. "It's not funny!" I said getting up.

"Yes it is. Why are you still running from me?"

"I'm sure even in the dark you can see the expression on my face."

"Can't we put that aside for this morning? We need this."

"I need an apology."

"For what?" He said sounding insulted.

"For everything! How dare you get all huffy with me, and you were over here raw-dogging with your ex." Derrick sighed out loud and plopped down on the bed. "Now move over!" I said trying to push his body over. He laid there like dead weight and wouldn't move when I pushed him. When I tried to get on his side of the bed he moved over to that side. "Move! Stop playing! I'm sleepy!" I whined.

"Touch it!"

"No!" I whined.

"Kiss it!"

"You've got to be joking! Stop playing Derrick I'm sleepy!"

"I can put you back to sleep."

"Stop playing!" I said laying across the foot of the bed.

"I need my woman!" He said diving on top of me.

"You have too much energy. I'm tired!" I said yawning.

"Help me burn off some energy." He said putting his face in my chest. I laid there looking mad. "Chantel!" He sang. When I didn't respond, he collapsed on top of me. "If I apologize right now it won't seem genuine."

"But making love to me right now will?" I hissed

"Yes."

"No, it will pleasure you too much to pleasure me." Truth be told I was getting that itch myself. It's been killing me to hold out, but this wouldn't be solved by me giving in.

"Ok fine. Can I kiss you?" He said putting his lips on my cheek.

"No, you'll use your kiss against me." I said turning my mouth away from him.

Then he started kissing my neck. "There's other places I can kiss you. Although I want those lips I settle for anything I can get." He said as he continued to kiss me. My resolve to hold out was weakening by the minute. Each kiss was making my body respond. I tried to tell him to stop but only an in auditable sound came out. When I had completely thrown in the towel and I was ready he backed away. "No! You're right! This isn't right! I should wait until I can genuinely apologize." He said while saluting me.

"Derrick! I will kill you right now if you don't stop playing with me!"

He laughed, "Chantel! Why are you so violent? I'm not feeling very loved right now. I think we should go to sleep and get a real apology." He laughed

"You can be replaced by machinery!"

He started laughing, but I was getting mad. He's playing entirely too much! He kissed me and only went in enough to tease me. I tried to bring him in with my legs. "I apologize for being a hypocrite. Do you forgive me?" He said bobbing at heaven's gate.

"Yes! Yes! Come on!" I said raising my hips.

He scooted his back. "Tell me you love me!"

"I love you Derrick."

"Tell me you need me!"

"I need you Derrick."

"Tell me that you'll never stray again!"

"As long as you don't!"

"What is this return evil for evil?"

"Call it whatever you want!"

"Tell me..."

I cut him off, "I'm about to tell you to get off of me if you keep playing!"

He laughed then he kissed me. I went back to sleep satisfied and worn out.

****

"This must be Chantel, nice to meet you. I'm Dale," an older gentleman said with eyes like Tim's.

"Yes I am, nice to meet you." I said

"Derrick she's pretty!" Derrick nodded acknowledging his compliment. "I see why you're holding up my whole development for her."

I looked at Derrick, "our house is holding things up?" Then I yawned.

Dale smiled, "long night?"

"I'm sorry. My flight got in this morning; it's hard to sleep on a plane." I explained.

"We need to resubmit our plans to the city for approval on everything, but what's a little nepotism if you can't use it for good?" Dale said

I looked at Derrick, "this is my Great-Uncle."

"I thought he had eyes like your Grandfather. Nice to meet you." Uncle Dale turned his attention to the model of the development. He explained to Derrick how he would have to rescale things. Derrick asked a few questions looking at the model, and then he made some suggestions that made Uncle Dale's eyes sparkle. Uncle Dale got excited and asked Derrick why he didn't go into architecture. Derrick said it wasn't challenging enough, and then he chuckled. Uncle Dale rolled his eyes while he smiled imagining the changes. Then Uncle Dale asked me how the album sales were going. I told him that I was amazed with how well things were going. Dale was nice and very smart, but he didn't have that edge to him like Uncle Frank and Uncle Jeff did. A woman came in and he introduced her as his daughter Sharon. She gave me a huge hug and said that Gwen talks about me all the time. She took us into the office; on the computer, she showed us the planned look of the community. There were going to be actual security guards at the station twenty-four hours a day. In front of Iron Gates, that gave me a measure of comfort about staying in Oakland when I blew up.

We did a virtual walk through of the neighborhood and it was going to look amazing. Although it was going to be a community, each house was separate and huge. She showed us what the structure of our home would look like. She said certain variables would have to be chosen; but for the most part, she showed us the plan. My heart started pounding; this whole thing seemed completely over my head. I grew up very basic and this house was gonna be massive. I looked at Derrick, he looked at me then he held my hand. As we were leaving Sharon got a call from her son Ryder so she went back in the office. Derrick talked to his uncle while I walked out of the trailer on site. I waived hello to Derrick's

Uncle Timothy. I couldn't pinpoint an emotion. I felt all over the place. I stood by the truck waiting for Derrick. He watched my eyes as he approached me. He opened the door but didn't say anything. "You wanna call your dad and tell him we're running behind?"

I did as I was told and then I took a deep breath. "I don't know Derrick! It's an awfully big step."

"Ok" he said listening to me gather my thoughts. I loved that even though he may have known my thoughts he was giving me the time to express them. He took me to his place since it was the closest. I went straight to the bedroom and laid on his bed. He sat in the chair next to the dresser watching me. "In the end this is your house or is it our home?"

"Our home," he said.

"How are you prepared to spend all that money on a home for us, but you can't answer a simple question about our future? It gives me anxiety."

"Isn't the house a gesture in the right direction?"

"So why can't you say, Chantel five years from now I see us together?"

"I don't know."

"So why build a home that you're not even sure I'll live in?"

His eyes rolled around the room. "I guess it's the next best thing to making you have my baby."

I popped up! "What?"

He smiled and I thought I was gonna melt on the bed. "Say for some crazy reason you left me. I'd still have the home you designed. I'd still have a home filled with you. My piece of you that lives on."

"You want to have a baby with me?" I asked in shock.

"Yes" he said watching me.

I felt all warm and fuzzy inside. "Really?"

"Yes," then he cleared his throat. Uh oh! Is all I could think. "But you're not ready." He said watching my eyes.

"How am I not ready?"

He exhaled, climbed on the bed and put me in a bear hug. I knew this meant he was about to say something I didn't like, but he was gonna try to say it as nicely as little Malcolm could. Sometimes they're too direct! "You need the space to deal with your family first."

"What? I can't let them hold me back from anything!"

"You need to resolve your issues with your mother first. Your father for that matter too."

"You're the authority on unresolved parental issues?"

He exhaled, "your mother's sick. Clear the air for your own peace of mind before she's gone. It's not about her. No regrets Chantel."

"I want her to hurt just like she hurt us!"

"How do you think someone could cause someone else pain like that and not be in pain their self?"

"Now you're siding with Cyrus? You've got unresolved parental issues too! How about I make nice with my mother when you make nice with your father!"

His body flinched, he let me go and he got up off the bed. "You don't know what you're talking about."

"But you do? Who are you to ever tell me anything about dealing with my parents? You have unresolved resentment towards all of them and you don't think that would affect you as a parent to your child?" He started pacing, "you're not better than me Derrick. Please tell me you don't honestly believe you are!"

"Better than you? Is this supposed to be a competition?"

"You're sitting over here judging me and my family when your family has issues of its own."

"I never said my family was perfect. I don't resent Malcolm and if you ever thought that you read the situation completely wrong. I don't have an issue with my mother either."

"Yes you do! When you got mad at Malcolm, you were beyond livid! Remember I saw you that night! He hurt your mom I get that but your anger isn't normal screaming and yelling and you know it. You feel like he's a hypocrite."

He locked his eyes on me. "You need to know what you're talking about before you open your mouth. Malcolm and I have had our disagreements, but like father and son we've talked them out. I could never make you understand the dynamics of my parent's

relationship, and since it's none of your business I don't care to.

Say what you want about Malcolm and me but we are at peace with each other. You are not. Ever since you've found out about your father you're suspicious of everything I do. I will not carry the burden of your parents."

"I had every right to be suspicious. You were cheating on me! When have you ever been about me and only me?"

"Right now!" He barked
"Yes, just in time for your ex to show up claiming she thinks! She's still saying she thinks! When by now she should know unless you're lying to me about the last time you touched her."
"I don't lie to you!"
"You did the first time you told me you weren't cheating on me. Lied to my face."
He stood still, looked at me, almost smiled. "Get back on topic."
I cut my eyes at him. "I don't want to see her!"
"Do it for me, please!"
I felt like someone threw a heat ball on me. I erupted in tears, which startled Derrick. "Don't ask me to let her in, Derrick she's evil!"
He rushed to the bed and put his arms back around me. "We can't choose our biological parents." He squeezed me tighter. "One time I pleaded with my mother to tell me that Malcolm was really my biological father."
"Really?" I said pulling back my tears. "What did she say?"
"That she knew exactly when I was conceived and that there was no way possible that I could be Malcolm's son, but I'm still doing my own investigation." He smiled at me.
"What about your biological father?"
He squeezed me tighter. "He left and never came back."
"I know you could find him. Find him, maybe we could do this together."
"He died a little while after that. He was spiraling out of control." He said
"Did you bury him?" He blew air and didn't answer me. So I asked again as if he didn't hear me.
"He used to take us to the San Francisco zoo and the beach all the time. He loved taking us to Golden Gate Park."
"Are you saying that would be better?"
"Yes" he said holding me.
"I don't want to let her in Derrick! I don't! She doesn't deserve anything good from me!"
"This isn't about her, it's about us."
"You're scared I'll end up like her?"
"I think it's interesting how children judge their parents for their faults and before they know it they're repeating them. I know there are parts of me like him. Those parts I hated I can't let them be

me." Then he took a deep breath. "That night when Brooklyn was here." He held me tighter. "I couldn't believe she came here. I couldn't believe she was acting like that. I've had to snatch a female up before. That night I wanted to hurt her like she was hurting me. I...." He swallowed, "my tears weren't for her. I know that's what you thought."

"It looked like it."

"I saw my father's face in the mirror. There's not too much I wanna understand when it comes to him. I see how he haunts Drew; I don't want anything to do with that. As a child I always wanted to be with Malcolm. I went with David because Drew wanted to. I was just there."

"I can't remember my mother ever hugging me. My brother always took care of me, and I he. If she had to choose to save one of us by gunpoint I know she would've chosen Cyrus. That's fine I guess, but how can a mother carry you for nine months go through labor and then hate you? What was so horrible about me, or my brother that we didn't deserve to have people who loved us around? Treated with any kind of human decency? I really don't want to talk to her Derrick."

"I'm not saying it has to be today, but soon." I didn't say anything. "Are we good?"

I know it shouldn't have but it made me angry that he wouldn't let it go. I don't want to talk to my mother. There is no excuse that she could give for her actions. I DIDN'T WANT TO DO IT! "Are you ready? DJ's waiting."

"I guess."

I was quiet the entire way to my father's house. DJ and Mario came bolting out of the house as we pulled up. DJ barely let Derrick get out the car as he started explaining the problem with the car they built together. Derrick blank stared at him. He told DJ he knew how to fix the problem, and he could've walked him through it over the phone. Mario chimed in that he told him that. DJ told him to shut up and then he asked Derrick to look at the car with him. Normally my little brother's admiration for my man tickles me, but today it was annoying. Little Adon was sitting at the table working on his homework. Seeing him made me think of Cyrus and me. When we came we did our homework, chores, and then we'd go out and play. Outside of the chores, our mother didn't care what we did. "What you working on baby?" I said giving Adon a kiss on the forehead.

"CHANTEL!" He yelled standing up and wrapping his arms around my waist. I could never get tired of his reaction to me. "Can you come to my school? Nobody believes that you're my sister."

I blushed, "sure baby. When do you want me to come?"

"Tomorrow," he said with a mile wide smile.

"I'll have to see, where's mom and dad?"

"Daddy's in the backyard, mom's laying down. Go knock on the door." He said returning to his homework.

I knocked on the door and Maria told me to come in. She was laying on top of the covers on her bed under her throw blanket. She smiled really big when she saw me. "What are you doing here?"

"I just got in this morning. DJ needed Derrick's help with something on the car."

"Have you talked to your father?" She gave me a look.

"Not yet, what's up?"

"I'm pregnant." She had an embarrassed look on her face.

I smiled, "still trying for that girl huh?"

Maria started crying. "I don't want to have another baby. I'm getting too old for this!"

I frowned, "you're not old."

"Older than I want to be having a baby. I had to work really hard to get back to the perfection you see in front of you." She laughed really hard, I smiled. Then her eyes turned sad. "I don't wanna do it."

"What did he say?"

"We're not agreeing."

"What are you going to do?"

"He won't get fixed, he doesn't want me to have surgery. I gotta be sneaky about birth control, but he caught me slipping." She blew air.

"So you gonna have it?" I said with pleading eyes.

She rolled her eyes. "This could be our breaking point. I love your dad, but I can't take too much more. I'm the breadwinner, mom, cook, maid, and wife. Now this? He's no help with the baby either. It's all on me. I'm not a spring chicken I can't keep doing this."

I felt bad for her, and I really couldn't tell her anything. I've never been pregnant. I don't have a husband, and.... "I guess I should go talk to him." I said standing up and kissing her cheek.

"Don't bring it up until he does, and he will. I don't care what you tell him." Then she rolled over.

When I walked in the backyard my father was punching a sand bag. I guess he was working off some steam. He was sweating like crazy and going to town punching and punching. I guess he felt my presence cause he turned and looked at me. "Hey baby how you doing? When did you guys get here, I thought you weren't coming until later?"

"It is later dad." I sat in the chair off to the side. He gave me a kiss on the cheek. "How's business? Your record selling good?"

"Phenomenal, stupendous, beyond fathom!" I said gesturing big.

"You making fun of me?"

"Yes! Sells are good, better than anticipated. I gotta go to LA to do another TV interview and then I'm gonna do a few performances locally."

"Locally? When? Why am I just now hearing about this? I'm not opposed to flying out with you, you know."

"Daddy, my manager books everything. I get the high level details."

He eyed me, "I saw your backup singers from the club with you on that one show."

I rolled my eyes, "so are you jealous? It's not time to bring you out yet. I'm still promoting. Once I have an established name then I can show you off."

He looked irritated. "Did you change over the address like I told you to?"

I blew air, "Yes!"

"What's wrong with you?"

"Why would you hide your royalties check from Maria? She's been breaking her back for this family and you hide your money from her? I don't like it daddy!"

"There's just something's you won't understand little girl."

"Make me, cause I don't like it."

"I love Maria, and she's a good woman, but if I'm the head of the household how she gonna put me on an allowance? I'm the MAN!" He said all indignant.

"Seriously daddy? You know why?"

He looked me up and down, "what would you know about it?"

"I've got eyes I can see. How many trips to Oakland land you right at the Casino in Richmond?"

"San Pablo!"

"Whatever! You know what I'm talking about! Only a woman deeply in love could put up with some junk like that from her man. And even then I can't say that love is enough."

My daddy looked angry, "figures you would be on her side."

"I'm not on anybody's side. Right is right daddy."

"Oh well since you think Maria is perfect. Did she tell you she's pregnant and she doesn't wanna keep my baby? How could she look at you guys and say this one doesn't live?" He spit on the ground glaring at me.

"She's upset, give her a minute to digest it."

"I can't stay with a woman who kills my baby. She needs to ask your momma about that."

"Is that why you guys broke up?"

He exhaled, "I'm old fashioned. I don't want birth control. I think every life is a gift from God whether I'm practicing my faith or not. I think everything should happen naturally."

Fire started turning in my stomach. "You know what else is natural?" He looked at me. "A man taking care of his children." I got up angry. "I CAN'T BELIEVE THIS!"

"What?" My daddy asked.

"YOU MEAN TO TELL ME YOU PULLED THIS SAME STUFF ON MY MOTHER! YOU DIDN'T WANNA WORK CAUSE YOU WERE TOO BUSY TAKING CHANCES AND RISKS TRYING TO GET DOUBLE OR NOTHING! SHE DIDN'T WANT TO HAVE KIDS DID SHE?" I was up and pacing.

"Chantel calm down."

"ANSWER THE QUESTION!"

He lowered his eyes, "no." He said lowly.

I don't know why that relieved some of the pressure on my chest.

"SO SHE DIDN'T WANT KIDS IN THE FIRST PLACE, BUT YOU KNEW SHE LOVED YOU SO SHE WENT ALONG WITH YOUR RIDICULOUSNESS! DID YOU GET HER PREGNANT?"

"Baby calm down!"

"ANSWER ME! DID YOU?"

"Yes."

"DADDY IF THAT'S THE WAY YOU'RE GONNA BE, GET A JOB! THAT'S TOO MUCH ON ANY WOMAN TO BARE! AND YOU'VE GOT THE NERVE TO GET MAD ABOUT TAKING PREVENTATIVE MEASURES TO MAKE SURE SHE DOESN'T GET PREGNANT!" I stood up to go to the house

"Chantel!" I didn't respond I kept walking, "where are you going?" When I still didn't respond he said; "now you're acting like your mother!"

That stopped me dead in my tracks. I gave him evil eyes! "YOU ARE AN UNREASONABLE PATHETIC EXCUSE FOR A MAN! HOW DARE YOU TREAT THESE WOMEN BADLY BECAUSE YOU DON'T GET TO CONTROL EVERYTHING IN THEIR LIVES! GET A JOB OR GIVE MARIA YOUR ROYALTY CHECKS! OTHERWISE I'M CUTTING YOU OFF FROM ANY FUTURE PROJECTS! YOU WANT HER TO KEEP THE BABY! THEN HELP HER!"

"GIVE HER MY MONEY? YOU MUST BE CRAZY!"

I ran in his face. "MARIA PROVIDES THIS BEAUTIFUL HOME FOR YOU AND FILLS IT WITH THE FAMILY YOU MAKE TOGETHER, BE A MAN! THE LEAST YOU COULD DO IS SUPPORT HER SO SHE CAN FEEL LIKE THE WOMAN FOR ONCE!"

"YOU THINK IT'S OK TO JUDGE YOUR FATHER? HOW DARE YOU TALK TO ME LIKE THIS! IF IT WASN'T FOR ME…"

"IF IT WASN'T FOR YOU WHAT? YOU NEED TO GROW UP!

I CAN'T BELIEVE YOU'RE MAKING ME SIDE WITH THAT HORRIBLE WOMAN! WHY WOULD YOU MAKE A WOMAN WHO DOESN'T WANT KIDS HAVE THEM? AND THEN YOU CALL YOURSELF LEAVING HER CAUSE SHE DIDN'T DO WHAT YOU WANTED HER TO DO? AND LEAVING HER WITH THE TWO KIDS SHE NEVER WANTED! MY LIFE IS ALL YOUR FAULT!"

"IF IT WASN'T FOR ME YOU WOULDN'T BE HERE!"
"AND I ALSO WOULDN'T BE IN THIS HORRIBLE PAIN!
YOU MAY HAVE CAUSED MY BIRTH, BUT YOU'VE ALSO
CAUSED A LOT OF PAIN! HERE'S YOUR CHANCE TO FIX
IT AND YOU'D RATHER GO BLOW IT IN A PLACE WHERE
THE HOUSE ALWAYS WINS? I'M NOT TALKING TO YOU
UNTIL MARIA TELLS ME SHE KNOWS ABOUT THE
MONEY AND YOU'RE SUPPORTING HER!"
"CHANTEL!"
My brothers were standing at the fence looking over. I didn't know
how much they heard, but I also didn't care. I went in the house
and I told Maria to get up cause I was taking them out to dinner.
All except my so-called daddy.
****

"You look fabulous! Burgundy is such a good color for you." The
makeup artist said.
"Thank you, I think I'm starting to agree with you." I said
"This blouse makes your skin pop! So I'm accenting your makeup
with hints of gold. You look amazing!"
I blushed, "thank you."
"AND YOU ARE DONE!" She stepped back and looked at me.

"You look amazing sweetheart."

"Ok, ok! We're running behind schedule so let's get going." The
stage director said
When I walked into the studio my heart dropped. I knew that head.
When he turned around I wanted to run. "Hey Gerard how you
doing?" Caprice said having no clue about the panic session going
on inside my body. They hugged, and he came to me for a hug.
Gerard seemed normal where I felt like a deer caught in
headlights.
The stage director clapped her hands together. "Let's move it
people! You've got thirty minutes to make a miracle happen in
here."
"I only need ten!" Gerard called out
She smiled, "a little over confident aren't you?"
"I know how to do my job you should focus on yours." He shot
back with a grin.

Really? Flirting? Do I have to watch this? "Where do you want me?"

He smiled at me, it was like he was trying to use his eyes to hypnotize me and make me forget how unfulfilling he was last time. "Right over there in the chair."

"You're Chantel's assistant right?" The stage director asked Caprice. When she said yes she asked her to come with her to confirm some information. They walked over to the side.

Gerard fixed the lighting, and then he told me to smile as he started snapping away. I smiled slightly, and then he told me to look normal, which I did. He told me to look down and then look up like I didn't understand what he just said. He smiled as he snapped. Then he told me to look down and then look up at him like I wanted him. He loved the look I shot him but I was giving him a "you can't be serious" look. As he came to adjust the lighting he put his camera close to me and said in my ear that he wanted to see me. I shook my head no, when he asked me why. I told him I have a boyfriend and I got my period. Then he said, "Walk through mud…" when I gave him a give me a break look then he smiled and kept snapping. Then he told me he still wanted to see me. I said a simple no. He continued to flirt with me the entire time he was shooting me. Once Caprice looked at me I could tell she was trying to read me. The stage director came and ushered me to the sideline for my interview. She stood next to me, "I wanna sink my teeth into that man." I gave her a lost look. "Oh come on! You're trying to tell me you don't think Gerard is sexy? I saw you two." I bucked my eyes at her, "you saw what?"

She smiled but didn't respond, my interview was a lot of fun. Most people wanna know what Shameless is really like. He told me not to make him look soft by telling everybody how kind and considerate he is. So I focus on how funny he is. I told them they'll see it when his behind the scenes movie comes out. During my interview I could see Gerard and Caprice talking. I wanted to know what they were talking about. I wanted him to go away. When my interview was over, my interviewer and I talked to the audience and we signed autographs. It was so weird to me that people were excited about me. It was happening right before my eyes and the feeling was amazing. I dreaded walking backstage but I did. Gerard's eyes floated all over me with approval. My stomach turned the closer I got to him. "You ready?"

"For?" I was lost.

"Lunch" he said with a grin.

I looked at Caprice, "the label thinks that Gerard is a gold mine. He's done amazing work for them with other artists. He's rallying to be your primary photographer." She watched my eyes.

I looked at him, "why would you do that?"

"We can discuss it over lunch. You ready?"

I huffed then I looked at Caprice, she had a question mark on her face. "Does JoJo know about this?"

"Yes, but no one thought it was a problem. Am I missing something?"

Gerard smiled and raised an eyebrow at me. "No," I said feeling defeated.

Our car service took us to the vine for lunch. There were celebrities everywhere, and a few of them looked at me as if they knew who I was, that was amazing.

Everything was business at first and that was fine. Then Caprice excused herself to go to the bathroom. "Are you gonna come see me?" He said leaning in on the table.

"Gerard I have a boyfriend, that was a mistake."

He smiled, "what's your man got to do with me?" When I didn't smile, he touched my hand. "I'm sorry. You were gone so fast. We barely got a chance to know each other. Can we start over?"

"We are starting over cause that night was random and can never happen again. I almost lost my boyfriend over that. I have no intentions of jeopardizing what I have with him for lust with you."

Gerard sat back, "ouch!" He drummed his fingers on the table. He put his hands up. "Ok, what can I do? Guess I have to wait until you're single."

I shook my head at him and sat back in my chair. After awhile Caprice came back and she looked flustered. "We have to go." Then she turned her face sympathetically towards Gerard. "I hope you understand."

"Of course." He said as he signed the slip for our bill. "Where can I drop you?"

"We need to go back to our hotel." She said, her face was serious and kind of worried. When we walked out of the restaurant paparazzi were snapping pictures of us the entire time. I didn't think anything of it. In the car she gave someone over the phone play by plays of our location and everything. When we pulled up to the hotel a guy opened our door. He looked familiar so I figured he was Mitigated staff. He told her to call JoJo as he walked with us inside. "Chantel, we need to grab all of our stuff. We're leaving this hotel."

"What's going on?" I asked as I kept moving cause I was doing as I was told.

"Someone called in that they spotted Kevin." She said walking quickly.

"Why are we running from Kevin? Does he want to hurt me or something?"

"Kevin isn't stable, we aren't taking any chances." The guy stayed in the hallway while we grabbed our stuff. When we walked out he took our bags and walked us to a waiting car. Caprice was on the phone with JoJo confirming that they were on the same page about my calendar. My phone rang, I answered without checking my caller ID. "You're going to Sasha's house." His voice rumbled in my ear.

"Malcolm, am I in danger or something? Why is everybody so panicked?"

He was quiet for a minute. "When you get to Sasha's house. Call me back at work from her number."

"Ok, bye" I said, my heart was pounding. Sasha wasn't home when we got there but she pulled up right after us. I hoped she wasn't angry about our sudden invasion of her privacy. She smiled as she walked up to our car. "I'm so sorry!" I said as soon as she was in earshot.

"Don't worry about it, come in." She told us. The driver told her something lowly, and she told him to do something. I couldn't hear them, but I could tell she was directing people. "You know where the rooms are. Make yourself at home."

"Can I use your phone to call Malcolm?"

"Of course."

I went into my usual room and I shut the door. Malcolm answered on the first ring and started talking immediately. "We've been watching Wade. Once they released him he's been bouncing around. He's out there with his producer friend. It wasn't alarming until someone spotted Kevin. I need to know you're safe."

I smiled, "thank you Malcolm. You're always good to me." I don't even know where the tears came from. Malcolm was silent. "I'm sorry. I'm a ball of emotions." Malcolm still didn't say anything I imagined him blank staring at me while trying to get away from me. "I'm sorry." I tried to pull myself together.

"You're safe Chantel take care." Then he hung up. But in Malcolm language that was, "don't be scared baby girl. I care about you. You're safe with me, and even though your daddy is a worthless piece of crap! I'll take care of you as if you're my own."

I dialed Derrick's number, he answered on the first ring. "How is she?"

"Derrick?"

"Chantel? Why are you calling from Sasha's?"

I was confused, why would they move me without Derrick knowing about it? "Malcolm told me to come here. Where are you?"

Derrick sighed. "I'm at the hospital."

My heart sped up, "why?"

"Don't freak out." He said waiting for my agreement.

"I'm not agreeing to that." I spit at him.

"Chantel I need to lean on you in this moment, please hold me up." He pleaded.

"Fine! Whatever! What's going on?"

"Brooklyn showed up at my place early this morning." My heart started pounding. "She was really upset, there's a lot going on in her life right now." I guess I was supposed to feel bad for her. I didn't say anything. "When I told her she had to leave she started going crazy. Talking about we had to be cordial at least for the baby. I told her she wasn't pregnant. We went back and forth."

"Did she look pregnant? If she's pregnant there's no way she wouldn't be showing right now."

"She's gained a little weight but she was wearing baggy clothes."

"Did you see a stomach?"

He exhaled, "I asked her to take the test you left at my house. She started screaming and carrying on."

"So what, you should've made her take the test anyways! She's going to...."

He cut me off, "Chantel! She tried to kill herself right in front of me!" I sat on the bed, more like fell. Derrick was quiet for a minute. "I'm at the hospital, they're gonna keep her under psychiatric evaluation for a couple of days. I'm flying her mother and her sister out here to be with her. THIS IS TOO MUCH!" He yelled.

My man was hurting, "I'm coming home. I'll call you once I've landed."

"You have to work!"

I could tell he needed me, but would never ask me to cut out work. "I'll have JoJo move stuff around. It doesn't matter, I'm coming! I love you Derrick! I'll see you in a little bit." Then I hung up. When I called JoJo, he said as soon as he heard, he knew this was going to be my answer. He said he was already moving things around. Sasha and Caprice were talking when I came out of the room with my bags. Sasha asked me what happened, so I told her about Brooklyn. She got her keys and told me she'd take us to the airport. Caprice said I should wait until JoJo said he had a flight out for me. I told her I wanted to be at the airport. If he couldn't get me a flight, I'd drive either way I was out of there on the first thing smoking. Caprice huffed, and then she grabbed her bags. There were three guys outside, Sasha simply said, "We're going to the airport." And then two of them got in the car that brought us and pulled up behind Sasha to follow us. As we were pulling out,

Sasha's boyfriend pulled up. Caprice sat up straight and hit my seat. I saw his pictures around the house, but they did him no justice. When he spoke he had an accent, I looked at Caprice who was openly drooling. With her looking at him like that, it wouldn't have been a good idea for us to stay anyways. Sasha was looking at Caprice while she told her boyfriend she was taking us to the airport. He said he'd make her dinner. She told him not to pour her milk, and that she would do it; cause she did not like soggy cereal.

Then she shook her head and said he couldn't cook to save his life.

The car couldn't move fast enough, but Sasha was driving quickly without breaking any laws. "What happened to the other girl?" Sasha asked

Caprice blew air, "she eloped with Shameless' bodyguard."

I reached behind me and squeezed Caprice's hand. "I doubt she'll come back to Mitigated, but she's happy."

"She gave up everything for a man?" Sasha shook her head. "I hope that works out for her."

"You wouldn't do it for your man?" I asked

She looked like she was thinking. "It depends on the man. If he's the right man for me, I shouldn't have to give up too much to make us work." She exhaled. "Relationships are hard."

"Amen!" Caprice said, "If you're giving up everything how is that supposed to work?"

I cut my eyes at her cause I knew she was referring to Cyrus. "You have to make a choice. If you can't do what's needed to make the relationship work let it go! Hanging on creates drama and mess." Sasha frowned, she started to say something but Caprice cut her off. "I still love him!"

"So what! One day my niece is going to be old enough to understand what's going on. You guys need to let it go. I don't want her hurt because you're holding on to something that won't work."

"Your niece is not my fault! Why would she get pregnant knowing about me? She put her child in that position not me. I don't owe her anything!" Caprice said folding her arms and looking out the window pouting.

"Don't be that selfish! My niece didn't have a choice but you do."

"So you're brother and Caprice were together?" Sasha asked. Since we were sitting in beautiful LA traffic I told her the whole story. Caprice interjected only to expound on points she felt I glazed over. Like how she was first, they were in love, how she messed up by getting pregnant, etc. Sasha listened to the whole story. "You're not supposed to get emotionally involved when you're on assignment; and you're definitely not supposed to sleep with anyone. Malcolm's not running an escort service."

"I got caught up! Oh and trust, Malcolm let me have it when Derrick told on me. I would've lost my job if I had that baby."

"I know working for my cousin is great, but what's so important about your job? There are other jobs."

Caprice blew air. "My job allows me to live comfortably. Most importantly I can provide for my little sister."

"You have a sister?" I looked at her in disbelief.

"Yes, both of my parents are lifers. We were put in the system young. At first we were in foster homes together, but then we got separated. As soon as I turned eighteen, I tried to get guardianship for my sister. I needed a job and a place to live. What job can an eighteen year old get that will provide all that. I barely graduated from high school. I was hustling and I eventually got my sister but by then she had so much hatred and hurt on her heart, her only escape was to get high. I'm not gonna lie, I smoked from time to time; but I didn't really have the time to sit still and be high cause I constantly had to hustle. My sister got involved with the wrong guy. He had her strung out and selling herself to support their habits. When I found her I lost it. It was either him or my sister, and my sister is alive. She was all messed up and back in the system because she needs constant psychiatric care. I found a home for her up North by Eureka. In order to pay for her to be there and not on the streets hurting herself or in a government funded facility, I had to hustle big time. I was getting in over my head when Curtis found me. He saved my life and referred me to Malcolm. At night I sleep easy knowing my sister is ok. She's all the family I have!" She said wiping her tears.

"Does Cyrus know about this?"

"Not completely."

"Why don't you ever tell him the whole truth?"

"At first it was because I was on assignment. And then too much had happened, I was scared to go back to try to undo all the half truths."

"You sold yourself short by underestimating my brother!"

She cut her eyes at me. "Your brother has supported the both of you. Until now he hasn't even come close to my salary at Mitigated. The bill for my sister isn't cheap; I can't leave her hanging like our parents did us! I can't!"

We were quiet for a minute then Sasha cleared her throat. "That's a sad story Caprice. I can only imagine how traumatic your life has been; but I got a question," she looked at Caprice in the rear view mirror. "Your sister deserves a better life right. But what about her niece? She is oblivious to it now, but eventually she's gonna understand. What are you trying to teach her?"

"Rosa is not my child, I'm not teaching her anything!" Caprice snapped.

"Cyrus is her father. What he does affects her. What he does teaches her. If you love him you love all of him, and that includes his child. If you want what's best for him, you want what's best for his child. I know it's only my opinion but you need to leave him alone. I can tell you first hand how this will mess with Rosa's head when she's older. Parents with their lies and secrets hurt their kids in ways they can't seem to understand. Stand down Caprice."

"Sasha no disrespect but you need to mind your own business. Chantel you too! I can't help it if Cyrus keeps coming back to me. I love him and I will not turn him away."

Sasha cut her eyes at me. "Caprice with all **intended** <u>disrespect</u> you are a selfish whore who's gonna end up twisted up if you keep going like you're going. You're not invincible, and Sherrell may not be a Latour, but she's connected to them. I'm pretty sure Sherrell has been holding them back. It only takes one word from them and its lights out for you. There are three names you don't screw over Wallace, Latour, and Cardell. That girl is doubly covered but you're too selfish to yield. Why should anyone care about your sister if you don't care about others?"

"I love my sister, I love Cyrus, and I love Chantel. We've all been through the same stuff. And look at us we're coming out on top, going against the grain. Anybody outside of those three I DON'T CARE! NOT MY PROBLEM!"

"If you love me, you should love who I love."

"You don't understand!"

Sasha looked at me. "Chantel, you wanna believe she's your friend or that she loves your brother, that's on you. The only two people she truly loves is her sister and herself. How could she truly love your brother and speak of his child that way? If it wasn't for you she'd be walking to the airport! Don't trust her! She's mean and full of hate. " Then she turned the radio on and tried to calm herself, but I could see her gripping the steering wheel.

JoJo called me and said my flight didn't leave for two hours. He told me to check-in and then he wanted me to find a corner to chill out in. I asked what if someone recognized me. He exhaled and said if that happened then I needed to stay visible. He said he was going to call Caprice and let her know how things were gonna go. Sasha gave me her shades; they were fancy and fit me perfectly. I thanked her and then we laughed as I admired my reflection in the mirror. Sasha thanked me for going to be with Derrick. She said when everyone kept telling her I was family she was hesitant at first. She said she could tell that I really loved Derrick and she was happy to call me family. She said she feels bad for Brooklyn though. She shook her head and said she wasn't like this before. She told me Brooklyn had the nod way back when, and she wondered what happened.

When we got to the airport Sasha circled the airport until the men were waiting for us. One took our bags and stayed with us. The other stayed close by. When we went through the security checkpoint the guys had no boarding passes but somehow they glided through. Every time someone looked at me I got nervous about them recognizing me. I hated feeling afraid of what I had wanted for so long. To be recognized as someone worthy of love and admiration. We found a table in the corner of a restaurant. "I feel stupid and obvious wearing these glasses in the corner of this dim lit place." I said to Caprice.

"BJ it's your call." Caprice said looking at her menu.

"Just don't forget to put them on when we walk out of here."

"Uh oh!" Caprice said looking up at the monitor.

"Looks like the playboy photographer Gerard has moved on to greener pasture. These pictures were taken hours ago of Gerard and the new singing sensation Chantel Shaw." They showed pictures of us at our table alone. "Look at that chemistry!" Then they showed pictures of he and I getting in the car. "Do we even have to ask where they're going? You go Chantel! Gerard Pavlik is HOTT!"

I wanted to scream. I looked at Caprice completely pissed. She shrugged, "we know the truth. It doesn't matter what they think."

"It matters what Derrick thinks. I don't want him getting the wrong impression."

"Chill out! Don't forget who his momma is. He's aware of the media circus and the games they play." Caprice said disregarding my inner panic.

What if Derrick figures out Gerard is the one. Will it make him mad all over again?

We got on our flight without incident. Caprice dropped me off at the hospital and she kept my bags for me. Derrick was standing in the hallway talking to the doctor when I walked up. He hugged me and squeezed me tight. "She's asking for you." The doctor told Derrick.

Derrick shook his head, "I can't go in there."

"She's sedated so she should remain pretty calm." He assured Derrick.

"So now you guys have upgraded to having people do the dirty work on their selves for you?" The woman said as she approached us with a cocky walk.

"Not now!" Derrick growled.

She took out her badge, "I'm following up on the report I received. You have to talk to me." She held up paperwork.

"Can you tell her that her mother and sister are on their way?" He pleaded with his eyes.

"No! I can't go in there. What if that sets her off?"

"I don't know what else to do Chantel." Derrick sounded very defeated.

"Ok," I heard myself say.

I pushed the door open slowly. "Derrick?" Her voice pleaded.

"No, it's Chantel." I said walking towards the bed where she could see me.

"Where's Derrick?"

"He has to talk to the police. He wanted you to know your mother and sister are on their way." Her neck and wrist were bandaged. Her hair was wild all over her head. She had gained a little weight; I couldn't tell if that was weight gain or a baby. "How's the baby?"

"They stole my baby!" She said with her eyes wandering around the room. "When they put me under they took my baby out. I heard her cry even though I couldn't wake up. Those Wallace's are very sneaky. Tell them that her name is Derricka. Please tell them to give her back to me. She's the only piece I have left of him." She started crying.

"Brooklyn," I rubbed her foot gently. "Why would you try to take yourself away from Derricka. She needs you."

Brooklyn started crying, "he doesn't love me anymore. He don't want me no more, Derricka deserves better. If her own daddy doesn't love her mother...." She started crying. "I wanted to go to sleep forever, but then I heard her cry. I knew I had to be strong for her. Now they won't tell me where she is. They keep putting medicine in my IV to make me sleepy. I'm not crazy, but they're trying to make it seem like it."

I tried to keep the "she's crazy" look off my face. "How did they take her? Did you push her out?"

"I'm not crazy Chantel. They cut me open." I didn't say anything. She slowly kicked the covers back, and then she raised her gown. Her stomach was bandaged like she had a C-section. "They cut her out." Then she turned her back to me and laid on her side. She moaned from the pain of the position and went back to laying on her back.

316

The room spun, "wait a minute. Did you get prenatal care? How far were you?" Brooklyn didn't answer. "Brooklyn?" I walked closer to the bed. That fast she fell asleep. I put the covers back over her and then I sat in the chair shaking my leg. When Derrick finally peeked his head in the room I jumped up and pushed him back in the hallway. "She's sleep."

"Ok," then he grabbed my hand and we walked towards the waiting room.

"Does your mother know about this?" He gave me a what do you think look. "She keeps insisting she's not crazy."

"She's not," he said matter of factly.

"She said you had the hospital take her baby girl out. She said her name is Derricka."

Derrick looked shocked, "ok she is crazy."

"She's insisting that she's not and that you guys are drugging her on purpose."

"You heard the doctor say they sedated her. She was too upset earlier."

"I asked her if she pushed the baby out. She said they cut the baby out. Then she showed me her stomach and it was bandaged just like her neck and wrist." I said staring at Derrick's face.

Derrick's eyes rolled around. "You believe her?"

"You know how crazy people can almost make you believe them. I just need you to tell me it's not true."

"It's not true," he said quickly. He adjusted in his chair. "She was reminding me of my grandmother. She's having a hard time right now, she's not crazy." He shook his head.

"Why would a sane person say you stole their baby?"

"She's sedated. Those drugs can make you say anything."

"Subject change real quick." Derrick looked at me. "Do you guys know about Caprice's sister?"

"Yep" he said looking at me.

"Why don't you tell me anything? Why do I have to keep finding things out?"

"It wasn't my place to tell you. She's my employee, and there is a measure of confidentiality I have to maintain."

"What about my daddy? You knew about him didn't you?"

He exhaled, "I'm not going to take him from you and your brother. With something like that you have to learn on your own otherwise

you could end up blaming me. If you're gonna be mad at someone I prefer it's them and not me."
My heart started pounding. "Do you think I slept with Wade?"
"Nope!" His face turned to stone. "You have to choose me. I understand the part I played in that. That was your gimme. If you cheat on me now!" He shook his head. "It would suck to be you."

Chapter 18

"Derrick PLEASE tell me what's going on with my baby!" A middle-aged woman came rushing in the waiting room. My heart was pounding cause her voice came out of nowhere, and the urgency slapped me out of my sleep. I was sleeping with my head on Derrick's shoulder, and Derrick had his head on mine. The woman looked startled when she realized I was there.

She was followed by a young lady who looked at me and then at Derrick. Then she stared at me. When I stood up, the girl smiled really big. "OH MY GOD MOM! IT'S CHANTEL SHAW! OH MY GOD! OH MY GOD!" She almost screamed while she jumped up and down excitedly. "You know my sister?" She said almost dancing in place.

"Brooklyn is sleeping, the doctors have had her sedated. She's been saying some pretty off the wall stuff. You can go in the room and see her." He said standing up.

"Thank you for sending for us. Is her boyfriend here?" Her mother said looking around.

"What boyfriend?" Derrick asked as nonchalantly as he could but we all looked at him cause the directness was there in his voice.

"Oh maybe I don't know what I'm talking about. Let me shut up! Sheri you coming?" Brooklyn's mother said walking to the door.

"You go ahead, I'll catch up." She said waving her mother on. She had the biggest smile on her face and stars in her eyes. "I have your CD!" She smiled.

"Sheri, I don't think this is the right place or time for this. You need to go talk to your sister." Derrick said

"Ok," she said walking to the door.

"A!" Derrick said stopping her walk. "What boyfriend? A boyfriend out here?"

"Yeah, I don't know much though. She said he was crazy, I thought they broke up. Maybe they got back together if our mom is asking about him."

"What's his name?"

She stood there thinking for a minute trying to remember.

"Maurice" she said then she walked out.

I exhaled; I don't know why I was bracing myself for a familiar name. When Sheri walked out the waiting room Derrick immediately got on his phone. He didn't say hi, hello, or any kind of greeting he started talking. I don't know who he was talking to but he was visibly upset. I sat there watching him talk to whomever trying to understand if he was upset because he wasn't the only rooster in her hen house or what his emotion was. He was going back and forth with someone, and then I guess other people were added to the call. Completely bored with the scene I got up and started pacing, Brooklyn's sister and mother had been in the room a long time. I prepared myself to be the villain when they came out. Her sister wouldn't look at me the same way when they came out of the room I'm sure. I stood in the doorway halfway watching Derrick while watching Brooklyn's door. Derrick looked at me when my stomach grumbled. He gave instructions to whoever was on the phone and then he told me he'd take me to the cafeteria to eat. As we were passing Brooklyn's room her mother and sister were coming out because nurses and a doctor were going in. Her mother said they needed to do another evaluation. She asked if we were leaving and Derrick said we were going to eat. He invited them to come, in the elevator I noticed that sparkle wasn't in Brooklyn's sister's eyes anymore, but I couldn't get a good read on her. I couldn't tell if she was mad at me or not. When we got to the cafeteria everything looked like cafeteria food. Derrick suggested leaving to eat somewhere else worth eating at. I thought her mother and sister would object not wanting to be too far from Brooklyn but they agreed. Derrick was holding my hand and Brooklyn's mother kept looking at our hands, but again I didn't know what that meant. As we approached Derrick's truck he chirped the doors unlocked. Brooklyn's sister and mother walked a little faster and when Brooklyn's mother climbed in the front seat Derrick started to say something. I squeezed his hand telling him it was ok. I could see him biting his tongue; I wondered how this was going to set the tone for our morning or day for that matter. No one had any suggestions or special request so Derrick drove; we pretty much rode in silence. Sheri's back was to me and she looked out the window. When we pulled into Gonzalez's I kind of figured we'd end up here when no one had any other suggestions. There was a fancy car in the parking lot and a few other cars. When we walked inside the owner was very happy to see Derrick. He told him that Malcolm was in the booth over to the side. A guy I didn't recognize popped his head around the corner and smiled at Derrick. When we got close he stood up and hugged Derrick. Malcolm was sitting on the inside of the booth. Derrick introduced me to "Dude" then he asked him when he got out. Dude said he got out less than a week ago. Then Derrick introduced Brooklyn's mother and sister to him. They both seemed to remember Malcolm and said silent hellos. I said a very excited hello to Malcolm as he greeted me with his normal nonchalant hello. Which only said to me, that he was happy I was here supporting Derrick. I've learned you gotta speak Malcolm's language; if you don't speak it he can seem pretty scary. Malcolm asked how Brooklyn was doing, her mother got a little emotional as she said she doesn't understand what's going on. She said Brooklyn's been all over the place lately and she didn't understand why the sudden change up. Malcolm told her he didn't understand either, but he would get to the bottom of the situation. Brooklyn's mother swallowed hard, then she said Malcolm being involved made her nervous. Malcolm didn't say anything I doubt he cared to hear her explain why but Dude asked why. She explained that when they were younger a lot of people told her they couldn't believe she let Brooklyn date Derrick because of the reputation that Malcolm had. Then she said that Amber seemed pretty normal to her and that they never had any real problems then she flashed a quick and sad smile at Derrick. Dude asked what that meant and she said after Brooklyn and Derrick broke up they learned of the physical aspects of their relationship when Brooklyn moved on to her next boyfriend. Brooklyn's mother slightly laughed at the memory. "All that time we thought you were so respectable and you were turning our daughter out." She said. I looked at Derrick and his expression never changed. He seemed like he was listening and collecting information for the first time; although I'm sure he's heard it before. Malcolm asked what the next steps were going to be for Brooklyn. Derrick told him they were doing another evaluation as we left the hospital. He said they'd release her soon, and it'd be up to her family what they wanted to do next. We ordered breakfast and then Derrick started asking questions about her boyfriend, her mother didn't really know too much; but you could tell her sister wasn't saying anything.

"Sheri you're awfully quiet!" Derrick said. She was pushing her food around her plate taking little nibbles here and there. She nodded acknowledging Derrick's statement but still not speaking. "Come on." He said telling her to get up and walk with him. They went to a booth on the other side of the restaurant to talk. I kept my eyes on them, while Malcolm watched me. Dude engaged Brooklyn's mother in conversation. Then Dude said so many things have changed since he went in. He said his brother is married, Drew has a son and is engaged, and then Dude asked Malcolm if he and Amber had gotten married. Malcolm cut his eyes at Dude like he was an idiot. Dude put his hands up like he surrendered. Then Malcolm looked at me and said he needed to talk to me. I said ok, and then he looked at Dude and Brooklyn's mother. Dude invited Brooklyn's mother to join him in a separate booth across the room. Malcolm leaned forward on the table, "what's going on with your father?" I didn't understand what he meant. "He's shopping your little brother's around, he's thinking about working with Wade."

My mouth dropped open, "WHAT?"
"Your grandmother has been through enough. Otherwise I wouldn't say anything. Your father is in over his head. He's making amateur moves and your brothers will pay the price. What affects them affects your grandmother."
"The last time I talked to him, we got in an argument."
"About?" Malcolm's eyes were locked on me.
I exhaled, "he's an idiot! I can't believe I came from such horrible people!" I exhaled trying to stop the tears that were begging to pour out. "My step mother is pregnant and stressed out. He won't work, he doesn't want birth control, and he won't be the man she needs him to be. He even had the address changed to a PO Box for his royalty checks so he could blow his money in peace while Maria breaks her back to provide for them and raise his children. I told him I wasn't working with him anymore until he told Maria about the royalties. I guess he figures if he can get my brothers into the business he won't need me."
None of my information seemed to hit Malcolm like it was brand new information. "What do you want to happen?"
I digested his question, "can you do something to protect them?"

His eyes stayed glued to me. "What do you want to happen? Don't answer my question with a question."

"I want Maria to get his royalty checks. I don't want my brothers out until they're ready, if they're ever ready. I want him to man up and be worthy of me calling him daddy." An unruly tear fell down my cheek. "What does it say about me if both of my parents are screwed up?"

"You can't choose your parents, but you can choose the person you want to be. You have to learn to accept them for who they are, accept the parts of them that are like you. And be mindful to be better, it's easier said than done." He watched my eyes.

"You've been taking care of me all these years." I watched his eyes, but he had no reaction. "Do I even need to acknowledge him? Knowing that he's a sorry excuse for a man depresses me. And then my mother..." I exhaled again to catch my breath. "Derrick wants me to talk to her. I don't want to talk to her! Now that she has nobody and is near death she wants to have a heart to heart. I don't want to do it! Malcolm, she can never give back what she's taken away from me. Doesn't every child deserve to be loved and cherished as a gift? I never had that! If it weren't for my brother, I wouldn't know love at all. It feels like Derrick's telling me we can't move forward if I don't do this and I don't want to!"

"He knows how you feel, you guys need to talk."

I could feel my anger burning inside my stomach. "Its his way or no way."

"Unfortunately he gets that from me. You still need to talk. I can't tell you one way or another on that one."

"Would you ever say anything against your son?" I wasn't really asking, cause I knew the answer.

"You guys need to talk, and the clock is ticking your mother's health is deteriorating as we speak."

I exhaled, "does Ms. Laverne still work at the kiosk in the mall?"

"Yes."

"I need to go visit my momma!" I said as tears came rushing out of my eyes.

Malcolm rolled his eyes, "Derrick." Derrick looked at him. "I'm gonna take Chantel to the mall. You'll pick her up from there." Derrick's eyes darted to me; he looked like he was reading me. Then he went back to his conversation.

During the car ride over to the mall, Dude shared that he and his brother grew up with Derrick and his brothers. Dude said that Malcolm tried to warn him about easy money, but he was too dumb to listen. He said he was thankful to be alive unlike most of the people he ran with.

I started jumping up and down as soon as I laid eyes on Ms. Laverne sitting in her normal seat. She had the biggest smile when she saw me. I ran past Malcolm and I squeezed Ms. Laverne like my life depended on it. Malcolm rolled his eyes again. Then he told Ms. Laverne to show Dude how to answer the phones and he could cover them while we went out for coffee. She gave him a list of callers who were directly transferred to Malcolm and the only numbers they could call from when that happened. Otherwise he needed to take messages and she'd follow up when she came back. Since I had no makeup on and very ordinary clothes I doubted that anyone else would recognize me. We went to the coffee shop and sat in the two accent chairs with ottomans. We sipped our coffee while I told Ms. Laverne everything. I told her I was in desperate need of some parental guidance. "It sounds like you and Derrick need to call off whatever it is that you have going on." My heart sank.

"That's not the advice I was looking for." I said sadly.

She touched my hand, "you aren't ready. In relationships sometimes you have to do things you aren't ready for. You have to eat crow. I don't agree with how he's doing it, but I understand his point. You need to resolve your issues with your mother. Not for her, but for you. You're so angry with her, that you can't even see what's good for you at this point. Talking to her isn't about her, it's for you. You need to be able to move forward past the biggest pain you've ever felt. You shouldn't resent Derrick for trying to help. You will end up transferring those ugly feelings to him. I don't wish that on you baby, you've come so far. Do you believe in God baby?"

"My mother never introduced him. My dad does but the thought of anything like him makes me angry these days. Yussef talks about him all the time though. I like some of the things he says, but I can't say I do or I don't."

"God is real, and he can help you with this; but you've gotta give it to him. Forgiveness is not easy especially when you have to extend it to yourself."

"Why do I have to forgive myself?"

"First you have to forgive yourself for feeling what you should feel when a parent comes to you with news like your mother did.

You're mad at yourself for caring. It's ok to care about your mother baby. I know you don't like it, but she gave you life. The way she raised you wasn't right or ideal, but she didn't give you guys up. You could've been in the system separated from your brother. I know that's reaching for a silver lining, but lets take whatever we can get at this point ok sweetheart."

Tears poured out of my eyes. "Ms. Laverne I don't want to forgive her! What mother chooses her man over her kids? I've never felt pain like that in my life. Parents are supposed to protect you, keep you safe. Not hand feed you to evil! I can't forgive her for that."

"Then you need to hit the pause button on you and Derrick. You need to sort all those feelings out before you take that into a relationship. Don't you think Derrick deserves better than that? Cause I know you do."

"I can't let Derrick go! I love him! I can't do that!" I said feeling backed into a corner. "I feel even more confused now than when I came to you."

"You're confused because you know I'm right, but you're fighting against me." She shrugged

We talked a little longer until I calmed down enough to pull it together. When we got back to the office Dude went in the back with Malcolm and I sat at my old desk. I felt like little Chantel again waiting to get a glimpse of Derrick, like I always used to. Ms. Laverne asked me to man the phones while she ran to the bathroom. Then the phone rang, the caller ID had a series of zeros.

"Thank you for calling Mitigated Staffing Solutions, how may I direct your call?" Saying that greeting took me back to the olden days when things were simpler.

"Chantel!" The caller said, but it wasn't Derrick.

"Yes, how may I help you?" I said even though sweat popped up on my nose.

"Baby why we gotta be like this?" The caller said.

"Who is this?" I asked a little panicked.

Malcolm walked out of his office with his headset on. I exhaled when he told me to keep going. "You know who this is."

"I really don't!"

"It's Kevin." He paused for a reaction when I didn't have one he kept going. "You don't appreciate all of the things I've been doing for you?"

"You've been doing stuff for me?"

"You don't think its been Derrick taking care of business on your behalf do you? Malcolm has him too soft. A business man, doing things legitimately." He laughed, "he's too soft to get his hands dirty anymore."

"What does that mean?" I said sounding irritated.

"Anyone so much as raise an eyebrow at you, they're out of here. Isn't it ironic that they had the same name?"

"You're the one?" I said in shock.

"I can't either agree with or deny your statement. Just know that anyone who causes you pain will know pain." He said in a deep voice.

"Kevin! You can't go around killing people. I never asked you to do that nor do I want you to."

"SSSShhhhh! You can't be saying stuff like that over the phone. You never know if these lines are tapped or not. I just want to make sure you're safe. And I FINALLY want my date with you."

Ms. Laverne came out the bathroom; she was looking at everybody and my chest moving up and down. "Kevin I don't want this! Please don't hurt anybody else."

"I got a question for you. If Derrick is so in love with you, why was he still seeing Brooklyn? Do you know who she is?"

"I know who Brooklyn is. You don't understand our relationship, but please…"

"Derrick is too soft! You could've been rid of Brooklyn a long time ago, but he lacks the conviction. She's his plan B, you know that right? I wouldn't need a plan B if I was with you. You'd be my only plan."

"Kevin, please turn yourself in. I don't want any of this."

"I can't decide whether your mother lives or dies though. We need to discuss that…. SHOOT! You need to meet me so we can discuss next steps, I don't trust this phone."

"Kevin, I can't meet you." I said looking to Malcolm for direction.

"Derrick isn't there. Tell Malcolm Derrick is there and then meet me on the other side of the building. I can avoid their cameras a lot easier on that side."

"What cameras?"

"Stuff you don't know about little girl. You coming?"

Malcolm shook his head no. "I can't Kevin."

"WHY CAN'T YOU?"

Malcolm pointed to his chest. "Malcolm won't let me go."

Malcolm gave me a thumbs up.

"MALCOLM!" He growled, "What he got to do with me? The student has become the master! He can't touch me! Listen Chantel, I'm gonna come for you. I want one date! That's all I've ever asked you for. I think I've been putting in enough work to show you I'm worthy of at least one date."

"Kevin I can't go out with you and you know that."

"All I know is Laverne burst my bubble when she told me you were underage. My opportunity was stolen from me when she did that. We could be..." I could see him licking his lips. "We could be great together! You'll be saying Derrick who?" He chuckled.

"Kevin, please hear me. You make me uncomfortable when you say stuff like this. Please don't hurt anybody else. Please turn yourself in."

"We can discuss all that when we finally go out. I'll come for you since it appears you've got a lot going on. Don't stress about anything! You hear me! Anyone who even looks at you wrong is gone. I'm mad at myself for relying on Malcolm to protect you. His operation is really shabby."

"Kevin please don't." I pleaded.

"Don't worry, I'll make sure you're safe." Then he hung up. Derrick came around the corner with red eyes. When he saw our faces he looked at Malcolm. They went in Malcolm's office. I put my hands on my face and started crying. Ms. Laverne rubbed my shoulders, but she didn't say anything.

Then my cellphone rang which scared me. It was JoJo and he apologized for interrupting me with work stuff. He said a killer opportunity just came up, and then he asked if I could play the electric guitar. I told him I would have to refresh my memory, but I would say yes with practice. Then he told me about the project. One of the headliners requested me specifically. That made me excited. He gave me the list of artists who signed on and it was all my favs. He said it was all female and all black. He said we would perform on a show focusing on empowering black women, and

they only wanted artists who presented their selves in a dignified manner. I felt honored to be considered especially since I'm the extreme rookie. He said I'd have to go to New York in a few days though. I swallowed; I didn't know how things were going to be at home to say yes I could go. I told him I'd have to get back to him. When I got off the phone Ms. Laverne was on the edge of her seat. I told her what JoJo said and she gave me an excited hug. Torrie Rowe, Meredith Bling, Alexa Kords, and Jennifer Scott have agreed. I told her that Jennifer suggested me and that floored me; there was no way around it. I was gonna be star struck. I loved all of Jennifer's work. All of the artists involved have been roll models to me. I was happy to have a happy thought. When Derrick came out of the office he looked drained like if one more thing happened he'd snap. He reached for my hand but didn't say anything. Ms. Laverne told me to come back soon. While we were walking I kept looking at Derrick's face. I saw mostly anger but there was emotion in his face, not a normal look for him. When we got to the car I hugged him. He accepted my hug, and then he got in the truck. When we pulled into my garage he said they were still cleaning his place up. He said he wasn't going back there either way. When we walked in the door Cyrus and family were visiting with my mother. I rolled my eyes and pulled Derrick by the hand. Cyrus yelled out that he thought I was going to be in LA. I told him last minute change of plans, and then I shut my door. I asked Derrick if he needed to shower, he shrugged. I put him in the shower then he asked me to lay down with him. He was tired but he couldn't sleep. "She was mad cause I wouldn't kiss her."
"When did you stop kissing her?"
"When she moved away."
"When you were kids?"
"Yes."
"Was she pregnant?"
"I don't think so." He said exhaling hard.
"Why don't you know for sure?"
"Nothing is one hundred percent." He exhaled again. "I'm sorry Chantel. For all of this! It seems like everything is getting messy when it's supposed to get easier." He put me in a bear hug, and then I felt tears drop on my face. I didn't know what to do, Derrick doesn't cry.

"Did I ever tell you I wanted to join the circus?" I pulled my face back to look at him. I wiped his tears. "I always thought it was cool how they did all those acrobatic flips and stunts. I was really little but I thought I could do it. Cyrus reminded me that I was afraid of heights, but I didn't care I was gonna do it. Shelly told me to run away to join and I was game. I had never been to the circus personally but I knew the circus was my life long career. So of course I convinced Cyrus to go with me. We didn't go to school and we went to the local pop up circus tent. I was so determined to get inside and show them my tumbling cause I had been practicing. When we didn't have money to go in through the front, I convinced Cyrus to sneak inside around the back."

Derrick grinned, "You were the sneaky one."

"Yes! We crept along the back and inside the tent. They had this part of the tent sectioned off like dressing rooms and stuff. There were elephants and everything. I was so excited I knew I was home. Right? Then we crept along to where we heard the most voices. I peeked in saw people. I didn't pay attention to how they were dressed or anything. I told Cyrus when we got in the middle of the room we had to dazzle them with our stunts. We counted to three and then we ran in." I swallowed and made my voice shake. "Well what had happened was," I swallowed again. Derrick's eyes smiled at me. "I had never seen a clown before!" Derrick started laughing. "I was horrified! I screamed to the top of my lungs and I left Cyrus in there all by himself." I laughed, Derrick did too.

"What happened to Cyrus?"

"He ran away behind me, but apparently he knew about the clowns, but he wanted to see my reaction to them."

"Didn't you see clowns on the signs for the circus?"

"It didn't register to me. They were a lot scarier in person than the caricatures on paper."

"So how you doing now? You still scared of clowns?"

"Not like I used to be. I'll be alright as long as I know they're coming."

He pulled me in tight and squeezed me. "I love you!" He kissed my nose. "Thank you!"

I laid there with Derrick until he fell asleep. I knew he knew I was creeping out, but I hoped he would stay asleep. As soon as baby Rosa saw me she got off my mother's lap and ran to me. We shared a loving embrace and then I sat on a stool at the counter. Cyrus was showing our mother one of his many home videos of baby Rosa when she was a newborn. He was looking in the bookshelf most likely for another video. He looked at me then he asked Sherrell if she could help him find the other video. He said he thought it was in their room. Sherrell smiled at me and then they ran up the stairs and shut their door. I wouldn't be surprised if they both had glasses to the door trying to listen.

"I still hate you!" I said in a low tone.

"I know, I can't really tell you how I feel. At least you know how you feel."

"Maria's pregnant."

"Who?"

"My daddy's wife."

"Oh, I keep forgetting her name. Good for her, at least he has someone who doesn't mind having a whole tribe of kids."

"She didn't want to have it, but… I guess only you could go through with the alternative."

My mother exhaled, "I never wanted to be a mother."

"Tell me something I don't know." I blew air.

"I wanted to do whatever it took to make your daddy happy. I loved him so much!" I rolled my eyes. "I don't know where your brother comes from. That boy has a huge capacity for love unlike any other. He definitely doesn't get that from me, and you remind me of your father. Always wanting to sing and make everything happy."

I rolled my eyes, "I'm not like my father."

She smiled, "so you met the other side then." She chuckled, "even with that I was willing to roll with him until the wheels fell off, as long as we stopped having babies. Not only did he leave me, but also he left you guys with me. Like he was gonna be able to come back and forth when he felt like it. He started dating someone new and he really wanted to put my nose in it. When I started dating Reggie he suggested we move away. So we did. Your father did not get the last laugh."

"There's nothing funny about the way you raised us. You changed our last names, everything. Are your parents alive?"

"Barely, they're both in homes. My father has dementia and my mother has Alzheimer's, neither one of them remembers how much they hate each other. They don't remember me either so at least they won't have to know when I'm gone."

"Aunties? Uncles? Cousins?"

She shrugged, "I wouldn't know. My parents moved out here when I was young, it was just us as far as I know."

"I still hate you! At least I know why I hate you! How dare you come here only after you have no one else! If Reggie were alive, you wouldn't be sitting there right now."

"You're right about that, but that isn't the current reality. The children I hated are the only people I have in this whole world. Talk about ironic!" She chuckled.

"That's funny to you?" I could feel the acid in my stomach turning over.

"It's ironic like I just said."

"You don't have me! You might have Cyrus but you don't have me! I hate you!"

"There's a thin line between love and hate."

"Meaning what? You had some kind of love for us?" I said while rubbing baby Rosa's back.

"Its weird, I feel sorry for what I've done. I wasn't trying to cause you guys any pain. I'm proud of the hard workers you've become. You definitely don't get that from your daddy. But yet, I still never wanted children and I only had you two to make him happy. Two was my limit! It was two with the idea of him in the picture. I didn't know how to be a mother. We never bonded! I kind of bonded with Cyrus, but definitely not with you. Some women are cut out to be mothers I wasn't. You can testify to that."

I guess this interaction was supposed to make me feel good, but all it did was make me angrier. I wanted to put the baby down and beat her in her face.

****

"I'm so happy all you lovely ladies could make it. Torrie is running a little late, but she will be here. Did everyone get a chance to look over the music?" The guy said. I had extreme butterflies in my stomach Meredith Bling knows my name and said she loves my CD! That's what they all said and I can't believe someone like each of them listens to me. I'm completely star struck and honored to be here. "Chantel can you do us a favor?" The guy asked me, "since we're waiting for Torrie as usual can you play your interpretation of the song for us?"

My face started stinging. I walked to the back of the room and plugged in my Gibson guitar Derrick bought me. I turned the volume down on the amp so I wouldn't blast everyone out the room. The guy pointed at the music on the table, but I told him I didn't need it. I had been practicing and practicing hoping that I wouldn't look like the amateur of the bunch. I wanted to scream everyone was looking at me. I closed my eyes and played. Derrick and I went over the music so much I was seeing it in my sleep. When I peeked at everyone they were bobbing their heads to my rhythm. I smiled and closed my eyes again. I heard fingers snapping and people saying, "Owe!" When I was done they stood up while applauding me. Torrie was standing in the doorway sizing me up. "You guys started without me?"

"You're late Torrie!" The guy said

"The dog ate my homework, blah, blah, blah!" She said while rolling her eyes and taking a seat next to Meredith.

"Anyways, Chantel I liked that rendition but the timing is a little faster than we wanted." He said

"I like it better that way. The song has more roots." Alexa said

"I guess, but it isn't what we had in mind. Are you guys singing or rapping?" The guy asked

"How about we record it both ways and then we vote." Jennifer said

"Well, I already know I'm voting for the slower tempo." Torrie said

"Yeah, because you can't keep up!" Meredith cut her eyes at Torrie.

Torrie sucked her teeth. "I thought we were past all that." Torrie sighed.

"Of course you are, it happened to me."

"Do we have to do this right now? Can't we talk about this later?" Meredith glared at her. Torrie sighed, "Meredith I apologize for all of the pain I caused you and your family. I was in a bad place back then. I've done a lot of things I'm ashamed of. Please accept my apology even if you don't forgive me."

"Whatever Torrie! Cross me again and I'll finish the number someone started on your face!" Meredith said in her New York accent.

Torrie looked mad but she didn't say anything. Her appearance in person was a lot rougher than television, but that's what makeup is for.

We went over the song as a group and confirmed who was singing which parts; meanwhile our managers were a few doors down going over rights, etc. Alexa and I were staying longer to work on the music. We had lunch in the studio and chatted in between working. Alexa asked how I liked touring with Shameless. I told her I liked it, but I wasn't looking forward to doing it again. She said she couldn't wait to see Shameless' movie, she said the commercials were pretty funny. Looking down at her piano she asked me if Dwayne Reed showed up much during the tour. I told her I only saw him when we were in New York. She sighed and asked what's the deal with Dwayne. I shrugged cause I couldn't answer that, she matched my shrug and went back to playing music.

****

"This place is really nice!" I said taking my shoes off in the doorway.

"Thanks honey. This will be your bedroom." Amber said pointing to the guest room.

The room was huge bigger than my room in my apartment, and I had the master suite. The bed was huge and I loved the colors.

"Wow! Did you decorate this place all by yourself?"

Amber laughed. "No, I had the same interior decorator who did my house do this place." Then she gave me a key. "This is your key to the door. Don't forget the guest code to the alarm otherwise the police will be here faster than you can scratch your head."

"How does Mitigated watch you here?" I asked

"Mitigated is everywhere. As long as I know I can take a shower without someone watching my naked behind I don't worry about it." She laughed. Caprice knocked on the front door. Amber let her in then she came back in the room. "What did you say to get on Sasha's bad side?" Amber asked Caprice. I didn't expect her to go in like that. Caprice relayed the last conversation we had with Sasha. Amber's face changed and then she started sizing Caprice up. "I see!" Then Amber started walking away. "Let me know when you guys are ready for dinner."

Caprice looked at me, "am I that bad?"

I sighed, "How can you love my brother and not love the extension of him?"

Caprice got angry, "I'm sorry I asked." She took her bag and put it in the closet. "So just because she got pregnant and kept hers she gets my man?"

"He's not your man, he loves Sherrell." I said as gently as I could. Caprice looked at me like I betrayed her. "You don't know what you're talking about! "

"If you say so Caprice, don't say I didn't try to warn you." I shrugged.

I could tell she was about to say something but she bit her tongue. We went out to dinner with Amber and her friends Corey and Kimmy. Kimmy said she was glad I was down to earth, she was tired of divas. I made a mental note to avoid diva like tendencies. Caprice was mostly quiet all dinner, but it was obvious she was upset about something. When we got back to Amber's place her friends came up for a nightcap. Caprice excused herself and went to bed. I had a good time with Amber and her friends. We were drinking and talking. Kimmy asked what it was like touring. I told her we had a lot of fun, the movie didn't show everything of course. Then Kimmy said she couldn't wait to see the new movie with Dwayne Reed and a bunch of other folks in it. Amber shifted in her seat, and then Kimmy asked Amber if she was going to see the movie. Amber replied that she saw it already. Kimmy started laughing but Corey looked like he was searching her face to make sure she was ok. She said she was happy for Dwayne and that his career was going so well for him. Who knew an assistant coach could build a career out of his brief moments on camera. Kimmy said it was because he was gorgeous and a nice guy. She said if he was only one of those things he wouldn't have made it as far as he has. Then Amber said I should look to do movies when the opportunity presented itself. That was her way of slightly changing the subject. I hadn't thought of being in movies. The thought made me nervous, so I continued with the subject change. When I went to bed that night my mind was racing. I had a lot of work to get done in a small window of time to get it done in.

When my alarm went off, I cursed at it and then I hauled my bones out of the bed. Caprice was already up and I could smell breakfast cooking. I instantly thought of Amber and hoped that the smell of food in the morning didn't bother her. After my shower I went into the kitchen, Caprice was washing dishes and Amber and I came out at the same time. Amber was wearing her dance clothes. I was happy to see a genuine smile on her face. Caprice made breakfast for everyone and then she cleaned up behind us. I could tell Amber was watching her, she kind of moved her eyes around the room like Derrick does. She thanked Caprice for breakfast, and then she asked us if we needed a ride. Caprice said JoJo was on his way to pick us up. Amber said she doubted that we would see each other tonight so she hugged me and told me to have a good day. I guess that's the kind of stuff people who love each other do for each other. Caprice was still very quiet but she was doing her job so I decided to let it ride. Talking to her was going to take more of the little bit of energy I didn't have to spare. More studio time, this time it was for a soundtrack for an upcoming movie. I met the writer Natalie and the Producer. They told me about the movie, they played the music, and then we went over the song and how they wanted me to sing it. The Producer kept saying he wanted raw emotion; the song was a mad at the world song. The star of the movie was finding her man with another woman. When I initially started singing the Producer stopped the session, he said I wasn't singing the song right. This went on for a long time. I'd start and then he'd stop me. I was completely flustered and feeling like I couldn't do it. So when he told me to go again I was trying to take the frustration out of my voice. I was surprised when he didn't stop me. When I got to the chorus he told me to skip it and to go on to the next verse. So I sang the second verse just like I did the first one. I was waiting for him to tell me to stop. He told me he liked it and to do the verses over the same way. FRUSTRATING! I never had to go over my own music this much, but I guess when I chose the music it was easier to go with my own mind. Natalie told me to lighten my voice for the chorus, cause I still was in hard mode. I didn't know what she meant, so again the frustration but I guess I finally found what she was talking about. I recorded the chorus more times than I wanted to think about. AND THEN THE STINKING STUPID BRIDGE! How many ranges were they asking for in this one song? I was SO HAPPY when Aleisha showed up. I asked her to come in the booth with me and be my visual guide since she seemed to understand what they were saying. I calmed down a lot with her in the booth. Then they played back for me the raw and uncut version of the song. I bucked my eyes at Aleisha when I heard the whole song. Yeah, I sounded mad. This song didn't sound anything like any of my other songs. I was a little amazed and then I felt like they may actually know what they were doing. I drank hot water with lemon and honey while Aleisha and two other girls I didn't know harmonized on the background vocals. I was ready when I went back in the booth, we worked on the intro and ending to the song. When someone said it was five am the next morning I couldn't believe it. I hadn't seen daylight and had been working. When I started to feel that sleep headache I knew it was true. I didn't have time to sleep. I only had time to take a shower at Amber's and then get back in the car. When I arrived on set people were talking fast and pulling me in every direction. They picked out my clothes and then I sat in the chair for makeup. I chatted with Natalie while they worked on me. JoJo sent Aleisha back to the hotel, I left Caprice at Amber's and BJ assisted me. Funny how I needed sleep like the rest of them but I had to keep pushing. I didn't know what to expect when I saw Gerard, I was hoping this one time he wouldn't be my photographer. Fortunate for him, he was all business. I don't think I would've been able to put up with his nonsense otherwise. Natalie was a short flower child seeming girl. Her whole appearance seemed very down to earth like. Her black hair was pulled into a slick ponytail. She was very sweet and naturally loving, but don't cross her. Natalie and the Producer had it out a few times before our session was over. Natalie said her day was done after my photo session and I was happy for her. I had an interview to go shoot. It made me feel warm and fuzzy when she volunteered to go with me. She said we could be delirious together. She was my only trooper in this marathon of madness. The good thing is that my clothes were on set and my makeup and hair would already be done. We cat napped in the LA traffic to the studio. That forty minutes felt like heaven but an ugly tease of sleep. BJ gently tapped my shoulder when we arrived. Natalie invited me to her house to have dinner with her and her family. She said her husband was making dinner so by the time we were done it should be ready. I looked forward to a home cooked meal, it had been a minute. Some how my interview went well, and I found the clarity not to display how tired I truly was. I was energetic and upbeat, another positive interview. When we got back in the car, we went to Natalie's apartment; the building was nice but not fancy like I thought it would be. Natalie introduced me to her very tall and handsome husband. They were the cutest couple, I asked what he did for a living and he said he was a physical therapist. He mainly worked with the Lakers. I told him I thought he was a player himself. He said he played in school, but he had to figure something out when he didn't get picked up. He said this line of work was the next best thing. As we sat down to eat, Natalie's cell phone rang, she looked at it funny then at her husband. She answered it with a weird tone that made her husband and I stare at her. Then she laughed and gave her phone to her husband. She told him that he turned off his phone so his friend Desmond called her phone to talk to him. She said she didn't know he had her number. When he hung up he said his friend was coming over. I texted BJ and told him that a friend of theirs was coming over, cause I knew his alarm would go up since he wasn't inside the apartment. We started eating without Desmond and the food was delicious. Ken went to answer the door and he came back with his equally tall friend Desmond. When Desmond saw me he immediately started singing my song off key to me. We had a good laugh, and then he happily shook my hand and said it was nice to meet me. Now Desmond was cute, but since I don't follow basketball I don't know if he's a player and I just don't get it. He helped himself in the kitchen, this was definitely not his first time here. I wanted to hang out longer, but the bed was calling me. And since I knew I had to get up in the morning I thanked Natalie for everything, said goodnight to the men, then I ran out to the car. I think I was sleep before my head hit the pillow completely.

Again I was not happy when my alarm went off, but this time at least it was time to go workout. Caprice was still one word answering me, and at this point she was on my nerves. I focused on my workout, got a good burn in and then I showered and got dressed. I met with the label to discuss my next project. I had so much recorded material I already knew that I had a good five or six songs ready to go already. JoJo was so good, and I was happy I had him in my corner fighting for me. We walked out of that meeting all smiles. Natalie called all happy and gushy. She said Desmond was asking about me when I left. I was shocked cause he didn't seem interested when I was there. When she asked me if I was single I told her it was complicated, but I wasn't really available.

She sighed and said oh well. She said Desmond was going to be disappointed.

At the airport I had enough of Caprice's attitude. "ENOUGH!"

"Oh I'm sorry is something bothering her royal highness?" Caprice said full of attitude.

"Don't do that. Either tell me what's wrong or let it go, but don't play the game."

"Cyrus loves Sherrell and not me!" I looked at her like I was waiting for her to go on. "You don't know anything about love."

"I think we both know you don't know what you're talking about." I said

"Really? You know so much don't you!" Her eyes turned evil. "It's funny how you can run into a random female and get an emotional reaction from your man, but you never loop back around and ask him to clarify who the female is. You're so busy looking at Brooklyn, that you never made him explain who Quesha is."

I remembered immediately. My replacement at the smoothie stand. "What about her?" I also remember seeing Reggie trying to get at her. How was I supposed to be concerned about someone who would consider Reggie?

"I'm saying, you judge me and your brother; but you don't know what's going on in your own nonexistent relationship. Mister will not commit to you still runs the show, and you go along with it. At least I know what I'm signing up for. I know everything! You get a few credit cards and a couple dollars and equate that to the ultimate expression of love and trust!"

I looked her up and down. "You're just jealous because in your whatever you wanna call it with Cyrus, he never broke you off; and now that he finally could break you off he won't cause he has a girl and a child! You're not even second your last! AND for your information as IF you didn't already know! Say what you want about my relationship, but at the end of the day we all know WHO Derrick loves! You don't have the same. Cause if you did, maybe you wouldn't have time to follow me around." I said rolling my eyes.

"Female! Before you get all high and mighty about me following you around you actually might want to ask yourself who's best interest am I paid to protect? Yours or his? You step out of line and all of a sudden it will seem like you're crazy supposedly trying to kill yourself in the man who LOVES you living room!" Then she stood up cause it was time for us to board. "You're so STUPID!"

Chapter 19

"Hey Cadence this is Chantel, how are you doing?"

"HEY! I'm good! How are you? I was just watching your video. You look amazing. Nothing like that shy little girl who worked for me."

"Thank you."

"My mother loves to tell people how I used to be your supervisor, yadda, yadda, yadda. People keep asking me what you're like."

"What do you tell them?"

"I tell them that you're great of course." Then she laughed.

"I don't think Bob likes that I used to date Cyrus, but hey! Its my past, he doesn't need to know how recent in the past that was."

"You're gonna mess around and end up in trouble." Then I took a deep breath. "Listen, I'm trying to track someone down and I was wondering if you could help me."

"If I could help you?" She sounded suspicious, "who?"

"That girl Quesha you hired to replace me. What can you tell me about her?"

"Oh my goodness! You went WAY back didn't you. We never got all that close." She started snapping her fingers, "what was her name? What was her name?"

"Anything you could remember about her would be fine."

"Her last name was Wilkins, but I can't remember too much about her. She was good enough for the job, but she and Shelly hit it off."

"Is Shelly still out here?"

"Last I knew Shelly was an office manager at a storage unit facility off 98th and San Leandro Blvd. I don't know if she's still there, cause that was a long time ago."

I wrote down the information and thanked her. I talked to her for a while after that. When she asked about Cyrus that was my cue to get off the phone with her. I grabbed my keys and made my way over to 98th Ave. I parked in the parking lot. I took a deep breath and I wondered if Shelly would be receptive to me or if she would have an attitude. Now that time has passed you know how you look back and realize that what you thought was there was never there? Shelly was always talking down to me, treating me bad; she was never a real friend. Now I need something and I don't know how she'll be. I'm not the same Chantel she used to know. When I walked in the door a young girl greeted me. I smiled and asked her if Shelly was in today. She said yes and that Shelly would be back in a minute she was closing out someone's storage unit. I sat in the chair waiting for Shelly. When she walked in the door her belly was undeniable. Instantly I felt a little jealous not even knowing the situation. She was having a baby, and I felt like Derrick was dangling the possibility in front of my face, but as usual he shows me something to take it back. I stood up and smiled at Shelly, I could tell she didn't recognize me at first. She started to walk away and then she stopped and looked at me again. She stood still and I could see all the questions all over her face. "Chantel?" I smiled, "Congratulations!" I said gesturing towards her stomach. "What are you doing here?"

I still couldn't read her mood. "I'm looking for Quesha, I was told that you guys are friends." I didn't see the point in beating around the bush.

"What do you want with Quesha?" She asked

"I want to talk to her. Can I get her phone number?"

Shelly sucked her teeth; she walked over to her desk and pulled out her cellphone. "Hey girl! Guess what! Chantel is here asking for

your number… I know gurl… For real?…. Ok, I'll tell her…"

Shelly started laughing that loud ghetto laugh and my breath felt like fire. "She's gonna come down here to talk to you. I don't know why though."

"What's wrong with you?" I said, the girl in the office sat at the desk, trying to act like she wasn't listening.

"You disappeared and then you show up out of the blue not to see how I'm doing or ask anything about my life."

"I said congratulations, what else am I supposed to say?"

"You don't even care!" Shelly hissed at me.

"Let's be real Shelly you've never liked me. I wasn't gonna walk in here acting like we were best friends. You always wanted my brother and you gave me your sorry excuse for friendship, just to be closer to him. I'm sorry if you thought I should've come in here in some other way. I'm trying to be as real as possible."

Shelly got angry and started yelling about my brother was a user and a bunch of noise I didn't want to hear about. As I stood up to walk out of the office the girl said, "OH MY GOD! YOU'RE CHANTEL SHAW!" She started jumping up and down real excited. "Can I take a picture with you?" She wasn't really asking as she ran towards me with her phone in hand. She threw her arm around my neck and then she put her cheek next to mine and snapped the picture. She was too excited. Shelly snapped at the girl but she didn't care, you could tell she was used to it. Shelly barked at me telling me the office was closed and I was going to have to go outside. I asked her when Quesha would get here and she snapped at me saying in any minute. When I walked out of the office Derrick pulled into the parking lot. "What are you doing here?" His face was stone.

"Why are you here?" I asked completely shocked. "Where did you come from?" I said looking around

Derrick glared at me, "What are you doing here?"

"I'm waiting for someone."

"Who?"

"None of your business!"

"Chantel! Get in your car and go home!"

"You can't tell me what to do!" I said as he got out of his truck.

"I'm not one of your workers!"

"Chantel!" Shelly yelled as she walked out the office not even looking in my direction. I guess she thought she was going to come out and tell me something about myself. When she looked up and saw Derrick she turned on her heels bumping into her office helper and very clumsily pushing her back in the office and slamming the door shut behind them. You could hear her locking the door after she closed it. Good to know Derrick still put the fear of God in her. "Chantel, get in your car and go home!" He said walking into my face.

Derrick looked angry but I couldn't understand why. "Derrick, I'll be home in a little bit." I said looking at the green car that pulled into the driveway and paused.

Derrick got angry and grabbed my arm; he took my car keys out of my hand. He threw them to a guy I didn't recognize, or know that he was standing there. "Take her car to her house!" He told the guy then he took me to the passenger side of his car. His grip was firm on my arm but he wasn't hurting me. If I tried to fight him I knew his grip would only get firmer. He firmly sat me in his truck and then he slammed the door. He looked at the green car and then he got in his truck. I can only assume that was Quesha in the green car although she never got out while we were there. He burned rubber as he pulled out of the driveway. "What were you doing there?"

"I was waiting for somebody."

"Who?"

"None of your business!"

He cut his eyes at me, his jaw tightened. "None of my business!" He shook his head, "none of my business!"

"What's wrong with me being at a storage unit place?"

"You tell me, since you're the smart one."

"Stop it DERRICK! STOP IT! WHO IS QUESHA?"

He glanced out the window, "nobody" he said lowly.

"I'm tired Derrick! Tell me the truth, who is she?"

"I TELL YOU EVERYTHING!" I wasn't expecting him to yell, I jumped really hard. "THAT'S WHAT YOU WERE DOING THERE! WHAT ARE YOU AN UNDERCOVER REPORTER NOW? WHAT ARE YOU HOPING TO FIND OUT BY TALKING TO HER? I'VE BEEN GOOD TO YOU CHANTEL! THAT'S ALL YOU SHOULD BE WORRIED ABOUT! MY PAST IS NONE OF YOUR BUSINESS!"

"What? How is your past none of my business? My life is an open book to you; but your past is none of my business? You're wrong! You're so wrong!" Derrick pulled into my garage. I jumped out of the truck, and ran to the elevator. Derrick parked and was walking fast to the elevator when I pressed the button to close the doors. I ran to my front door as Derrick came up the stairs. I saw Derrick jogging to the door as I put my key in. He pushed the door open when I tried to slam it shut. There was fire in Derrick's eyes when he came in the door. "WHY ARE YOU SO CONTROLLING?"

"You have no idea what controlling is! If I wanted to control you I could!"

"You already do! I can't make any moves without you being all over it."

"All I'm doing is trying to protect you."

"Protect me from what? All I can see needing protection from is your family's nonsense! I'm tired of this!"

"Tired of what?"

"You! You won't commit to me! You're forcing me to deal with my mother, but you won't do the same! I HATE YOU!"

"How you figure I'm not doing the same?"

"You won't even go to the cemetery where your father is buried, but I have to go and talk to that evil woman to appease you! You don't answer any of my questions, but you know all of my business. Please explain to me how this is supposed to work? Everything is stacked in your favor."

"So going down there is supposed to even things up?"

"It was a start!"

"What have you done?"

I rolled my eyes, "what?"

"Are you searching for justification for something you've done?"

"You know good and well I haven't done anything."

"So then where is this coming from?" He said, I could see the wheels of his brain turning.

I huffed, "I asked you a question first. Who is Quesha?"

Derrick sucked his teeth and glared at me. "Nobody!" Then he sighed, "I told you we went out a few times she did nothing for me, I stopped calling her. Why were you at the storage place?" He gave me a look like this was the last time he was gonna ask me.

"I wanted to talk to Quesha."

He gestured with his hands to keep talking, although I could tell that wasn't the answer he was expecting. "And?"

"That's why I was there, I wanted to talk to her. I wanted to hear her side. Your answer is too vague."

Derrick rolled his eyes real slow then he set them on me like he was burning a hole through me with his X-ray vision. "HOLD ON!" He did a deep scary chuckle. "You mean to tell me that you went there to talk to some girl I smashed way back in the day? Why wouldn't my explanation of who she is be enough for you? Why would you think there was more to the story than what I've told you?"

"See! Cause you never said you had sex with her. You said you went out a few times and she did nothing for you."

"You want me to spell out all the details for you?" I put my hand on my hip. He did a mad laugh, "I took her home. It was our third date, I knew I wasn't calling her again I wasn't feeling the whole setup. We're sitting in front of her house and she starts kissing on my neck. I didn't stop her but it didn't change anything. She started pulling at my clothes and she unbuckled my belt and unzipped my pants. Then…."

I screamed putting my fingers in my ears. "Ok! OK! Stop!"

"This is what you wanted to hear? I'm holding back some huge secret about that girl. She got a taste and wanted more, and I said no. Not even sex was gonna keep my attention with her."

I felt completely dumb; I searched Derrick's eyes. "Is there anything I would want to know about your interactions with her that you're holding back from me?"

Derrick clapped his hands together once and the sound rumbled off the walls. The sound of it scared the life out of me. "I swear woman! I swear!" He paced, "You want me to start with the details again? I honestly don't know where..." He looked at me, "who said there's more to it?" His eyes were burning a hole in me.

"Caprice said..."

He cut me off, "CAPRICE? That no good, don't know how to keep her legs closed, sorry excuse for a female said something and I gotta deal with this? CHANTEL! Please tell me you did not let that girl get in your head?" He said in a sarcastic and angry tone.

Ok now I feel stupid. "Ok, well what had happened was..."

He squinted his eyes, "what had happened was?"

"Yeah, you see... Um! Um!" Now I'm pacing trying to tell the story without feeling as dumb as Derrick was making me feel. I exhaled, "I messed up! I let her get in my head about Quesha. I thought there was more. I honestly didn't connect the dots that you slept with her. She made it seem like there was more to your relationship than what you told me. I should've come to you. I was afraid that you were going to lie to me and I was going to have to do my own detective work."

Derrick hadn't taken his eyes off of me. "Tell me about the whole conversation." So I told him everything from A to Z, I left nothing out. The level of pissed didn't change on Derrick's face. He told me I need to come to him right away with stuff like that. Then he dialed Malcolm on his cell phone. He told him to draw up the paperwork cause Caprice was fired! Malcolm said that was fine then he told him what Amber said when he talked to her a few minutes ago. Amber agreed with Sasha that Caprice was dirty, and she didn't want to be around her anymore. Malcolm said he was just about to call him to tell him that she was fired. Malcolm said he was going to call Cyrus, Cyrus was a grown man; but he wouldn't let him walk into that trap without at least warning him first.

When Derrick got off the phone I watched his eyes, "so tell me something." Derrick nodded at me to go ahead. His face had completely relaxed and he was almost smiling. "Who did you think I was there to see?"

Derrick squinted then licked his lips and smiled, "Jajuki." He chuckled a little bit.

"Who?" Then I remembered, "You mean Jaloni?"

He chuckled, "yeah what I said Jajuki."

I chuckled, "ok. Why would he be there?"

"He kicks it with Shelly from time to time." He said watching my face.

I frowned, "they date?"

"If you wanna call it that."

"Is that his baby?"

"I think so, but it's not their first."

"WHAT?" I said in disbelief.

"It's their second." Then he looked at me, "does that bother you?"

"Heck yeah that bothers me! How she gonna go behind me like that?"

"You guys barely held hands in high school. You moved up to me. Let her have him, he's a loser."

I crossed my arms. "That's not the point!" I said pouting.

"What's the point?"

"I don't know..." I huffed. "Oh, that she shouldn't go behind me!

I don't care if it was high school; I bet you she won't let him watch my videos. I bet you she be heck of jealous when he talks about me."

"Why is any of that your problem?"

"It's not, but..."

"Butt is what you get beat on." I rolled my eyes at him. "Are you ready for Saturday?"

"Yeah" I said nonchalantly.

"How are you ready? I haven't seen you practice."

"I got it, don't worry about it." I said shooing him.

"Hey! Hey! You don't understand what you're up against here. It's us against them."

I smiled, "ok."

He shook his head, "you better not be the weak link on our team or I'm never gonna let you hear the end of it."

"I know how to play baseball Derrick." I pretended to be annoyed by him.

"We're playing against Malcolm and all of them! It's

the soldiers against them! If you're on the soldier's team you gotta be good!" He said getting excited something he rarely does.

"Can we play for the fun of it?" I said putting my arms around his waist. His face dropped as he sucked his teeth. "Why everything gotta be so serious with you guys?"

Derrick huffed, "you think I'm bad…. wait 'til Saturday… you'll see."

I smiled at him, "you were jealous."

He tried to get away from me, but I wouldn't let him go. "It's nice to know you care."

He looked down at me, his face was serious. "Of course I care, I love you!" Then he kissed me.

****

They weren't playing. They had uniforms, The Soldiers against Team Malcolm. Most of the family came to watch and have the coliseum staff wait on them hand and foot. While the rest of us came to play. Amber and Tracy were out of town on business trips, and Andrew's son was spending time at a friend's house. However, Sasha was in town and she brought her father with her to play. Our team Roster: Derrick, Darryl, Drew, Yussef, Cyrus, Tanisha, Sasha, Pearla, Ryder, and me. Team Malcolm was everybody else.

Malcolm, Ethan Sr. (Derrick's cousin), Richard (Sasha's dad), Malachi (Derrick's uncle), Timothy (Derrick's uncle), Tim (Derrick's cousin), Tina (Tim's sister), Jade (Derrick's aunt), Franky (Derrick's cousin), and Sonny (Jade's husband). Derrick informed me when we were doing our team huddle that I was pitching. "Can she even throw? We got to beat Malcolm D-Rick! I know that's your girl and all, but we can't leave this game to chance! Chantel can you throw? Chantel can you throw?" Darryl was a little excited.

"Get a grip man! She has to be good otherwise he knows what's at stake!" Drew said to his brothers.

"But seriously, all jokes aside. You got this? I'm kind of a sore loser." Tanisha said with no smile.

Everybody was looking at me. I swallowed, now I regretted not practicing like Derrick told me to. Derrick looked at me like "I told you so!" I didn't say anything I looked at everybody.

"AW HECK NAW!" Darryl shouted, "we're gonna LOOSE!"

"She's fine!" Derrick said, "she better be!"

"Lets just go have fun you guys." Sasha said breaking our huddle.

They tossed a coin and our team was up to bat first. Malcolm took his place on the pitcher's mount. Uncle Malachi was the catcher and everyone else was in out field, while Juan was the umpire. Tanisha was up to bat first; Uncle Malachi was talking mess the whole time. When Tanisha FINALLY hit the ball, it was a pop up. Malcolm stood there shaking his head like she was going to have to do better than that. Tina caught the ball. Sasha went up to bat and Malcolm struck her out. Sasha was angry and Darryl was giving her a hard time about going for Malcolm's fastball. It was my turn and my heart was beating out of my shirt. "FRESH MEAT!" Uncle Malachi yelled. I rolled my eyes as the out fielders

started coming in field like I wasn't any smidgen of a threat. They were laughing at me and ready to come in. I took my stance, which made some in the audience laugh. Malcolm didn't even put a spin on the ball. He tossed the ball to me. I KNOCKED THE CRAP OUT OF THAT BALL! HOME RUN! "THAT'S RIGHT CHANTEL! I'M SORRY I DOUBTED YOU! YOU'RE ON THE RIGHT TEAM! TAKE YOUR TIME! RUN REAL FANCY!" Darryl screamed like he was losing his mind. Everybody cracked up laughing. "SOLDIERS!" Darryl yelled as I came in for my home run.

Malcolm said I got away with that one time, it would not happen again. Cyrus actually got a hit, but they tagged him out before he got to first base. First up to bat was Tina, "Chantel don't go easy on her just because she's a girl! No mercy, ok! NO MERCY!" Darryl yelled. Tanisha was our catcher, and she signaled for me to throw the ball low and fast. Strike one! I could hear people whistling after they saw my fastball. The Soldiers came to the edge of the dugout to watch me pitch. I guess Tina thought she was getting a hit off of me. Nope! Not today! When Ethan came up next he stuck he tongue at me. Tanisha told me to throw it high slow. Ethan cursed cause he went for it. After a foul ball and two more strikes

Ethan was out. Then Richard came up to bat he was a browner and male version of Sasha. She told me to humiliate her father. He laughed like it was impossible, but when I struck him out he had fire in his eyes.

Yussef was up to bat when our team went up, as if he could read Malcolm's mind, Malcolm threw the ball hard and fast. Yussef hit the ball right down the middle; Malcolm had to jump to avoid the ball that was hurling at him furiously. Yussef hit first base he started to run for second, but he changed his mind. Malcolm glared at Yussef, and Yussef had a mile wide smile the entire time. He made kissy faces at Malcolm; Darryl went up to bat next. Darryl talked mess the entire time up to bat, and he talked even more mess walking back to the dug out. Sasha and Tanisha gave him a hard time about striking out. When Drew went up to bat everybody got quiet. Neither one of them smiled, there was definite tension. Malcolm threw the ball hard and fast, you heard the impact when the ball hit Drew's leg. Drew turned a little red, he spit then he smiled. Yussef advanced to second and Drew walked to first base shaking his leg. My baby was up, I held my breath watching him walk up to the plate. Yussef rallied for Derrick to bring him home. Malcolm almost grinned at Derrick, Derrick switched from his right to his left side. The crowd oohed, Malcolm rolled his eyes. Malcolm threw a fast hard ball, Derrick backed up. They started laughing. Malachi stood up shook his hand for a minute. Derrick told Malcolm to calm down. Malcolm huffed and threw another fast hardball. Derrick tapped the ball and took off running. Malcolm and Malachi dove for the ball. Everybody was laughing at them. Tanisha went up to bat, bases were loaded. Tanisha smashed the ball, it looked like Tim was gonna catch it. He missed it, Malcolm cursed as Derrick made it home. Drew told him next time he'd want to be more careful about the runs he gives up. Then he flipped him off. Malcolm rolled his eyes as his team mates gave him a hard time about giving up runs. Sasha got a hit but she still got out before she got to first base. Pearla made it to first base, and Ryder struck out. My heart was pounding; Malcolm did not take it easy on me. He struck me out.

In the bottom of the fifth inning Mitigated Staff came out of everywhere and they said we had to go. I was in the middle of pitching. I heard Darryl asking if it was Toya, Phineas, or Kevin. The seriousness on everyone's faces was alarming. It seemed like

they went from playful to drop dead serious in the drop of a hat. Everyone got on the party buses and we left. We went to Malcolm's lounge and restaurant in Berkeley Shylight. We went upstairs to have our victory meal. I was holding baby Rosa when Malcolm addressed the room telling everyone they played well. Then the argument started about who actually won. We were ahead by three runs. Everyone was going back and forth about who would've won. Drew said his peace then he had to go pick up his son. Malcolm walked out with him then he came back. Malcolm told Derrick to come with him, and then he grabbed Yussef and Darryl along the way. They left for a few minutes. Pearla, Paulette, Liz, and Sherrell encircled me. "So we hear your girl got fired." Pearla smiled real big refusing to hide her excitement.
I sighed, "yeah."
"So what does that mean? You guys gonna still hang out together or is she completely gone?" Liz asked her eyes fixed on me.
"We didn't end on good terms. And I doubt that getting fired will restore warm and fuzzy feelings. She's got a lot on her plate. I don't know if we'll make up."
Pearla sucked her teeth. "Girl if you don't wake up and smell the coffee. That girl wasn't ever your friend. She may have loved your brother, but she put herself first. And you gotta know she isn't gonna just let this go. Everybody needs to stay on alert."

****

Cyrus has found his niche amongst my team of supporters and promoters and it has worked out nicely on all parts. Financially things are going so well that he put a deposit down on a house within the same development that Derrick and I are going to be in. He said the offer was so sweet he couldn't pass it up. He was excited and he wanted it to be a surprise but he told Sherrell right away. All I know is Derrick and I were cuddling watching TV when we heard Sherrell start screaming! She came running out the room down the stairs and she dove on Derrick and I saying she was getting a brand new house. Cyrus stood so proud at the top of the stairs while she told me about the house as if I wasn't there when it all happened. Derrick chuckled and congratulated her. Sherrell was talking a mile a minute, she was overjoyed. Every nuance in the planning of their family home excited Sherrell. Cyrus told her he loved how much she appreciated everything he did for them. We all knew that was a comparison to Caprice, but we let it ride on the air. Even that didn't steal Sherrell's thunder. When Cyrus bought her a slightly used luxury car you would've thought he put a million dollars in her hands. She cried for days when he told her she didn't have to work anymore. Sherrell made sure Cyrus had everything he needed, they were a perfect team. Things really picked up with them now that Caprice was out of the picture. Cyrus being Cyrus though, I could tell that he missed Caprice sometimes. I was happy that he reached out to me whenever he felt weak instead of giving in to her constant pleading. Cyrus was overall happy with Sherrell. They were so happy that they were even discussing having another baby. When I asked him if they were going to get married he said they talked about it, but they agreed that they didn't need the paper confirmation. He said he didn't care either way, but Sherrell was fine with things the way they were.

****

"Right there is perfect!" I told Sharon.

"Ooh! I like that! That's going to be nice. A double sided fireplace in the dining room and next to the kitchen is a lovely touch." She said typing information into the computer. "This house is going to be amazing!" She said.

Structurally the design of the house is finished. Now I get to pick out all of the upgrades, fixtures, and the fun stuff. "Has Derrick given you a budget for the house?"

Sharon smiled, "UN huh" she said nodding her head.

"Can I ask what?"

"Not my place to tell you. You gotta get it from the horse's mouth. I will say that you are LOVED!" Then she chuckled.

"Oh really?" I smiled while cutting my eyes at her.

"Can I ask you something?" Sharon lowered her voice.

"Sure."

"Are you two going to get married?" I frowned. "I know it's none of my business, but I'm just thinking this is an awfully big purchase, and you aren't engaged. Is this your engagement ring?"

"Honestly, I don't need a marriage as long as the commitment's there is all I care. We're working on the commitment, but I don't think we'll be getting married."

"Don't you want to have children?"

"Derrick and I are proof that children don't have to come from marriages."

"I guess I'm old fashioned. How will you handle this house if you guys should decide to go your separate ways?"

"My name will be on the house as well. It's not like he can kick me out, if that's what you mean. I trust Derrick to do right by me."
"Love can be sticky, that's all I'm saying."
Sharon's words were echoing in my head as I drove away. My cellphone rang; the car said it was Auntie Lorraine, I told it to answer. "Hello Chantel how are you?" She said overly calm.
"I'm good and you?" I said
"I'm ok. I was trying to reach Derrick but he's not answering. Do you happen to know where he is?"
"He's in a meeting right now, do you want me to relay a message?"
"Can you reach Darryl for me, neither one of them are answering. Tell them that she's ok first of all; but Dionne is in the hospital. She has pneumonia, but she's going to be ok."
"What hospital is she at?"
"Brookside Hospital in Richmond, room 104."
"I'll be right there."
"Oh no honey I know you're busy. Just let them know for me ok."
I called Amber who picked up on the second ring. She asked me to pick her up and she'd call her boys and let them know. Darryl beat me to Amber's house. So we rode in his car, he seemed normal. I guess I didn't know how I expected him to be. She said Dionne was going to be ok, but he got there awfully fast to be so calm and his normal silly self. Derrick called me as we were getting off the freeway. I could see the signs pointing to the Richmond, oh excuse me San Pablo casino. I zoned out for a minute thinking of my father. Derrick said hello a second time, I snapped out of it. I told him just like Auntie Lorraine told me. Then I told him I was riding with Darryl and his mother. I could hear his irritation through the phone.
He was upset cause I left my car at his mother's house. I rolled my eyes and asked him how long before he got to the hospital. He said he had to secure my car first then he'd be there.
By the time the hospital released Brooklyn she seemed pretty lucid again. That also meant she was depressed and quiet. Her mother convinced her to come home for a while. Derrick said he'd have her apartment packed up and shipped back home. I tried not to be irritated by all the extras he was doing for her. I guess in one way it was the least he could do. He was shelling out a lot of money for

her and her family. When her insurance ran out, and the doctor really felt Brooklyn needed to stay, guess who volunteered to foot the bill? He had her mother and sister in a hotel and he got them a rental car. He paid for all their meals. I asked him why they couldn't stay at Brooklyn's place and drive her car, but he didn't want to go into it. Not to mention he broke the lease on his place cause when he said he wasn't going back there he meant it. When he wasn't sleeping in my bed he crashed at Malcolm's. With everything going on he had me taking all kinds of self-defense classes with these random people who he'd bring to my gym. When I would say I was tired or complain he'd tell me to man up and deal with it. NO PATIENCE these days! And his lack of

patience has affected our intimacy; I'm never in the mood. ESPECIALLY when I got the impression that he and Brooklyn might've been fooling around right before she tried to kill herself. Actually he wouldn't give me a straight answer and had the nerve to act irritated when I asked him point blank about it. I look forward to my time away these days. I love Derrick with everything in me. He's my motivation when I'm nervous. My sense of protection when I'm scared. My definition of what love feels like. On the other hand his ambiguity about us is getting on my nerves, it's hurting every aspect of our relationship. It makes me feel stupid to put so much love and trust in someone who can't say that they'll be with me for the long haul.

When we got up to Dionne's room Auntie Lorraine was in the hallway asking a nurse for some water. Darryl was real quiet all of a sudden. He hugged his great aunt and then moved behind me. I gave her a hug and she kept looking at Darryl. Darryl sighed; he told her he knows he hasn't been coming around, but it's been a lot going on. She didn't say anything she kept looking at him. He kept explaining more to fill the silence. Amber smiled at me and told me to come with her. She told me he was in trouble with his auntie and he was gonna have to do some fancy footwork to get on her good side. We went in Dionne's room and she was sitting up looking out the window. She smiled at Amber and I. She told us we were such pretty girls. When Darryl walked in the room Dionne smiled real big, "David! My baby! Come give your momma some suga." She said extending her arms.

Darryl took a deep breath, "hi momma." Then he gave her a hug and a kiss.

Then she looked at me then she looked at Amber. She put her hands out to me. "I know you love my son. I don't know all you young folk's business. But David's with Amber now. They got a family, you need to go find a man of your own."
Amber leaned in to Darryl, "who's she supposed to be?" Darryl shrugged.
"Amber!" Dionne said firmly out of nowhere.
"Yes ma'am?"
"Be nice to Patricia it's not her fault."
"Yes ma'am." Amber said smiling at me. Then she gestured that she'd tell me later.
Andrew and Derrick walked in together followed by Auntie Lorraine who kept cutting her eyes at Darryl making him feel bad. "Seems like your brother always forgets, why don't you two remind him to come see us?"

"I remind him, but he's really busy. "Andrew said smiling at his little brother.
"You're not busy?" She asked him.
"I am." He said straightening his face.
Then she frowned, "yeah cause I haven't seen that baby in a minute. Nor have I met the woman you've vowed to spend the rest of your life with!"
Andrew's face dropped cause now he was in trouble. Everybody started laughing at him. "Auntie! I'm gonna bring her, its just been a lot going on."
"It's always a lot going on!" Then she looked at Derrick. "Come here baby." She put her arms out and hugged him. "Derrick is the only one who comes regularly and he made sure we've met the lady in his life." Derrick actually smiled, and then she smacked him up side the head and we all laughed. "But you're living in sin!" Derrick laughed while rubbing his head. "They are too!" He said pointing to his brothers.
"Not un! I'm marrying mine!" Andrew said
Derrick sucked his teeth. "Fine! Me and Chantel will get married too." He laughed I didn't. Andrew caught my non-smile.

"Auntie you already know mine. You knew her before I did. I can't get credit for picking a good girl?" Darryl said trying to make his voice sound like he was pleading.

"OH! So because you went across the street and turned out a good girl, I'm supposed to excuse your absence from my life?" She put her hand on her hip.

Darryl looked at Amber, "I didn't see that turning on me." Then he put his arms out to his Great Auntie, "Auntie! I'm the baby. Go easy on me. You know I'm not wrapped too tight. Can't I get a little time off for being on good behavior?"

"Boy! You're related to me, crazy knows exactly how crazy is. You better bring your behind around! Don't make me come looking for you! Cause if I have to look for you, I will find you. And it will SUCK TO BE YOU when I do!" She threatened.

"Yes ma'am." Darryl said lowering his head.

I was quiet the rest of the time we were there. When they would laugh I'd courtesy smile, but I wasn't in a laughing mood. As we were leaving Andrew put his arm around my neck. "You ok?"
"Yep!" I said
"I saw your face. You don't wanna get married?"
Fire burned in my stomach. "I don't care about a wedding."
"Then what's wrong?"
"If you don't get your raggedy arm off my woman!" Derrick said halfway joking.
Andrew removed his arm. "My bad! I was just talking to my sister in law, but it's cool! Sink or swim on your own."
"About what?" Derrick eyed me.
I ignored him cause I knew Drew was gonna tell him. I walked ahead to Amber. I hugged everyone goodbye and then I waited for Derrick to unlock his truck. He chirped the doors then he talked to Andrew. I rolled my eyes at the thought of how fun this ride home was gonna be. Then Amber got out of Darryl's car. She said something to Derrick and then they came and got in Derrick's truck. I was happy cause that meant he had to be on good behavior. Amber said Darryl had a sudden change of plans and he was going to Vallejo instead of back to Oakland. I asked Amber if she was hungry, Derrick cut his eyes at me. I stuck my tongue at him. She said she had a roast in the slow cooker and we were welcome to

come have dinner with her. Amber's house had antique furniture and a real classic look to it. We sat at the table in the kitchen to have dinner. Amber explained that Patricia was the girl that Derrick's father was seeing before they started dating. Derrick was not interested in the conversation. I asked her if Derrick looked like his father, cause honestly I saw Malcolm more than anyone else. She looked at Derrick to ask him with her eyes if it was ok to show pictures. He looked away and she told me she would be right back. Derrick looked at me the entire time she was gone. He wasn't frowning, but I didn't know this look. Amber sat next to me and showed me her pictures, some of them I had already seen of the boys when they were growing up. I hadn't seen a picture of his father ever. As soon as I laid eyes on him I saw it, that was his father. Derrick looked a lot like Amber, but they all did, but this man was definitely Derrick's father. Derrick didn't look at the pictures he watched my face for a reaction. I loved looking at pictures of Amber when she was little. She had the same face; only her body was a little girl's. It seemed like Amber and her sister Jade and cousin Sophia were the three musketeers. They were always together, made me wish I had a sister; but I wouldn't trade Cyrus in for a hundred sisters so I guess its better this way. When it got late we gave Amber hugs and then we left. Derrick said goodnight to the Mitigated staff outside watching the house. When we got in the truck Derrick looked at me, "you don't want to get married."

I blew air, "you can't even commit to me. What I look like hoping to one day be your wife?"

He started his truck. "I'm not committed to you." He said it like the thought was ridiculous. "So then what are we building?"

"A house that you know better than to bring any of your tricks in." I said turning my body away from him.

"Let's talk this out, apparently you're not attracted to me anymore. You don't want to marry me. Do you even want to be with me?"

I gasped and looked at him. "What do you mean I'm not attracted to you? WHY ON EARTH would you think something like that?" I watched his face to see if he was trying to run game on me or if he was speaking from his heart.

"I know things have been stressful, and I've been pushing you; but we're up against a lot. I don't think Caprice would ever be stupid enough to come against me. By the gumption she had to say the things she said to you leaves room for a lot. We gotta be ready for anything and clearly Kevin is that stupid. Then there's the whole Toya mess, and those detectives watching everything we do. Then there's work and the stress that brings, we've been going through a lot. Since I've been pushing you about everything else, the last thing I have energy to push you on, is whether or not you're gonna give me the love I need right now. I shouldn't have to ask you for that; all of this is so that we can have the love. I thought we were clear on that. I need you to talk to me and stop shutting down. We won't last if we keep going like we're going."

The thought of him saying that put butterflies in my stomach. "I'm sorry." I said

He fought the irritated feeling coming up on his face. "What are you sorry for?"

"You're right I should've thought about the big picture."

"Chantel!" He stopped at the light, "if you don't stop it I swear!"

"Why are you mad at me, I'm agreeing with you." I said feeling tears well up in my eyes

"Where's your voice? Why are you hiding from me? What are you afraid of?"

"That you'll stop loving me." I said quietly.

"Why would I do that?"

"No one outside of my brother has ever consistently loved me. You didn't even love me enough to say I was worth it to say no to other females. I'm waiting for you to change up, show me who you really are. I can't fall apart when you leave me."

"After all these years you don't know me at all!" His face was stone.

"After all these years you should understand where I'm coming from."

"Just because I understand doesn't make it ok. You're doubting me, what are we even doing? If we don't have it together by now its hard to say we'll ever have it right."

"Are you breaking up with me because I wasn't putting out?"

He cut his eyes at me, "don't do that! Don't play dumb! Talk to me!" He barked

The fire in my stomach traveled up my throat and out of my mouth. "You're still in love with Brooklyn! You can lie and say you're not, but why else would you do all that you did for her and her family? You're not forth coming when it comes to her. How do you think that makes me feel when I'm watching you and I know how you are. You haven't even told me what happened when she came over your house. All I know is you won't look at her. You're acting so guilty! THEN YOU WANT ME TO TALK TO MY MOTHER! I do it and you tell me to do it again! I HATE HER! We will never be best friends or anything like that. You had a mother who loved you, and even though Malcolm is Malcolm you grew up with a father figure who you knew loved you. ALL I EVER HAD WAS MY BROTHER! THERE WAS NO ONE ELSE TO LOVE ME! SHE OPENLY ADMITS TO NOT LOVING ME, TO HATING ME! And yet YOU think there's some conversation or bonding moment I'm supposed to have with her. It makes me mad at you when you do that. You don't get it; you don't understand what it feels like. Your mother looks like love! You have aunties and uncles who love you; you have a whole network of a family. ALL I EVER HAD WAS CYRUS!" I cried from my toes. "Then I finally have a real daddy just to find disappointment in him too. He says he loves me, but not enough to be good. All I know is disappointment and you want me to have blind faith in you. I try but it's not good enough. I guess I'm not good enough. I guess this is what I expect my life to be, existing."

Derrick peeked at me. "Yeah like that..." I looked at him with questions on my face. "I know I told you to talk but I didn't expect you to say all that." He smiled, "I expected you to say," and then he made his voice all whiny and sad. "Derrick, I don't know what you want me to say. I don't get mad I don't feel anything." I rolled my eyes at him. As I continued to cry my eyes out. "I honestly don't know how I'd feel if the shoe was on the other foot. My thing is I don't want you to carry the woulda, coulda, shouldas, but did nots. I want you to be free from all the stuff they tried to set you up with. I love you Chantel! I don't want to be with anyone else. I have the same parental issues you have, it helps that I have a mother like mine; but it doesn't change who my biological father is. He didn't want me, and I was old enough to recognize it. Nothing changes that. I have separation anxiety whenever you're not right here with me. I try to pull it back; I'm not the emotional one. Drew is mister emotions. I don't know how Tracy puts up with him. My point in having you talk to your mother is so that you can let her evilness die with her. Release your anger and be done with it. You can't carry that anger around with you and think you will be ok. When we have kids I need you to be free to love them and me for that matter. Stop holding back because you've only had Cyrus. That was a long time ago, now you have us. And you've had us for some time now. When does the gravity of the past ten plus years sink in? You have love now Chantel. When do you accept that?"

I clapped my hands, "good points. I will open my mind to that. However, I can accept and acknowledge all the love that your family has shown me. I appreciate it, I do; but YOU still won't commit to me. You shrug your shoulders when I ask about the future. You've got too many rules. What if I do the same to you? Show you how it feels."

Derrick shook his head, "you don't get it. "

"No you don't get it! You wanna be free to throw your little tantrums whenever I'm not up under you. Seems like you need a stay at home wife."

"I never said I don't have issues; but I'm trying to be with you. Just being honest, this is the longest I've gone without sex ever. I feel like I'm dying, please don't refuse me tonight. I'm telling you what I need. I need you to tell me what you need."

"I need you to tell me, show me, make me believe that it's going to be me and you. Tell me that you're gonna love me five years from now. Tell me you're never gonna leave me! Let me know that what I feel at this moment won't be taken away because someone from your past pulls at your heart."

Derrick got quiet; as we rounded the corner my cellphone rang. It was Cyrus; he said Maria was in labor. He asked if I was going to the hospital. I looked at Derrick. I told Cyrus I'd call him right back. I told Derrick Maria was in labor. He closed his eyes for a minute then he said let's go. I called Cyrus back. He said baby Rosa was sick so Sherrell was staying home even though she didn't want to. Cyrus got in the truck extremely excited. He was talking so much Derrick was pulled into his conversation. You wouldn't know we were just arguing or having a deep conversation moments ago. Derrick reached for my hand and my heart melted. I squeezed his hand.

When we got to the hospital Maria was almost ready to push. DJ and Mario were pacing in the waiting room. I went in the delivery room and my grandmother told me to hurry to her side so that we

were out of the way. Both of my aunties were on either side of
Maria while my father was dying as Maria tried to break his hand.
I snuck and took a tasteful picture of the moment with my phone.
Seeing Maria in so much pain broke my heart cause she didn't
want this. Grandma said the baby would be here in a second. The
doctor got ready; I was silently having a fit. I couldn't imagine
going through any of this and not wanting my child afterwards.
When the baby slid out it changed from grey to green to pink to red
to normal. He had a head full of hair. They took him to the side
and cleaned him up then Maria started breathing again and a tiny
baby slid out. It wasn't breathing and emergency staff rushed in the
room and told us to get out. My father fell on my grandmother's
neck. His cry was so painful, I forgot about how angry I was with
him. I wanted whatever was hurting him to stop. Medical staff was
running into the room and a alarm was going off. Cyrus came
running when he saw us in the hallway. Then everyone came out,
there were too many of us in the hallway. One of the nurses begged
us to go in the waiting room. Maria's family wanted answers, but
we couldn't tell them anything. My daddy said they didn't know it
was twins. Everybody was pacing waiting to hear. Even with all
the emotion and nerves in the room my Auntie Tania's jealousy
was obvious. Fortunately my grandmother was on top of it and
pulled my aunt's collar. After that my aunt ignored my existence,
which was fine by me, cause I already had forgotten hers. I told
myself to watch her though, cause this time if she ran up on me I
had something for her.
The doctor came in the waiting room and we encircled her. She
said Maria was fine, she said twin A is healthy and strong. She said
twin B is very small and weak. She said fortunately the baby was a
fighter and they had a strong team working with her. Then the
doctor told my father to go be with his wife and their son. She said
once they're confident in my little sister's stability we could come
see the baby but no more than two at a time. My daddy let Maria's
family go in to see her. He stayed on my grandmother's neck
crying his eyes out. My grandmother snapped on him. She told him
to man up, everybody's eyes got big. She ripped him a new one,
she said everything I said to him. It was like he was hearing those
words for the first time with the way he responded to her. I stood
there in disbelief, but my siblings shared the same expressions on
their faces.

After awhile the doctor came and said the baby girl had a strong heartbeat. The delivery was stressful for her, so far she looked good. Her weight is really low she was barely three pounds. It took a lot of convincing but we convinced grandma Rosa to go to daddy's house and get some rest. I told DJ and Mario I would be back tomorrow. Derrick and I held hands walking out the hospital. Cyrus was on the phone telling Sherrell how much he loved her and the baby. It was one of those moments where you appreciate everything you have. I told Derrick that whole scene was so scary. He agreed. When we were alone in my room we put everything out there no holding back. I told him how much I loved him, why I loved him, and how much I hate being separate from him. Instead of telling me he loved me he explained the things about me that he loved that I didn't notice. He told and showed me how much he loved me. He told me he wants to marry me, but only when I'm ready no pressure. He said asking him about five years was so limiting because he wanted forever.

****

"I needed to go, and you can't even go right now. It's ok Derrick I'm gonna be with my family." I said trying to calm him down. I was on my way to my daddy's house to see the twins. Alexandria had been home for two weeks now and I finally squeezed a visit in to my schedule. Derrick keeps saying things are getting hectic but he's not explaining how or why he's on red alert. He was stressing about me riding with my brother. I told him Cyrus and I would be fine. I told him I wasn't going anywhere except to the house and then I'd come home. He didn't really have a choice in the matter cause we were already almost there. I didn't think it would be such a big deal, otherwise I wouldn't have left. When I got off the phone

I told Sherrell we couldn't sneak away for a girl's pamper moment. She looked a little disappointed but she also said she understood. Cyrus and I were talking business a long the way and he told me that the boys don't want to work with dad. He said at the hospital they were begging him to take them on. He wanted to know what I thought about that. I told him to talk it out with JoJo but I was all for it. He said daddy was speaking for them but they weren't under contract or even in agreement about anything he was trying to set up for them. They told him daddy knew the creative side, but he was lost on the business side. He said their projects weren't moving no matter what they did. I knew part of that had to do with my conversation with Malcolm, I smiled internally.

When we walked in the house my daddy was holding Alexandria, Ria for short. And Alexander was in the swing. My daddy was singing to Ria, and showering her with tons of love. Maria was laying down resting but not sleep in their bedroom. I took my precious baby sister from my father and I hugged her up. She was staring at my face like she was taking me in. Little Rosa was saying hi to the baby and giving her kisses. I took Ria with me as I went to check on Maria. She smiled real big when she saw me. She told me to come in and shut the door. She patted the bed next to her and she sat up. When I sat next to her she hugged me real tight and kissed my cheek. She thanked me for having her back and planting the seed for my father to get some act right. I sat there in disbelief that he told her. She said he told her that he felt everything happened with Ria the way it did so that God could get his attention and show him to listen to me. I frowned at her at first because the conversations I've been having with Yussef about God reflected God in a different light. Why would God punish their child because my dad's an idiot? But I let it go cause it motivated him to do the right thing. She said the hardest part right now is trying to convince my daddy to confess that he's doing right by her. She said he's embarrassed and ashamed. She said he goes to a support group on Tuesdays, which has been helping him, sort out his addiction. She thanked me again, she said now that he's come around he's been giving her his entire checks to use for the house as needed. And she said that with the money they've gotten they've paid all of their hospital bills and she's been able to take the needed extra time off work.

With her words I felt like I had a daddy again. We cried together, cries of reflection and happiness. Maria said my daddy has been helping with not just the babies but Adon too. She told me that life feels so much better and she feels like she can breathe. I was so happy for her. Then she told me that I had to somehow continue to play dumb though. I couldn't let on that she told me.

I played basketball in the backyard with Adon and he was getting really good. I kept looking over my shoulders though. I kept feeling like someone was watching us. It could've been any of the neighbors looking out their windows. When the feeling wouldn't go away Adon and I finished our game and then we went back inside the house. I called Derrick and I told him we were on our way home, and he said he would meet us at the apartment. We weren't on the freeway thirty minutes when the low tire pressure light came on in Cyrus' dashboard and then you could hear the tire. I got butterflies in my stomach. Cyrus told us to stay in the car, and he started changing the tire. A car pulled up behind us, and I looked at Sherrell and her eyes got big. It was two Mitigated Staff members. Darryl was on the phone confirming their identities, car make, and model as they approached. They were coming to help Cyrus with the tire. As they finished the tire Cyrus was thanking them, I was calling Derrick to let him know what happened. I started telling him when all of a sudden I heard pops and I saw sparks. I screamed as I saw both guys going down and someone grabbing my brother. I dropped the phone in my lap. I started to get out the car and Cyrus yelled at me telling me to stay in the car. Derrick was yelling something but I couldn't focus on the phone, all I could think about was my brother. A man's voice called out to me and instantly I knew it was Kevin. He was telling me to come out of the car we didn't have much time. Cyrus told me to get in the driver's seat and drive off. When I looked at Sherrell she was balling her eyes out and poor little Rosa was screaming cause she didn't understand what was going on. My door opened and the person grabbed me. I stood up in the doorway between the door and the car. Caprice had on all black and her hair was pulled back. "I got her let him go!" She said to Kevin.

He blew air, "yeah right! You know we got thirty seconds left before the next guys show up. Lets kill them and take her. Stick to the plan!"

"That was the plan before it involved Cyrus. Let him go!"

Kevin got angry; he twisted the gun he had pointed at Cyrus' head. "Caprice we don't have time for this. They all die, otherwise it will get too messy!"

Caprice gestured towards the car, "kill them, I don't care. But don't touch him! You want her, she said pointing her gun at me. I want him!"

"Caprice! Don't be heartless!" I said trying to calm my tears.

Caprice looked at me with evilness in her face. "DON'T YOU EVER TALK TO ME!"

"We don't have time for this!" Kevin barked, "GIVE HER TO ME!"

"GIVE ME HIM!" Caprice yelled back.

Kevin shot one of the windows out the car. I screamed, I didn't know if Sherrell or little Rosa were hit. Caprice was focused on Kevin, I hit her with the car door and jumped back in the car and shut my door. I reached over and started the car. Caprice broke the window and she started pulling me out the window. Kevin screamed at her to let me go. I guess he forgot about Cyrus cause lightning fast Cyrus jumped in the driver seat and stood on the gas. I don't even know what Cyrus was saying but he was yelling. Sherrell was trembling with her body over little Rosa. I asked her if she was hit and she said no. The baby was scared and screaming but she was fine. I started looking for my phone; it had fallen on the floor and a little under my seat. The call was still going but Derrick wasn't saying anything. "Derrick!"

His voice was deep and scary, "is everybody ok?"

His calmness scared me. "Yes!" I said crying my eyes out.

"Tell Cyrus to slow down and to take the next exit. Turn the dome light off."

I did as I was told, "how did you know the light was on?"

He didn't answer my question. "Tell Cyrus to turn left at the light, and then make a right on the corner. Tell him to run the red light." I told Cyrus to do as Derrick said. "Tell Cyrus to turn on his high beams and to drive slowly down the street. Tell him not to hit the breaks until he passes the stop sign then to come to a complete stop." The street was a business park and all the businesses were closed. It didn't look like anyone was on the street at all. Cyrus did what Derrick said. Four cars came out of nowhere. Derrick told us to go with them and he was almost there. The people in the cars looked straight ahead, they led us to a big building we stopped in the parking lot. Two of the cars had two people in them. In the parking lot Cyrus grabbed Sherrell and the baby, he was crying his eyes out.

The girl looked at her watch, "he's coming! We gotta move!"

"Who's coming?" I yelled .

"We gotta separate them." Another guy yelled.

"No!" Cyrus barked.

"Cyrus, listen to me." The girl said calmly but forcefully. "If you want your wife and child to live we gotta get them out first." A truck pulled up right in front of them. "They can't stay with you or she will kill them."

Cyrus kissed Sherrell and little Rosa. He begged the girl to guard them with her life. She assured him that that's what she was going to do and she had every intention of living. Sherrell was still trembling when she got in the car. They drove away and onto the street as if they were a regular car. "Where are you taking them?"

"Malcolm's house." Cyrus shook his head to agree, I threw my head in Cyrus' chest and I cried my eyes out. "Cyrus! You're up next!"

"Wait why do we have to separate?" I asked clinging to my brother for dear life.

"We have to get him out of here! Kevin will kill him!"

Everything started spinning. "Go!" I said as the next car was pulling up.

"No! I gotta make sure you're safe Chantel!"

"They got me Cyrus go! I'm going to see you in a few minutes." I put on my best brave face.

Cyrus still refused to go, then one of the guys said, "if you don't go, Kevin will kill both of you. We can move you around easier one on one. Your sister is safe with us!"

Cyrus hugged me so tight. He told me he loved me, and then he got in the car. I watched the car drive down the street. Then I saw a car round the corner, it sped up and came at the building full speed. One of the guys grabbed my arm and we ran into the nearest car. Everyone ducked while they drove away. I could only assume that car was Kevin, my driver sat up enough to see over the dashboard and he drove away. I sat on the floor silently crying my eyes out. When the car stopped they unlocked the doors, Derrick opened my door. His face was angry but concerned. When I reached out for Derrick my hand was shaking and I couldn't stop it to save my life. Derrick put me in his truck and then we pulled off. Derrick looked at me but he didn't say anything. His phone rang and he put it on speaker. Malcolm's voice came booming over the speaker.

"Sherrell and the baby are here! Pearla's gonna take them."

"Ok."

"ETA on Cyrus?"

"Dude has him."

Malcolm exhaled, "how is she?"

Derrick glanced at me again, "she's shaken."

"You wanna call me when you get there?"

Derrick exhaled, "I already know!" Derrick started cursing. "You couldn't get to her?"

Malcolm didn't speak right away. "I know son." He paused, "he already messed her up. She won't ever be the same. It's beyond our control. You gotta let her go."

Derrick kept cursing! By the look on his face I knew they were talking about Brooklyn. "Did you get to her? Talk to her mom, her family, anybody!"

"Her mother hasn't seen her in two days."

Derrick looked at me then he started cursing again. "Why didn't they say something? Maybe we would've seen this coming!"

"They don't know son." Malcolm paused. "You know this game. What's their next move? Think about it."

I guess it takes being a man to appreciate the way they were talking to each other. Derrick was yelling, and although Malcolm wasn't "*yelling*" the deepness in his voice was heavy and thick. I didn't understand everything they were saying but whatever he was saying it calmed Derrick and refocused him. Malcolm asked Derrick what Caprice actually thought she was going to do with Cyrus. Derrick blew irritated air and he told him he had no idea. When we got off the freeway and started up the hill, I recognized that we were going to Uncle Frank's house. At night the house and everything around it seemed darker. Derrick got out the car, he greeted the dogs. He brought me out the car. The dogs greeted me, and then Derrick sent them off. Uncle Frank met us at the door. He told Derrick to take me to the basement. There was a coat closet with a false door on the back. When Derrick opened it cool air hit my face. He turned on the light and then we walked down the stairs. I asked Derrick if Sherrell and the baby were going to be ok. He said Caprice wants Cyrus; he said they were going to deal with her before she goes after them. He told me he was going to go get Cyrus and I'd be safe there while he was gone. I got really scared and Derrick hugged and kissed me. He told me I was safe. The basement looked like a living room or a nice sized studio. I sat on the couch holding myself. Caprice was prepared to kill my niece how ruthless could she be? I saw no traces of my friend in her face at all. I guess I was stupid for ever thinking, no believing we were friends. The fact that she was so attached to my brother said that something about all of that was real. I sat on that couch afraid to move, the whole situation was unreal to me. Caprice had a gun in my face; Kevin had a gun to my brother's head. I tried to think about something else but all I could see was that gun. I don't know how long I was down there, but the door opened and Uncle Frank called me snapping me out of my freak out. I ran to the stairs, his eyes were iced over they weren't sad or mad. He handed me a phone. "Hello?"

"Baby, Kevin has your mother. What do you want me to do?" Derrick was calm but I could tell he was waiting for me to tell him how to respond.

My heart was pounding out of my chest. "Do you have Cyrus is he safe?"

"Yes, he's right here."

Then he put Cyrus on the phone. "Chantel!" I could hear that he was hanging on by a thread.

"Is she hurt?"

"I don't know. I don't know what to do. I'm stuck!" Cyrus' voice pleaded with me to be a voice of reason.

"She's going to die anyways, but she can't die like this." I heard myself say. "What can we do?"

Cyrus started crying, "I don't know! I don't know!"

"Let me talk to Derrick," he gave the phone back. "Derrick is it too much to ask to secure my mother?" I exploded in tears as soon as I heard the words come out of my mouth.

"O.." I heard rapid pops outside. Uncle Frank took the phone, then he pushed me and I stumbled backwards a few steps. He shut the door to the basement then I heard the closet door shut. My heart was pounding double time. My mind kept focusing on the loaded gun Kevin had pointed to my brother's head. I don't know how much time elapsed while I was sitting there. Uncle Frank broke my trance when he called my name again. I ran up the stairs, he put his hand on my shoulder and patted me. He told me Derrick was outside waiting for me. When I walked out the door Derrick was petting the dogs who looked at me when I stepped out the door and then awaited instruction from him. Derrick hugged me then he opened the door for the backseat my mother was sitting on the other side of the car wrapped in a blanket. She looked at me in a way I've never seen her look at me before. It was a look of love and concern. She asked me if I was ok. Cyrus was in the front seat with the same look on his face. When I sat down my mother threw her arms around me and my heart burned. We sat there holding each other and balling our eyes out and then for the first time ever my mother kissed me. I cried harder! All those times she's come to our apartment I didn't realize how thin she's gotten. I never paid her much attention. Then she said, "thank you." Derrick got in the car and then he looked at us. He smiled then he drove. Derrick broke the news to my mother that the guys who grabbed her were working for Kevin. My mother looked shocked, she sat quiet for a long time. We met Derrick's Uncle Jeff at an office in Sacramento. He gave Derrick keys and then we drove for almost an hour. We arrived at a house at the end of a cul de sac. It was an ordinary looking house. Derrick went inside then he opened the garage door. Cyrus drove the truck into the garage. The house was completely empty and clean. Derrick said this was one of his uncle's rental properties. Cyrus asked when Sherrell was coming. Derrick said she was already in transit, but it was gonna take a couple of days for her to get to us. Cyrus tried to relax a little. My mother sat on the floor watching Derrick while he was on the phone giving orders. She swallowed hard then she told me he was pretty intense. I smiled she patted the carpet next to her for me to come and sit next to her. I was reluctant for a second. Then I blew air, I told myself to suck it up. Our relationship turned a corner last night. "Carmen, we're gonna have a physician come check you out and set you up with your meds. How are you feeling?" Derrick asked my mother.

"I'm tired, but I'm ok." Then she exhaled, "thank you. I still don't understand what's going on, but I do know you kids didn't have to come for me especially when I'm knocking on death's door as it is."

Derrick looked at me. When I opened my mouth he walked away. I told her I didn't want her to die like that. Then she faced me and held my hands. Through huge sincere tears she started apologizing for everything. We sat on that floor crying and going back and forth. She even told me about the dishes I used to make that she really used to like. Cyrus said that JoJo was canceling my calendar for the next two months. I felt a little sick thinking about all the money I was going to lose. Cyrus said my PR rep was on top of everything. Derrick said Malcolm talked to grandma Rosa and convinced her to let him send her away. He said my family is going on a vacation, and that they were already in the air. He said

Mitigated was at our apartment packing everything up. I asked him how they got in the apartment. Derrick exhaled, Cyrus looked at Derrick. "I own the building."

Cyrus cut his eyes at me. "You knew about this?"

"Did you hear me ask him how they were inside? Of course I didn't know."

"Why is that a big deal?" Our mother asked.

"Derrick has had a hand in every aspect of our lives since they met. His mother owned the last place we stayed in. We both in some way work for his father. We were trying to stand on our own."

"So what was I supposed to do, deny your application because I owned it? It was a convenient coincidence."

"Then why didn't you mention it?"

"I don't report my business to you." Derrick shot back.

"Why does it matter? You're not going back there." My mother said.

"Right." I said letting it go. "Now we're all homeless."

"We'll have beds by tonight, but we'll need linens and necessities to make this space livable for the time being. Do you guys feel up to some shopping?"

"When is the doctor coming?" My mother asked.

"In an hour."

My mother exhaled, "I'll probably need to take my meds and then pass out. Which room will be mine?"

When she stood up she moved real slow. We looked at all the bedrooms. She told Derrick she wanted the smallest room since it was closest to the bathroom. Cyrus claimed the room with it's own bathroom. We said the room between their rooms would be for little Rosa. Derrick and I took the master suite. This house was all one level which was nice, four bedrooms and three full bathrooms. It had vaulted ceilings and the kitchen was the showplace. Everything in there was brand-new. We waited for the doctor as he left our bedroom furniture arrived. A full bed for my mother, a crib for the baby, and two California Kings. One for Cyrus and one for us. My mother used the blanket she had from Derrick's car to lay on her mattress until we came back with linens for her bed. Derrick told her we weren't expecting anyone while we were gone. He said if anyone showed up shoot first and ask questions later, then he laid a gun next to her bed. Seeing the gun reminded me that we were under hostile circumstances and not to get too comfortable.

Derrick's navigation system took us to the stores we needed to go to. He paid cash for everything. I was so happy about the toothbrush and toothpaste that I couldn't wait until we got home to brush my teeth. I brushed them in the parking lot with a bottle of water to rinse while Derrick and Cyrus loaded the pots, pans, plates, glasses, cooking utensils, linens, etc. etc. into the car. Then off the top of our heads we planned out our meals for the next five days. Derrick agreed to make breakfast, Cyrus was on lunch, and I was on dinner detail. We had two and a half carts full of things since we needed everything. I couldn't wait to get in the bed and sleep. When I brought Cyrus toilet paper etc. for his room, I saw that he also now had a gun. All of this ammunition around the house was making me nervous. When my mind kept flashing back on the car window that shattered after Kevin shot it out, I said nothing. Derrick secured the house and then when he laid next to me I felt at peace enough to go to sleep.

"How do you know she's still here?" I heard Kevin saying.

"They would've left if they were gone." Then she saw me. She snatched me out the back of the closet, "where's Cyrus?" She yelled at me.

"I don't know!"

"Chantel?" Kevin called out.

Caprice pulled her gun out and put it up to my head. "AW HECK NAW KEVIN! CYRUS ISN'T HERE! EITHER WE GO GET HIM OR SHE DIES RIGHT NOW!"

"CAPRICE! PUT THE GUN DOWN!" Kevin commanded.

Caprice started screaming and acting crazy. Then Kevin approached both of us, and I tried to run. But no matter how hard I run I can't get away. I run to a door, I open it and instantly I start falling. When I woke up Derrick was watching me. I told him how vulnerable I felt and he assured me that we were safe. I slept a lot better when Sherrell and little Rosa made the trip out to us. Derrick had them doing a lot of changing up and switches as they took the train, the bus, and then car service to Uncle Jeff who then brought them to us. Once I knew everyone was safe then I could finally get a good night's sleep.

Chapter 20

"Oh my God Chantel!" Her eyes rolled back in her head. "This tastes exactly the way I remember it!' My mother said chewing on her food.

I smiled a satisfied smile. My mother's appetite was far and in-between these days. She said food tastes like dirt, and every once in awhile she would have a taste for something and then food would be good to her. I was excited when she got excited about dinner. She was having a better day today, so this meal was a happy occasion. Derrick suggested that we sit at the table as a family and have our meals, just like they do on TV. Just before Sherrell and the baby arrived general furniture arrived for the house. TV's, the dinette set, and couches. It was awkward at first, but after the first couple of tries we got the hang of it. At the end of the week it started to feel more natural. I watched her eat to see if she was putting on a show, not that she's ever done that before, but there's a first time for everything. She was really eating and enjoying her meal so I was happy. I sat there for a minute taking in my family and I couldn't believe that my family included my mother. Since we're pretty much stuck together we have no choice but to sit and talk. Derrick and Cyrus go out in the backyard a lot and we hang out all over the house together. I never knew there was a humane side to my mother. She was purging so much information about herself. She told Sherrell and I about the night she met my father.

My father was playing at a local nightclub that she happened to go into one random night after work. She said from the moment she laid eyes on him she wanted him. She said he was so pretty, she couldn't believe that he was looking at her. She said she gave him a hard time cause at first she honestly thought it was a joke or a bet. Like he and his friends were trying to see who could get the most numbers or something. She said she left the club without giving him her number. When he showed up at her job the next day she said she still didn't believe it. She said he had to stalk her before she gave him her number. She said after their first kiss she was hooked. Anything my father wanted he could have. She said she loved him so much that when he asked her to have his baby she didn't scream no at him like she thought she would. She said she loved my daddy so much that when she stopped taking her pill she couldn't believe it. She said she never wanted to have kids, she said she wasn't cut out for the job. She never thought she would be on her own with two kids. She said before she could wrap her mind around the gravity of what happened with Cyrus she was pregnant with me. She said Grandma Rosa pitched in a lot to help with us cause my mom wanted to chase my dad around and she wasn't into the baby scene. She said she was back in that club watching him play and it wasn't even four weeks after I was born. She said she was trying everything over the counter to keep from getting pregnant, and it worked for a year. Then when she found out she was pregnant the third time she didn't tell my father. She worked extra hard to slink away and have her abortion. It was no use my father figured it out and that was the end for them. She was devastated and he left her with two kids she didn't want to have in the first place. She cried out loud wishing she could take it all back. When she said she wished she could have a do over with raising us, my heart bled cause I found myself wishing I grew up with this woman instead of the one that I did grow up with. I was so tired of crying, but being with my mother and feeling her hugs, etc. left me confused. I was enjoying her attention and affection, but I hated the circumstances surrounding it. At times I would just cry and cry. Sometimes at night Derrick would hold me as I cried my eyes out asking why everything had to be so messed up for me to FINALLY have my mother. Knowing that the clock was ticking made everything more urgent as well. We didn't have time to build up to things, we had to go in and go hard. When I told my mother how much I hated her she laid there agreeing with me like we were talking about someone else. She told me there was no way I couldn't hate her, then she asked me point blank what happened the last time Cyrus beat Reggie up. I told her how he would stare too long. Try to stay in the bathroom while I showered stuff like that. That night we were sleeping and he came in our room in only his boxers. I awoke to him kissing me and rubbing all over me. He covered my mouth trying to keep me quiet, but the commotion on the bunk bed woke Cyrus. I told her how Cyrus drug him out of my bed and beat Reggie until she came and stopped him. She cried while I told her that story, she said there was no excuse for the blind eye she turned to all of that. I appreciated that she didn't try to excuse her behavior or act like it didn't happen. I was finally getting the closure I needed. Something's don't change though, when we told her about our little sister, my mother listened but she couldn't honestly show loving concern for my father's family. She was still so hurt that he left her like he did. Her heart was hardened to him and she wished nothing good on him.

"Yeah Chantel, you put your foot in this meal." Cyrus said putting a fork full of pasta and shrimp in his mouth.

"Derrick have you heard from Pearla? Are they ok?" Sherrell asked.

Derrick blew air, "Kevin maybe crazy but he isn't stupid!"

"He's stupid enough to come after Chantel, who knows how far his stupidity goes."

"You've got a point, but they're fine for now. Malcolm has everyone on high alert. Kevin knows that messing with them will be a useless depletion of his resources. I don't know how many he has on his team, but he'll never be stacked up like Mitigated, so he has to use his resources wisely."

"How long before he finds us out here?" I asked

"He won't, you guys don't need to be worried about him. I'm here!"

"Let's change the subject." Cyrus said, "What's the first thing you wanna do when we get to leave?"

"See my momma." Sherrell said with a smile.

"Take Rosa to the park." Cyrus said smiling at his baby girl.

"Get back to work." I said

"Check in with my family." Derrick said

"Be happy that I'm still alive." My mother said, everybody got quiet for a minute. My mother looked towards the kitchen,

"Derrick what were you making earlier that smelled so good?"

Derrick smiled, "my specialty. Peach cobbler!"

My eyes rolled in my head. "Oh my goodness you guys are in for a special treat! He makes the BEST peach cobbler ever!" I exclaimed, "I had to make myself eat dinner cause all I wanted was a big bowl of cobbler with vanilla ice cream."

"Its that good?" My mother asked with a big smile.

"The crust is buttery and flaky, the peaches are sweet and cinnamony, but not too sweet. You guys I kid you not, you will never have anything like that ever again in your life."

Derrick smiled at my description of his dessert. "Thanks babe."

"No, thank you for making it." I smiled real big.

When we finished dinner, we let our food digest and then we dug into Derrick's cobbler. We sang Derrick's praises, and then they told me my description of his cobbler wasn't good enough. I kept getting a sinking feeling while watching my mother finish her meal. Her appetite was the best it has been since we got out here. I was scared and Derrick could see it all over my face. I made my mother take a bunch of pictures with us, I made her hug me. Then I'd close my eyes and put the imprint of her embrace on my mind. When she got tired, I followed her to her room, I was Chatty-Cathy. At one point she looked at me with huge sandbags under her eyes, she begged me to let her sleep. Reluctantly I sat there quietly watching her breathe. Then I got my notepad and pen. I wrote more poems and bridges for songs. My hand seemed to have a mind of its own. I wanted to wake her up and show her. I was afraid that tonight was all we had. Derrick stood in the doorway watching me, he didn't say anything. I knew he was there, but I didn't want to look at him. I was focused on her and I only inhaled and exhaled when she did. I thought Derrick would get tired and go away, but he didn't move. Then at about three my mother's eye popped open. She asked me why I was staring at her. Derrick chuckled and I told her I was concerned. She tried not to snap at me as she told me to get out of her room and she'd see me in the morning. Derrick lightly laughed at me as I walked out of the room defeated. I didn't relax until Derrick put his arms around me, and then I fell asleep fast and hard.

My mother pushed my shoulder, "wake up sweetheart!" she kissed my cheek lightly. Derrick stood next to her with a plate and a glass of orange juice. "I made you guys breakfast." My mother said with the biggest smile. Cyrus and Sherrell stood in the doorway with goofy smiles as they waited for me to wake up. I smiled, sat up, and Derrick put my plate in my lap. When I looked at my burnt toast, charred bacon, and I don't even know what that's supposed to be on my plate I smiled bigger. "You made this yourself?" Derrick gave me a goofy toothy grin, "she insisted on cooking it herself."

I swallowed big, "so what do we have? Bacon, eggs?" I looked at my mother she smiled real big. "Toast, and what's this?" I said pointing to the orange goop on my plate.

"Grits" she smiled.

"Oh, I see!" I said with a smile.

My mother was very proud of her plate, and everyone was looking at me with the same look. I swallowed my last taste of untraumatized taste buds then I took a fork full of food towards my mouth. Derrick flinched like he was reliving his experience, I swallowed again. My mother watched with the biggest grin. I put a fork full of the eggs and grits in my mouth. I caught myself before I went into a full out dramatic reflection of what was happening to me. Everything was salty, and then mixed with burnt flavor, and it looked like she took everything in the cabinet and put it in these grits. I tried to keep the nastiness of this food out of my expression, but when Cyrus and Sherrell fell out laughing I told my mother I was sorry as I swallowed the nastiness. Derrick turned his head as he belly laughed as well. "FORGET ALL YOU GUYS! I TRIED!" My mother said laughing a little herself.

"Thank you," I said getting out of the bed and hugging her. "At least now we know you didn't cook because you can't, not because you didn't want to."

"Thank you baby," she said hugging me back.

Derrick put my orange juice in my hand, "I'll take this. I'm gonna go have a bowl of cereal." He said taking my plate away.

"Chantel! You should've seen it! We were trying to be nice and suffer through it, and then Rosa put a fork full of food in her mouth." Tears were coming out of Cyrus' eyes he was laughing so hard. "She started crying!" Cyrus and Sherrell fell on my bed laughing.

"You kids ain't right!" My mother said still laughing. "I'll give my grand baby some cereal."

Cyrus started laughing harder. "I don't know that she'll trust eating anything from your hands again!" He couldn't breathe he was laughing so hard. "I'll feed her."

Then Rosa walked in the room holding her baby doll. "Come here baby." My mother said to Rosa. Rosa looked at my mother and frowned, and then she reluctantly walked to her grandmother. My mother sat on the bed, and I put Rosa in her lap. My mother apologized to Rosa for serving her nasty food. I brushed my teeth then we sat at the table happily enjoying our bowls of cereal.

My mother went to lay down, Rosa was watching her morning shows, and Cyrus and Sherrell disappeared into their room.

Derrick and I cleaned the kitchen while laughing about the breakfast my mother made. I asked him why he didn't try to save me. He said he did, but my mother insisted that at least one of her kids would like her food. We laughed some more, then my mother's physician called Derrick. He said he was two blocks away. Then Derrick's face turned serious. He asked me if I was going to be ok, he didn't think we had much time left with her. I told him I didn't know, I never in my life imagined getting along with her better yet, loving her. Derrick put his arms around me, and he told me that he was glad that we had this time together. The doctor came in the door like he did everyday with his briefcase full of meds, and things. The physician Truman was Derrick's cousin Jennifer's husband they were both doctors; Truman had a private practice while Jennifer worked for a big corporate hospital. Truman asked how my mother was last night and this morning like he normally does. I told him about her appetite last night, and that she attempted to make breakfast this morning. Truman wrote it all down and then he said they were all good signs. Then he knocked on my mother's door. He went in for a little while, when he came out his face was serious. We were in the living room watching TV with Rosa when Truman came in. He said he needed to move my mother to the hospital. It felt like he punched me. He said it wouldn't be long before she was gone. If she died in the house the coroner would have to come and there would be a lot of undue attention on the house. He said he had his nurse alert the hospital that she was coming. Derrick gave me sad eyes, and I looked at Rosa who had no idea of what we were talking about. I knocked on Cyrus' door, he slightly opened the door. I told him we had to take our mother to the hospital cause it was almost time. His face immediately dropped, and he said they'd be ready in five minutes. Derrick dressed little Rosa while I hurried in the bathroom to wash up. I only had two pairs of pants and two shirts, and pajamas. So it wasn't like I had to make huge decisions about what clothes I was wearing.

I put on my hat and shades and then I got in the car with Cyrus, my mother, and Truman. Derrick, Sherrell, and little Rosa followed us. I held onto my mother wishing in my heart that she didn't have to go. The hospital staff met us at the door with a wheelchair for my mother. Cyrus picked her up and put her in the chair. Truman talked to the nurses at the ER desk, and they advised him that they had a room set up for her already on the third floor. Truman told Cyrus and I to go with my mother and he'd tell Derrick where we were. When the nurses left, I took off my hat and glasses then I grabbed my mother's hand. I told her I didn't want to go back to being a motherless child. That made her cry harder, she apologized again for everything, and I apologized too. When Derrick came by the bed, she thanked him for coming to get her and for taking care of her like he has. She said she knew I was in good hands and she was happy that he was in my life. Derrick's eyes looked sad, then he sat down. Staff came in checked my mother's vitals, put the oxygen tubes on her nostrils, and they gave my mother an IV and medicine to make her comfortable. I didn't realize she was in pain; she was dealing with it quite well. Once the medicine kicked in she relaxed a lot. Derrick told Cyrus he would go to the waiting room with little Rosa so Sherrell could come in. Sherrell kissed my mother and then went to my brother to comfort him. My mother asked them if they were going to get married. Sherrell said they didn't need the paper their commitment to each other was solid. My mother smiled then she told them to go get married. She said it wouldn't change anything, but it would give them the paperwork to back up their commitment, Sherrell agreed. Then my mother told me not to be stupid. She told me to marry Derrick too. She told me to have as many pretty babies with Derrick's curly hair and dimples as I could stand to have. She said if my father would've taken care of her even a smidgen of the amount that Derrick does there would've been a whole tribe of us. I told her I was scared to have a baby. I wanted them, but I was afraid of me. She told me that dysfunction dies with her. She said I was already ahead of where she was and that I didn't have to worry about being a good mother. She said I was good to Rosa and she wasn't even my child, she reassured me that I would be a good mother.

While my mother was resting the new nurse came in to check my mother's vitals, etc. She looked at the three of us smiled and went back to doing her job. Then as she started to walk out she stopped

turned and looked at me. "Are you…?"

Butterflies hit my stomach, "NO! People ask me that all the time though." I said

"Oh" the nurse said then she walked out the room.

I looked at Cyrus, "what should I do? If I put my hat back on it will look suspicious."

Cyrus told me to stay put and he'd go talk to Derrick. When Cyrus came back in the room he said the nurse was telling her coworkers that you looked just like Chantel Shaw, and they laughed at her asking her why you would randomly be in Citrus Heights. I didn't know where we were, but as long as they didn't buy into it I relaxed a little. Derrick took really good care of little Rosa. She was all smiles as she played with the little toy structure they had in the waiting room with Derrick. I could hear her laughter before I entered the room. I thanked him for everything. He asked if I was hungry, and even though I had only eaten a bowl of cereal that morning, I wasn't hungry. Derrick made sure little Rosa ate and she wanted for nothing. I kissed him and thanked him so much. When I walked back to the room, I heard one of the nurses tell the other nurse that I wasn't tall enough to be Chantel Shaw. When little Rosa got restless Sherrell went out to put her to sleep and Derrick came in the room. Truman came in the room with sad eyes. He said my mother's heart rate was slowing and then he explained what was going to happen. I squeezed Cyrus hand while Truman was talking; I wanted to scream to the top of my lungs. Derrick switched places with Sherrell and we said our goodbyes to my mother as she took her last breath. My brain felt like it was fizzling, I sat down and cried my eyes out. Truman called the time of death, and then he told us he'd be right back. Cyrus was crying a deep painful cry, and Sherrell was rubbing his back while she cried as well. Truman came back walking real fast; he said the nurses were obsessing over whether or not I was really me. He said they were on the Internet looking at pictures of me. He said he didn't know how long they had been at it, but he said the whole hospital was buzzing with the news of me being there. He said he would deliver my mother's ashes to Malcolm's house, he didn't think it was a good idea for us to stay too much longer. Cyrus took Sherrell and I by the hand and he told us it was time to go. I kissed my mother's cheek one more time; she looked like she was sleeping. I told her I'd see her when she woke up and then we'd have all the time in the world together. Then I walked with Cyrus and Sherrell. When we walked out of the room, majority of the staff was looking at us. I put my eyes on the floor and I followed Cyrus' lead. Derrick grabbed my hand with little Rosa in his other arm. Derrick gave the baby to Sherrell and then he took out his phone. He told someone on the phone we have been compromised. My heart started beating. I didn't know what happened to make him say that, but I was waiting for instructions. When we were close to the house he told us to grab essentials only. He said we weren't coming back to this house. I grabbed my notepad and all my song doodles. We grabbed all the diapers, wipes, etc. for Rosa. Derrick went in my mother's room I assumed to get the gun he left with her whenever we went to the store. We got back in the car then we went to a house. A woman was standing outside with her garage door open. When Derrick pulled in he said hello and gave her a hug and kiss. Derrick introduced her as his cousin Jennifer. She told us to transfer to the SUV next to us while Derrick was tinkering under the hood of his truck.

This truck was brand new, "when did it get here?" Derrick asked Jennifer about the truck.

"A few hours ago."

Derrick walked around the truck. He lifted the hood, got on the ground looked underneath, and then he walked around the truck checking everything. Then he got on his phone, and then he hung up. He thanked his cousin for everything and then he got in.

"Derrick is everybody in your family white?" Cyrus asked.

Derrick smiled, "on my mom's side most of them, not all as you know."

"Seems like we keep meeting new white people. Your family must be pretty big."

"Yeah, Poppa and Nana, my grandparents, had a tribe; and then the tribe grew. We used to get together every summer until Poppa died. We're just an American family, we don't see color." Derrick said matter of factly.

"How were we compromised?" I asked.

"Caprice is my guess. Kevin was a field worker; he only knows what we showed him. Caprice was closer cause she had worked with us longer. We were suspicious of her once the goon came up dead. Some things weren't adding up with her. I'm pretty sure Kevin has it out for her since they didn't get you when they could've. She's probably all around rogue at this point. That also means she doesn't care about anyone else she wants Cyrus and she'll take out anyone who stands in the way of that. Kevin will stand down for a little bit. He likes to pop up, he's not much of a chaser."

"What does she think she's supposed to do with me? I told her we were done!" Cyrus said completely angry.

"Why does Toya act the way she does, why is Kevin obsessed with my woman? Sometimes you can't ask crazy people why. When they lose it, they lose it." Derrick said

"Where are we going?" Cyrus asked

"Up North! Just sit back and ride." Derrick said as he drove on. We drove about eight hours maybe a little less. When we hit Portland, Derrick turned on the Navigation and took us to a Post office. He came out with a small box that had keys, cash, a garage door opener, and cell phones in it. He gave us each one, he said we could call our families on these phones, and not worry about traces on them. Again we pulled up to a random looking house this one had a upstairs and a downstairs. When Derrick pulled into the garage he told Cyrus to come with him as he secured the house, he told us to stay in the car. Sherrell immediately called her mother. I could hear her mother screaming into the phone. She said she was worried sick about her. She said police came to her house questioning her about Cyrus and Derrick. Her mother said she went to our old apartment right after the police left looking for her and the apartment was completely empty. She said it was move in ready for the next tenants. She said someone shot up my car and Sherrell's. She said the police had them towed or at least she thought they were police. She said Pearla would only tell her that we were ok, but wouldn't say anything more than that. Sherrell looked at me like she didn't know what to say. I shrugged cause I didn't know what to tell her. Sherrell told her mother that one of my fans has become obsessed with me, and it wasn't safe for us to stay there anymore. When Sherrell told her mother that Malcolm was taking care of us, her mother calmed down a lot. Then her mother asked how she could reach her, she said this phone came up as unknown on her caller ID. Sherrell told her she didn't know, she didn't even know how long she'd have that phone. She promised she'd call as often as she could. Then she let her mother talk to Rosa. Rosa got very excited when she heard her grandmother's voice. When Derrick and Cyrus came back out to the car, Derrick looked at the phone then he looked at me. I told him she was talking to her mother. Derrick looked at Cyrus; he closed his eyes and shook his head. Then Derrick said we needed food for the house. He said this house had furniture already. Cyrus was jumpy and quiet, when I asked him what was up he looked at me. He had sad eyes, but he didn't say anything. I know he was sad about just losing our mother last night, but this sadness made me think it was something else. When he wouldn't speak, I walked away. I started picking out apples, and other fresh fruit. It made me a little sad to keep checking myself whenever I reached for something I thought would be good and healthy for my mother. I felt heavy and like I was in a movie that someone just hit pause on. I was stuck and tears were pouring out of my eyes. I was so happy I had my shades; I didn't want to scare anyone. When Derrick touched my shoulder he turned me around and put me in a bear hug. I buried my head in his chest and cried my eyes out. He rubbed my back and told me it was ok. Cyrus switched places with Derrick, and Derrick and Sherrell got everything else we needed. When Derrick was out of eyeshot, Cyrus whispered in my ear that Caprice may find us out here. He said Derrick told him to be prepared for her to pop up. Cyrus' voice got heavier as he said he's going to have to do what he has to do.

****

"Cyrus Daniel Shaw do you take this woman to be your wife?" The judge said.
"I do" Cyrus said with the biggest smile.
"And Sherrell Latasha McCants do you take this man to be your husband?" The judge said.
"I do" Sherrell said with a smile as big as Cyrus'.
When the judge pronounced them as husband and wife little Rosa clapped as her parents kissed. Derrick and I held hands and smiled at each other. I always thought if I wasn't working I would go crazy. I always thought I had to be on the go, but being under Derrick these past few months has been wonderful. We've had a couple of minor disagreements but nothing life threatening. Derrick has been great helping me with all the emotions that keep popping up out of nowhere regarding my mother. He shared with me how he dealt with his father's passing, I could see him opening up to me in a totally different light. Only a fool would doubt his love for me after all of this. I could see how I was holding back this whole time. I know I told him I was waiting for him to push me away. I was holding on to him pushing me away so hard that I convinced myself that I let go when I really hadn't. I stared at Derrick with the biggest smile on my face. This is the face of the

man who loves me. What did I do to land a hottie? A real man, and deals with me like a real man should. He looked at me then he kissed me. We picked up takeout from this Italian food place not too far from the house. We had little Rosa sleep with us so she wouldn't bother her parents in the middle of the night. We said as soon as this whole thing was over they would have a ceremony for our families.

The next morning Sherrell called her mother and told her that she got married. Whenever Sherrell called home Derrick would look at Cyrus, and Cyrus' eyes would turn sad for a moment. Derrick told me that he's sure Caprice was watching Sherrell's house. Once she was aware of the wedding we needed to be ready. After a week of everybody being extremely jumpy we started mellowing out.

****

"Yeah?" Derrick sat up at the knock at the door.

Sherrell and Cyrus walked in the room with the lights out, "Rosa has a 104 fever," Sherrell said with her voice shaking.

Derrick turned on the light next to the bed. My poor baby was red and lethargic, she wasn't feeling well earlier in the day. Derrick rubbed his massive hands over his face pulling himself out of his sleep. Then he looked at Cyrus, "you ready?"

"The house is ready, I'm ready." Cyrus said looking stressed.

Derrick got up, "Sherrell. I'm gonna take you guys to the hospital. You're here on vacation, give them all your accurate information from California. Chantel you and Cyrus are going to stay here." Then he looked at me. "Pay attention!"

"Ok," I said kissing him goodbye. "Cyrus you know where all the bread boxes are, you got this." He said looking him in his eyes.

Derrick picked up little Rosa and she rested her head on his shoulder. I watched out the window as the truck went down the street and around the corner. Cyrus was pacing around the house. He triple checked all the doors and windows, I made breakfast. Derrick called every ten minutes to make sure everything was still quiet. Cyrus and I were sitting at the table eating bacon, grits, toast, and eggs in our mother's honor. I put a drop of red food coloring in the grits to make Cyrus smile. When he sat at the table he looked at me then he smiled really big. We started laughing at the recollection of that breakfast, I couldn't breathe I was laughing so hard at Cyrus' imitation of Derrick trying to swallow those horrible grits.

Then you know that feeling when the house is sealed and then a door opens? Cyrus' eyes went to the garage door. I saw light from the side door in the garage and then it closed. Cyrus told me to go under the stairs. I shook my head no, Cyrus stood up and took our plates and put them in the sink. He quietly walked back to me grabbed me by my arm and he made me go. We tiptoed to the stairs then he opened the door to the storage area, I wouldn't go in until he went in. I heard light taps on the doorknob. Cyrus went in the first door then he went in the second one that led to a small section kind of under the house. The second door wasn't obvious. It was completely dark in there, I was trying not to breathe too hard when I heard the squeak of the floor board right in front of the staircase. I wished I could see Cyrus' face, I couldn't tell how he was feeling. I was happy I was in front of the door though. He couldn't jump out and think I would sit in the closet while he went out there. I know he was probably thinking he could talk some sense into her and get her to stop this. When I knew as soon as she realized he wasn't going with her she'd probably try to kill him. The part that made me sad is that I knew Derrick had no intentions of letting her go once he had her. I heard the floorboard again; I assumed she came back down the stairs. I couldn't tell where she was, but when Derrick called my phone again it wasn't on silent. I grabbed it and turned it on, but I didn't speak into the phone. I heard the door open to the storage under the stairs. I could hear movement outside of the door. Cyrus started moving, and I grabbed his hand. We heard the board squeak again but it kept squeaking. Then I heard movement in the storage area again. It was only a matter of time before she found the door. This was it; I could hear her hand moving over the door, I closed my eyes. Then I heard the garage door open. Why would Derrick bring Sherrell and the baby here, if he knows why I haven't spoken a word? I heard the storage door close then I heard movement in the storage area. I deflated cause she was in the way of Derrick getting to me. It was quiet then I heard her hands on the wall then the door opened she reached in and pulled me out. She put her hand over my mouth and I bit the mess out of her hand. "LET ME GO!" I yelled.

Cyrus crawled out, "Caprice let her go!" He yelled.

"CYRUS!" Caprice exclaimed.

The storage door opened and my heart dropped cause it wasn't Derrick, but I did see a gun. I backed away from the guy. Caprice didn't appear to know who it was either. She put her arm around my neck and a gun to my head, and she told us to go. It was awkward getting out of that space especially with her holding me like that. She made Cyrus go first then me while she held on firmly to my neck. Once my eyes adjusted to the light I realized I was looking at Dude. He had a gun to Cyrus' head. I was confused, he looked angry and crazy. "What's going on?" I said through tears. Caprice was just as confused, "Dude? What are you doing here?"
"WHAT ARE YOU DOING HERE? I came here for her!"
"ME?" I said in disbelief.
"Her?" Caprice said matching my surprise.
Dude had Cyrus positioned like a shield to cover him. "Yes, its nothing honorable you understand." He smiled, "but I always wanted to do a star."
"Dude! I will kill you!" Caprice barked.
"At least the feeling is mutual, I'm not leaving without her. We don't have time for this song and dance. Move your head to the left just a smidgen more so I can kill you, handle my business, kill her, and be gone."
"Whatever Dude!" She said keeping her gun at my head, "I don't believe you!"
"I don't care what you believe! You're wasting my time!" Dude said looking for a way out of the situation.
Cyrus' eyes were red and fixed on Caprice. Dude and Caprice were looking for ways out. "I can't believe you actually came here!" Cyrus was angry.
"I need to talk to you." She pleaded.
"We have nothing to talk about. How could I forgive the way you've endangered my family? You know how much family means to me!"
"Cyrus…"
Dude interjected, "seriously you guys! We don't have time for emotional conversations. I don't know where Derrick is but I'm not stupid enough to be here when he gets back!"
Caprice looked around the room, "Cyrus come so we can talk. I'm gonna kill him real quick and then we can discuss everything. I

know you married her probably because of the grief you're going through right now, but you love me! We're gonna go away from all of this." She said still looking around.

"After you kill everybody right?" She blank stared at him, "what could I possibly want with you after you kill the people I love the most?"

"You want me! You'll want me!" She said moving around.

"And when I don't?"

"But you do, I'll do it! I'll have as many babies as you want. We can be a family, just come with me."

"How could I love someone who threatens my family?"

"We are a family Cyrus!"

"As touching as this is, I DON'T HAVE TIME FOR THIS!" Dude said moving backwards with Cyrus.

Caprice's grip got tighter, "STOP MOVING! STOP IT! I SWEAR TO GOD I'M GONNA KILL YOU DUDE!"

"This make you mad?" Dude said kind of dancing with Cyrus in front of him,

Caprice screamed then she loosened her grip enough for me to move my arm up. I hit her arm, which she wasn't expecting, and then I hit her arm with the gun. She squeezed the trigger and she shot the wall. Cyrus eyes were wide it looked like he wasn't breathing. I grabbed her hand that held the gun. This crazy girl was strong but I wasn't going out without a fight, and I could tell she wasn't expecting me to fight back. I dug my nails into her wrist while pushing her hand away. I remembered how she laid Reggie and Shameless out. She hit me with her left fist once, then twice in the same spot. When she started to come for the third hit I head butted her, and she dropped the gun. I went for the gun, and Dude shot her. His gun had a silencer on it. Caprice hit the wall and slid.

"CAPRICE!" Cyrus yelled before he could pull it back.

Her shoulder was bleeding but she was alive. I put my gun on Dude, "STAY BACK!"

He smiled and put his hands up, and then he handed his gun to Cyrus. "Finish her!"

Cyrus started balling and shaking his head. "Baby! Please come!" She said with tears streaming down her face.

"Think about it!" Dude said to Cyrus, "it's her or your wife and child!"

"Does she have a another gun or something?" I yelled still looking at Dude.

She had three more guns, clips, chloroform, handcuffs, and a knife. Dude's cellphone rang, he smiled at Caprice. "You know what this means!" He answered the phone. He told the person on the phone that Caprice was shot and bleeding on the wall, but she was alive. He looked at Cyrus and I, and then he agreed. His face turned cold and his eyes turned black. When he got off the phone he looked at me. "Chantel and Cyrus go upstairs. Go to your rooms, turn on the TV or something but don't come back down here." His voice was strong and deliberate.

"Cyrus! I loved you from the moment I saw you!" Caprice said through tears. "Kevin killed my sister, because I let you get away!" She cried, "You are all that I have left! I'm sorry for killing our child. If I had to do it all over again, we'd be just like Brandy and Paul. Married with a baby and none of this!" I took Cyrus' hand to make him come with me. "I was the first woman you wanted to marry. I know you married her because of your mom. Remember you told me it was only me. I LOVE YOU!"

"Just not enough to love all of me. You would've killed my

daughter. MY BABYGIRL! I CAN'T FORGIVE YOU FOR

THAT!" Cyrus said as he let me pull him up the stairs.

"Cyrus! I LOVE YOU!" She said, "Please tell me you love me too! PLEASE!"

When we got to the top of the stairs Cyrus looked back and said, "NO! I CANNOT LOVE SOMEONE WHO HATES ANY PART OF ME! My daughter and my sister are parts of me! My blood runs through them! Hurting them is like killing me!" I pulled Cyrus in my room and then I turned on the radio.

****

By the time Derrick brought Sherrell and little Rosa home Dude had the downstairs sparkling clean. The spot where Caprice shot the wall had been patched up and painted. I could only see it because the paint was still drying. At first they told Sherrell to bring the baby in our room and to wait for them to say it was ok to come out. They left for a long time and when they came back Derrick and Dude made dinner. I was looking at everything when I came downstairs. Derrick was

watching but he didn't say anything. The scary part is that he and Dude were completely unfazed while the three of us were completely shaken. Derrick said we were going home in the morning. I asked him where home was, and he said one of Malcolm's buildings. I asked him what about Kevin and he said they were working on him, but without Caprice his reach was going to be a lot shorter. When I asked him if Caprice was really dead, he stared at my eyes. When he started to open his mouth to respond I cried harder, and I touched his face and I closed my eyes. He hugged me tightly and kissed my head. We packed our few things and we piled into the truck to go home. We put movies on for Rosa in the rear row while Sherrell pretty much held and kissed Cyrus all the way home. Cyrus was really quiet, but none of us were talking all that much. When we drove through Citrus Heights, Derrick's cousin Jennifer told him she had his truck shipped to Malcolm's. Derrick told us that we were stopping at Sophia's to have dinner. When we got there Sophia greeted us at the door. I thought I looked normal but when I saw her, her eyes glaze over with sadness, I knew I didn't look like I was ok. She gave me a huge hug and she did the same with everyone. Then she told us to go to the banquet room. When we walked in JoJo, Jeff, Randi, and Sophia's daughter Sabrina were in the room. Everyone stood up immediately and came to hug us. Which only made me cry more. Sabrina was instantly in love with little Rosa. Everyone was quiet at first not really knowing what to say. The fact that we left as five adults and came back as four was heavy enough; let alone wrapping my mind around what happened to Caprice. "So when do we get back to work?" I asked trying to break the silence. Everyone erupted into lively chatter. JoJo said they had to give something, so my PR rep spun the fact that my mother was dying into the reason for my absence. JoJo said my fans were very sympathetic about my loss. With that said he suggested counseling for Cyrus and I. Cyrus seemed receptive to the idea, but I rolled my eyes I didn't want to be judged. Derrick said his parents

separately go from time to time and he can see how it's helping them. I let the idea of Malcolm opening up to anyone sink in. JoJo said I had another month and a half downtime so I could definitely make use of the time. I didn't say anything cause it felt like they were telling me I needed it more than just making a suggestion. Cyrus on the other hand took the information readily, he and Sherrell seemed like they were gonna jump up and run there right away.

Sophia brought in dish after dish. We had a nice spread. Everything was delicious! Then she reminded Derrick about her parent's anniversary party in a couple of weeks. When Darryl came he pulled Jeff, JoJo, and Derrick to the side. He looked like he was bringing Derrick up to speed on a lot of things. Derrick's face was always serious so I couldn't tell if it was good things or bad. The way they were talking it seemed like they were moving things around. Sophia sat next to me taking Derrick's chair. "So what do we think about the woman in my little brother's life?" She said looking at Randi. Her face was blank and I didn't know where the comment was coming from.

Everyone at the table looked at Sophia. "I like her?" I said not knowing what to say.

"Randi, you've been around for some time now." She blank stared at Randi.

Randi stirred in her chair a little bit, "yes I have."

"You love my brother?"

"Yes I do." She said turning a little red from the embarrassment. Sophia looked at me, "there's no point in asking you. You radiate love all over you."

"I do?"

"Only a fool would question you about it, but you've been sprung off Derrick since the beginning so it's not new." She said nonchalantly. Sophia grinned while raising an eyebrow. "Both of you should know that if you're here that speaks volumes about your relationship with my family. I don't fall in love with everyone and I will let you know if I don't like you."

"Sasha's the same way." I said

"That's right, I raised my baby to be real and to leave that fake stuff to the phony females. Glad to know she hasn't forgotten her roots." Sophia smiled

Sabrina had Rosa cracking up, her laughter made us laugh. I looked at Derrick's face and he looked stressed. He tried not to look at me, but I was watching him. Something told me that the warm and fuzzy feeling we had was about to be strained. We went to Malcolm's when Malcolm walked out the house with Derrick he had his hands in his pockets. I jumped out the car and ran to Malcolm, he looked at me like I was crazy. Which in Malcolm language said "girl what is wrong with you?" Then I threw my arms around him and squeezed him tight. Malcolm stood there being hugged his body was stiff. "Thank you Malcolm! Thank you for everything you've done for me and my family."

I looked at Derrick and he was smiling at Malcolm, Malcolm looked like he wanted to be anywhere but in my arms. "Ok! Ok! That's enough." He said wiggling out of my arms.

I kissed his cheek then I got in the car. Malcolm blank stared at Derrick who was cracking up at his father's reaction to my affection. We got in the car and drove down the skyline hills and around the city to Harrison St. We pulled up to a building that had a lobby and multiple floors. The garage was gated; Derrick parked next to his truck. Derrick gave the keys to the new truck to Cyrus. Then he pointed to the other keys, he told them they were in unit 4B. Cyrus said thank you as he carried little Rosa to the elevator. We were across the hall in 4F. I hugged Cyrus and Sherrell goodnight in the hallway then we went our separate ways.

****

"Chantel, you didn't have to come all the way out here just to fly back with us." Grandma Rosa said hugging and kissing little Rosa to death.

I smiled, "that's what your lips are saying, but your actions are showing something completely different." I laughed.

"Besides we haven't done anything with just us girls." Sherrell said.

Grandma Rosa looked at BJ and Ronald. "Do you feel like you're alone with them in tow?"

"Pretty much, they give us space to talk or whatever. BJ has been around for some time now. Derrick has to be there for his mother's event tomorrow or else he'd be here."

"What event?" My daddy asked.

"She's having a fundraising event for her school. There's going to be all kinds of celebrities there."

"Why aren't you going, you could network."

I sighed, "I'm not ready for all of that yet." I felt heavy in my chest. "Too many people," I swallowed. "It would be too much!" I looked down as my eyes betrayed me and watered up.

Auntie Tania sucked her teeth, while Maria and my Grandmother gave me sad eyes. "It's ok sweetheart take as much time as you need." My grandmother said rubbing my back.

"Don't tell her that! The world doesn't stop moving because you're going through something. Show business is business, you better find a way to push through and get the job done! You're going to mess around and end up being a has-been!"
"Tania stop that!" My grandmother said.

"I'm just telling her the truth. She hasn't been working this whole time. Her career could be over and you guys wanna be over here holding her hand like it's ok! It's not ok, SUCK IT UP!"

Sherrell shot me eyes to say she'd get on her if I wanted her to. I could see all her Oakland attitude begging to come out. I gestured with my hand to tell her I got this. "So that we're clear! My business is being handled! Trust Cyrus isn't here because he's also handling business for me. Maybe you didn't notice, but even with all the drama going on in my life my sophomore album has dropped, sales are through the roof, my songs are in heavy rotation on the radio, as well as my videos. My business is being handled. I know you don't care, but I just lost my mother! I'm not going to run around the country with my heart hurting like this. I may decide to give this all up and focus on working behind the scenes. The spotlight is ok for awhile, but I can't see spending my whole life under a magnifying glass just so you can say that's my brother's daughter on the screen."
"Chantel you are so stupid! If you're not in front of the screen who would want you?" She spit at me.
I cleared my throat. "Maybe you haven't noticed, whether I'm singing them or not, I write hits. Yes, being in front of the screen you get a lot of notoriety. Honestly, as long as the fat checks keep hitting my checking account I don't need to be in front of the screen. That's what you don't seem to get. I don't expect a high school drop out who only got by on her looks to understand any of that. Speaking of which, how are you surviving now? Your 'hey-day' has long past!"
Tania started laughing that; you crossed a line laugh, as she stood up. My grandmother told her to sit down, but she shook her head and kept coming. "You are so disrespectful, and it looks like I'm gonna have to embarrass you in front of everybody!" She said coming for me.
"Leave Chantel alone!" Adon yelled, as she got closer to me.

I stood up and moved away from the table, she paid no attention to my stance etc. Everyone was yelling at her telling her to sit down. BJ and Ronald looked at me and I put my hand out to tell them I got this. They sat at their table watching looking like they were ready to jump up if things got out of control. I could tell by the look on her face she just knew she was going to handle me like she used to and I would be embarrassed especially since Cyrus wasn't here to protect me. When she crossed the invisible line I drew on the floor I charged and I kicked her in the middle of her chest, which sent her flying backwards. As she was falling I was still coming. I kept tagging her face! I heard someone say, "oh my God Chantel!" I could tell everyone was in shock. Auntie Tania wasn't expecting any of this from me she laid there covering her face while I punched her hands. "QUIT DISRESPECTING ME! I'M NOT THAT SAME LITTLE GIRL WHO WOULD TAKE YOUR CRAP JUST BECAUSE YOU FEEL ENTITLED TO DISH IT! I WILL MESS YOUR LIFE UP IF YOU EVER DISRESPECT ME AGAIN!" My cousin Larry gently picked me up off his mother. He had a goofy grin on his face.

My auntie scooted backwards as she looked at me in disbelief. She had knots coming up on her head and face, she was embarrassed and didn't say anything. My grandmother and Maria smiled at me while trying to contain their approval of how I handled her.

Sherrell gave me a high-five then she shot Auntie Tania a look.

"Chantel! That's still your aunt." My daddy said.

I rolled my eyes, "she's not my aunt!" Then I locked my eyes on him. "Are you seriously going to sit here and side with her? You know she was wrong!"

"I'm saying that you should show your aunt respect, because she's your aunt."

"Daddy seriously? She is disrespectful and she has no love or respect for me as her niece. I don't care how old you are, you have to give respect to get it. Why do you defend her? Does she speak your thoughts?"

"Sometimes she does." He said matter of factly.

Maria inched her chair away from my father. "What about today?" I said

He sighed, "I know you lost your mother, but you guys weren't even close."

"Daniel!" My grandmother said like she wanted to take him over her knee.

My eyes filled up with tears. "You are such a disappointment!" I blew air to talk, "she was still my mother. And you only get one! Maybe when you die I shouldn't feel anything because you're a selfish jerk! That woman loved you and would've done anything for you. Matter of fact she did. She had your baby twice when you knew she didn't want children. Then because you don't get your way not only do you leave her, you left us with her! You moved on to your next victim. You have the nerve to sit there and talk about my mother like she wasn't nothing because she didn't take your crap!"

"How are you defending her? You know she hid you guys from me! You know I was looking for you guys! She was the evil one!"

"None of that was right, however you played a part in that too! You better hope that Maria never gets tired of your crap, cause I'll make sure she takes you for everything!"

"You're blaming me for your mother's behavior?"

"I'm blaming you for yours! And the fact that even after her death you have the nerve to sit there and talk about my mother like she was nothing! Say whatever you want about her, but she loved you, and proved that she would do anything for you! You show my mother respect by respecting the fact that she's my mother and I have the RIGHT to grieve her for however long I need to!"

"Are you going to disrespect our mother like that?" DJ said his eyes were red.

"What? No! Maria is my wife!" My daddy said.

"Yeah but you threatened to leave her just like you did Chantel's mother." DJ said

My daddy looked at Maria, "you told him that?" He was angry.

"No, I didn't say anything." Maria said

"You can thank your sisters. They told me everything." DJ said

My father looked at both of his sisters and you could see how hurt he was. "You guys told him that?" His voice shook, both of their eyes hit the floor.

"Wait a minute!" Mario said standing up. "You left their mom, why?"

"Because she got rid of her pregnancy. Because he was more than likely doing the same stuff he does now lay up on his butt and write songs all day!" DJ said, his eyes were on fire.

"You left her with two small kids with no help cause you didn't get your way?" Mario said getting angrier.

"Chantel's mother was a piece of work! You can't blame him for leaving her!" Auntie Tania spit.

"WHY CAUSE SHE DIDN'T TOLERATE YOUR CRAP! SAY ONE MORE THING ABOUT MY MOTHER! ONE MORE THING! NOT EVEN YOUR SON WILL SAVE YOU!" I barked.

"Carmen got the short end of the stick, I just wish that she would've let me help her." My grandmother said touching my hand to calm me.

"So! You were going to do the same thing to my mother?" DJ asked looking his father in his eyes.

"Killing my child is a deal breaker for me." My father said feeling right in his stance.

DJ looked at Maria, "mami I told you, you deserve better!"

"You told her? You've been talking about me behind my back?" My daddy looked at his sons and then Maria. "A real man says what he needs to say!"

DJ sat up and looked my father in his eyes. "Like you've ever been a real father to me. Thank God for Cyrus and Derrick! Otherwise I might not know what a real man looks like!" My father looked like his face cracked. "The most ambitious we've ever seen you be is when Chantel came around and you were pushing her to get her career going. You let your sisters run your house from across the country and they don't even respect you or your children. You let Auntie Tania put her hands on Chantel when she was wrong and you defended her. Larry, you shouldn't have interjected. You let your momma walk over there talking mess, and then she crawled her behind back over here where she should've never left. It's none of her business how Chantel conducts her business. Chantel being a better daughter than you ever deserve is going to take care of you no matter what and they know that. And as long as you're taken care of so are they. Your dumb behind will defend them to the death even when they're wrong. I'm telling you now, if either one of them ever rises up to my mother I will not hold back because they're a woman and especially because they're my aunt. You are too old to be acting this way!" He said to Tania, "and you do nothing! You sit there looking pathetic! I hate that I have your name. You disappoint me at every turn!" He said to my father.

"You will not sit here at this table and talk to me like this!" My daddy barked.

"What does it matter to you? You're not footing the bill. And even if you were, it would be with the money from Chantel! What you gonna do? I know you're not crazy enough to run up on me!" DJ said like he was wishing my father would say otherwise.

"DJ please! I don't want you guys to fight!" I said

"No! No!" My father said standing up. "You think you a man now! Let me show you how a man gets down!" My father said walking around the table.

BJ and Ronald smiled like this was going to be entertaining. Then the waiter walked into our private room, "is everyone's food ok? Can I bring you anything else? A dessert menu perhaps?" He asked oblivious to what was going on in the room.

"No, can you bring the check." My grandmother said. DJ stood up as my father approached him. "Seriously Daniel! Estoy muy decepcionada! (I'm so disappointed!) Este es tu hijo! (This is your son!) Esto es lo que quieres ensenrle? (This is what you want to teach him?) Cuando un hombre se enoja utilize su puno! (When a man gets angry he uses his fist!) Basta! (Stop it!)"

"No, es la abuela ok (no its ok grandmother), nunca me enseno nada, (he has never taught me anything.). Lo unico que puede hacer bien es luchar y hacer bebes! (The only thing he can do right is fight and make babies!)"

I didn't know what they were saying but by the way their words were hitting my daddy I knew they were on him. My grandmother stood up with little Rosa on her hip, "Sit down Daniel!" My father hesitated then he went and sat down. "Tania got what she deserved! Daniel clearly you have not listened to a word I've told you over the years and now you see. Your children see it all! Do you want all seven of your kids to look at you this way?" I started counting, and sure enough Ria made seven, good grief! "You have a lot to make up for. Your father would be so disappointed in you. In all of you for behaving as you have. You weren't raised to be such users and meddlesome people! I'm disappointed!" Both of my aunts started crying and begging my grandmother for her forgiveness.

Sherrell looked at me and shook her head. I thanked my brothers for having my back and I hugged the three of them tightly. My father sank in his chair real low with his eyes on the floor not saying anything. We put our hats on when it was time to leave the backroom. Everyone wore a hat so it wouldn't seem so suspicious that I had one on. We got in the limo bus and all you heard were the sniffles of my grandmother's children. When we got to the hotel Grandma Rosa said goodbye to her children and then she came to the room with Sherrell and I. My brothers came to our room and we sat in the room playing cards and having a good time. DJ said he was going back to school and he was going to focus on his education and get a job from there. He realized that he didn't really want to sing or be a part of the music industry period. Mario said he wasn't sure yet. I told him to focus on school and if the other part was meant to be it would happen for him. Adon said he wanted to sing just like me. I told him he had to go to school first and there was no way around that. Grandma Rosa told us about our grandfather, she told us he would be so angry with all of them if he knew how they were acting. The boys walked Grandma Rosa to her room, they packed all their stuff up and came back to Sherrell and I's room for the ultimate slumber party. Adon helped Maria bring the babies to our room as well. In the middle of the night, BJ knocked on our door. He said we needed to get to the airport right away. No one asked questions we had our stuff ready to go and we were out. My daddy came down with the rest of their things and we got on the airport shuttle and headed to the airport. Everybody was quiet and looking around. Ronald and BJ pointed out a few guys waiting by the curb for us. They were spread out but they were alert. As we got off the bus BJ assured my grandmother that my aunties were safe, but it was time for us to get back to California. Ronald told us to go through the security checkpoint and they would take care of our bags. There weren't very many people at the airport so we glided through security. When we sat down in the little restaurant to have breakfast my father was holding Alex and waiting for someone to look in his direction. No one was enthusiastic about him, he exhaled real hard then he stood up. "I know saying I'm sorry doesn't cut it, but it's a start. So, let me start by saying I'm sorry for my behavior. Thank you all for the reminder of how selfish I am." He frowned. "Chantel, I know your mother loved me. I regret that I never got a chance to sit down and talk to her about what happened. When she started dating Reggie that was a wake up call for me. I didn't want some other man-playing daddy to my children. When I finally had the conviction to apologize and make things right you guys were gone. I feel extremely guilty about her passing cause if I would've done right by her she'd still be alive." His face looked pained, "I've been wrestling with this feeling since you guys told me she was sick. I feel like it's my fault. I know what kind of woman she was. She was down for her man, faithful, and hard working. I know saying I'm sorry doesn't cut it, and the fact that I could walk to the ends of this earth and it wouldn't matter because she won't be there troubles me. I've been having dreams about her ask Maria. I…" He took a deep breath, "I know sorry doesn't cut it. You and Cyrus growing up without me isn't all her fault. I didn't have to be evil about everything; I didn't have to do half the things I did. I was hurting and I thought I was right. My ignorance forever changed everyone's life. I brought that same stupid attitude into my relationship and marriage with you Maria. I've been blessed with two of the most forgiving and loving women and still it takes the anger of my children, the near loss of one for me to completely open my eyes. Then my own mother's disappointment…" He swallowed, "I can do better and I will be better. You guys don't have to forgive me now, but please don't shut me out." He pleaded. "Ok" DJ said and then he turned his back to my dad to resume eating.

"Give them time Daniel." Maria said while breastfeeding Ria under her discreet draping.

My daddy exhaled and sat down. I bumped DJ under the table; he tried to ignore me so I bumped him again. We argued with our eyes, I gave him a look that said talk to him, and he gave me a look that told me to do it. We went back and forth then Mario stood up. "I don't know Chantel's mother but knowing my mother and knowing Chantel I have no doubt that she was just as beautiful as my mother." He smiled at me, "dad I'm going to accept your apology on the condition that my mother remains happy with you. I have noticed a change in you since the twins were born. You seem to be making my mother happy unlike you ever have. So as long as she's happy with you, I'll stop hating you."

My father's face looked pained, "you hated me?"

"Oh come on! If your mother isn't happy no matter how much she tries to convince you other wise you can see it and feel it." DJ spit at my father.

Everyone sat there quiet for a little while, we ate in silence then we went to our gate. Mitigated staff was pretty much surrounding us. BJ said they spotted a couple of Kevin's guys at the hotel, they were too close. He said he had to change our itineraries and we'd spend pretty much all day flying, but they had it under control and he had a good team with him so we could relax and follow their lead.

When he said we'd spend all day flying he wasn't kidding. We connected so many times it was ridiculous. I was happy I wasn't in charge of keeping track of how all of that was going to run. When we got to my daddy and Maria's house BJ went over the new security system placed in their home. And the cameras placed outside. After BJ and team went back outside DJ and Mario broke the news to our father that they didn't want to work with him. It seemed like he expected it but I could tell his feelings were hurt. He took the news surprisingly well.

Chapter 21

"What's up Chantel? You ready?" Darryl said standing in the doorway.

"Yeah let me grab my sweater." I said as I hurried down the hallway. "Ok let's go."

"Nice outfit." He said as he spun me around.

I had on a simple but nice knee length dress, "thank you. I wasn't sure how dressed up everyone was going to be."

"You're fine." He said double checking the door after I locked it. Then I knocked on Cyrus' door, I could hear music coming from inside. Sherrell opened the door while dancing in place to the music. I could hear her family inside laughing and having a good time. "You're gone?" She said reaching to hug me.

"Yep" I said hugging her.

Cyrus came to the door to hug me goodbye, then he said hey to Darryl. "Where's my baby?" I asked.

"With my mom, come in and say hi real quick." Sherrell said moving out the way

I looked at Darryl and he said it was ok but he wanted to get on the road so to be quick. Little Rosa was in Sherrell's mother's lap. I gave them both hugs and kisses. I went around the room hugging everybody and saying hello. Liz introduced the people I didn't know. Pearla told me she liked my dress. I had a quick conversation with them then Darryl and I left. "So how you holding up?" Darryl asked.

"Ok I guess, some days are better than others." I sighed.

"D-Rick said you've been really quiet." He glanced at me.

"I guess so, sometimes it doesn't seem real. Everything has been happening so fast. I can't believe the last few months of her life I FINALLY had the mother I always wanted. It isn't fair." I tried to keep my emotions in check.

"You should see someone, you'd be surprised how much talking to someone can help."

"You too Darryl? Why does everyone keep pushing for me to see someone! I don't want to be judged."

"Judging is part of human nature, but it can help."

"How would you know?" I said crossing my arms.

He whispered, "I don't know if you've noticed, but I'm a little crazy." I laughed. "See I knew you didn't notice, but I am!"

"You crazy? Never!" I said smiling.

He exhaled, "behind all the laughter there's a lot of pain. If my family was normal, I'm sure I'd be the perfect comedian. Everything pisses me off so much that all I can do is make it funny. It's the times when I can't find the humor in things that makes it all bad."

"When can't you find the humor in something? You always make me laugh, and Derrick laughs at you too. He doesn't laugh at too much."

"All this craziness lately. Drew is stressed, D-Rick is stressed, and Malcolm is Malcolm." He said watching the road. "Then I got my own woman problems, heartbreaking situations."

"I'm sorry," I said feeling guilty about my contribution to the stress.

"What are you sorry for?"

"I feel guilty for Kevin, maybe if it wasn't for me that would be one less stress."

"Kevin isn't your fault. Whether you were here or not he would be trying this mess. He came in looking to run things, it actually helps that he's got some kind of crush on you. It gives him a weakness that we exploit."

"How?"

"He's lost so many men trying to get to you. Now that he's lost Caprice he's feeling the affects of it. Kevin isn't your fault. There's always someone looking at our setup thinking they could do it better or something like that. Kevin's been the first real challenge in a long time though, but ain't nobody worried about him." Then he laughed, "I bet he thinks, better yet, I know he thinks the only reason you're not together is because of D-Rick. Have you seen that fool's teeth? I don't know what kind of chicks he was pulling before but he needs to get that fixed."

I laughed, "I never got close enough to really notice his teeth. Kevin's not ugly, very very average at best though."

"Averagely Fugly!" He laughed. Then his phone rang, he answered over the speaker, "WHAT UP D-RICK!"

"Hey," Derrick said, "it's confirmed tonight is hot. Where are you?"
"Walnut Creek, on our way to Uncle Jeff's."
"We need Detective Dartnell distracted." Derrick's tone was straight forward and all business.
"Where that big ole biscuit eating he-she at?" Derrick didn't respond. Darryl exhaled, "where is she?"
"She's following Sophia right now. Sophia's at the restaurant getting her stuff for tonight. Momma said they're gonna load up and then once Andre gets there they're going to get going to Sacramento. Let her tail you and Chantel for a little bit. Take her out to Sacramento, but let her think she's getting something."
"Alright" Darryl said getting over on the freeway to get off on the next exit.
"Hello beautiful, you ok?" Derrick's voice turned tender I smiled.
"I'm good. How are you?"
"I'm good. I told JoJo to keep your calendar clear for the wedding. It seems like everyone wants to work with you around that time, and that's our time."

"I haven't met Tracy, you sure it's gonna be ok?"

Darryl shot me a look, "Chantel you're family. Drew got you on the list. Besides you're going to meet her tonight after we handle some business." Derrick said, then as if he could see in the car, "What D?"
"How many times we got to tell you that you're family Chantel?" Darryl said
"I don't want to assume." I said
He took a deep breath, "you've been around way longer than Tracy. You're family and I don't wanna discuss this again. You hear me? FAMILY! END OF DISCUSSION!"
Derrick didn't say anything, "no matter what?" I said
Darryl made an exhausted sound, "no matter what!"
I reached over and pinched his cheek. "You look so cute when you're irritated." I teased.
He wiggled his face free, "ALRIGHT! ALRIGHT! ALRIGHT! Yeah, yeah I'm cute, I'm lovable, and you couldn't imagine your life without me. I get it! Just remember that!" Darryl said

shrugging me off. "Like I was saying you need to see somebody about that."

"About what?" Derrick asked

"He said I need to talk to somebody, same thing you've been saying. I'm not gonna lie, I can see how therapy has been helping Cyrus. I didn't know but he saw Caprice slumped over after Dude shot her. I didn't go back out the room until you guys said it was ok to come out. I can see how that would mess with someone." I exhaled, "it's just that this lovely anger helped me beat my auntie down. I loved that moment! I don't think I would've done it if I wasn't angry."

"CHANTEL!" Darryl gasped, "you put hands on somebody?" He faked a surprised expression.

I smiled big, "yep!"

He adjusted in his seat, "tell me everything. Don't leave anything out!"

Derrick blew air, "you two go ahead and bond. I'll check-in in a little bit."

"Ok love you babe!" I said

"Love you!" Derrick said

"Love you babe," Darryl said mimicking my voice.

Derrick chuckled then he hung up. I told Darryl the story and he was completely into it. He asked me who Derrick had me working with during my self-defense education; he got a big smile when I went down the list. In the most hilarious way he told me about some of the incidents he's had. He even made me laugh about him breaking Jamie's jaw all those years ago. I told him the story that Jamie told me about three big guys, and he blank stared at me. "He didn't give me my credit?" I shook my head no, "I otta go break his jaw again for lying. I felt his jaw crack upon impact, it was beautiful!" He smiled at the memory.

"Please don't. I don't even know him anymore. If it helps he followed your instructions and left me alone."

"I guess, but if I see him on a day when I feel like knocking somebody out. It sucks to be him."

"Darryl when do you not feel like knocking somebody out?" I asked

He thought about it for a minute, "maybe every other Tuesday." He smiled. "You got a point, so he better stay clear of me. Let's go inside."

I didn't see anybody, there were cars in the parking lot but there were workers inside the restaurant. I hugged Sabrina and told her she was getting so tall. I told her she was going to be tall just like her big sister. Sabrina got the biggest smile, she told me she hopes she does. You could tell she looked up to her big sister. Darryl talked to Sophia for a minute and then he said we were leaving. Sophia gave me a hug and then we left. I had my passenger side mirror down and I couldn't see anything. I asked Darryl if she was following us, and he said she was. A few good turns and Darryl parked on the street in downtown Walnut Creek. When I hesitated he assured me that people wouldn't recognize me as quickly out here as they would in Oakland. We made it a few steps when two little blonde girls came quietly bouncing up to me asking for autographs and pictures with me. Darryl shrugged and smiled, while he took the picture for them. They were sweet though; both of them said they were sorry for my loss. I thanked them, and then I walked closer to Darryl. We went inside Tiffany & Co. Darryl asked if Katie was in today. "She's finishing up with another customer, is there something I can help you with?" The sales guy asked as he pointed to a brunette who was ringing a customer up. The sales guy wasn't enthusiastic about talking to us. You could tell his greeting was fake and forced.

Darryl glared at the guy and then he waved him off. I asked Darryl what we were doing there. He said he needed some trinkets for his chicken heads as gifts when he leaves in the morning. I shook my head at him, and he smiled real big. Katie came around the counter and she gave Darryl a big hug. "This is my sister Chantel, Chantel whenever we shop here we only allow Katie to work with us." Darryl said

Katie blushed, "nice to meet you." I said to her, "Why is that?"
"When his brother came to purchase his engagement ring I was the only associate who was glad to help him. That one sale changed my life; I get excited when I see Andrew or any of his family come in. They ask for me by name now." She smiled
"Yep all the cousins, and everybody only come to Katie."
"So what can I help you with today?" She asked

"I got some time to kill, and I need some more parting gifts."
Katie smiled then she looked at me again, "lets look at this display case." I could tell I was starting to look familiar to her. "Have you come in the store before?"
I looked at Darryl and smiled, "no this is my first time here."
She said ok and kept walking. She pointed out some pieces through the display window. Darryl said chicken heads not wives. She smiled then she looked at me again. I put my finger to my mouth to say quiet, and then the light bulb went off. She got real excited and then she pulled herself back down to happy existence. "CHANTEL SHAW?" She whispered excitedly.
I looked at Darryl who had surprise all over his face. "What you know about her?"
"I have both of your CD's! I love your music!" She said
Darryl backed up and looked Katie up and down. "You listen to her music?"
"Why is that shocking?" I asked
Darryl shrugged, "I didn't see that coming. What your man think about you listening to her music?"
I shook my head at Darryl cause that was not smooth. "He likes her music too." Then she turned her attention to me, "can I tell people that you buy from me?"
Darryl's face turned serious, "not yet Katie. We got some red tape to get through and then you can tell it on the highest mountain." Darryl said
"Aren't you in here with the wrong brother?" A female voice said from behind us.
I turned around and Darryl looked at the woman very annoyed.

"See it's people like this we'd rather avoid." He said pointing at the woman. "What do you want?"
"I'm looking for Toya, have you seen her?"
"No, but I'm looking for her." Darryl said
"I bet you are," then she turned her attention to Katie and I.
"Detective Dartnell," she said extending her hand to Katie. They shook hands, "could you be a doll and give us a minute? I need to talk to my friends." Katie walked away. "Chantel what are you doing in here with Darryl? Are you switching brothers?"
I looked at Darryl and he was shaking his head at her. "You should know better than that." Then he whispered, "We're casing the joint. Tell all your boys to get ready cause the Wallace's are going to hit

downtown Walnut Creek with a vengeance. They won't know what hit them."

"Stop playing!" She said sounding annoyed.

"I'm not playing, Malcolm is going to buy those foam bats that you get from the toy store. Then we're all coming down here and we're going to spread out. Then randomly we're gonna hit people. Mostly old people and babies. If you come I promise to personally hit you." He made a kissy face at her then he bit his lip, "you are so sexy! Those baggy men's slacks, the way your stomach falls over the top of your pants and you don't even care who see it. I think its down right sexy how you have stopped washing your hair. I thought all white girls washed their hair everyday."

"You should know white boy in black man's clothing."

Darryl faked hurt, "Detective Dartnell! Can I call you D for short?"

"No!"

"D, your comment hurt me!" He fake cried, "Just don't tell nobody. My momma will be so disappointed to know that I didn't come straight from the motherland like she ordered. You gotta help me D! You gotta help me!" He grabbed her arm as he pleaded with her.

Detective Dartnell turned red, and then she started laughing. "Why do you always have to be so silly?" She said trying to stop herself from laughing. "This is serious business!" then she straightened up. "I need to talk to LaToya. I know how much you guys LOVE her, but she said she has some important information for me and then she disappears. I know you guys have something to do with that."

"Why can't she be running from you guys, aren't you guys looking for her for another reason?"

She blew irritated air, "I don't care about the hit and run thing."

"You just care about busting us. We clean D, CLEAN! Smell my hands, I just washed them. We're clean!"

Then she looked at me, "I'm sorry to hear about your momma sweetie. I had a momma once before too. I can't wait for your next project I know there's gonna be some tear jerkers on that one."

"HOLD UP! HOLD UP! D? YOU LISTEN TO CHANTEL TOO?"

"I sure do! I even like her better than Torrie these days. Her music was more relatable when she was dating your daddy. Now she's full of gimmicks no heart and soul to her anymore."

I looked at Darryl, "D! Why you telling our business though? Malcolm don't wanna be linked to that skank no more. You've hurt me to the core. Now if you will excuse me, we need to purchase something's for my chicken-heads and then we'll be on our way."

She handed me her card, "when they turn on you like they did poor little LaToya, you call me and I'll make sure they rot in jail."

"Thanks?" I didn't know what to say to that.

Katie helped Darryl pick out a few nice pieces and then she showed me other pieces. She wrote down my ring size, she said if I see something I like in the future it helps if she knows how to have it sized. When we got back in the car Darryl pointed out a tan sedan that always stayed far back. He said that was D. Eventually I asked him about Malcolm and Torrie, Darryl's demeanor got very serious, it was kind of scary. He said he didn't want to talk about it. Thank goodness we were ten minutes away from our destination cause he stayed quiet the rest of the car ride. When we pulled up to Uncle Jeff's big beautiful house Darryl sat there for a minute. "My parents are a very sensitive subject for me. I apologize if I made you feel uncomfortable."

"No, I get it. Mine are too."

"Everybody else can be quiet, but it seems that whenever I get quiet it's a real problem."

"Its alarming because you're never deathly quiet. I get it, don't worry about it." I said patting his hand.

"By the way I wouldn't call what Malcolm and Torrie were doing 'dating'. They kicked it HARD for a while. Then he cut her off! It's in the past, I don't like talking about it."

"Got it, say no more." I said patting his hand and unlocking my door.

Then we stood up, "can I at least get a hug? I'm feeling emotional right now." He said jokingly but I knew he was serious. I hugged him, and then we went inside. Sophia and Amber were already here setting up the buffet tables for a little later. I asked Tina if she needed help setting up and she thanked me. We talked about the baseball game and how much fun it was and how we needed to do it again.

Uncle Jeff and Auntie Lauren thanked me for coming; they had nothing but concern in their eyes. I thanked them for everything they did for my family and me. They told me not to mention it.

They said that's what family is for. I chatted with Sharon for a little while, then crazy Lanie, her boyfriend, and her family   arrived. Eric and Zoey had me cracking up, which was a lovely distraction from my thoughts. Uncle Frank pulled me to the side to discuss business; he asked how everything was going; and if I thought I'd be ready to get back to work in a few weeks. Amber was watching us interact, I wondered if she could see the worry in my eyes. Derrick said the night was hot. I hoped he was ok, and I kept checking for that feeling I got the night before my mother passed away. Late in the evening Amber disappeared but I got so happy when I saw Derrick. My excitement surprised him but I was too happy to see him. I told him I was worried, he kissed me and told me he loved me too. When Andrew and Tracy came inside I could see pride all over him as he introduced Tracy to everybody. By the time he got to me, I know all the people she was meeting overwhelmed her. I didn't expect to have a major bonding moment, but it was nice to finally meet her. She wasn't as extra-extra as Toya was. She was pretty, but girl next door pretty. I was happy he found a woman who made him happy, but I was even happier that she wasn't Toya or a Toya type.

****

Sherrell and I visited the development regularly and at her urging we took pictures of the stages. She said she had a photo album that she was going to put all of her pictures in to hold on to the memories. When the model units were built Sherrell talked with the interior decorator constantly about her design concepts for the model that was just like the one they were having built. I loved watching Sherrell look at something the decorator would bring; she'd explain where she got it and how much it cost. Sherrell would take it all in, she'd study the piece whether it was a vase, decorative piece, or a painting. Then she'd come home and put together a sometimes better version of the piece. She's amazing, and she said this was a new talent that she was very happy to possess. Their condo was full of things for the new house. I loved how creative and thrifty she was. She had a whole concept planned for little Rosa's room. She said as soon as they were settled they were going to have another baby. Sometimes I sit back and think, my brother is married! And faithfully married at that, I honestly didn't know if that day would ever come around. Sherrell was always down for my brother from the beginning. She never pushed him too hard, I don't know how she dealt with that Caprice stuff, but I'm so happy she did. We had a ball together too. I told her that it was nice to finally have a real sister.

My last week before heading out east Derrick and I spent it inside mostly. It was getting hard to do anything around our place because it seemed like people were looking for me around here. I was so happy construction was moving full speed ahead on our house. I will never take for granted taking a leisurely walk around my block again. Derrick keeps telling me he's going to miss me. We even got in the dumbest argument about who was going to miss who more. When we realized what we were arguing about; we then teased each other about who picked the dumbest argument to ever have. We were a wonderful mess; I wondered how long it would last though.

Out of the blue I got a call from Brandy, it was so good to hear from her. She and Paul were in New York, not too far from Lewis. She said Lewis is talking about buying a place out in or near the Bay so they would be moving too. I was happy to hear that she was coming home. Then she said that the three of us needed to get together. I swallowed hard and I told her that Caprice and I weren't friends anymore. She got quiet and then she said we'd discuss it more when I came out to New York. I planned to meet her son and spend a little time with them while I was in the studio with Lewis. Derrick sighed real heavy, "I'm gonna miss you." He said staring into my eyes.

I kissed him, "I'm gonna miss you more! I know I should be ready, but I don't feel ready. Is it wrong that I wanna stay up under you?" "In a perfect world it would be ok to exist like that. But we gotta keep moving." Derrick said kissing my forehead. "Call me when you land."

We hugged and kissed one more time then BJ and I got on the plane. I knocked out as soon as we sat down. Derrick and I had a long night last night, and I barely got any sleep. As we were coming down the escalator a woman was holding a sign for

"Bernard James," BJ pointed in the direction of the sign. I followed him and the woman smiled, she held out her card, which looked like an ID, and BJ scanned it. As I got off the phone with Derrick, a cameraman noticed us after we got my luggage. "Chantel Shaw!" The guy behind the camera said. The light on his camera was so bright I squinted to see where I was going. I waved hello. "What brings you to the big apple?"

"I'm going to go work with my big brother and some other business ventures." I said happily.

"Shameless' movie was hilarious! It looked like you guys had a lot of fun on tour."

"We did, I'll never forget it."

"Will you tour in the near future?"

"Probably not any time soon. I've got too many projects coming up." BJ told me to come on because they were finished loading our luggage and it was time to go. "Thank you guys for being so nice. Everyone who does your job isn't always nice." I blew them a kiss then I got in the car.

"This is Teresa, she's going to be assisting you in the spaces I can't follow you into." BJ said

"Nice to meet you Chantel. No need to worry we have a whole team out here." She said in a very professional tone.

"Should I be worried?" I looked at BJ.

"No, the Mitigated presence is very strong here as well."

After I checked into my suite, we went straight to the studio. I got extremely excited when I saw Brandy. She was still carrying some baby weight and she looked GREAT! I hugged her tightly, and then she introduced me to her son little Pierce. He was adorable, I showed her pictures of little Rosa and how big she's gotten. I was telling her about some of the cutest conversations we have. She asked when Derrick and I were going to have one of our own. I told her we needed to take care of business first. Lewis came out of the booth and gave me a big hug, when he asked me where Caprice was my heart sank a little bit. I told him she didn't work for me anymore. He asked me if she was on the same level as Wade? I told him I didn't know, cause I didn't. Then Brandy explained that since they've parted ways Wade has been petty about most things. She said he eventually found new artists to work with and some of them are doing well. He learned his lesson about sticking to one artist, but none of them are the cash cow that Lewis was for him. She said she had to convince Lewis and Paul to reach out for backup cause Wade was ignorant and coming at them with

ridiculous stuff that was starting to hurt Lewis' reputation. Then we went to the far end of the room and I told her everything. Brandy was shocked and hurt for me. She cried a little with me. She didn't say she couldn't believe it, but she wondered when Caprice started working for Kevin. I told her what Darryl said about Kevin, and she got on my case as well for thinking that Kevin was my fault. She said he was going to be up against Malcolm even if I wasn't a factor. I told her I couldn't wait for her to move back to the Bay. Lewis planted himself in the middle of our conversation; he was in a good mood. "I know we're supposed to be here tomorrow night, but I forgot about the thingy I got tomorrow. Please come with me, I'm trying to be on good behavior."

"What about work?"

"We're already done. Once you go in and put your spice on it we're finished."

"I wrote a few songs for my mother. Some not so obvious, I wanna know what you think."

Brandy touched my hand with sad eyes. "I'm sorry to hear about your mother." Lewis said with sad eyes as well.

"Sure, let's go. I could use the distraction."

"Did you bring a dress?" Brandy asked

"No, but I can have a few looks brought in. What are you wearing?"

"I don't know my stylist is dressing me."

I texted Derrick and told him there was a change in schedule.

I ended up in this edgy asymmetrical dress. It was leather and the shoes were so BAD that they looked like they hurt! I wore this short jet-black wig. I was in love with this purple and black outfit. It was still sophisticated but this look matched my mood more than anything else did. Since everything else was so dramatic my makeup was simple and clean. When everything was said and done, Teresa high-fived me, and she told me I was sizzling hot. I shot BJ a look when Teresa continued to check me out after the initial compliment. I was not in the mood! Lewis was wearing baggy jeans, a button-up and a yellow puff leather jacket. Our looks kind of complimented each other. We took pictures together when we arrived, then I sat at our table while Lewis walked around mingling. My shoes were not going to let me make a proper round. Then Wade came out of nowhere and sat next to me scooting his chair in as close as he could behind me. "Hey miss popular, how are things going?" I could tell he was tipsy, I was nursing the drink

I had cause I had work to do the next day and I didn't need even a slight hangover slowing me down.

"Hi Wade," I said unenthusiastically.

"I miss you, do you miss me?"

"Wade! You're talking to Chantel, not Ka-kari."

"Karquisha! And I know who I'm talking to. You was supposed to be my future baby momma."

"Don't you got enough of those?" I spit at him.

He smiled, "there's always room for one more."

"Well I ain't the one!"

"Ok, but we can at least get a practice session going." Then using both hands he palmed my butt like it was a basketball.

I jumped out of the chair like it was on fire. "WHAT IS WRONG WITH YOU!" Then I slapped him as hard as I could. "DON'T YOU EVER PUT YOUR HANDS ON ME!"

When I looked up Lewis was already almost to us, and it looked like he saw everything. There was fire in his eyes. Wade stood up angry about my reaction; he didn't even see Lewis's fist coming on his right side. Wade stumbled spilling his drink. Lewis was coming to finish him when BJ and Paul grabbed him and held him back.

There were a few guys holding Wade back as well. "This ain't over!" Wade yelled

"Trust me! I know it ain't over!" Lewis said

Chapter 22

I love the curves of his face. I love to watch him sleep. He looks so peaceful. Earlier this morning was amazing, and now I feel overwhelmed with love and vulnerability. Derrick opened his eyes and stared back at me. I smiled an embarrassed smile. "You nasty!" Derrick said with an evil grin

"Isn't that the pot calling the kettle black? I learned it all from you." I said kissing him.

"I didn't teach you that." He shook his head like a little boy.

"Well you took me there, how about that?"

"Whatever Chantel, you took me there, that's it that's all." Then he smiled.

"We gotta go pick out colors for the house."

Derrick exhaled a little irritated air, "do I have to?" He whined, "I thought you and Sherrell had that covered." Sherrell and I seemed to be living onsite these days. Cyrus' house was going to be ready before ours, so in preparation we were there for all the final touches on their house. We stood in the living room taking in Cyrus' soon to be home. He put one arm around Sherrell and one around me, then he kissed little Rosa. He said words couldn't describe how beautiful this moment was to him. His best women all together in one of his biggest financial adventures. I tried not to be grossed out as I watched them celebrate with hugs and kisses. I got it, they were beyond excited and I could see how that could get physical.

"If you don't want a say, that's fine, but I don't want to hear any complaints if our room looks too girly for you. Or the rest of the house for that matter."

"Just stick with derivatives of blue and grey and you should be good." He sat up and smiled.

"Blue? Why blue? I like burgundy, it's my signature color."

"Burgundy is just a fancy red, makes me think of the forty-niners I don't want that." He said shaking his head.

I exhaled, why does everything have to come back to football with him and his brothers. "See! This is why you need to come with me. Sherrell is dragging Cyrus down there for the same thing, just not today. We can go have breakfast afterwards." I was leaving tonight for the annual awards ceremony tomorrow.

Derrick exhaled cause he knew I wasn't going to let him slide. We showered then we parked at the model homes and then Sharon walked with us to our house. She had a small keychain looking book full of colors. She had the book marked at each primary color and then the mix downs from there. The walls were just sheet rock and nails. The down stairs floors were cement and the stairs and upstairs were base flooring. The living room and the bedrooms were going to be carpeted and the rest were going to be marble tile and hardwood. I had to do some extra begging to get Derrick to agree to the marble because at first he said no. When I saw how pretty they were in the model unit, I had to have them. When I offered to pay for them myself, that's when he started coming around. He didn't want me paying for anything on my own. We agreed on the basic premise for the house. It was a sandy beige color, light and warm. I picked accent walls for the living room, dining room, family room, game room, theater, music room, and the bedrooms. I kept pinching myself, this was real. I was going to share this mansion with the man I love! We've come a long way from the one bedroom Cyrus and I got together when we struck out on our own. Derrick was outside talking to his uncle and the landscaper about the front and backyards. When we had the basics settled Derrick came inside, he looked impatient. I knew he was hungry so I told Sharon I would come back. She was used to me being there almost daily. When we got in his car he asked me

where I wanted to go. I knew if I didn't pick he'd say Gonzalez's, which was fine, but I wanted something different, so I asked if we could go to the place in Richmond he goes to. He smiled and said yes, but then we'd have to go by Auntie Lorraine's since we were right there which was fine with me. I hadn't been over her house in a couple of months, my schedule was kind of all over the place. Most of my appointments had been local thank goodness. I lived for mornings like this morning with Derrick. Five minutes on the freeway and the caller ID from his phone called out "Call from

Sherri." Derrick hissed at it, I looked at him like he better answer it when he hesitated like he wasn't going to take the call. "Yes" he said sounding defeated after he told the car to answer.

Sherri immediately started talking, "Brooklyn is tripping again! She's saying she wants to come out of the rehab. How long is it paid up for?"

I held my breath and I shot Derrick evil eyes. "For as long as she needs to be there. When I talked to her doctor Monday he said she's in no way ready to come home." I slammed my body in the chair! When he did WHAT?

"I know but we can't really make her stay in if she doesn't want to stay."

"Not true if she's a danger to herself and or others she has to stay."

"Right, but isn't using drugs one of those arguable dangers?"

"Depends on who's arguing and how they're arguing."

Sherri exhaled, "I know this is messed up to ask, but I have to." Derrick wouldn't look at me. "Can I have her car?" He didn't

respond, "my car is breaking down, and I got to get to work. It's

just sitting here not being used, mom said I needed to ask you first since you bought it."

"WHEN WAS THIS?" I erupted.

"I'm on speaker?"

"I'm in the car." Derrick said to Sherri. "Chantel we'll talk about it in a minute."

"Anyways can I have it?" She said

"You drive it you bought it. I'm not replacing it if you damage it."

"Why are you still paying for anything for her? She's your ex?" I spit at him.

"Chantel hold on!" He said putting his hand out to me.

I slapped his hand, "NO YOU HOLD ON! This doesn't look good! You need to explain this all to me and explain it now!"

"You mean explain why he was out here while you were in New York?" I could hear her smile through the phone.

Derrick stared at the dashboard like he was trying to choke her through the phone. "You will be dealt with in a minute!" His tone sent shivers through my body cause it was ice cold, but my heat melted that ice. He hung up the phone as Sherri tried to backtrack her comment cause she realized she just messed up.

"You cheated on me!"

"No!"

"Look at me and tell me the truth!"

He kept his eyes on the road, "I'm driving!" As he shook his head. "Everything was going too good, of course something dramatic has to happen now!"

"I can't believe you cheated on me, after all that we've been through! You pull this on me!"

Derrick shook his head, "I didn't cheat on you!"

"Then what then? You weren't going to tell me about your little trip down south. You're still footing the bill for your ex! How else would I see it?"

"Chantel, please calm down! You leave tonight, can we enjoy the day and we'll discuss it later?" He said firmly like I was someone who worked for him.

"You're making me mad! There is no enjoyment left to this day. You better start explaining or else we can kiss everything goodbye!"

"You're working my last nerve! This isn't you! Since when do you act all loud and ridiculous?" He said putting his hand on mine.

I snatched my hand away. "Since you started having secret rendezvous with your ex! If the shoe was on the other foot you would be completely pushed out of shape. Stop trying to flip this on me!"

"Fine! Fine Chantel!" He growled, his foot got heavy on the gas. I stared at him unaffected by his anger. "I thought Kevin had her! Her stupid addiction that he started her on is what saved her life. Mitigated staff found her in a crack house high as a kite while we were on our little adventure. I had her put in a safe house, but she's too messed up. She needs professional help! She kept trying to run away and giving my staff the blues. So I went out there to convince her that she needed to go to a hospital. It was the only way she would go."

"Kevin?"

"Her boyfriend Maurice equals Kevin."

"What about the car? You haven't even replaced mine, but she gets a new car? Why would you ever buy a crack head a car?"

"It just kind of happened, it doesn't mean anything. Besides it wasn't new. It's a very used less than a thousand in value car. A bucket, it doesn't mean anything."

"It means EVERYTHING! What happened that night?" Derrick shut down, he focused on the road. "Derrick! I asked you a question!" He wouldn't respond to me, it was like he clocked out. "You're still in love with her!"

"I'm in love with you!"

"Prove it! Let her go! Tell me what happened!"

"I can't!"

"You can't let her go, or you can't tell me?"

"Can't talk about it!"

"Your little secret is worth losing me over?"

"If I lose you over something this ridiculous you were never mine in the first place." He was too calm.

"Well I guess I wasn't ever yours if you were still in love with her in the first place. I guess you were just passing time with me."

"STOP IT!" He roared. "I HATE WHEN YOU DO THAT! THIS IS A DUMB ARGUMENT TO HAVE!"

"Isn't it!" I said calmly, "and yet you can't open your mouth and be straight with me. I'm not playing this game with you." He pulled into a parking space in front of the restaurant. "You might as well take me home, I'm not hungry any more."

Derrick looked at me, and then he huffed and got out the car like I wasn't nothing. I watched him walk in the restaurant and be seated like he was going to eat with or without me. I put my purse on and I got out of the truck when he went to the bathroom. I walked quickly the two blocks over to the Bart station. From the top of the El Cerrito Del Norte Bart station I watched his truck pull around. My train was pulling around the corner, and I was thankful to at least have him sweat it out for my whole Bart ride. When I got off at Lake Merritt station I walked up and out to a cab. Derrick followed the cab back to the condo, when I walked inside the building he drove off. Sherrell and Cyrus weren't home, so I went inside our place and finished packing my bags. Then I called an Airport shuttle and I went to the airport. I was able to switch to an earlier flight, as I was waiting at the gate BJ made his presence known but he didn't approach me or anything. I got an early check-in at my hotel, I thought about staying in my room crying my eyes out, but then I called Natalie. She was near my hotel she volunteered to come pick me up so we could hang out and get a little shopping done. I couldn't shake my angry feeling, I was furious with Derrick and if he really thought this is just the way we're supposed to exist I wasn't doing it. Natalie kept asking me what was wrong; I kept saying nothing and changing the subject to anything other than how I was feeling. Then she took me by her husband's job and of course Desmond was there. He smiled really big when he saw me. He started singing one of my newer songs, his voice wasn't bad either. "So I take it you like my latest project?" I said forcing a smile.

He held onto his smile, "yep. My girl plays your CD nonstop! If I didn't like it I'd be tortured." I felt a little relieved to hear he wasn't flirting, even though I saw Natalie's head whip around when he said his girl. "You're from The Bay, what part?"

"East Oakland for the latter part. You know the area?"

"Sure do. I lived in Alameda, Hercules, West Oakland, and El Cerrito."

"There's a list!" I said not wanting to devote any of that to memory.

"I used to shop at Oakland mall all the time."

"Oh yeah? I worked all over that mall. I don't think there was a side of the mall I didn't work on."

"Then I've probably seen you before."

"Possibly," I shrugged.

"Let's go." Natalie said

"Where are you going?" Her husband said.

"Dinner" he looked like he was pouting. "When are you leaving cause I'm hungry now?"

"Give me ten minutes," he said hurrying inside.

"Can I come?" Desmond asked

"What about your girl?" Natalie snapped at him.

"It's just dinner, it's not like we haven't all sat down to dinner before." He said

"You are ridiculous!" She shook her head.

"Does that mean I can come?"

"As long as it's ok with Chantel, I don't care."

"Why should I care? I got a man and he's got a girl."

"Right" Natalie said not sounding so sure.

As we walked to Natalie's car Desmond was full of excited chatter. I found myself a little irritated cause Derrick never talks this much, even when he's excited. And let's just face it, I love everything he does, except for when he cheats on me and puts his ex in front of me. I locked eyes with BJ and Ronald for a moment then I got in the car with Natalie. We went to a Cantina on Sunset Blvd. The food smelled delicious as soon as we walked in the door. What I liked about being out here was that most of the folks out here are used to seeing celebrities and especially at this time of year, no one paid too much attention to me. Plus I wasn't so recognizable that people noticed me everywhere yet. The awards ceremony was tomorrow and I had so many nominations I lost track.

My eyes darted around the restaurant until I spotted BJ and Ronald. Even though I was mad at Derrick I wasn't stupid. Kevin has to know I'm out here, I was a little nervous. Even though it has been quiet as far as I know, I knew that there was still the possibility of having him pop up at any moment when he felt we were weak and defenseless like he did on the side of the freeway. Desmond kept flirting with me, Natalie and I exchanged looks. "Would your girl be ok with you acting like this?" She asked him. "We have a open relationship."

"Completely open cause she doesn't exist." Natalie said

I put my hands over my mouth cause I was embarrassed for him. "You need to mind your own business." He said

I felt like somebody was watching me. I looked up just in time to see Derrick walking smoothly to the table. "Derrick!" I said straightening up even though I didn't do anything wrong. Natalie grinned at me, she recognized the name. "This is Natalie and her husband, and this is..."

"Desmond," he said flatly cutting me off.

Desmond smiled, "are you a fan?"

Derrick tilted his head, "you are weak! Heck Naw! You used to fool with Toya. I know who you are."

"Toya who? Who are you?" He asked searching his memory bank. Derrick put his eyes on me, "we need to go."

I stood up; he didn't have to tell me twice. "Natalie, I'll see you tomorrow."

"Seriously! Who is he?" Desmond asked Natalie. I heard her tell him that he was most likely my man.

I turned my back to him in the car. Derrick didn't say anything to me. There were all kinds of personal security buzzing at the hotel, but it's something about the way Mitigated staff members stood that let you know who was who. It's not like they were wearing suits, but they were always nicely dressed never raggedy or homeless looking. The men always had fresh haircuts, and the women always looked nice and put together. They weren't taking any chances I could tell. Derrick opened my door and I didn't even ask how he had the key. I crossed my arms and stood in the middle of the floor. Derrick's face was serious as usual. We were having a good old fashion stare down. When he stood in my face I slapped him as hard as I could. Derrick didn't flinch he kept staring at me; my hand was stinging so I knew it had to hurt. When I reached up like I was going to do it again he grabbed my wrist. "I know you're mad, but I don't respond nicely to being hit. Keep your hands to yourself!" Then he squeezed my wrist and let go.

I turned on my heels and walked towards the bedroom. I felt another slap in me, but I wasn't that stupid. I was angrier than I thought I'd be. I kind of felt like he didn't understand how much he hurt me, and if I hit him at least he'd get the point. He warned me so, I'm gonna go in this room and get ready for tomorrow. This hotel had a whole spa kit next to the whirlpool bathtub. I figured I might as well indulge. When I put the bath salts in the running water, the room came alive with a tranquil aroma. I dropped four bath beads in then I put the bubble bath in, the label called it milky bubbles. I put my iPod on shuffle and jazz flowed over the speakers in the bedroom. Only thing I was missing was candles. I sunk in the tub and turned on the jets, which created more bubbles. Just when I thought the bubbles would rise too high they stopped just above the bathtub. I could feel my body relaxing; the jets worked my body like a massage. I felt the stress lifting off me. My body tensed when I heard the bedroom door open. I didn't have to open my eyes to feel Derrick's presence. "Why do girls like stewing in their own juices?" Derrick said turning his nose up at my bath. I didn't respond, I shot him daggers with my eyes. "So this is what you do now? You don't like something with us, you go running across the state and then out with some other guy?"

"Should I do like you and wait until you're out of town on business and then go lay up with my ex?"

He cut his eyes at me, "I didn't touch her!"

"I guess it's your word against my imagination. Funny how if you would've stayed home like you were supposed to we wouldn't be having this issue right now. Or if you had to go you could've waited for me. I would've gone with you. After everything we've gone through over these past few years seriously this is where we are today? I want to beat your face in!"

"Where's all this aggression coming from? Just because I had some people show you something's don't get it twisted." He glared at me. "Stop making me angry!"

"You know what Chantel, I don't know what to tell you. You're not always gonna like everything I do. I don't like everything you do."

"What have I done?"

"You won't go to therapy!"

I exhaled and slapped my hand on the water. "WHAT IS IT WITH THE THERAPY THING? I TOLD YOU I DON'T WANT TO GO JUST TO BE JUDGED! WHY IS THAT SO HARD TO UNDERSTAND!" I yelled

"YOU WON'T EVEN TRY! LOOK AT HOW IT'S HELPING YOUR BROTHER?" He yelled back.

I could feel the vibrations of his deep voice on the water. "Cyrus and I are two totally different people!"

"You're getting angrier and angrier! It doesn't take much to set you off."

"Oh I'm sorry! When was it ever ok to sneak away to go hump on some other female? Last I checked I was never ok with stuff like that. And you're buying her cars, supporting her. " I frowned, "what part of the game is that?"

"You knew about me paying for her stuff before, this is not new!"

"I DIDN'T LIKE IT THEN EITHER!"

"You never said anything!"

"I didn't know how!" I said getting angry at the tears that were starting to sting my eyes. I told myself to blow air, whatever it took, but don't cry!

"That makes my point, how are you supposed to communicate to me how you feel if you don't know yourself?"

I put my finger up to my face, "hhhhmmm! I think I just told you!"

"Yeah, but you have to be angry to tell me."

"Whatever Derrick you're not blaming this on me. You knew you were doing wrong otherwise you wouldn't have snuck off! You won't tell me what happened that morning! You have no idea how much you've hurt me. I can't even talk to you."

"Then shut up and listen!" I glared at him as he leaned against the counter. I was confused because him telling me to shut up sent something through my body. I was supposed to be angry, but I felt

419

Carey Anderson

extremely turned on. I cursed my body for betraying me. I didn't care what was happening under these bubbles he wasn't getting none from me. "When we get back to Oakland I want you to go see Joanne. I have been as nice about this as I could be but you're going! We can talk out this whole Brooklyn thing there."
"We don't need therapy! Why can't we discuss it now?"
"We're too angry!"
"Why does that matter?"
"Cause we'll end up tearing this hotel down!" He said with his eyes fixed on me.
"I'm not one of your workers Derrick, you can't just order me around."
"But I just did!" He had an "and?" expression on his face.
I growled at him and he could've cared less. He went in the bedroom and turned on the television. Eventually I got out the tub. I left my towel in the middle of the floor just like he HATES! I walked out the bathroom naked and I rolled my eyes at him He looked over my body then he rolled his eyes. I sat at the foot of the bed in his way to put lotion on. I could see him in the mirror glaring at the back of my head. I took my dear sweet time putting my lotion on. I saw Derrick's eyes get caught up in the dance between the lotion and my hands on my body. Then he glared at me again. When he went to the bathroom I heard him suck his teeth. I smiled cause I knew he knew I did it on purpose. I got under the covers of my King sized bed and I stretched out. I was dozing off when he pushed me on my side of the bed. We wrestled for a minute, and then he had me pinned on the bed. When he came in to kiss me I snapped at him like I was going to bite him. I was still angry but my body betrayed me and gave in to him. I tried not to let him enjoy it. I tried to be mean about getting mine, I was even madder when he finished at the same time I did. I turned my back to him and he hugged me anyways. I tried to scoot away and he put me in a bear hug.

****

Derrick insisted on escorting me to all of my appointments, interviews, and PR events. Even when I went to "The Salon" on Rodeo to get my hair and makeup done. He was on the phone mostly but he was right there the whole time. I was wearing a dress designed by Amber's friend Gabrielle, Amber warned it would be sexy and she wasn't lying. I told her to keep it classy, but she had free range with the design. If my breast weren't taped up under this dress I'd be afraid of a boob slip up. Sheer asymmetrical lines went across this dress just above and below my breast. It was sequined and gorgeous! When I took the dress off the hanger it was heavy and it felt like good quality. This dress stood on its own, I wondered if it was too much and then Derrick told me I looked nice. So I relaxed a lot.

I made sure I had my acceptance speech, and my backup speeches in case any or all of my nominations came through. Aleisha and JoJo met us in the lobby of the hotel to ride over to the ceremony together. Aleisha's project had just dropped but we were convinced that next year was her year. Aleisha and I got out the car together and Derrick and JoJo followed behind us. Aleisha and I took a few pictures together, and then we took pictures by ourselves. When I walked in on the arm of Derrick I heard someone cat calling. "Uh oh! We got a wanna be gangster in the house!" Wade sang out as he approached us. "I was starting to think you didn't exist anymore!" Staff came out of everywhere begging Wade to find his seat before the ceremony started. Wade sucked his teeth then he walked away slowly. Then a argument broke out on the far right side of the lobby, the staff hurried in that direction, the stuff that happens behinds the scenes never ceases to amaze me. JoJo reminded Derrick to be cool. Wade's seats were in the middle of a long row; it wasn't like he was going to be getting up for anything so it didn't make a difference. We were seated with Lewis and Paul, he actually came to this ceremony unattached, I smiled at him. I could see the progress he was making.

"And the winner is… CHANTEL SHAW!" No matter how many times that happened, each time was like a shock and a surprise. I was so happy my makeup was waterproof cause I was extremely emotional. Thank goodness I came prepared, I went on that stage so many times it wasn't funny. I was overwhelmed that the world liked me so much that they recognized me in this fashion. In the end I brought Lewis and Aleisha up on stage with me. And then Lewis brought us up with him. I didn't feel like it, but JoJo said we had to at least show our faces at one after party. So we went to the party on the roof of a Hotel across town. I was over it before we got there. There was still tension between Derrick and I, I tried to keep that between us as much as possible; but there will be no dancing for us tonight. I was talking to a veteran artist who had powder around his nose and was high as a kite. He was trying to convince me why I needed a pick me up to get me through the night. He said half the people in the room weren't as happy as they were pretending to be. I felt bad, because that included me. I didn't need a pick-me-up to get me through the night at least. Derrick gave me space to mingle but he was never too far away.

My feet were hurting so I sat at a table to the side while I people watched. Wade came from nowhere and sat at my table. "I want to apologize about the other night, I get very hands on when I drink." I rolled my eyes. "Why do you keep doing that?" I gave him an irritated look. "Acting like the rest of these hood rats? What happened to my innocent jewel?"

"I was never your nothing!" I spit at him.

"Come on admit it! You were feeling me at least at first. That's why your boyfriend stopped coming around." He said smiling at the memory.

"Whatever Wade! You can imagine whatever you want! I don't have time for this or you!"

He frowned, "Eeewwllll! See what happens when a female gets a little money and a name for herself. Everything that made her real disappears!"

He was getting on my nerves. "Like I care what you think of me!

You have no idea what I've gone through! I'm not in the mood for you right now!"

His face turned evil, "you will care what I think of you. I was holding back a lot because of what I thought we had, but now," he took out his phone. "Its about to rain down on you, you won't ever forget this conversation!" Then he walked away telling somebody all bets were off.

Derrick came over to the table and he asked me what that was about. I told him what happened, he looked at me then he looked at Wade. He called someone and asked them what Wade had. As Derrick was talking a ghetto shadow cast over our table and I looked up at straight ghetto fabulousness. Her hair was over done and crunchy, her press on nails were so long I didn't want to imagine how she went to the bathroom. She sucked her tongue, "I see you're still trying to push up on my man!" She said wiggling her neck and waving her hands in the air.

Derrick turned around and chuckled. "What's this?"

"Wade's baby momma," I waved her off.

"The name is Karquisha! Get it right!"

Derrick chuckled again, "no it's not."

"You trying to be funny? My name is Karquisha!"
"Ok, so what do you want?"
"She keeps disrespecting me trying to push up on my man!"
Derrick waved his hand like he didn't have time and two guys
came out of nowhere taking her away from us. I told Derrick I was
ready to go, I was tired of faking the funk. In the limo ride
Derrick's phone rang. As he was listening his eyes darted to me.
JoJo sat up which alarmed me. Derrick said we were flying out
first thing in the morning then he hung up. JoJo opened his hands
to ask what was up. Derrick gave me sad angry eyes. "Your father
is in the hospital, he's been severely beaten up!"
My breath felt like fire, "what?" I said reaching in my purse and
looking at my phone. I had missed calls from just about everyone. I
looked at Derrick in disbelief, "Wade?"
"Wade?"
"He just threatened me, did he do this?"
Derrick took his phone back out, and JoJo got on his. When we got
to the hotel Derrick told Aleisha and I to go with Ronald. BJ got in
the limo and a few other guys. Ronald escorted us through the
lobby, which was full of groupies trying to get to celebrity rooms.
Aleisha comforted me while I cried my eyes out in my room.
Cyrus called me from the hospital. He said my daddy was going to
be ok, but they were keeping him for observation. My daddy and
Adon were going to the store on an ice cream run. Adon told Cyrus
they were almost in the car when guys came out of nowhere. Cyrus
said Adon had a few knots but he was fine. My daddy had a
concussion, broken hand, and a few broken ribs. Adon said the
guys said something about my daddy not honoring his contract. I
knew it was Wade, but how did he have guys planted at my
parent's house? Cyrus said Malcolm brought our grandmother to
the hospital. I told him I would be there in a few hours. When
Derrick and JoJo walked in the room just before sunrise, they were
big and angry looking. I asked Derrick if he wanted to change
clothes. He was about to say no then he changed his mind. JoJo
and Aleisha left to get their things from their rooms. When I asked
him where he went he looked at me, "JoJo and I were here all
night." Then he kissed me and led me out the door. I didn't know
what that meant, but it didn't look like he was willing to discuss it

either. Aleisha had the same look I had. I asked her if JoJo told her anything and she said no. Basically he gave her the same answer Derrick gave me.

Mitigated was waiting at the airport when we landed in San Jose. When we got to the hospital Juan was waiting for us by the door. He told a guy to take us up to the room while he talked to Derrick and Joseph. Malcolm was comforting my grandmother when Aleisha and I walked in the waiting room. I fell to my knees when I looked at my little brother's face. Both of his eyes were blackened and his entire face was swollen and his nose and lips were busted. Adon hugged me, he told me he was fine and I should see the guy he was fighting. I kept saying I was sorry, even though no one could understand why. Cyrus said he couldn't worry about what I meant with how bad Adon looked. I was afraid to go in the room; I couldn't move myself to go. Malcolm's strong hand led me up and out of my seat and down the hallway. He told me I was stronger than this and to get it together. My father's face was worse than Adon's. Maria said he was in good spirits, his pain meds were working. Malcolm didn't say much, but I knew he came with me so I would stop falling apart. I went back to the waiting room with Malcolm, he told me he was going to take my grandmother back to my parent's house. A few minutes later Darryl walked in the waiting room. "Whoa! I thought the elephant man died!" He said Adon was the first to laugh, "Do I really look like the elephant man?"

"Your head is pretty lumpy!" He started laughing, "Looks like bugs asked you if you wanted one lump or two." Derrick smiled at Darryl, while Adon and the rest of my brothers were cracking up. "Looks like you're a little G!"

Adon's chest swelled with pride. "I went out fighting!"

Darryl sat next to JoJo; the three of them started talking lowly then my brothers joined the conversation. They kept their voices low, so Aleisha and I only heard low rumbles. Darryl said hi and bye to Aleisha and I. Then Derrick pulled me to the other side of the room. He told me things were going to move fast. He told me to remember everything he's shown me, follow instructions, and not to be scared cause someone was with me. I asked him what he meant and he kissed my forehead and put his arms around me.

"It's my lucky day!" Detective Dartnell said happily. "Derrick!"
She said waving her hands for him to come with her. "I gotta take
you in." She said with a mile wide smile.

Derrick looked at JoJo, "call my lawyer."

"Why are you taking him?" I said grabbing his arm.

"We got a homicide not too far from where you two were last
night."

"Why aren't you looking for the people who did this to my brother
and father." I said pointing at Adon. "They live here why are you
worried about what happened in LA?"

Detective Dartnell jumped when she looked at my brother. Sadness
flashed across her face. "Who did that to you baby?"

Adon hung his head like someone yelled, "Action!" He inhaled
then exhaled. "My dad and I were going for ice cream when some
guys jumped us. We tried to fight back, but..."

She looked at Derrick, "who did it?" Derrick shrugged. "I'm gonna
find out who did that to you. Lets go Derrick!" She said

Derrick walked out with her. I felt scared and vulnerable. JoJo
suddenly looked real big. He told us to stay put! Then he walked
away. When Kevin walked in I thought my heart was going to
stop. Kevin flashed his gun under his jacket at Cyrus and told him
to be cool, and then he sat next to me. There was fire in Cyrus'
eyes. Then he looked at Adon's face. "I did not authorize this." He
said

DJ and Mario stood next to Cyrus now as tense as he was. "Then
who did? Why should I believe you? You took my mother!"

Kevin stared at my face for a minute, "we haven't been this close in
a long time." He shook his head, "what was your question?" He
looked like he was really happy to be sitting next to me.

"Who did this to my brother and my father?"

"Wade went around me and made the call. He's been dealt with. I
wouldn't knowingly do this to your father and brother I know how
much they mean to you."

"What do you mean dealt with?" I asked

He gestured with his hands, "dealt with. I don't know how else to
say it so you understand. You don't have to worry about him no
more."

"You're trying to set Derrick up for that?"

He blew air, "Derrick set himself up. He should've known I'd
handle this. Wade crossed a line."

"You took my mother! You knew she was sick!"
He reached for my hand and I snatched my hand away. "I didn't
hurt her. I wasn't gonna hurt her. I'm not the savage, Derrick is the
one leaving bodies behind." He said irritated and adjusting in his
chair.
"He's been protecting me!"
"You don't need protection from me. I'm not gonna hurt you."
"But you're killing people just to get at me? It doesn't make any
sense. Why would you do all this?"
"I don't condone beating up little kids. I'll make sure this is taken
care of, but we need to go."
"Where am I supposed to be going?"
"We need to talk." He said standing up and reaching for my hand.
Cyrus pushed his hand back. "She's not going anywhere with you.
Why would she go anywhere with someone who held a gun to my
head."
Kevin shrugged, "it wasn't personal. I haven't acted like that since.
Can we go now?" I shook my head no at him. "What do you mean
no? Do you have any idea of what I've gone through to be standing
here?" His voice got angry.
"Do you have any idea what I've gone through behind you chasing
me?"
"I'm gonna make that up to you, but all these Wallace's die! They
took my cousin out behind some bull! And he was married to one
of their daughters. This is a cold blooded family."
"You talking about my sister!" JoJo said standing in the doorway.
"White women are the devil!" He spit.
I frowned at him. "You are one to talk!" A voice came from behind
JoJo. "You have no right to call anyone anything!" Uncle Frank
said as he walked in with his son Franky behind him.
Kevin's eyes bucked a little, then he sat back down. "You in
trouble now!" Joseph said dancing like a kid behind his uncle.
Uncle Frank looked at him and he straightened up. My poor
brothers didn't know who they were looking at. Uncle Frank
gestured to my brothers. "Gentlemen have a seat." Cyrus sat next
to me and the others filled in the other chairs.
Kevin smiled, "look at the head nigga in charge! You came all the
way out here for little ole me?"
Uncle Frank squinted at Kevin, "N bombs, really?"

"You came all the way out of Fort Knox to be here? I wish I would've saw that coming! You know how many men I lost trying to get in that gate?" Kevin was excited

"Are you done?" Uncle Frank said patiently waiting.

"No! Since I know this is the first and last time we'll talk I got some stuff to get off my chest." And then he proceeded to go on and on about stuff that my brothers and I know nothing about. Uncle Frank was letting him talk, calming Franky as he got impatient with the long drawn out story, until he went too far.

"You should be happy your daughter turned a new leaf. Cause she was my target before Brooklyn. I planned on using her as a distraction and weakness for you, but in the end I had to use Brooklyn. I'd say that tactic worked pretty well, women seem to always be a man's downfall. I planned on sending you pictures of your little girl Gwen on her knees, and strung out." He said laughing to himself.

I could tell that pissed Uncle Frank off but he didn't turn red or anything. He looked at me like, "no this fool didn't!" Franky stood up like he was done with the whole scene, Uncle Frank shook his head. "Stuff like that is exactly why you die today." He said matter of factly. "Your cousin was a sorry excuse for existing. He was a coward and sneaky, you've killed people for less than he did." Kevin rolled his eyes, "he was a snitch!" Kevin gasped. You could tell he didn't want to believe it, but he knew it was true. "He had to go. Besides, that was before we went straight." Uncle Frank said, as if he was popping his collar.

"Yeah right!" Kevin blurted still angry about his cousin.

"You're the one still dealing trying to keep up. You will never be like us! Now you'll never be anything else!"

Kevin sucked his teeth then he turned to me. "Chantel, it's now or never!"

"Never!" I said full of attitude.

Kevin slapped me so hard my ear started ringing. Cyrus jumped over me and tackled Kevin. My heart stopped beating cause I knew Kevin had a gun. Not only that, Cyrus wasn't a soldier. He did pretty ok on his own but I knew Kevin was beyond his league. I should've been quiet and not have gotten smart, I jumped up to help my brother even though JoJo was right there. I saw Kevin reach in his jacket and I threw my body on Cyrus. He was all I had and I couldn't handle it if he was hurt because of me. I started screaming to the top of my lungs. I could hear and feel movement all around me, but I was waiting for the sting of the bullet.

Someone hit Kevin hard, I don't know with what or how. His body jerked really hard. I kept my eyes squeezed shut while I cried out; time seemed like it stood still. Someone was picking me up, but I refused to let go of Cyrus I couldn't hear what was being said either. "Chantel! Chantel!" Mario yelled while smacking my head. I opened my eyes and Kevin, Uncle Frank, Franky, and JoJo were gone. Nurses were standing in the doorway. "What's wrong with her?" One asked
"We're sad about our father, do you know when he's going to get to go home?" Adon said letting his jacked up face speak for him.

"The doctor is…." DANG IT! SHE RECOGNIZED ME! "OOH! OOH! PATTY! OOH! OOH!"
I got up and off Cyrus, and as soon as he stood up he grabbed me and squeezed me tight, both of our hearts were pounding. We stood there for a long time without speaking I was crying my eyes out. Eventually DJ, Mario, and Adon joined in the hug. I was the only one crying but still. I could hear the nurse telling the other staff who I was. "I GOT IT!" Aleisha said, we turned to look at her. "Adon you look like a light skinned version of Martin when he got in the boxing ring! Un huh that's what you look like. I've been trying to put my finger on it this whole time!"
We looked at Adon and he did look like that. Even though I was just balling my eyes out, now I was cracking up. Everybody laughed. The nurses with no filter came in and asked for autographs and took pictures even though my face was a mess cause I had been crying, etc. When the nurses cleared the room, DJ and Mario were aw struck about how smoothly JoJo dropped Kevin. They said while the nurses were coming to investigate my screams from one direction, Uncle Frank threw Kevin's unconscious body over his shoulder like a sack of potatoes and they walked out the exit door on the other end of the room. Aleisha said JoJo texted her and told her to keep us inside and that it was completely crazy outside. It was weird cause from where we were the outside was still. Ronald came with a couple of pizzas that we devoured and thanked him for. Mario asked him what was going on. He said some of Kevin's people were trying to save him, they didn't understand they were too late. "If Frank has to come out to

handle business it's a wrap." Ronald said, then he explained that if Derrick didn't go into custody with Detective Dartnell it would've been difficult to defend the fact that he didn't kill Kevin. Although Derrick was coming for Wade, by the time they got to him he was gone. Derrick realized the setup that was in place, and he had to make sure he stayed visible. Police custody was the most visible he could be when they determined time of death for Kevin.

"Where's BJ?" I hadn't seen him since the hotel in LA.

Ronald dropped his eyes to the floor, "he's gonna be ok." He said shaking his head.

"BJ is the one that be trying not to laugh at our jokes?" Mario asked, I shook my head yes.

Maria came in the waiting room as Ronald got a phone call. She said my daddy was looking good and they were going to release him in the morning. Then she gave Adon some more pain medicine, and then she called her sister to check on the twins. I asked Maria how she was so calm about this whole thing, and she said, "You reap what you sow. Malcolm has assured me that NOTHING like this will ever happen again. Daniel needed to understand he doesn't know the business, and when you get involved with people like Wade stuff like this happens. He needs to stick to what he knows, making the music, and let his son handle the business. I'm just happy that everyone is ok. This whole thing could've been a lot worse."

Ronald said we were green and that he'd take Cyrus and I home. I sat in the seat latched onto my brother and cried. I kept seeing Kevin's gun, my mouth almost got my brother shot. Cyrus kept assuring me that it was ok and he was ok, but I couldn't stop crying. When I thought about Sherrell and little Rosa I cried harder. I almost cost them a husband and a father.

Chapter 23

"It's nice to finally meet both of you. I've heard so much about you." Joanne said, her face was kind enough. I don't know why I expected her to look mean and like she was going to scold me at any minute. Her office wasn't too small, but it wasn't big, it seemed like Derrick and I's tension filled the room, and made it stuffy. I nodded my head but I didn't say anything. Then I noticed that Derrick actually looked nervous. I looked at him like I didn't understand. He was the one putting his foot down and demanding that we "HAD" to come here. Yeah, so I'm scared to go to sleep, and the lack of sleep makes me cranky. Every time I sleep I have nightmares. Even though my daddy and Adon's faces were pretty much healed up now, I still kept expecting to see them all swollen and jacked up. Although I feel like I've been holding back, Derrick keeps saying I've been impossible. Which hurts my feelings but I'm so angry with him. "It's nice to finally meet you." I said out of the manners I've developed, not that I was raised with any.

"Why do you seem so nervous Derrick? I don't bite." She said with a smile.

Derrick actually smiled; it was a nervous smile but a smile nonetheless. "There's so much riding on this."

"Oh really? Like what?" I liked that her tone was kind and not fake.

He gestured between the two of us. "We haven't been getting along. There are a lot of things unsaid." He inhaled and then exhaled, "I don't know how much longer we can continue like we have been." I felt like he shot me.

Joanne looked at my face, "you look surprised. You guys haven't discussed this?"

"NO!" I said shooting Derrick daggers.

"Ok so Chantel tell me how you two met."

I exhaled, and I shot daggers again. "Ok, but first let me say," then I turned to Derrick. "How much of a coward are you to bring me here to tell me you want to break up with me!" My statement made Derrick visibly angry, but that was my intention. He hurt me and I wanted to hurt him back.

"Chantel sweetheart that's not what he said." She was trying to help.

"I should know how he's feeling before anybody else does." I snapped

"Just like you would come to me about how you were feeling all the time. You let that snake that was planted to divide us, steer you towards some other guy, and make you doubt me! If you would've been listening this wouldn't be a surprise. Maybe I didn't say we're on the verge of breaking up; but it shouldn't be a surprise." Derrick said flatly.

"Ok, lets redirect the energy. I need to get up to speed on your relationship. Chantel can you tell me the story of how you two met?"

I couldn't stop staring at Derrick; it felt like my heart was going to fall on the floor. How could he leave me after everything we've been through? I can't imagine life without him. Not now with all these traumas swimming around my brain. How could he leave me? I started crying, "I can't even do this right now!" I said waving my hand.

"Ok," Joanne said like she understood. Derrick why don't you tell me your version.

Derrick licked his lips and adjusted in his chair, he looked like he was getting comfortable to tell a good story. "I was walking through the mall and I saw her. She looked so innocent and sweet; she was offering samples from the smoothie stand. She gave me one, smiled at me, and kept it moving. I was a little disappointed that she didn't notice me, but then I liked that. I developed this addiction to smoothies." He smiled at the memory, "Sometimes when I had no reason to be at the mall, I was there just to get a look at her and watch how she handled herself. When I said her name it seemed like it surprised her that I noticed her."

"Did you ask her out?"

Derrick smiled, "Chantel was like this beautiful rose bud. You look at it and it's beautiful, but you know when it finally blooms it's going to be breath taking. You have to give it time to get there. So I didn't ask her out I did one better, I brought her in to Malcolm's office. If she turned out to be annoying or impossible Malcolm would fire her and oh well. I knew I was in trouble when he liked her."

"When did you make your big move?"

He chuckled, "I kind of fumbled through that. I told her I liked her but that it wasn't going to work. And where she could've acted crazy, she one upped me; and made me feel horrible when she cried. Then she started dating this loser, probably to make me jealous." He looked at me, "it worked." I rolled my eyes.

"So things moved slowly with you guys. Sounds like you've grown a lot together."

"Yes."

"It also sounds like you're looking for her to be that same person she was when you were teenagers."

Derrick smiled, "well yeah!"

They shared a laugh, I was still hurt. "That's a little unrealistic, how have you changed since you first met?"

Derrick sat there quiet for a long time, but I could understand why. He hasn't changed all that much. If anything his changes were centered on his interactions with me, but he hasn't changed.

"Besides having a obvious weakness for her," he said pointing at me. "I smile more."

"Is that true? Does he smile more?" She asked me

"Yep" I said flatly.

"So Chantel, why did you agree to come here today?"

"He made me."

"Why did he have to make you?"

"Cause I didn't want to come here for you to judge me."

"Why do you think I would judge you?"

"Cause," I exhaled like I was explaining something simple. "I sit here telling you everything. You say something nice, and then you go home and say 'GURL THAT GURL CHANTEL IS A MESS!' I'd rather not."

"You're describing a girlfriend relationship. I'm a paid professional. For one I can't discuss you with anyone else. What's said in here stays in here. And for two my goal is to help you, not to judge you."

I exhaled in defeat, I hoped that was true cause I was about to explode, "he used to come to the smoothie stand all the time. I thought he was extremely sexy and unlike any guy I had ever met. I was floored when he knew my name. I didn't think he liked me, I thought he felt sorry for me." Derrick frowned.

"Why would he feel sorry for you?"

"I didn't feel very pretty back then. Even today sometimes, I feel like it's the makeup. I've learned to stop speaking on it and put my best foot forward." I exhaled, "back then my brother and I were a team and our focus was moving away from our parents, we didn't spend money on clothes and stuff we wanted. I made due with the little bit of clothes I had, that my mother didn't take from me. We worked and went to school. We worked two jobs each and I was exhausted. Working for his father," I started crying. "Working for Malcolm changed my life! I didn't have to work two jobs anymore. I could study more, and I could get a good night's sleep, well as good as could be expected until we moved out. We were able to move out a lot sooner than we thought. Malcolm has taken such good care of my brother and me. I owe him my life! Even when he found my father for me, I know he saw all my father's faults but he let us find out without throwing us in the middle of it. He's been protecting us and setting us up for greatness."

"Why don't I get any credit for that?" Derrick asked

"Cause even when I wasn't dealing with you he was there." I said, "he gave me fatherly advice all the time. I feel like he's more of a man than my biological father is."

Four hours and extremely dry mouths later, we had only scratched the surface. At least I wasn't shooting Derrick daggers by the time we left. As we were wrapping up to leave they informed me that Derrick booked the rest of her week, and that we were coming back tomorrow, I was relieved to hear it. Cause I really needed to know and understand so much more.

****

We were staring at Derrick waiting for him to talk when he was ready. "I was sleep and she buzzes my door." Derrick started shaking his leg. "I told her to go away, but she stayed on the buzzer. I noticed that she was slurring and she seemed off. So I let her come in." Then Derrick stood up and started pacing. "Her eyes were glazed over, I kept telling myself this is Brooklyn. My first crush, my first like, my first piece, my first love. The person in front of me was a reflection of that, but it wasn't her." His voice cracked, he continued to pace. "She…" He took a deep breath, "she was talking really fast and acting crazy. She opened her coat and she had a little stomach, I was confused. If she was having my baby how could she be high? She started arguing with me and I lost it. I cursed her out! I went real bad on her, I..." he took a deep breath. "She took me there! I grabbed her, I pushed her, and I even choked her a little bit." My mouth was literally open. Derrick's never put his hands on me. Outside of slapping him I don't think I've ever pushed him either. Seeing how upset he was about it had me in tears. "Malcolm's never hit my momma. No matter how much a female pushes me unless her name is Toya or she's a Toya type I normally can walk away. When I got a hold of myself and I told myself to calm down, she lost it saying I didn't love her anymore. She asked me to kiss her and I would not, and could not do it! She went in the kitchen and grabbed a knife. She started slicing herself up. There was blood everywhere. Then she sliced her stomach, and she told me that she killed the baby then she started screaming. There was so much blood and it was everywhere, when I called 911 then she cut her neck." Derrick cried a little bit. I got out of the chair and I hugged him. I could tell Derrick was trying to hold back and be a man, but this was a safe place. "I thought she was going to die! Just because I couldn't stand to be alone." He inhaled and exhaled. "I think I'm cured." He said trying to laugh as a rebel tear fell. "I feel like her life is wasted because of me. Maybe if I pay for her treatment and make sure she's not a burden to her family she can at least somehow return to them. She could recover and get better. I'm not in love with her, she's not the same person anymore."

"Derrick she had and still has a choice in all of this. You can't hold yourself responsible for what's happening with her." Joanne said in a warm motherly tone.

"I know that makes logical sense, but it doesn't seem to work in my head. I can't look at her."

"Derrick," I said and waited for him to look at me. "Nothing could be worse than those grits!" Derrick fell in his seat and he belly laughed while wiping his face.

Therapy was surprisingly good. The weight on my shoulders felt like it was getting lighter and lighter. At the end of the week Joanne asked if I would come back, and I found myself booking a regular appointment with her.

As usual Derrick was right. Derrick knew, but never knew in such detail, how traumatic life was with my mother and Reggie. Until now he knew the basics, no affection, or concern. I touched on the molestation issues but never told him about how bad Reggie was.

For example I shared about Reggie touching himself and saying my name, while I was trapped in the shower. How my mother would only react to say I was instigating his behavior. She always had Reggie's back, never ours.

I never knew that Derrick physically fought with David his biological father. He said he was emotionally disconnected from him and only really tolerated David's presence for Andrew who always seemed to need him more than he could relate to. There were so many things about his father that he didn't speak on, that whenever he talked about him I was in awe. He didn't get how Andrew was so attached to David. But he understood that Andrew minimized the negatives and focused mostly on the positives, something he couldn't bring himself to do. That reminded me of Cyrus with our mother. It was like he waited for her to come around.

Derrick shared that Auntie Lorraine helped him a lot, he said talking to her filled in the blanks about who his father and grandfather were. He didn't like the fact that dealing with Brooklyn made him feel like he was loosing control. He said after the incident with Brooklyn he couldn't stand his reflection for a while.

****

It was an unusually quiet evening, I made dinner then Derrick and I felt restless. I told him I felt like singing and he agreed that tonight felt like a night that should be filled with music. I took out my notepad but nothing was coming out, I threw my pen down completely frustrated. Then Derrick emerged from the bedroom dressed nicely with his saxophone in his hand. He smiled at me and told me to get dressed. I had to check myself because I almost opted to stay in. He looked so good to me standing there dressed nicely and like he owned the room already. This definitely felt like the ultimate foreplay and I was game. I put on what felt like the perfect dress; it was majestic green chiffon and flowing, one shoulder, with a empire waistline. I put my hair up and I clipped a flower barrette on the side. Derrick played music while he waited for me to get ready. When I walked out of the doorway suddenly he wanted to stay in, like he could feel my vibe. I wasn't having it, I was happy to be going outside. Since I was in a playful mood I messed with him the whole car ride. I hiked up my dress and flashed my garter at him. I kissed on him and grabbed at his clothes. Derrick was right there with me with fifty million hands all over my body.

"How you lovely ladies doing tonight?" The women responded, "thank your man for bringing you to The Place Where The Jazz Is Played." The audience applauded. "We've got a special treat for you guys tonight. We've got alumni in the house!" You could hear the whispers; the audience was trying to figure out who was here. "I bet you guys are wondering who." The audience erupted with pleads, the MC laughed. "You'll see in a minute. Ladies and gentlemen give it up for Narration and guest." The audience applauded, Narration played the introduction. It was a song from my album; Derrick played the lead vocals on his saxophone. The audience went wild, I could hear people telling him to "go ahead!" and screaming "D-Rick!" stuff like that. He was so good, I wanted him to perform with me on stage, but he refused, he would only go as far as the studio.

For the second chorus I joined him on stage and I promise it seemed like the lady in the front was about to pass out. We played a small impromptu concert; it was just what I needed. Gus was overjoyed when we showed up and offered to perform free of charge. We told him we owed him so much that it was our pleasure. Then we made plans to discuss when we could plan a small concert at his venue. I loved the idea of that, then my brothers could get a taste for performing and my daddy could play his heart out in front of a live audience like he's always dreamed of doing. I gave Gus Cyrus' card and I told him we would be in touch. After the nightclub cleared out Narration played for Derrick and I as we danced to their song. Things were good again, and I was so happy that our relationship was out of the woods. I love Derrick with all my heart, and now that there wasn't anything unsaid we both felt free to love each other. And tonight was unlike any other night. We barely made it in the door as we were all over each

other. Derrick is the master torture artist, when I felt like I couldn't take it and I needed to feel him. This fool wants to stop to talk! Yes TALK! He had to have the Barry White voice on while he spoke, the deepness of his voice mixed with my excitement to drive me

insane. Our night was so passionate and unlike anything we've experienced before. Words cannot express that night, all I could say is it was magical.

Once someone posted footage on the internet the concert went viral. My sales spiked again, I completely didn't expect that. Our performance also drove more business for The Place Where The Jazz is Played. Other local musicians remembered our spot and it seemed like that place was always hopping. Gus told us no matter who it was Derrick and I came first.

****

"You ok?" Sherrell asked me as I took another swig of my water. "I think I'm coming down with something." I said sitting on the couch.

Sherrell felt my forehead, "you're warm. You might be fighting an infection. We should get you home before your fever spikes." she said taking my keys from me.

"I'm sorry girl," I said curling up in the front seat.

"It's ok, I got everything I needed. Can you believe we move in Saturday?"

I moaned, "I gotta be there! This is a important moment, I gotta be there!"

"It's Tuesday, medicate today, tomorrow, and Thursday you should be coming around. By Saturday you should be good."

"Ok doctor mom."

"When do you guys move in?"

"The weekend after the wedding. We get the keys the morning the day before the wedding." My stomach started cramping. "Pull over!" I barely made it out the car. I was vomiting on the side of the street.

It took us a minute but we made it home. Everything I ate all day came up. I had a fever and the chills. I haven't been sick in years. I didn't know how to act, Derrick laughed at me and said I was the worst patient ever, cause I kept trying to do everything myself.

"Your soup and tea are on the night stand. Water bottles are next to the bed." Derrick kissed my cheek, "ooh! You're clammy!" He rubbed my back. "I gotta go into the office and then I'll be back."

"Can you bring me back some cake?" He sucked his teeth. "I know Tracy was sending a cake today. I want a piece, a small one."

"I'll see what I can do. Promise to stay in bed."

"Un huh."

"Hard headed!"

"Whatever!" I waited thirty minutes after he left and then I started the water to take a shower. Then I heard the front door, I ran back to the bed even though the water was still running. I was breathing hard and sweating and I put my head under the covers.

"You're so hardheaded." Sherrell said.

I was cracking up, "I need to be clean!"

"You need to rest."

I exhaled, "I need to go to the store."

"What do you need, I can get it for you?"

I swallowed, "a pregnancy test."

"WHAT?" Sherrell erupted in excitement. "I thought you had the flu."

"I had to keep the charade up." I showed her my damp washcloth that I kept laying on my head and face when he wasn't in the room. Sherrell ran to the store, it seemed like she went and came back in five minutes. I asked where the baby was and she said with Cyrus she thought I was contagious. She said there was no point in disturbing their bonding time until I took the test. Even though I drank like four bottles of water it took forever before I could pee. Sherrell was running water, tickling me, anything she thought that would make me have to go. Finally I was able to go, I took the test then I got in the shower. As soon as I stopped the shower she was knocking on the door. "Hold on! Hold on!" I put my robe on then I approached the test. My heart was pounding "POSITIVE!" I screamed. Sherrell barged in the bathroom and started screaming with me. We screamed and did a happy dance. "Oh no! Sherrell!

It's gonna hurt isn't it?" My eyes pleaded with her to lie to me.

"I'm not gonna lie, it's gonna hurt! Just remember many women survive it. You'll be fine." She rubbed my back, and then she got excited again. "How are you going to tell Derrick?"

"I was thinking that I'd tell him when we do the final walk through and we have keys in our hands."

Sherrell frowned, "what if he gets really excited and tells people?

It's supposed to be Andrew and Tracy's day the next day."

"True, but at this point if I say anything it's all bad I don't know how long I can hold out."

"Tell him the next day after the wedding. I'll help you plan." Sherrell excitedly clapped her hands.

Then we went to the mall, when I walked in the office Ms. Laverne was so happy to see me. She rushed over to hug Sherrell and I. Then she held my hands out to take me in. She raised an eyebrow at me. "What?" I smiled innocently.

"You're a more top heavier than normal." She said eyeing me.

"I am?" I said shooting Sherrell a "SEE!" Look cause that meant Derrick would figure it out.

"Un huh," she said putting my hands down. Then she smiled, "you got something to tell me baby?" She started getting antsy waiting for me to spill it.

"I took a test today and…"

Ms. Laverne screamed and spun me around. "I'm gonna be a grandmother!"

Ok, that made me cry. I thought about my mother and how she told me to have as many pretty babies as we could manage. I think she would be as happy for me as Ms. Laverne is. "Is Malcolm here, I haven't told Derrick yet. He can't know."

"Chile'! Everybody is so amped up about this wedding, it's like they forgot they got work to do, businesses to run. I won't say anything. So, who knows?"

"Just us three." I said, "I'm scared!"

"Already? It's too soon to be scared."

"Shouldn't I freak out now, and then have bliss later?"

"You can have whatever you want. How long have you guys been trying?"

"We weren't." I said flatly.

"Well you weren't trying not to." I felt embarrassed. "Oh honey, babies happen. I'm just happy that you weren't kids when this happened."

"Me too!" It had to be that night! I KNEW THAT NIGHT WAS TOO GOOD!

Ms. Laverne got excited and she decided it was quitting time. She said staff would just have to come back tomorrow to get their mail. We spent the rest of the day window-shopping.

****

"Everything looks perfect!" I said listening to the sound of my hands clapping echoing off the walls. I hugged Derrick; I couldn't believe our home was completely built. Everything was even more beautiful than I imagined it. My marble entryway, and kitchen. My wooden floors sparkled like they were laminated with the shiniest sparkle dust. I smiled an evil grin as Derrick looked at my Entertainment room that had a burgundy accent wall with the beige paint. I knew he was going to think of it as a forty-niner room but I needed one room that reflected me. The kitchen walls were grey; the appliances were chrome and black. The tile in there was grey, black, and white. The window in the kitchen was huge and a beautiful view of the Bay. All of the windows on the back of the house were huge and captured the most beautiful view of the Bay like picture frames. The sunroom which was off the family room had the indoor small pool already installed. The massive outdoor pool with the waterslide and waterfall would be installed later. The full basketball courts, lawn, barbeque, and picnic area were up next on the installation list. Derrick gave me permission, shaking my head, to spend my money on furnishing the house as long as I didn't drag him through the experience. Amber gave me the number for her interior decorator Shasta a few weeks ago. We had a ton of ideas already.

Of course Derrick's discerning eye noticed some things that were a little off. Uncle Dale and Uncle Timothy said they'd have it taken care of first thing Monday morning. Then Derrick told me he had a surprise for me. He covered my eyes and led me through the house. He opened a door and told me to open my eyes. In the Five-car garage there were three brand-new burgundy colored cars. A sports car, a luxury sedan, and a luxury SUV. He said there was one for each mood I may be in. I screamed and thanked him, and then Uncle Dale and Derrick sighed like they were relieved. He said he had been stashing them there for a minute and every time I came out to the house it was Sharon's job to keep me out of the garage. I told him I knew he loved me cause he bought me forty-niner cars. He frowned at me and then he pointed at me while talking to his Uncles, "See! I told you she was going to say that! I can still take them back!" He said faking an attitude.

Sharon and I did the happy dance together, and then the piano arrived. I had no idea he scheduled it's delivery already. It sat perfectly in the middle of the music room. The keys seemed like they were begging Derrick to tickle them. Derrick played for a little bit then he kissed me goodbye. I could see him consciously pulling himself away, he whispered in my ear that we needed to break the house in. I told him he was on, and then we kissed. He told me he'd see me at the rehearsal dinner at Sophia's tonight.

The restaurant was full of Wallace's and Tracy's family. Tracy was glowing and completely beautiful. She looked so happy and everyone looked so happy for them. I kept looking to Sherrell to reassure me that I could hold on to my secret for twenty-four more hours. I kept telling myself all I had to do was make it to the hotel room tomorrow night. I thought for sure Derrick would've caught on by now, my chest seems to be on its own growth schedule. That was the only noticeable feature but it was a big deal at least to me. I think he was too distracted to notice. Even at the dinner he was kind of all over the place, his face was serious as usual and he kept making eye contact with his brothers like something was going on. I kissed him goodnight and I told him not to get into any trouble with his brothers and cousins. He kissed me deeply and told me he would be on best behavior.

In the car Sherrell and I kept shooting each other looks from the front and back seat. Then we'd giggle or something. "What's up you guys?" Cyrus said very suspicious.

"Nothing!" We said in unison, and then we started laughing.

"Right! Come on spill it!"

"What on earth do you speak of my dear brother?" I was grinning from ear to ear.

He looked at me in the rearview mirror. "Chantel!"

"If we tell you, you can't tell anybody! Especially your loud mouth father cause he'll ruin the surprise."

"Ok! Ok! I promise! Spill it already!"

"I'm pregnant!" I blurted out and then I covered my mouth cause it felt weird to hear it.

"WHAT?" That's not what I thought you were going to say," he said excitedly. "I thought you were going to say you were going to take a year off or something like that. This is even better! CONGRATULATIONS BABYGIRL!" Then he made a wounded sound and shook his head. "My little sister has sex. YUCK!"

"Un huh!" I teased him.

"GROSS! SHUT UP CHANTEL!" He screamed while Sherrell and I cracked up laughing at him.

****

We got to the hotel around two-thirty, Derrick looked thoughtful when we walked into the hotel lobby. As soon as he saw me his eyes lit up. He hugged me and kissed me, "I love this dress!"
"Thank you, should I take my bag up now or later?"
"We could go now," he pointed Cyrus and Sherrell in the direction of the ceremony location. Cyrus passed me his keys and he smiled at me real big. I stuck my tongue at him and told him to be cool. This hotel was beautiful and fancy. "In the morning we should get a couple's massage," he said talking faster than he normally would. "I think we might be too busy for that." I didn't know what else to say. I thought you had to get carefully executed massages when you're pregnant, and how could I dance around that. I've made it this long I can make it seven more hours. I can do this! I can do it!
"Why would we be too busy?" Then he squinted his eyes at me, "are you on your period?"
I smiled, "no I'm not." I thought he would see it all over me. His eyes kept bouncing around the room. "What's wrong?" He seemed nervous.

"Nothing!" He threw his hands in his pockets. "Let's go back down stairs, I'm supposed to be directing people."
"Ok," I said relieved that I made it through this moment without spilling the beans.
In the elevator he kept looking at my breast. "You brought the girls out to play."
"It fit differently when I bought it." I said shaking them.
"Stop that! You're gonna make me stop this elevator!" I smiled, "you're gonna have to wear the bra again."
I smiled to myself; he thinks I have a pushup bra on. I chuckled a little. We kissed goodbye in the lobby, and then I found my seat next to Sherrell. All of the groomsmen were out and chatting with everyone. Dude was an Usher, and standing next to his brother you could tell they were related. They spoke in the same manner and they laughed the same way.
When it was time for the ceremony everyone took their seats and places. The ceremony started right on time. Amber was glowing as she walked down the aisle on Malcolm's arm, she winked at me. The entire wedding party looked beautiful. Tracy was a beautiful bride, her dress was gorgeous and everything seemed like the right touch of beautiful. I couldn't take my eyes off of Derrick, he looked so handsome. The ceremony was short and SWEET! I was

so happy to say I made it through the ceremony. I told myself I would be partying too much to worry about slipping up now. It was all down hill coasting from here.

They told us to stay out with the family during the portraits. I got emotional when they said it was time for a family picture and they included Cyrus, Sherrell, and I. It was hard to pull the emotion back, fortunately everyone kept misting up so my behavior didn't stand out as weird. Derrick was being weird though, I was afraid he figured out my surprise. He kept talking fast or looking serious. Darryl kept laughing at him, which was a dead giveaway that he knew. I told myself to continue to play the role, and then I'd do it just like I planned it in my brain. After dinner I had to use the bathroom again for the millionth time. This time when I came out Derrick was waiting. He led me back out to where the ceremony was held, all the chairs were gone. The sky was so beautiful; I couldn't take it anymore this seemed like the perfect moment to tell him. I turned to Derrick and then he dropped to one knee, he held out a ring box, "Chantel. I love you, will you?"

I blinked my eyes, cause I wasn't expecting a proposal. That's why he didn't notice! He's been nervous about this. "Yes!" I said completely surprised. He kissed and squeezed me tight. "BUT!" Derrick frowned at me like he couldn't believe I said but. "I gotta tell you something."

He eyed me, "ok." I could tell he had no idea.

I got butterflies; it was going to come out of my mouth. "I've been meaning to tell you that I'm not wearing a pushup bra." He was clueless, "ok."

"We're going to have a baby." Then I covered my mouth, for a second I thought, what if he wasn't happy?

The BIGGEST smile I've ever seen flashed across his face. "WHAT?" Derrick said laughing out loud. "Don't play with me! Don't play!" He said completely smiling. "Are you serious?" "Yes!"

Derrick picked me up and spun me around. "You make me so HAPPY! I love you!" Then he kissed me.
"I love you!"

MORE FROM THE AUTHOR

Thank you for allowing me to entertain you. I hope you have enjoyed reading my current release. If you have not read Volumes I – VIII of the Wallace Family Affairs series, please do so. Click here for a list of all the background stories. Once you have read the background stories, please checkout the current date series Together We Are Strong. Stay tune for more to come shortly.

Wallace Family Affairs
At Last (Click here)
Tracy's Complications (Click here)
Distorted Mirrors (Click here)
Sometimes Love Isn't Enough (Click here)
Love Is Just Enough (Click here)
Just A Friend (Click here)
Invisible (Click here)
Look Beyond Your Eyes (Click here)
No Regrets
First You Laugh Then You Cry (Click here)
A Heart That's Taken (Click here)
Abandoned (Click here)
Last Words (Click here)

Together We Are Strong
Season 1 Present (Click here)
Beyond The Wallace's ~ I Knew You When (**TBD**)
Season 2 What Comes Next (Release **TBD**)

Standalones
Secrets & Lies ~ (**TBD late 2016 release**)
Anthology **Short** Story (Where Love May Find You Collection) ~ (Click here)
Waiting (**TBD**)

Hopefully you've enjoyed all of the background stories for our lovely Wallace's and Latour's. Please tune in for more from the "Together We Are Strong" Wallace & Latour Family Episodes on Amazon.

www.ingramcontent.com/pod-product-compliance
Lightning Source LLC
Chambersburg PA
CBHW060806030726
47503CB00002B/360